Time. Space. Life. Death.
Do I determine my fate? Is my destiny written?
Can both be true?
Only one thing seems certain.
I must do what's necessary to survive.

"I might really get to visit the past." Jo's face beamed. "Do you know how long I've dreamed of this? Only all my life and then some."

Having absorbed everything in silence up until this point, Erik frowned. "Temper your enthusiasm until you hear the catch."

"What catch?" Jo asked.

"Remember that arriving in the past causes an alternate timeline to unfold from that point onward," Maya said. "If we go back, we can never return."

Lines creased Jo's forehead as she processed the statement. "You're saying that if we travel to the past and then return to our own time, it won't be the same."

"Affirmative," Bob said. "The new timeline's future may or may not resemble the present you know now. Predicting the degree to which the timeline will differ from ours after the passage of 200,000 years is well beyond the capabilities of the most sophisticated AI."

"On one hand," Maya said, "if the timeline plays out similarly enough to ours, we'll encounter different versions of ourselves. The closer that future is to our present, the greater the chances our different selves will be living our lives. We won't be able to resume them."

"On the other hand," Erik said, "if that future isn't anything like what exists now, our lives may not exist to resume."

Books in the Beyond Saga

Beyond Cloud Nine
Beyond the Horizon
Beyond Yesterday
Beyond Existence

Upcoming books by Greg Spry

Destalis

Upcoming short stories by Greg Spry

Bears in Space
Goodbye, Mars

BEYOND YESTERDAY

THE THIRD BOOK OF THE BEYOND SAGA

GREG SPRY

www.beyondyesterdaybook.com

www.beyondsaga.com

ISBN-10: 0-9908224-6-X
ISBN-13: 978-0-9908224-6-2

Written by Greg Spry
www.gregspry.com

Published by Beyond Innovation Books
www.beyondinnovationbooks.com

Edited by Jon Harrison, jonvt@comcast.net
Proofread by Richard Lawhern, www.lawhern.org
Overall book cover design by Tobias Roetsch, www.gtgraphics.de
Character designs by Aaron Page, aaronpage.deviantart.com
Starship designs by William Black, william-black.deviantart.com

Printed by CreateSpace, an Amazon Company
Printed in the United States of America
First Paperback Edition Published June 2017
First Paperback Edition Updated July 2017

One—Terra Incognita
Aryana, Fomalhaut Trinary System, September 2283 CE

The pitch-black horizon brightened to a deep sapphire, announcing the alien dawn. As Aryana's sun crested the mountains in the distance, the sky exploded into a kaleidoscope of color no artist could hope to capture.

Sitting on the edge of a steep cliff, Commander Maya Davis squinted until her corneal implants, or i-cite, dimmed the blinding glare. The tension in her muscles lessened as the breaking day banished the night. Despite her passion for space exploration, Maya had never quite conquered her fear of the dark.

Maya bit her lip to subdue any lingering fright and leaned back on her forearms. A vast ocean surrounded her, pockmarked by more island chains than she could count. New Jodhpur, the colony the starship *Serendipity* had traveled twenty-five light years from Sol to establish, rested on the largest landmass in sight.

She had teleported out from the colony to this island with its spectacular view, wanting one last glimpse of the breathtaking scenery before shipping out to the next star system.

Goosebumps of elation popped up on her skin. This moment—right here, right now—was why she had joined the Interstellar Expeditionary Force.

Patches of vibrant algae, mold, and bacteria thrived atop every island.

The tough organisms grew in exotic shades of indigo, scarlet, and tangerine, a result of the blue-white light absorbed from the blazing sun.

No grass, bushes, or trees sprouted up from the dirt compacted by this super-Earth's high gravity. The flora and fauna that grew on the terraformed planets and moons of the Sol system could never have survived the radiation here.

The planet's strong gravity had also shaped the low mountains to the west. No snow capped their flat peaks. Instead, the slopes looked as if a painter had dotted them using a rainbow of acrylics.

Aryana's landscape reminded Maya of a simulation she had played as a kid. In the sim, she had skipped among giant gumdrops, candy canes, and lollypops growing straight out of the ground. She had driven mini candy cars along roads of jelly beans and gummy bears. After arriving at a ginger bread house, she had taken a bite out of the car's licorice steering wheel.

Her stomach gurgled. In her rush to beat the sunrise, she had skipped breakfast.

Maya reached out and touched a clump of shiny fuchsia lichen. It felt hard and smooth, as if glazed in a kiln. Nothing here was sweet or edible, of course. Someday, perhaps, the IEF would discover a candy planet. The chances were slim, but it was fun to imagine.

Behind her a soft whirring noise stole her attention.

Looking back over her shoulder, she watched a wormhole three meters in diameter appear above the ground. A shiny black boot emerged from the reflective sphere.

Once the rest of Ensign Nicolaus Kepler had exited the phase portal, it shrank and disappeared behind him.

"There you are, Commander," Kepler said, his speech muffled by the breathing mask he wore over his nose and mouth. The breather filtered the excess carbon dioxide from the air.

After hustling over to her, Kepler stopped and bent forward, panting. Once his breathing evened, he stood up straight and saluted. "Ma'am, I'd like to request a moment of your time."

Maya raised her voice to ensure he heard her clearly through her own breather. "My duty shift doesn't start for another hour, Ensign."

"I apologize, ma'am, but there's a matter that requires your attention."

Maya chuckled at his intrusion. The real reason she had ported out here was to have a moment alone. Even when off duty, colonists and subordinates continued to hound her about construction bot breakdowns, hydroponics malfunctions, climate control glitches, work shift schedules, food ration disputes—the list had no end.

"Very well, Ensign," she said. "At ease."

"Thank you, ma'am." As Kepler relaxed his body, he almost keeled over in exhaustion. "I don't think I'll ever get used to the gravity here, even with the daily gravite injections."

"One-point-three gees are tough on the human body. So what did you want to discuss with me, Ensign?"

Clearing his throat, Kepler spoke in a business-like tone. "The flow rates have decreased in the underground water pipes to the colony's fusion generators."

"How much has the power output dropped?"

"Seven percent at last report, ma'am."

"That's within tolerance, but if it gets any worse, we'll have a problem." Maya tapped her cheek in contemplation. "The AIs might've miscalculated the pressure ratios. I'll take a look at it first thing after breakfast."

Counting on his fingers, Kepler listed off other issues requiring her attention. After reporting the last one, he said, "The city engineers are begging the skipper to leave you behind, Commander."

"They'll manage just fine once we're gone."

"I'm sure they will, ma'am." The view caught Kepler's eye. He shuffled over to the edge of the cliff and stepped out onto a short ledge.

His jaw dropped as he stared out over the ocean. "Too fused . . ." he whispered, conveying his awe with popular slang.

Maya smiled, recalling her own doe-eyed optimism after graduating from the IEF academy. Kepler held the position of operations liaison aboard *Serendipity*. Maya had filled the same posting on *New Horizons* to begin her career. With their shared histories and the ensign's eagerness to take on the multiverse, she had developed a soft spot for him.

She held her palm up to block the overpowering sunlight. Her fingers split the rays of electric blue, creating a lens flare effect.

As Fomalhaut A climbed higher, its warmth turned to scorching heat.

A radiation alert popped up in Maya's i-cite. "The UV dosage is approaching safety limits, Ensign. Enable your bioshield."

Kepler nodded. "Yes, ma'am." The space around his body flickered as emitters woven into his uniform shrouded him in a force field. A fraction of a second later, the distortions disappeared, and the field became invisible.

In her i-cite, Maya activated her shield as well. Her skin cooled.

"I'm amazed the radiation doesn't fry every living thing, ma'am," Kepler said.

"The organisms here thrive on UV light," Maya said. "They absorb it as their main source of energy."

"I guess they never go hungry."

"Scientists used to think that a young, hot star like this one couldn't sustain life. But life has a way of defying expectations."

"Look what the sun's doing to New Jodhpur, ma'am." Kepler pointed at the settlement. "It's like the colony's putting on a lightshow."

The electromagnetic dome that protected the colony glowed a shade of deep violet. The secondary solar panels encircling the perimeter shone like big blue spotlights.

As Maya increased her i-cite zoom, she saw thousands of colonists and bots working to erect habitats, pave roads, and build greenhouses beneath the dome. Children scampered down streets and played in the new park.

"The colony does look like a big festive beacon," Maya said.

Kepler weaved a hand back and forth through the air. "Whoa . . ."

A slight shimmering—like the heat haze above asphalt in the desert—trailed his hand. The glare of the sunlight enhanced the prismatic distortion.

"It's the hypofield that prevents unwelcome guests from downshifting from hyperspace unannounced," Maya said. "The emitters were the first things we installed when we established the colony, along with the teleporter to make supply transport easier."

"Yes, ma'am." Kepler poked his index finger into the shimmering effect twice. "It's so fused." Drawing the bottom half of a semi-circle beneath the two dots, he completed a smiley face.

Maya's smile muscles fought against her frown.

"Also, Commander," Kepler said, "you got a couple messages in the latest transmission."

A mail icon popped up in Maya's i-cite. "You could've pinged me with this info, Ensign."

"Yes, ma'am." Kepler stared up at the sky and shrugged. "But then I wouldn't have had an excuse to come out here."

Maya shook her head.

"Oh, and Commander?" he asked.

"Yes, Ensign?" she responded, deadpan.

Kepler's grin stretched out his thin beard and cheeks. "Happy birthday."

"Thank you, Ensign." Maya opened the mail viewer in her i-cite.

The first message was from her aunt, Vice Admiral Brooke Davis-Sommerfield, who opened by wagging a finger. "Don't expect any singing." With her well-practical scowl, Brooke did her damnedest to project stoicism—it was part of her charm—but Maya knew that deep down her aunt cared more than anyone.

"Happy birthday, Squirt." Brooke referred to Maya by the nickname she had used the first time they met. Maya had been four years old at the time. After living in the Jovian system for six years, Brooke had returned to Earth. Brooke hadn't spoken to her sister, Marie—Maya's mother—since leaving, so Brooke hadn't known about Maya. Brooke had never been fond of children, but after spending time with Maya, the two had developed a bond. When Marie died, Brooke adopted Maya.

"I hope you're doing well out there on the frontier," Brooke continued. "Planning the defense scheme for the first interstellar phase gate is taking up most of my time these days. Well . . . I won't keep you. Be safe, and know that I love you." The vidsim ended.

Short and to the point as always, Maya noted to herself.

The next message originated from her uncle-in-law, Kevin Sommerfield, the director of the Scientific Society of the Interstellar Alliance. Kevin had earned the nickname "Modern Einstein" when he invented the FTL phase drive. Maya thought that if she were to look up the term "introverted scientist" in an encyclopedia, she would find Uncle Kevin's vidpic there. Kevin wore his archetypal lab coat like a second skin, and preferred tinkering in obscurity to the spotlight his invention had cast upon him.

Kevin had always shown her great warmth and understanding—far more than Brooke ever had, even though her aunt loved Maya like a daughter. Maya looked upon Kevin as her father. Her real father cared more about building his financial empire than playing any role in her life. Maya tensed at the thought of her father.

"Maya!" Kevin's virtual headshot shouted so loudly she flinched. "I did it. I got it working."

Maya sat up so quickly that she grew woozy in the high gravity. As she gripped the edge of the high cliff, her heart pounded in anticipation.

During the *New Horizons* mission ten years ago, she had led a team into the ruins on the Penphins' home planet. In a chamber within a tower that had remained undisturbed for 200,000 years, Maya had found a toy that a Mars-based company had invented in the twenty-third century.

"It took ten years," Kevin said, "but I finally managed to piece the metatoy back together." When he had first attempted to activate the toy, its brittle nanostructure had crumbled like a burnt log turning to ash.

He ran his hand through shaggy hair that had turned mostly gray. The stubble on his chin and the bags under his eyes suggested the project had been keeping him up at night. "The metatoy's too fragile to transform anymore, but I was able to transfer its data into the newer toy Caden gave you."

The mention of Caden flashed Maya back to the time she had visited him, after she had returned from the *Horizons* mission. When he had given her the newer toy, she had compared it to the one that was 200,000 years old. The serial numbers had matched.

Maya and Caden had enjoyed a brief romance, one of the few she had experienced in her life. Things had been magical until she received new deployment orders. Caden had wanted her to remain in the Sol system, but Maya wasn't willing to give up exploring interstellar space. They hadn't spoken since she had shipped out.

Thoughts of Caden weighed heavily on her. She knew she had made the right choice. However, she couldn't help but wonder if she would always struggle with romantic relationships, given the demands of her career.

"The newer toy's interface is active," Kevin said, "but I still can't access it."

Maya's shoulders slumped.

"But that's because it's showing a mind-blowing authentication prompt," he said. "Nothing I've tried has worked so far, but I have reason to believe you'll have better luck."

Me? Maya hung on her uncle's next words.

Kevin's thin, bearded face paled. "The prompt keeps flashing the same four-letter word. It's your name, Maya."

She dragged a hand down her face. As incredible as the notion seemed, she had suspected the toy somehow related to her personally. What were the odds of her finding it on a distant planet, then having the present-day version of the toy handed to her only months later?

For a decade she had stewed over the toy's origins. The mystery teased her curiosity like an itch she couldn't scratch. She wanted—no, she needed—to resolve the paradox of the toy's existence. Now, at long last, perhaps—

"Incoming war—"

That was all Maya heard over her neural comm before it cut out.

"Say again, *Serendipity*?" She tried pinging the ship without success.

Bright light whited out her surroundings.

Maya threw her arm up to shield her face. Whipping her head to the side, she clamped her eyes shut.

A concussive blast boomed in the distance, followed by a tremor that jarred the cliff. The ground beneath her shook so violently that she feared the tall, narrow island might collapse.

Her butt slid halfway off the cliff. Gripping the edge, she twisted her body and rolled back, avoiding a fatal plunge.

Maya sensed that the light had faded and cracked open her eyelids. Then the ledge beneath Kepler collapsed.

Flailing his arms in terror, the ensign plummeted. He turned, reached out, and sank his fingers into nearby stable ground. But his digits tore and slipped, lacking the strength to support his weight. In the time it took Maya to lunge a step toward him, he dropped out of sight.

Maya wracked her brain for how to save him. In one-point-three gees, and given the drag from the thick air, he would strike the crashing waves in a few seconds.

Interfacing with the colony's phase teleporter—she pinged the network three times before getting a response—she locked onto the ensign's position and opened a portal below him. Then she whipped her wave gun out of her hip holster. Setting the gun for sonic levitation, she gripped it with both hands, fell backwards, and pointed it up at the sky.

High overhead, the opposite end of the portal burst open. Kepler dropped out of it, limbs flailing.

Maya fired straight up at him. The acoustic levitation effect created by the gun slowed his rate of descent, reducing his momentum.

Kepler came crashing down on top of her before she could roll clear. Their bioshields repelled one another like magnets. Kepler tumbled away in one direction. Maya slid along the dirt in the other. She hissed through gritted teeth as sharp moss poked her in the back.

Her neurosensory implants numbed her pain.

According to her health monitoring sim, the impact hadn't broken or cracked any of her bones. Nor had it crushed or punctured any internal organs.

Kepler howled in pain. His bloodied hands trembled. When clawing to break his fall, he had scraped skin from his fingers and bent back his nails.

Holstering her gun, Maya rushed over and knelt beside him. "Take deep breaths, Ensign." She retrieved an auto-syringe from her belt and jabbed it into his neck. "You're going to be fine."

His shaking and howling ceased as the injected medical nanites took effect. In an hour, the medites would heal his fingertips, making them as good as new.

Maya pushed to her feet. "*Serendipity*, please respond," she mind-spoke. "New Jodhpur, are you receiving me?" The diagnostics in her i-cite detected interference due to neutrino jamming. "We must be under attack."

"The Greys?" Kepler asked as he lay on his back, taking deep breaths. Sweat drenched his pale face.

"Most likely."

"Like the attack near Epsilon Eridani."

Maya shivered at the memory of the horrific incident she had barely survived. "Let's hope not." Hurrying to the edge of the cliff, she stared out over the ocean and magnified her surroundings via her i-cite. Towering waves beat against the shorelines of every island.

She caught sight of a science bot that had landed on a small island nearby. Oblivious to what had happened, it went about its business collecting soil and lifeform samples.

"Did a Hyperflare blank a saucer, ma'am?" Kepler asked.

"I don't think so," Maya said. "Based on the garbled comm, I'd wager one of our 'flares intercepted a warhead meant for the colony." The shield dome surrounding the settlement flickered.

Maya rapped her finger against her cheek and thought out loud. "With the hypofield in place, the Greys couldn't have shifted anywhere near the planet. They must've fired the warhead from long distance—but they also had to have known one of our fighters would shoot it down. The warhead detonated too far away to threaten the colony, which suggests New Jodhpur wasn't the target."

She snapped her fingers in realization. "The piping."

With the color returning to his face, Kepler forced himself to sit up. "What about the piping, Commander?"

Maya turned to him. "The fusion generators supply power to the rad shield, but you said the water flow had slowed."

"Yes, ma'am."

"The Greys must've snuck onto the planet and plugged up the plumbing. Then they force us to blow up their warhead to divert our attention." *But divert us from what?*

"If the water levels drop too low, the generators will shut down. The rad shield will go offline."

"Which will force us to evacuate the colony. They know we couldn't get people off the surface quickly enough. With the comm down, it would take hours to get everyone into the underground shelters."

"Plus the civilians don't have bioshields, ma'am."

"People are going to die." Maya stomped her boot. "Every time we establish a new colony this far out, they try to drive us back."

Holding his tender hands close to his body, Kepler asked, "The IEF doesn't know why, Commander?"

"For a while, we thought we might be straying into their territory. But attacks against ships and settlements in different directions from Sol have cast doubt on that theory."

The ensign gave an absent nod.

Maya folded her arms. "The Greys lurked behind the scenes throughout our history, never destroying or conquering primitive humans. Then, three years ago, they gave up centuries of hiding and attacked the research outpost near Epsilon Eridani. We still don't know why."

With a series of pixelated flashes, the colony's rad shield tinted to a lighter shade of lavender.

"The shield's failing." Maya's muscles tensed. "If I were the Greys, I'd send in a team to finish the job. I need to get back."

"How, Commander?" Kepler asked.

Staring down at the turbulent ocean, Maya considered using her wave gun to levitate all the way to the colony. She had used the gun to slow her fall or cross short distances on plenty of occasions, but New Jodhpur rested a kilometer away. Theoretically, firing a burst every few seconds at the right angles would allow her to hop all the way there. But a slight miscalculation on any shot could send her plummeting to her death. She decided it wouldn't work in practice.

"I can't ping the ship or the colony teleporter because of the jamming," Maya said. "I was lucky to get a signal through to save you before losing all contact."

Biting her lip, she whipped her head around, searching for something that could help her.

The breeze picked up, flinging spores into her face. Maya's breather protected her nose and mouth, keeping her from sneezing, but her eyes itched and swelled. *Not now.*

With a thought Maya instructed her bio-implants to release antihistamine into her bloodstream. *You'd think modern medicine would've come up with a cure for allergies by now.* As the irritation in her eyes faded, she spotted the science bot.

The bot was taking off from the island. She tried to ping it, but the jamming blocked her attempts.

Pulling out her wave gun, Maya toggled it to sonic tractor mode, aimed at the airborne bot, and fired.

The bot slowed in its flight toward the colony until it stopped in midair. Shaking, its hyper-conducting magnets fought the unseen push-pull.

"Come on, come on." Maya gripped the handle with both hands.

Unable to resist the high-low pressure stream created by the gun, the bot slid through the air toward her.

A minute later, she had yanked the bot close enough to get a signal through to it. Interface menus popped up in her i-cite, giving her control of the bot as it flew to her.

When the bot reached the island, she instructed it to jettison the samples it had collected, lightening its load.

It wasn't until the bot was hovering over her head that her pulse quickened.

Kepler rubbed his neck—gently, given his tender fingers. "Ma'am, you don't really plan to. . . ."

Maya shrugged to hide her trepidation. "It's rated for up to a hundred kilos of return samples." Stuffing her gun into her holster, she stared at the bot. "Then again, that's per standard gravity. In one-point-three gees—"

"You might be close to maxing it out, ma'am."

Narrowing her eyes at him, Maya said, "Young ensigns would be wise not to comment on the weight of superiors."

Kepler winced.

Maya rubbed her palms together, then sucked in a deep breath and instructed the bot to descend to within arm's length. "Sit tight and heal up. Your bioshield and hydro-protein pills should keep you going. I'll be back for you—hopefully."

The ensign frowned.

Maya grasped the manipulator arms on either side of the bot and told it to rise. Increasing power to its levitator magnets, the bot lifted her off her feet. She could feel the force of the bot's magnetic resistance pushing against and through her. As Maya's feet flew over the edge of the cliff, she gulped and tightened her grip.

"Good luck," Kepler yelled from behind her.

Despite the angry sea below her dangling boots, Maya ordered the bot to descend toward the water's surface. A hundred meters out from the colony, she had dropped to only twice her height above the water. Her sore arms, weakening fingers, and sweaty palms strained to keep their hold on the bot's manipulators.

Feeling her left hand slipping, she adjusted it to get a better grip. She lost her grasp, and her left hand slipped free. With her heartbeat on rapid fire mode, she squeezed with her right hand to keep from falling.

The uneven weight caused the bot to teeter and flip on its side. With its magnetic emitters no longer pointed toward the planet, it dropped straight down.

Her face smacked the water first. As she completed the belly flop, the surface tension pummeled her stomach like a roundhouse punch. Stinging pain coursed throughout Maya's body as she plunged into the frigid ocean.

Two—Moribund
New Mars, Alpha Centauri System, November 2283 CE

Two officers saluted Vice Admiral Brooke Davis-Sommerfield as they passed her in the corridor.

Returning the gesture, Brooke bounded toward Base MAVEN's command center in the half-standard gravity of New Mars.

She stopped in front of a window that ran the length of the corridor. Alpha Centauri B, the star New Mars orbited, descended toward the cratered surface, setting the horizon ablaze in shades of amber and marigold. High overhead, Alpha Centauri A shined brighter than a full moon in Earth's sky.

The rocky landscape of New Mars filled Brooke with a longing for simpler times, before the Interstellar Alliance had terraformed every major planet and moon in the Sol system. Brand new habitat domes, each larger than a sporting arena, comprised Hues colony. The curvature of the shiny domes reflected the sunlight from the binary stars.

When none of Brooke's obnoxious, eager-to-please aides came rushing after her, she allowed her shoulders to relax. The higher she had risen in the ranks over the decades, the more difficult it had become to find time alone—and she lived for her solitude.

Absently, she ran her fingers over the three stars affixed above the left breast of her IEF uniform. Her rank as a vice admiral, duties as commander-in-chief of IEF Aerospace, and recent posting to MAVEN had kept her out of a cockpit for far too long.

"Your life's too valuable to risk out in the field," IEF High Admiral Westerberg told her before she left Sol. "We need you coordinating fleet maneuvers and planning defense strategies behind the lines, and the phase gate is top priority." Normally, an officer with the rank of commander would oversee the base, but Westerberg had placed her in charge due to the recent attacks by the Greys.

At first Brooke had seethed with anger over the assignment. She perceived it as a blatant attempt by Westerberg to keep her grounded. But after cooling down, she had seen the logic in his decision.

Pangs of nostalgia washed over her as she recalled her days as a combat pilot. Had it been ten years since she last flew a star fighter as part of any meaningful sortie? *Not since Gliese 581.* She scrunched her nose in disgust.

As if being relegated to a desk job hadn't been bad enough, her doctor and her husband had sided with Westerberg because of her health.

Shooting pain pierced her left arm and leg. She shook out her limbs until it subsided.

She focused her attention on the mountainous dome that dwarfed all the others. The Momma Dome, as the residents of Hues colony had nicknamed it, housed the classified energy source that powered the interstellar gate connecting Mars and New Mars across four light years. Despite being married to the man who had invented the gate, Brooke didn't know what resided beneath the dome.

But such details didn't affect her duty. She had taken command of MAVEN to protect the phase gate during its shakedown tests. Soon, she would be out of here and searching for ways back into a cockpit.

Brooke's mind grew heavy, and her muscles tensed. Drawing in a breath, she shook off the dizziness and nausea.

A flashing icon in her i-cite indicated an incoming message from her husband, Kevin. With a mental click, she played the vidsim. Kevin had recorded it hours before driving through the Mars end of the gate in the Sol system.

Kevin's headshot appeared in her i-cite. "Hey, Brooke." Sitting in the passenger seat of a rover, he ran a hand through shaggy gray hair. "I've informed Base MAVEN and Hues colony of our departure through official channels, but I wanted to send you a personal note before we leave. I know you think I should let someone else be the first to traverse the gate, but I couldn't pass up the opportunity."

He folded his arms and grinned. "It was never very fair that you got to experience hyperspace before me, using the drive I invented. So I'm stealing the spotlight this time."

A hint of a smile crossed Brooke's face. As much as she hated to see him risk his life, she would be the galaxy's worst hypocrite if she faulted him for it.

The vidsim switched to his view, ahead of the rover. Across a plain covered by rust-red dirt and patches of olive green grass rested the Mars end of the gate. The top half of a wormhole with a twenty-meter radius towered above the ground like a sun that refused to set. Around the circumference of the wormhole churned the salmon-pink hue of hyperspace. Brooke couldn't see the generator or nacelles, though. The machinery that maintained the gate resided kilometers away and in orbit, far out of sight.

Pointing at the gate, Kevin said, "We can't see New Mars, of course. That would be the equivalent of seeing a day-and-a-half into the future, which hasn't happened yet. Once Hues opens the gate on the exit end, the people there should be able to see us driving toward them."

Brooke glanced at the time in the bottom corner of her i-cite. Kevin had entered the gate over a day ago. Five hours remained until he emerged.

"Due to the time dilation effect," Kevin said, "the trip will be as quick as stepping through a door for me. But you'll have to wait thirty-seven hours to see my bright, smiling face. Once we finish this trial run, we'll be able to start sending colonists through to fill those domes."

The view switched back to Kevin. "Well, I need to get going. Try not to stress about my safety. I'll be there before you know it. Love—"

Before the vidsim ended, her right arm spasmed. She gripped her wrist to hold it still and sucked in deep, even breaths.

Just as the shakes appeared to have subsided, her body convulsed.

She lost all sensation below her waist and then fell.

As her shoulder thumped against the cold floor, she shuddered from head to toe.

Her vision and mind blurred, and she blacked out.

When Brooke awoke, she was lying on the floor where she had fallen. The health monitoring sim in her i-cite confirmed she had suffered another seizure due to the degeneration of motor neurons. Her implants had pumped meds into her bloodstream to subdue the seizure and relieve the pain, but they could do nothing to reverse the damage.

"There is no cure." The words of her physician echoed in her head.

The physician had given Brooke the bad news during her last visit. "Your nervous system has degraded due to the, shall we say, 'recreational activities' you engaged in in your youth," the pompous shrew had informed her. The physician hadn't really been a pompous shrew, but

Brooke sometimes had a tendency to blame the messenger.

Sitting on the edge of the exam table, Brooke snorted at the physician's euphemism. "Just say it, Doc. I was a drug addict, and now I'm paying the price for my spark use."

Kevin had only made things worse by saying, "You're sixty now. Few fighter pilots are still flying at your age."

"There might not be very many, but there are some," Brooke had countered. "Besides, sixty is the new twenty."

"But you're not a healthy sixty-year-old."

"There's no reason why a few faint wrinkles and gray hairs should keep me grounded."

"You're not facing the reality of your condition."

Brooke had scoffed in disgust. "I feel just fine."

Damn it all. She tensed in frustration as she remained lying on the floor in the corridor.

Once she regained feeling in her lower body, she felt warm and wet in the groin area. *Really?* She told her uniform to self-clean.

A young officer came bounding down the hallway as she was sitting up. When he noticed her, he rushed right over. "Are you okay, Admiral?" He bent down to help her stand.

"I'm fine, Lieutenant." Brooke waved him away.

"You look awfully pale, ma'am," the lieutenant said. "I'll comm for a medic."

"Cancel that comm." Brooke hopped to her feet. Piercing pain shot through her skull. She kept her mouth closed and gritted her teeth, suppressing any outward sign of the pain. "I sat down to rest for a moment. Something I ate must not have agreed with me. I've flushed my system and feel better."

"Are you sure, ma'am?" The lieutenant tilted his head, looking less than convinced.

"Quite sure." She glowered up at him, donning her best scowl. Despite standing over a head taller than her, he shrank back. After hesitating, he turned and continued back in the direction he had been heading.

"And, Lieutenant," she called after him.

The officer stopped and turned. "Yes, Admiral?"

Swallowing the guilt and embarrassment, she ordered, "Keep this to yourself."

"Understood, ma'am." He walked off.

♦

Brooke sat cross-legged at the situation table in MAVEN's command center. Thirty minutes remained until Kevin would emerge from the gate.

Lieutenant Emilia Tereshkova approached her. The young woman of no more than twenty-five had arrived on base as Brooke's chief aide the week before.

Tereshkova was a pilot with a specialty in starship helm operations. She had graduated first in her class from the academy three years ago, with commendations from both the Aerospace and Fleet divisions. Brooke had approved the posting, but she had yet to understand why an officer with such impressive credentials had requested such a role.

Tereshkova carried a tray from the officer's mess. "Your lunch, Admiral," she stated with a grating Russian accent. "Today, I wanted to bring it to you personally."

The sight of the travel box of Fruity Planets atop the tray dismissed Brooke's concerns, at least for the moment.

With a rare smile, she accepted the tray. "I can't remember the last time I . . . wherever did you find it?"

"The *Magellan* had a few boxes in stock, ma'am," Tereshkova said. "Before the starship deployed, I had them sent down."

When Brooke tapped the box with a finger, it morphed into a bowl. Planet-shaped marshmallows floated in the milk that filled it. "How did you know this was my favorite food?"

Very matter-of-factly, Tereshkova stated, "It's in the public record, ma'am." Black bangs dangled above her penetrating eyes. Brooke approved of her no-nonsense frown.

"You must've done some digging." Grabbing the spoon extruded by the box during its transformation, Brooke scooped up her first morsel and inserted it into her mouth. As the sugary cereal touched her tongue, she closed her eyes and basked in the sweetness. Her skin tingled in delight.

"No, ma'am. I've known since I was a kid."

Brooke blinked. "I'm curious, Lieutenant," she said after swallowing. Setting the spoon down on the tray, she asked, "Why would an accomplished pilot ask to serve on my staff?"

Tereshkova nodded. Apparently, she had been expecting the question. "I put in for this posting to shadow the greatest pilot of them all. I've got the rest of my life left for flying."

Brooke didn't know what to say. She had never excelled at showing gratitude, affection, or any other positive emotion.

Tereshkova stood at attention, staring at her.

"Thank you, Lieutenant," Brooke said. "You're dismissed."

Tereshkova saluted, turned, and exited the command center.

As Brooke finished her cereal, the chatter in the command center increased. Base personnel had begun implementing the gate defense strategy.

"Now deactivating the hypofield," the defense systems officer reported from a nearby control station. "All satellite and surface emitters have been disabled. The field is down."

The liaison to the phase port said, "Hues is now initializing this side of the gateway."

"If an attack's going to come, it'll be any moment," Brooke spoke up. "Stay alert."

Every officer in the room sounded off, "Yes, Admiral."

"No blips or gravity distortions detected," the remote sensing officer confirmed. "The threat board remains clear."

Brooke tapped her fingernails on the edge of the situation table. With each passing moment, her heart pumped more rapidly.

From the opposite end of the sit-table, the flight controller said, "The *Spitzer*, *Chandra*, and *Magellan* are now deploying fighter groups Epsilon, Zeta, Omicron."

Three-dimensional renderings of the starships in orbit appeared above the table. Thousands of miniature PF-77 Hyperflares swarmed from the ships. The phase fighters flashed, disappeared into hyperspace, and blinked back into reality, scattering into their assigned orbits.

To display the tangible renderings, or rends, emitters built into the table created tiny projection wormholes. The wormholes delivered nanites into the air that morphed into tangible shapes that a person could manipulate on a whim.

Brooke summoned a rend of the gateway promenade in the Hues colony phase port. With a shift of her irises, she rotated the rend, studying it from different angles.

The mini-promenade resembled an antique model train set she had once seen in a museum. Enlarging the rend, she observed a handful of technicians, officers, and civilian officials standing near the semi-circular gate. A crowd of several hundred people, the current populace of the colony, had gathered beyond the cordoned-off arrival area.

A rend of New Mars the size of a beach ball replaced the promenade above the sit-table. Ice covered the poles of the maroon world. An intricate latticework encircled the planet, representing the network of satellites and platforms. If an unidentified object violated the grid, the AIs would alert the fighters in orbit, which could shift on location in under a second.

However, space was vast. No defense grid yet conceived could guarantee the immediate neutralization of a threat, given the immense volume of space around a planet.

"This strategy still makes me nervous, Brooke," Admiral Westerberg had told her during the final defense planning session at IEF Command on Triton. "With the hypofield offline, a hundred times as many ships still wouldn't be enough. An enemy fighter could downshift anywhere and strike the colony before our units can react."

Brooke had given a slow nod. "I wish there was a better way, sir. All we can do is deploy our surface assets near the colony and base. With our orbital units, we cover the maximum volume of space without spreading them too thin. Then we cross our fingers and hope that no attack comes during the few minutes the hypofield is down."

Westerberg had interlocked his fingers and banged them against the conference table. "If only we didn't need to take the field offline."

"Our fighters and starships can shift in the presence of the field," another admiral had said. "Any spacecraft with the algorithm can circumvent it. Why can't the gate?"

"Unfortunately, even the slightest gravimetric fluctuation can collapse the gate," Brooke had replied, paraphrasing her husband's long-winded explanation. "The precision and power required to traverse the four-light-year distance are too great."

Shifting in her seat in MAVEN's command center, Brooke studied the rends. Her right hand shook until she dispersed meds into her system. For a moment, she feared the onset of another seizure, but the episode passed.

"Hues indicates one minute to arrival," the port liaison announced.

Sitting up straighter, Brooke switched to the rend of the promenade and magnified it.

The liaison said, "Arrival imminent."

The wormhole in the phase port wavered and rippled.

A hover rover emerged. Its boxy chassis flew out onto the promenade as if it had exited a garage.

As the rover settled down onto the pavement, two others joined it.

Kevin stepped out of the first vehicle. The lanky scientist's shaggy hair and lab coat blew in the artificial breeze. He waved to the crowd and all around, knowing Brooke was watching.

"Hues has begun gateway shutdown procedures," the liaison said.

"Reinitializing the hypofield," the defense systems officer announced.

Blowing out a prolonged breath in relief, Brooke sank back in her chair.

The rend of the promenade shrank away, replaced by a sector of space above the planet. Five of the hypofield generator satellites exploded in brief flashes of light.

Brooke jumped out of her seat.

Toggling to an overhead view of the cratered surface, the threat table showed three other generators exploding. Emergency klaxons howled throughout the base.

"Eight of the field generators have been destroyed," the defense officer yelled. "The losses have created a gap in the field near Hues colony."

The remote sensing officer shouted, "I'm detecting hundreds—no, thousands—of wormhole signatures in high orbit."

"Confirmed. Approximately two thousand dish-shaped fighter craft have appeared along with five motherships."

A rend of the enemy fleet popped up above the sit-table.

"The Greys," Brooke muttered. "Order the fleet to fire at will."

"All orbital units, fire at will," the weapons officer repeated over the comm.

Relativistic beaming emitters, heavy particle cannons, and lasers fired toward the Greys' fleet from the starships and platforms in orbit.

Without the hypofield to constrain the enemy saucers to conventional propulsion, they blinked away in rapid succession, upshifting to hyperspace. All friendly fire passed through the empty space they had vacated.

The saucers downshifted everywhere around the colony, littering the sky.

"All fighter groups and surface units," Brooke ordered, "engage the enemy."

Damn it, she thought with a scowl. The Greys had waited until right before the hypofield reinitiated to destroy the generators, which were most vulnerable during their power-up cycles.

Leaning over the sit-table, Brooke observed the battle on dozens of rends. Hyperflares materialized on the tails of saucers, making strafing runs on the colony. Spacecraft fired relativistic particles, streams of plasma, and zigzagging seekers at each other as they blinked in and out of reality. More often than not, friendly fighters blanked bandits before the latter did any harm. But every now and then, a projectile or beam pelted the shield dome protecting the colony, tinting the dome crimson.

Brooke kept watch on the promenade in her i-cite. Kevin and his welcoming committee lay on the ground, covering their heads with their arms.

As she studied the combat zone, a pit formed in her stomach. Her fighters were only achieving a two-to-one kill ratio. Also, the Greys seemed to be concentrating their assault on the west and north sides of the colony even though the phase port and generator dome were located at the south end.

Two explanations for the puzzling strategy struck her. Either the Greys had determined—incorrectly—that the colony's defenses were weakest farthest from the phase port, or—

"Second wave downshifting in low orbit," the remote sensing officer reported. "Two-thousand additional saucers on approach from the east."

The first wave was a diversion.

Brooke redeployed her forces to account for the latest enemy wave. As the battle continued to unfold, she squeezed her seat's armrests. Her units had outnumbered the first wave. However, the second wave had doubled the number of enemy forces. Considering the low kill ratio, the IEF stood a significant chance of losing.

To be precise, the tactical AIs predicted a thirty-seven percent possibility of defeat. That was much too high for her liking, so she issued additional orders.

All throughout the combat zones, Hyperflares struggled to blank saucers. Dogfights dragged on for seconds. Given the speed at which orbital hyper-combat took place, seconds might as well have been eons.

A tremor rocked the base. Then, on the east side of the colony, an intense flash signaled a massive explosion.

"Enemy forces have scored a direct hit," the defense officer shouted. "The colony's force field is failing in sections."

The sight of her husband cowering on the ground pushed Brooke to a decision.

She shot to her feet. In her i-cite, she ordered the hangar bay to prep her ride.

As she bounded away from the table, everyone in the command center stared at her.

Brooke stopped. "I'm going out there." Pointing at the next highest ranking officer, she ordered, "Commander, take charge until I return."

The commander gave a reluctant nod. "Yes . . . yes, ma'am."

"You'll do fine," she said, softening her tone. "You'll all do fine. Just focus and do your jobs." Brooke bolted out of the command center before she or anyone else had a chance to question her decision.

Halfway to the hangar bay, Lieutenant Tereshkova caught up to Brooke, matching her brisk pace through the corridor.

"I take it you plan to deploy, Admiral?" Tereshkova asked in her even tone.

"Word travels fast, I see," Brooke said without breaking stride.

"It's my job to know what're up to and attend to your needs, ma'am."

Brooke skidded to a halt. As her subordinate did the same, Brooke whirled on her. "You mean someone ordered you to keep an eye on me. Who? Westerberg?"

For once, Tereshkova hesitated. "Um, yes, ma'am. The high admiral said that in an event such as this one, I should respectfully request that you reconsider coordinating our defenses from your assigned post."

Throwing her arms up into the air, Brooke growled under her breath. *I haven't been grounded by a flight surgeon. Westerberg wouldn't order me to stay out of a cockpit without medical justification, so he's assigned me a damned babysitter.*

"Request denied." Brooke broke into a near-sprint toward the fighter bay. "We're getting pasted out there. Our forces need a competent field commander or else we might lose this one."

"I understand ma'am," Tereshova said, chasing after her. "May I ask if you've chosen a dash-two?"

"A wing mate will only slow me down."

"Ma'am, the regs prohibit solo deployments. All fighter teams must operate in pairs."

"I know the regulations, Lieutenant."

"Of course, ma'am. What I'm saying is that I'd be honored to fly with you, if you'll have me."

Brooke and Tereshkova stepped into a lift.

As it ascended, Brooke said, "I was blanking bandits long before you were born, kid. I'm afraid trying to keep up with me will only get you killed."

"I know I'm young, Admiral, but I'm an accomplished pilot. I flew against the Greys near Procyon—"

"And received a special commendation for it," Brooke said, folding her arms.

"Yes, ma'am."

After staring at the insistent officer for a moment, Brooke sighed in resignation. "I can't very well ignore regulations, can I?"

Within seconds after launching from MAVEN in a Hyperflare, Brooke had torched two saucers, and Tereshkova had blanked a third.

The fear and uncertainty that had gripped Brooke had given way to shudders of exhilaration. Between the feel of the gravgel pressing in on her and the tightening of her muscles during a high-gee turn, she knew she was back where she belonged.

MAVEN's flight controller, all starships in orbit, every fighter, and the planetary tactical network each synced telemetry to Brooke's Hyperflare. The suite of AIs that operated her fighter's subsystems processed, prioritized, and fed the data into her subconscious so that she didn't have to think. "Omicron, alter course to sector two-oh-nine and deploy in a battle spread formation," she shouted after identifying a weak spot in the second wave's formation.

"Epsilon group," Brooke barked over the comm net, "stop engaging in solo combat and work with your wing mates." Teamwork had become a lost art, given the frequent blinking in and out of reality by modern pilots.

Tereshkova shifted her Hyperflare kilometers behind Brooke's fighter and dispatched a saucer that had been heading in their direction. Brooke realized she had been wrong to try to head out alone.

"New target coordinates, Ensign," Brooke said.

"Received, ma'am," Tereshkova said. "Lead the way."

Brooke upshifted her craft to hyperspace, tracking four saucers harassing a pair of rookies in low orbit.

The moment her fighter emerged in normal space, her neurotronics read her intentions and fed them to her tactical AI. Targeting brackets auto-locked onto each of the bandits. Her Hyperflare unleashed volleys of seekers at each saucer before the thought to launch them entered her conscious mind.

Propelled by three-dimensional thruster arrays, the seekers darted up, down, left, right, backwards, and forwards through the vacuum of space faster than any spacecraft could maneuver.

A seeker struck one of the saucers before it could upshift. The explosive impact threw the saucer into a violent spin. Smoke trailed the craft as it shot off, helplessly, on a trajectory away from the planet.

The other three saucers blinked away into hyperspace before the seekers reached them. Having missed their targets, each seeker disarmed and followed paths away from friendly forces.

Prompted by tactical data and compelled by instinct, Brooke yawed her fighter one-hundred-and-eighty degrees and flew backwards.

As one of the three remaining saucers appeared in front of her craft's nose, she fired her particle cannons, scoring multiple direct hits. The bandit's shielding glowed bright red, and the craft exploded. Then bogey number three re-entered normal space above Brooke's fighter, diving straight at her.

Tereshkova's Hyperflare swooped into reality on Brooke's port side and forced the saucer to dart away. With a barrage of seekers, the ensign blew the bogey to pieces.

With the fighter wing under Brooke's direct command, the kill ratio increased. The Greys' numbers had thinned, and they were scattering more than attacking. The tide was turning in the IEF's favor.

"I recommend we fall back to base, Admiral," Tereshkova suggested. At low thrust, their Hyperflares flew a few kilometers above the surface on the outskirts of the colony and combat zone.

Brooke opened her mouth, intending to agree.

A warhead struck the ventral fuselage of her fighter before she could speak the words. With her energy harness clamping her into her seat, the impact drove her stomach up into her throat. Her brain pressed up into her skull, threatening to burst. Hit off center, the Hyperflare spun like a gyroscope with little air resistance to slow its somersaults.

"Admiral!" Tereshkova shouted over the comm net.

Brooke reached out to the fighter's AIs with her mind, but the warhead had knocked them offline.

As the Hyperflare tumbled, she stretched her hands out for the auxiliary control grips, hoping to manually fire her stabilizing thrusters.

She convulsed as she lost all motor control. Every muscle in her body felt like it was extending past the limit and snapping back again and again. Knifing pain pierced every part of her body.

Brooke howled in agony and vomited, spraying her helmet face shield as her fighter slammed into the planet's surface.

Three—Forestall
Aryana, Fomalhaut Trinary System, September 2283 CE

As Maya plunged into the ocean, the breather slipped off her mouth. She swallowed a lungful of cold water. Her bioshield remained active, but it wasn't airtight or waterproof.

She worked her arms and legs, fighting toward the surface. The water resisted her every stroke in Aryana's high gravity. Her uniform's thermal fibers warmed her, staving off hypothermia.

Maya reached down for her wave gun, hoping to use it to propel herself to the surface, but her holster was empty. Instructing her implants to reinforce her muscles, she found the strength to claw, kick, and then breach the surface.

As her head emerged she blew water out of her mouth and nose and then coughed. Microorganisms and particulates stung her eyes and left a rancid taste on her tongue.

She resisted the urge to gulp in the poisonous air. Instead, she fumbled for a medite injector within the compartments on her belt and then pricked her neck. Medical nanites rushed into her bloodstream, oxygenating her cells and killing off anything she may have swallowed.

Feeling her head clear, she located her backup breather and fastened it over her mouth. Then she swam for the shore, taking it slow to conserve her strength.

She stepped onto dry land, dropped to her knees, and keeled over in the sand. Panting, she sprawled out on her back and pushed strands of wet hair out of her face.

The rad shield surrounding the colony buzzed like an amplified insect zapper. Normally it emitted a soft hum when one listened closely.

Forcing her aching body to its feet, she hobbled toward the shield beyond the beach. The glowing wall of electromagnetic energy stretched meters below the ground and all around the perimeter of the colony. The shield wavered and fuzzed like an antique television set receiving no signal.

In her i-cite, she began looking up the resonant frequency of the rad shield. If she tuned her bioshield to the same frequency, she could slip through the barrier unimpeded. Before she located the frequency, she reached out and touched the shield. Her fingers poked through it with minimal resistance. *It should stop me cold with a mild zap. I guess it's lost too much power.*

Maya pushed through the shield, which was like stepping into a soap bubble. *If I can get in, so can anyone else.*

Once inside the atmosphere of the colony, she started to remove her breather, but then changed her mind. The bodies of IEF officers, adult settlers, children, and Penphins lay on the ground, not moving.

A Penphin had collapsed on the sod it had been installing in the new park. The stubby exobeing wore dark goggles over its bulbous eyes to protect them from the bright sun. Its head, snout, and body were thicker than those of its relatives back home—like the human colonists, the Penphins took regular gravite injections to strengthen their bones and muscles. It had folded and tied back each of its wide flipper-wings, or flings. The flings wouldn't allow it to fly in such high gravity.

Despite the many hardships they would have to endure, the Penphins had insisted on helping the humans settle their extrasolar colonies. Maya's admiration for these selfless workaholics had only increased since *New Horizons* had visited their world.

Maya touched the Penphin's smooth body. It felt warm. Its body expanded and contracted ever so slightly, barely breathing. *He's only unconscious. That's a relief.*

She found no one awake in the park, along the dirt road she jogged down, or in the city square. Every colonist and IEF officer was out cold.

Maya tried comming anyone within range. Then she attempted to connect to the colony network. Each attempt produced flashing red error icons in her field of vision.

Barring a freak accident, someone had intentionally subdued the colonists. And that someone was likely still around.

Instinctively she reached down toward her empty hip holster. *Why couldn't I have held on for another minute?* she berated herself. None of the unconscious officers she checked carried side arms.

She stared over the tops of the modular habitats and unfinished buildings at the flickering dome. Given the weakened state of the rad shield, an opportunistic enemy should have been attacking. Either *Serendipity*, aided by the fighter squads, was keeping the enemy at bay, or the saboteurs had something else in mind.

Why bother to attack? Once the rad shield goes down, the radiation will finish us off, anyway.

With that realization in mind, Maya rushed toward the power plant. The construction bots she passed went about their tasks, unaware of the crisis. An automated backhoe scooped heaps of dirt out of the ground as it dug the foundation for an elementary school. Fabrication bots extruded beams, supports, walls, doors, and pipes for a row of cookie-cutter condominiums. Tool bots flew around the site, welding, screwing, bolting, and hammering the pieces together. An android electrical crew exited a habitat after installing the wiring. A trash bot collected a stray soda can.

A vending machine rolled along a sidewalk, begging her to buy the taffy made right here in the colony.

Maya stopped the machine, bought a taffy bar and tore into it, ravenous. The tough, tangy sweetness satisfied her more than any meal had done in a long time.

As she munched on a second bar, she accessed the machine's bioware in her i-cite. The machine's sensor logs showed people collapsing, but otherwise revealed little in the way of answers. She interfaced with several other bots on her way to the power plant, learning nothing more.

At the plant, she squeezed between a pair of wall studs of the unfinished exterior and slipped inside. The bright blue light of Fomalhaut A shone through the rad shield and into the plant, tinting the interior purple. Beams, crisscrossing pipes, tall cylinders, and metal machines cast long shadows throughout the plant.

After winding her way through this industrial maze, she reached the three-meter-high control platform affixed to the primary generator. Two sets of stairs, one on either side of the symmetrical platform, led up to it.

At the bottom of the nearest staircase, she saw something that gave her a start. Two plant engineers lay passed out on top of the platform.

Climbing up, she knelt and checked the pulse of both the man and the woman. They were alive, like everyone else.

She rose to her feet and studied the instruments and displays projected above the control station. Rends of pressure gauges, power meters, dials, graphs, and data readouts hovered everywhere.

With a beckoning wave, she pulled a floating gauge within reach and enlarged it. The blinking gauge showed the water flow from seven of the twelve ocean pipes at critical lows.

She grabbed a power meter and turned it to face her. The AI responsible for power regulation was compensating for the loss of coolant by reducing the energy output. Once the amount of water dropped below the threshold point, the AI would shut down the generator to prevent it from becoming irreparably damaged.

A map of the subterranean pipeline infrastructure materialized at her command. As she rotated the rends of the ground tens of meters below the colony, she found all seven of the problem pipelines plugged with chunks of rock and welded shut at the ends.

Biting her lip in concentration, Maya input a series of commands she hoped would clear the obstructions.

Her gaze landed on a display pushed back behind the other instruments. From the blinking text and flashing warning icons, it seemed that someone had begun the process of overriding the safety protocols to force the generator to put out more power.

Were the engineers trying to keep the shield up? They had to have known that would be pointless. Without enough coolant or fuel, the generator would lose containment pressure and destroy itself. Not only would the shield drop, anyway, but the generator would be damaged beyond repair.

She glanced down at the unconscious engineers. The woman lay on her side at an awkward angle. It wasn't a posture someone would naturally end up in after falling. Someone had pushed the woman clear of the control station.

A flash of white light pelted Maya in the side. Her bioshield absorbed and dissipated much of the searing particle blast, but the force still threw her off her feet. She landed on the steps to the platform she had ascended and tumbled to the bottom.

Crying out, Maya clutched her left forearm. Her right foot throbbed. Health status displays in her i-cite confirmed she had sprained her elbow and ankle. Her implants pumped a numbing agent into her system.

As the pain decreased, she whipped her gaze around. No one stood atop the platform or anywhere else in sight.

Her ears caught the faint clanging of metal. Increasing the volume on her auditory implants, she recognized the sound of footsteps ascending the far steps of the platform.

She toggled her vision through the infrared, UV, X-ray, and other bands of the spectrum, but still saw nothing.

In the air along the path of her fall she noticed the weak prismatic shimmering of the hypofield. Maya composed and initiated a program to make the effect more noticeable to her i-cite.

A pair of indistinct figures stood atop the control platform. Despite their graininess, there was no mistaking the tall, lithe shapes of Grey exobeings.

The sight of them flashed Maya back to the Epsilon Eridani incident of three years ago. Her chest burned in anger at the memory. The Greys' destruction of the research outpost—and her near-death experience there—had taught her to loathe and fear them.

She had been a lieutenant commander then, assigned to oversee supply transfer between the starship *Sacagawea* and the new research outpost on the largest moon orbiting a gas giant. The Greys had drawn the *Sacagawea* away from the moon with a bogus distress call and then attacked the starship. With the ship occupied, the Greys had placed a small asteroid on a collision course with the outpost.

The *Sacagawea* had won the battle, but the Greys' fleet had critically damaged it in the process. This had left the vessel adrift in space, unable to reach the asteroid in time to deflect it or teleport anyone away from the moon.

Down on the outpost, Maya had managed to evacuate all but twenty-six of the more than four-hundred colonists aboard transport shuttles before the gigantic rock had slammed into the outpost. She remembered watching the collision as she retreated across the cratered lunar surface in a hover rover. The impact had launched plumes of dust and debris for kilometers in all directions, like an explosive dirt geyser.

The blast wave had caught up to the rover, slammed it into the ground, and buried it. Maya had survived because she had crammed herself into an armored flight suit she found in the outpost's launch bay. The other rover passengers, a young ensign and a pregnant colonist, were wearing basic EVA suits and died in the crash.

Every time Maya closed her eyes, she still saw the sphere-shaped droplets of blood floating around the corpses inside the rover.

Rescue teams from *Sacagawa* had dug her out almost a day later. After finding no other survivors, the crew had spent two months repairing the phase drive so the ship could limp back to Sol.

IEF Command had promoted Maya to the rank of commander for her valiant saving of so many lives—but she wasn't about to thank the Greys for it.

Atop the generator control platform, the shorter Grey stood interface-ing with the control rends. The controls flashed red and buzzed with errors, thanks to the last-minute encryption Maya had put in place.

The taller Grey descended the steps nearest to Maya, pointing the outline of a weapon at her.

Gritting her teeth, she pushed off with her good foot and arm, sliding backwards.

A loud click echoed throughout the plant. A whoosh of air followed.

Three nails flew over Maya's head and punctured the tall Grey, driving the genderless being backwards. Knocked off-balance, it rolled down the steps and sprawled out on the floor, likely dead.

The nail bot that had shot the tall Grey soared past Maya. The short Grey on the platform blasted it, reducing it to shrapnel.

Then a thick liquid poured onto the short Grey from high atop the generator, drenching the intruder in nanocomposite polymer.

The short Grey struggled to move under the fast-drying polymer. With great effort, it directed its weapon upward, searching for the fabrication bot that had doused it.

A hammer bot darted at the short Grey and pounded away at its shins. Meanwhile, an android plant technician rushed up the steps, pried the weapon out of the Grey's grasp, and bashed the exobeing over the head.

A quake shook the plant. The platform rattled. As Maya hugged the floor, both the android and short Grey tumbled down the steps together. Over the rumbling, she heard the loud hum of the power plant fall silent.

Every rend above the control station disappeared, signaling the shutdown of the fusion generator. The light illuminating the plant changed from violet to bluish-white as the rad shield dropped.

Fearing the worst, Maya covered her head.

The tremors ceased as quickly as they had started. The rends blinked to life, the hum of the generators returned, and the inside of the plant tinted back to violet.

Maya pushed herself into a sitting position. Gripping her sore shoulder, she stared for a moment at the corpses of the two Greys.

♦

Aboard *Serendipity*, Maya lay on a hospital bed in the starship's main infirmary. She rotated her left shoulder and her right ankle, wincing. An android physician's assistant had just injected her with medical nanites. The medites needed five minutes to heal the damaged bone and tissue.

Maya's stomach rumbled. The taffy hadn't held her over for long. *The moment the PA clears me, I'm going to wolf down a triple-decker bacon cheeseburger. We may only have fabricated meat and dairy onboard, but I'm so hungry I could eat the source protein blocks.*

Kepler hesitated inside the entrance to the infirmary. He stared at her like a timid animal, frowning with guilt.

With two fingers, Maya beckoned him to approach.

Hesitantly, Kepler approached the bed. "If only I hadn't gone out on that ledge, Commander."

"In the future," Maya said, "I recommend steering clear of unstable precipices."

"Good advice, ma'am."

Scanning Maya with wobbling irises, the physician's assistant gave an approving nod. "Everything appears to have healed as expected, Commander," the android said. "You're fit to return to duty."

The PA moved to the next bed to attend to the broken hand of a lieutenant. Like many of the colonists, the officer had suffered the injury after collapsing from the odorless knockout gas the Greys had pumped into the settlement.

Maya hopped to her feet, feeling as light as a synthetic fiber in the one-gee spin of the ship. She rotated her shoulder and ankle. They felt a bit stiff, but otherwise good as new.

Kepler rapped his mended fingers on the bed. "May I ask a question, Commander?"

"Sure, go ahead," she said.

"I've been wondering, ma'am. Why didn't you let the water break my fall? It had to be deep enough."

"In one-point-three gees from that height? At the rate you were dropping, the surface would've felt like concrete when you hit it."

"Okay, but why not port me straight to ground level?"

"The teleporter can't reduce momentum. No matter where I ported you, you would've emerged at the same speed. The only option was to port you higher so there was time to slow your fall. Otherwise—" She slapped her palms together.

Kepler flinched.

"Entertainment sims have been giving people the wrong ideas for centuries," Maya said. "They show characters grabbing hold of ledges to break their falls. They make you think a hero can port a plummeting damsel straight to safe ground. But here in reality, we have to deal with the laws of physics."

With an eager nod, Kepler soaked in her wisdom.

The hatch to the infirmary slid open. *Serendipity's* skipper, Captain Mbwana Yeboah, strode into the room.

Yeboah stroked his goatee as he approached her. "You're feeling better, Maya, yes?"

"Good as new, sir." Maya flexed her healed arm.

Nodding in approval, Yeboah clasped his hands behind his back. "Yes, that was quick thinking today. Hitching a ride on that science bot. Having construction bots to come to the rescue. Reversing the water flow and ramping up the pressure to unblock the pipes."

"So that's how you did it," Kepler said.

Maya leaned back against the bed. "Just another day on the job, sir."

The captain smiled. "Still fond of understatements, yes."

"I'm just glad we managed to save the colony, sir."

"Yes, another Epsilon Eridani might've convinced the IEF to pull back closer to home."

"The Greys almost got what they wanted, sir." Maya exhaled to dispel her anger.

"I never thought I'd end up facing them on my first mission, ma'am," Kepler said. "I've seen the reports. I've heard people talk. But a part of me wasn't sure that the Greys were real."

"I'm not surprised," Maya said. "Given that the Vril impersonated them in the invasion, skeptics still doubt their existence."

The captain said, "The two saboteurs in the morgue are as real as it gets, yes."

"But why did they use knockout gas, Commander?" Kepler asked. "Why not spread a more lethal biotoxin or plant charges on the generator to blow up the colony?"

"We don't know," Maya said, "but their tactics indicate the intent to discourage rather than exterminate us." She tapped her cheek with her index finger. "Even at Epsilon Eridani, they limited the asteroid to a velocity that gave most of us time to evacuate the outpost."

"Their ethics may not justify mass murder any more than ours do," Yeboah suggested. "Perhaps they have a moral code equal to ours, yes?"

"Or greater, sir," Maya said. "Sometimes I almost think they're out to prove their high-minded superiority—as if that's part of the point."

"That could be, yes." The captain turned to Kepler. "You're dismissed, Ensign."

After a last glance at Maya, Kepler exited the infirmary.

Captain Yeboah's grin faded. His irises were the color of molasses, and they stared at Maya as if she had contracted a terminal illness.

Maya stiffened her posture. "Sir?"

"Yes, the high admiral has ordered *Serendipity* to return to Sol," he said.

Maya held her palms up in confusion. "It can't be because of today's attack, sir. The report of what happened here won't reach them for almost three months. Comm signals don't travel any faster than ships."

"Yes, that's true."

"Then why, sir? Because of the Greys? Other attacks?'

"In part, yes."

"I can't believe Command would order us to turn tail, Captain. That's like conceding to the demands of terrorists. What about the colony here?"

"It'll remain with the usual defense systems and personnel, yes."

"At least we didn't come all the way out here for nothing." She placed her hands on her hips. "Still, sir, we should keep pushing out farther. We're supposed to be the first to travel a hundred light years."

"Yes, unfortunately, that honor will fall to the *Heinlein*."

"Wait, so another starship is assuming our mission?" She shook her head. "That doesn't make sense, sir. It'll take the *Heinlein* two years round-trip. We can do it in half that time."

Yeboah folded his arms and glared at her. "Yes, our recall has more to do with your performance."

"My performance, sir?" Her palms grew sweaty.

"They're not happy with you remaining part of the crew of *Serendipity*."

"I don't understand, sir. They'd cancel the mission and recall the ship because of me?" She thought about the message from Uncle Kevin. Had the IEF learned he had accessed the metatoy? *This can't be a coincidence.*

"The powers that be want you off this ship," Yeboah said. "The order came from the Alliance Administration—from Vice Administrator Saito. Yes, I can't say I disagree."

"You agree?" She grew lightheaded. "Space exploration is my life, sir. What else am I supposed to do?"

"It's been an honor serving with you, yes, but I'm afraid you no longer belong aboard this ship." The skipper extended a hand in her direction.

He wants to shake? Her chest burned in rage. *Sure, let's part ways amicably.* For once, she understood her aunt's perpetual bad attitude.

Yeboah's frown twisted its way into a grin. "Yes, you belong aboard your own ship."

Maya almost slapped her forehead. "My own ship, sir?" Her knees wobbled.

The skipper grasped her palm. "Let me be the first to extend the IEF's long-overdue congratulations, Captain."

Four—Recidivist
New Mars, Alpha Centauri System, November 2283 CE

With a gasp, Brooke flinched awake.

She found herself lying in a hospital bed in MAVEN's infirmary. A tube had been stuffed down her throat, forcing air into her lungs from a medical ventilator. When she looked at her legs, she saw new muscle and skin tissue growing over the exposed bones.

Her right arm refused to budge. A force field held it in place as her wrist and fingers reformed and reconnected. Her left arm was gone, but she could feel a warm, itchy sensation at the shoulder stub, an indication of regrowth.

An android nurse stood beside the bed, attending to the machines keeping her patient alive. The artificial woman studied rends of Brooke's healing organs hovering over the bed.

Glancing around the rest of room, Brooke found a full-fledged pity party. She wanted to growl at the people gathered around her, but lacked the lung capacity.

Kevin sat slouched in a chair next to the bed. As he ran one hand through his shaggy hair, he gazed down at her with a drooping I-can't-believe-I-almost-lost-you face. Leaning against the far wall with her arms folded, Ensign Tereshkova wore a concerned frown.

A familiar man whom she wouldn't have expected to see stood at the foot of the bed. With the faint lines on his forehead creased in contemplation, Lt. Commander Erik Maxwell focused on the rends above Brooke. He still wore his flight armor with his helmet wedged beneath one arm.

"You're awake," Kevin said, scooting to the edge of his chair. "Can you hear me, Brooke?"

Moaning, she gave a slight jerk of her chin to signal the affirmative.

"Thank the stars." Standing up, Kevin asked, "What were you thinking, getting into a cockpit?"

Brooke attempted a rebuttal and almost choked on the tube in her throat.

"Your respiratory and esophageal tissues have healed," the nurse said. "You shouldn't need assistance breathing anymore." She pried the tube out of Brooke's throat with all the gentleness of someone playing tug of war.

Following several coughs and gags, Brooke rasped, "I had to protect the gate, Kevin." Short on breath, she gulped air into her lungs. "And you."

"You know you're no longer healthy enough to fly," her husband said.

"I'm fine."

He frowned at her.

"It was recommended that the admiral coordinate the attack from the base," Tereshkova said as casually as if she were giving the time. "But given the admiral's accolades and green flight status, it was her prerogative to deploy." Standing up straight, she pushed her bangs out of her eyes and approached the bed. "Truth be told, we wouldn't be standing here now if she hadn't gone out there."

"What happened after I went down?" Brooke asked.

"The starship *Peacemaker* showed up and helped the fleet take out the motherships, ma'am. Colonel Maxwell and his fighter team launched from *Peacemaker*, overwhelmed the saucers, and forced the Greys to retreat."

"Thank you, Commander." Brooke studied Maxwell's square jaw and short, wavy hair. He had remained one of Maya's closest friends since their days together at the IEF Academy. During the years in which she had taught combat training, he had been her best student. After returning from Gliese 581, he had become the IEF's top-rated pilot in almost every statistical category.

"Glad to help, Admiral." Maxwell smiled and turned to Tereskhova. "You forgot an important detail, Ensign." To Brooke, Maxwell said, "After you crashed, ma'am, the ensign here blanked half a dozen bandits before they could finish you off."

Brooke's throat and chest tingled. She swore she could feel the medites crawling through her trachea and lungs, healing them. "Is that so?" she asked, rasping less.

"I wouldn't contradict a superior officer, ma'am," Tereshkova said.

Kevin nodded. "We can't thank you both enough."

In the lull that followed, Brooke activated her i-cite. It fuzzed briefly, but menus then popped right up.

She looked up the latest defense status and casualty reports. The *Magellan* had been destroyed, and the *Chandra* had taken a significant pounding. The battle had claimed the lives of three-hundred and sixteen pilots, along with one-hundred and forty-seven surface officers, techs, and support personnel. The colony was running on tertiary power, its force field dome barely strong enough to hold in air. Both the hypofield and gate remained offline. In short, New Mars was a war-torn mess.

Four colonists had been hospitalized for various injuries, but Hues had incurred no civilian casualties.

Despite this last bit of good news, Brooke tensed in regret, embarrassment, frustration, anger, sadness—everything she could feel to punish herself.

The beeping of the machines in the room increased.

"The patient needs to rest," the nurse scolded the visitors.

"Of course," Maxwell said. "One last thing, Admiral. *Peacemaker* is leaving our first officer behind to oversee the base."

"I should clean up my own mess," Brooke said.

"The skipper passed along new orders from Command for you, ma'am."

An encrypted message manifested in Brooke's i-cite. *Reassignment to Triton.* Brooke frowned.

"*Peacemaker* is departing tomorrow, Admiral," Maxwell said, pursing his lips. "Shall I set aside quarters for you and Director Sommerfield?"

Brooke glanced at Kevin, who nodded.

"Yes, thank you, Commander," Brooke said.

Cocking her head and raising her voice, the nurse said, "I must ask everyone to leave so that the patient can rest."

"Get well soon, Admiral." Maxwell saluted.

Matching his gesture, Tereshkova said, "It was an honor to fly with you, ma'am." The two of them exited the room.

Kevin bent over and kissed Brooke's forehead. "There'll be other gates. What's important is that I still have you."

Brooke held her husband's loving stare for the briefest of moments.

Then she averted her gaze, overcome by guilt.

"I'll come back as soon as they let me." Her husband stood and disappeared out the door.

The android nurse glanced at the entrance, prompting it to slide shut. "I thought they'd never leave." With her thumb and middle finger, she flicked a rend of one of her patient's kidneys. The organ spun like a top. "You did a number on yourself this time. As annoying as your entourage is, they had a point. You're an idiot for operating a star fighter with your nervous system in shambles."

These near-sentients are sounding more and more human all the time. Raising a regrown eyebrow, Brooke asked, "Is that your expert medical assessment?"

"You never did know when to listen to reason." The nurse sighed, blowing a strand of blonde hair out of her face. "You're still a pest, always trying to foil someone else's well-thought out plan."

The patient blinked up at the artificial woman. "What're you talking about?"

"Oh, come now. Are you getting slow and senile in your old age?"

"I'm not . . ." Brooke let her words trail off. In truth, she hadn't felt like herself while fighting to protect the gate. Her reactions had been milliseconds too slow. And how had she not even detected the warhead that took her down? Or had her AI alerted her? She couldn't remember.

"Me," the nurse said, pointing at her chest, "I cheated mortality some time ago."

Chills coursed through Brooke's limbs—the ones she still had or that had regrown, anyway. "Eve . . ."

This android was no AI or nurse. She was a human being—a mix of two humans, actually, whose neural patterns had been merged into a cyborg brain stuffed into a high-grade prosthetic body. Working on behalf of the Vril, Eve had almost killed everyone aboard *New Horizons* and nearly wiped out the Penphins just to influence the political climate back in the Sol system.

Brooke didn't know why this loathsome woman had chosen to pay her a visit now. But whatever the reason, Brooke knew it wouldn't be good for her or anyone else.

She tried pinging base security. Error icons indicating no connection popped up in her i-cite, but it came as no surprise. The Vril were always one step ahead of her.

"It took you long enough to recognize me." Eve reached into the front shirt pocket of her scrubs and pulled out a small box of candies. After dumping a handful of tiny pink sweets into her palm, she tossed them into her mouth.

"I've been wondering where you've been slinking." Brooke's throat was feeling better. "How many bodies have you been through since we last spoke? Shall I address you as Eve 492?"

The android's full mouth muffled her response. "I've lost count, so feel free to leave off the number."

"It's been ten years."

"It seems your decomposing brain can still do math," Eve quipped as she chewed. "Tell me. Have you taken up crossword sims yet? Maybe we should find you a nice retirement home. You can do your puzzles in a rocking chair."

Brooke's breathing grew heavy at the thought of her deteriorating health.

Eve dragged the chair closer to the bed and plopped down into it. "That's right, Brooke. I know the reality of your situation. You have another half decade at best before your body shuts down for good."

Try as she might, Brooke couldn't suppress the waterworks. Her eyes reddened, and tears trickled down the sides of her face. *Damn it. I don't want to feel sorry for myself in front of this bitch.*

"Sparking allowed you to cheat Death in your youth, but now He's catching up with you." Eve tossed another handful of candy into her mouth and leaned back. "If only you could go full prosthetic like yours truly, but your nervous system is too degraded for neural grafting. How's that for tragic irony?"

Eve shook her head. "Unlike almost every other human being from now on, you're going to die—and well before your time. The average life expectancy without cell scrubbing is damn near two-hundred years, but you're aging like a primitive from the twenty-first century."

"Either kill me or get out," Brooke spat.

"If I wanted you dead, we wouldn't be having this conversation. No, I think I'll stick around a tad longer."

"So why are you here? Have you found me a fountain of youth?"

Absently, Eve shook the box of candies. "And if I have?"

Brooke swore that her heart stopped for a moment. Cursing under her breath, she berated her overreaction. The desperation brought on by her present state had left her gullible. "Why should I believe you?"

"I've got the solution to all your problems," Eve said. "But wait a tad before you get too excited. My offer comes with a price."

"I'd rather die than owe you anything."

"The cost won't be payable to me," Eve said. "No, for accepting my charity, you'll reimburse Death with your most precious commodity, time."

"What the hell does that mean?'

Reaching into her pants pocket, Eve produced a case the size of a deck of cards and tossed it onto Brooke's chest. "See for yourself."

Brooke winced as the case struck her torso.

She grabbed the case with her right hand and held it up, at which point she realized the reconstruction of the hand had completed. Her fingers and wrist felt a little stiff, but otherwise functioned as well as the original.

As she shook the case, a number of objects rattled around inside of it. "What's this?"

"Your bittersweet salvation." Eve thrust out her chin. "Open it."

Brooke set the case on her chest and tapped the interface pad. The lid popped open, revealing six rectangular injectors shaped like old-fashioned cigarette lighters. "Spark injectors," she whispered. "But I can't go back to using or else—"

"Or else they'll run you into an early grave. But you're headed there, anyway."

Picking up an injector, Brooke studied it. Memories washed over her.

"If you spark and spark heavy," Eve said, "you'll feel like your youthful self again. Those ace piloting skills will return—"

"But my lifespan will shrink that much more."

"I'd guesstimate a year at most until you drop dead, flat on your face." Eve rested her chin on her fist in condescending contemplation. "To live a shorter, fuller life, or spend a prolonged period degrading to a vegetable . . . I don't envy the choice you face." She stood and sauntered toward the door. "But I know what you'll do once you learn of your niece's mission."

"What mission?" Brooke tried to sit up, but lacked the strength. "What about Maya?"

"We'll be seeing each other again soon." As the entrance slid open, Eve said, "I look forward to fighting on the same side for once."

"You're sadly mistaken if you think I'll join the Vril—"

"Join the Vril?" Eve laughed. "'Join,' she says. Times like these are why I love my job." She shook her head, beside herself. "Now, if you'll excuse me, I've got rounds to make." She whirled around and disappeared out into the hall.

Five—Transmigration
Generational Starship *Namtilla*, Interstellar Space, 201,171 BCE

Staring out a viewport at the receding Orion Nebula, Enki Namkuzu Alad Kishar flapped his wings, orienting his body in the microgravity of the ship. "Our homes are in the nebula far behind us?" Enki asked.

His mentor-progenitor, Tila Abgal Uanna Kishar, dipped her sharp beak in the affirmative. "Yes, my young novitiate." The aging geneticist puffed out her chest beneath a crimson garment. Tilting her head, she directed an amber eye at Enki. "Many cycles ago, the *Namtilla* left our home worlds of Anurash and Arala. The binary planets encircle one another like lovers who can never touch."

Grand Tila's chest deflated as she sighed. "It's a shame we've never seen them or flown their skies. Born on this ship, we've never known the joys of soaring through the open air with the suns warming our backs."

Each time Grand Tila told a story, Enki's scale-feathers stood on end.

"I shan't see our destination," Grand Tila said. "It shall be up to you and your generation to adapt us to an inhospitable world. At last you've reached an age that allows you to continue my work. This is why I've brought you here now."

The scientific emigration vessel *Namtilla* shuddered. Every wall, workbench, and piece of equipment in the hypergenetics laboratory shook.

Enki spread his wings to keep from tumbling through the air. "What was that?"

"The *Namtilla's* dormant engines have once again rumbled to life," Grand Tila said.

The violent shaking settled into a constant vibration.

"During the first leg of our journey from Anurash-Arala," Grand Tila explained, "the engines accelerated the ship to a velocity near that of light. We cruised at that speed for the middle leg of our trip. Now, the final deceleration phase has begun."

"I think I recall learning about this in my studies."

"Observe." From beneath her wing, Grand Tila extended a thin arm and pointed out the viewport. Spherical tanks the size of asteroids blocked Enki's view of the rear of the ship. "The ion drives expended half a moon's worth of antimatter in achieving such velocity. Now they require the same amount of fuel and time to slow us down."

Whirling from the viewport, Grand Tila floated over to the laboratory worktable. She flew beneath it and rose up through the circular hole in the center.

Enki swooped underneath the table and joined her.

Sealed vials and beakers, microscopes, and experiments in progress covered the table, affixed to it so that nothing drifted away. Within a thick glass case fluttered the hybridization of a flying spider and a long-billed wasp. Both were common insects found on Anurash-Arala. Replacement vertebrae for a bat raven grew in a vat. Next to the vat towered a scale model of the quadruple-helix DNA structure of their proud race, the Onaki.

The geneticist pressed a series of tiny buttons with eight needle-thin fingertips, enabling the monitor that wrapped all the way around the table. The monitor provided a three-hundred-and-sixty-degree view of the destination planet.

"Simple life can be found throughout the galaxy with relative abundance," Grand Tila said. "But this planet's full and complex ecosystem is as rare as that of our home worlds. While it isn't suited to support us, we can adapt to it. This world is why we've embarked upon our long journey."

With the eye on the left side of his head, Enki focused on the white clouds swirling over the blue oceans. With his right eye, he studied the greens and browns of the continents. "Its colors are very different."

Grand Tila nodded. "That's because of the planet's white star, which appears yellow from the surface. The oxygen and nitrogen molecules in its atmosphere scatter wavelengths of visible light, making the sky look blue. The world's plants absorb blue and red light and thus take on a green tint. Clouds of water vapor are the whites you see."

"It's strangely beautiful. . . ."

Enki's mentor-progenitor switched the monitor to show images of the indigenous life-forms.

Trees, bushes, and grass much shorter than those on Anurash-Arala grew on the ground. Colorful fish and other sea creatures filled the oceans, lakes, and rivers. Creepy bugs crawled and buzzed. Enki shivered at the sight of them. Scaled, slimy, and hairy beasts roamed the land on four legs, a strange but effective means of locomotion in the world's high gravity. Enki noted far fewer flying creatures in the empty skies than in images of his homes, but the soaring animals with beaks and feathers seemed most familiar.

"The following organisms are what I have brought you here to see," Grand Tila said.

The monitor displayed images of a hairy, bipedal animal. On its two legs, it walked erect with a slight hunch, carrying a stick with a sharpened stone affixed to the top end.

"Wow," Enki muttered. "Are these creatures intelligent?"

Chuckling, Grand Tila shook her head. "They show preliminary signs of complex thinking, but I wouldn't call them intelligent—not yet, at least. In many ways, they're similar to how we were thousands of generations ago."

"They're very strange."

"Indeed. Lacking wings, they cannot fly. As predators, their eyes face forward, so they lack our wraparound field of vision."

"Have we tried to contact them?"

"There wouldn't be any sense in trying. Any radio signal we sent would arrive only shortly before us. More importantly, they lack the means to receive, understand, or respond to any message."

"Then why are we interested in them?"

"These primitives are, expectedly, well-suited to the conditions of their planet. Our bones are long and brittle and will break in the strong gravity. We won't be able to fly in the thin atmosphere, so we'll struggle with basic movement. And we can't breathe the air."

Eyeing the hybrid spider-wasp, Enki said, "So we'll study them in order to create better adapted versions of ourselves."

Grand Tila puffed out her chest, clearly pleased with his deduction. "Correct, my young novitiate. But our work won't end there. We have chosen to cross this vast distance to solve a great mystery."

"What mystery is that?"

"The planet's diverse ecosystem presents us with the opportunity to answer a fundamental question." She pointed at the DNA model. "We seek to discover how life originated, so that we can in turn create it. Our science has reached the point where such a feat is within our grasp."

Grand Tila's chest deflated. "Still, I have reason to fear the consequences of that knowledge and the process required to attain it, beginning with our plans for the natives."

"Still grappling with your ethics, I see."

Enki looked up at the sound of the deep, powerful voice.

Mezhen Enkara Gaz Sumur, Advocate for the Pragmatic Faction and Grand Dignitary of the Caucus of Factions governing the expedition, swooped into the lab from overhead.

As Grand Mezhen halted in midair with expert precision, Enki shrank back from his immense stature. Enki found the penetrating eyes, hard scale-feathers, and sharp beaks of adults imposing enough. Grand Mezhen's long claws looked like they could rip right through the hull of the ship.

Grand Mezhen's novitiate, Gemekala Niggina Adamen Sumur, followed close behind him. When Gemekala's thoughtful stare found Enki, she bobbed her head in greeting. Enki and Gemekala had hatched near the same date, and often studied together.

Approaching the table, Grand Mezhen directed a fierce auburn eye at Grand Tila. "Many share your reservations about our colonization plan, but the Caucus of Factions made the decree before we left. The plan was born of necessity, so there's little reason to question it."

"A good scientist questions everything," Grand Tila said, "especially decisions made by bureaucrats."

"The inescapable fact is that we cannot colonize the planet without a labor force."

"We need workers or else we shan't survive," Gemekala said, nodding her head in agreement.

"That's right, my novitiate," Mezhen said. "We're too few in number to construct cities. Nor can we function on the surface without environmental shrouds. Unless your colleagues in robotics make a breakthrough before we arrive, we'll have no choice but to rely on the more advanced biological sciences."

Grand Tila sighed in resignation. "Of this I am all too aware."

"What do you mean?" Enki asked.

From beneath one wing, Grand Mezhen extended a five-jointed arm toward the grand geneticist. "Perhaps you should explain the situation to your novitiate."

"Very well." Grand Tila magnified the image of the bipedal primitive on the monitor. "The project you must help me complete, Enki, is to splice the genome of this creature with ours to create a hybrid that can perform complex tasks. Then we must domesticate our creations and make them smarter."

"These beings shall be our work force," Gemekala said. "They shall help us fashion a grand new civilization."

"That doesn't sound so bad," Enki said.

Grand Mezhen folded his wings in front of his body. "He is astute and pragmatic."

"That's a positive way to look at it, young ones," Grand Tila said. "But due diligence requires us to consider all sides of the issue. For many cycles, we debated the ethics of settling this planet and manipulating the genomes of the indigenous creatures. Would we have wanted a more advanced exospecies to claim our homes and alter our evolution? If we leave them alone, the dominant natives might become an intelligent race someday."

"That remains a possibility, but we must make decisions based on the current situation, not on a hypothetical future."

"Spoken like a true Pragmatic. If our survival required this of us, I could better accept it, but we have no such need. This mission was born of curiosity. The Scientific Faction argued against settlement—for observation only."

"And where would you have us observe from—the natural satellite lacking in atmosphere? Observing requires settling the planet, which can't be done without a labor force."

"But are we turning free-thinking beings into slaves?" Grand Tila asked.

"Slaves?" Grand Mezhen snorted. "Are the subsystems that run this ship slaves? Or are these things resources to be consumed and tools to be wielded by beings with the means to do so?"

"Inanimate objects and living beings are two different things."

Grand Mezhen pointed at the hybrid spider-wasp. "Is that concoction a slave, then? Was the meat I had for my last meal butchered from a slave, or from a domesticated animal?" He turned his head, directing an eye at Enki and Gemekala. "Do you think twice about swallowing an ant-fly? Or do you do it because you're hungry—and, most basically, because you can?"

"What can be done shall be done," Gemekala said.

Grand Tila leaned back, tight-beaked. "But should it?"

Enki didn't know what to think. The challenge of creating a whole new race of beings intrigued him, but he didn't want to hurt anyone, either.

"Our creations shall have education, culture, and purpose," Grand Mezhen said. "They shall worship us as their benevolent overseers. In turn, we shall celebrate them for helping us to construct a magnificent new society. Their existence could have no greater meaning."

"Only time will tell," Grand Tila murmured.

Six—Anachronism
Triton, Sol System, December 2283 CE

Leaning over the terrace railing on the ground floor of Base Reed, Maya basked in the fresh air. Waves crashed against the beach along the shore of Triton's largest ocean. She lived for space travel, but nothing compared to a warm breeze whipping through her hair on an Earth-like world.

The breeze caused her nose to twitch, but the air felt wondrous nonetheless.

Sol's golden rays shined down on her. Thousands of orbital mirrors redirected and concentrated the sunlight on the surface. The mirrors twinkled like daytime stars, sharing the lavender sky with the big blue marble known as Neptune. A collection of special reflectors encircled and tracked Sol's orbital path. Together, they enhanced the distant sun to make it appear as big as it looked from the ground on Earth.

When she bounced up and down, she felt heavier than the last time she had set foot on Triton. The moon should have weighed her down with eight percent of the Earth's gravity, but it felt more like a quarter gee. Planetary engineers had worked to increase the density of the core, resulting in the stronger pull and the creation of a magnetic field.

"You've put on weight," said a voice laced with playful sarcasm.

Maya turned to find Lt. Commander Josephine Ryder bounding

toward her out of the base. Thin blonde strands with pink highlights fell down to Jo's shoulders and framed her pale face. She still colored her irises pink and still preferred artificial fur-trimmed moon boots to standard-issue footwear, the regs be damned.

"Everyone here has put on weight," Maya fired back.

Shaking her head, Jo made a production out of looking Maya over.

"Hey," Maya said. "Aryana's gravity might've bulked me up a little, but it's all muscle."

Jo flashed a grin. "Sure, whatever you need to tell yourself."

Maya engulfed her best friend in a big bear hug.

As they released, Jo took a step back and twirled her hair. "Is it my imagination," Jo asked, "or are you glowing with a certain command aura?"

"I hadn't noticed," Maya said.

"Congratulations, Captain."

"Thanks, but I won't carry the rank until the promotion ceremony."

Jo folded her arms. "You still haven't learned how to take praise."

Maya sighed. "So how are the Penphins?"

"They're the same helpful, drama-free bunch as always," Jo said. "Ari says hi, by the way."

Ari, short for Aristotle, was the commander of the Penphin spacecraft that had greeted *New Horizons*. A type of telepathic empathy, or telempathy, linked every Penphin. They recognized each other and the world around them through feelings, so they didn't have the concept of names. Jo had therefore given him one.

"How is he?" Maya asked.

"Getting old," Jo said with a sad frown. "His people only live a fraction of our lifespan."

"I need to get out there soon."

"You'll be impressed if and when you do. Ari's heading up their program to design and build their first FTL spacecraft. They've made serious progress."

"If any species deserves to achieve interstellar flight, it's them."

"Amen to that."

Nodding, Maya asked, "How goes the excavation?"

Jo grasped her upper arms and shivered for effect. "Antarctica in the winter is a tropical paradise compared to the dark side of the Penphins' planet."

"I bet you wished you were back home in San Diego."

"No matter how much my pale skin fries, I'll never complain about sunshine again."

"I'm sure."

"Anyway, despite freezing our butts off, we managed to dig up half the tower plus five other buildings. We were making great progress until you screwed it up."

"Me?"

"My being recalled and your promotion can't be a coincidence. Do you know what the IEF Command briefing at 1300 hours is about?"

"I don't—well, my uncle had a breakthrough with the metatoy we found, but I don't know whether it's related."

Jo stroked her chin in thought. "Something tells me it just might be."

"I've got the same feeling, too."

Lt. Commander Erik Maxwell exited the base and joined them. His wavy hair was as short as Maya had seen it. When he saw her, he flashed his boyish smile, one that always came across as genuine rather than cocky.

"Erik." After Maya hugged him, she asked, "I take it *Peacemaker* still hasn't had any luck."

"Nope," Erik said. "We're beginning to think the Greys' home world is well beyond the fringe of human-explored space."

Maya nodded. "That's seeming more and more likely."

"You should see what this guy's been doing in his spare time." Jo said, patting Erik on the shoulder. "He's developed quite the green thumb."

"Really?" Maya asked.

Erik massaged his jaw in thought. "Up until the attack on New Mars, *Peacemaker* hadn't seen much combat, so I volunteered for a shift in hydroponics each week."

"And that's not all," Jo said. "He's been growing a bonsai tree, orchids, and that nasty pepper from the Penphins' planet in his quarters."

"Sounds like a rewarding new hobby," Maya said.

"Yeah, he's really been growing," Jo quipped. When neither Maya nor Erik laughed, Jo frowned. "You know, growing plants as a botanist and growing his skill base? Come on. . . ."

"Anyway," Erik said, "happy birthday, Maya."

"The big four-oh," Jo said. "How does it feel?"

Maya shook her head. "Technically, I'm only thirty-three."

Erik folded his arms and nodded in agreement. "You're right. Even though you were born forty years ago, you've only lived thirty-three of them. All three of us lost seven years to the time skip."

During the *New Horizons* mission, the starship had upshifted to hyperspace in 2265 and reemerged in normal space in 2272—seven years later—even though the onboard clocks had registered the passage of only six months. An act of sabotage had led to the time skip, the critical damage to the ship, and the deaths of hundreds of crew members. After many trials and tribulations, Maya, Jo, Erik, and the survivors had made it back home to Sol.

Jo's frown morphed back into a grin. "So the question posed by the 'How Old Are You' song is particularly applicable in our cases." She gave Erik a soft elbow poke in the chest. "C'mon, let's sing it."

"Not likely," Erik said, lightly pushing her away.

Glancing past Jo and Erik, Maya caught sight of her Aunt Brooke stepping out onto the terrace. Uncle Kevin followed her.

Brooke strode swiftly toward Maya.

"Hello, Auntie," Maya said.

"Hey, Squirt." Brooke pulled Maya into a firm embrace and damn near squeezed the life out of her.

With a gentle push, Brooke released her niece while keeping a vice-like grip on her upper arms. "You're looking well, Maya. I swear you haven't aged since the academy."

"I guess my implants are keeping the wrinkles at bay—but what about you? You look like you've shed a decade since the last time I saw you."

Brooke shrugged. "This is the best I've felt in years. I'm on new meds and an improved exercise regimen." She palmed a fist. "I feel ready to take on the galaxy."

Skeptical of her aunt's upbeat attitude, Maya gave a slow nod. "I'm happy to hear it." She tapped her cheek. "I heard you had an incident on New Mars, though."

"The Admiral turned the tide against the Greys," Erik said.

"It was nothing." Brooke waved her hand dismissively.

"I see," Maya droned, having already read the report of her aunt's crash.

After everyone finished their greetings, Kevin said, "I think it's time that I showed you why we brought you home, Maya."

Maya nodded. "I couldn't agree more."

Kevin glanced at Jo and Erik. "I'm not sure just what we'll discover, so. . . ."

"We'll see you at the briefing." Jo took Erik's arm and led him toward the base. "In the meantime, I have my lunch chaperone."

"I hear the mess is serving brussel sprouts," Erik said. "Delicious."

Jo stuck out her tongue. "Unless they're covered in chocolate on a pizza, no thanks."

The door leading to the terrace peeled back. Jo and Erik disappeared inside, headed for the officer's mess.

Maya followed Kevin and Brooke into the base and up to one of the many research laboratories he maintained around the Sol system. This particular lab was devoid of furniture except for a central workbench island and a ping pong table. Every one of her uncle's labs had a ping pong table. Fondly, Maya recalled the many times she had played—and beaten—her uncle as a teenager.

Zeke rested his forearms on the workbench, swiping a finger through one of his beloved 3D comic sims. He kept his mouth straight and his face relaxed, devoid of expression as usual.

As the newcomers entered, he deactivated his comics and stood up straight.

Other than his golden irises and eyes spaced too far apart, Zeke appeared human. But the resemblance ended on the surface. Zeke was a member of an advanced exospecies the IEF had yet to locate, a race somehow affiliated with the Greys.

Having found Zeke's DNA in a centuries-old ship belonging to the Greys, Vril scientists had grown him and others of his kind in a hidden base below the Martian south polar ocean. The Vril had hoped to learn how his people could manipulate human thoughts and actions in order to develop a defense against the abilities of Zeke's people.

But Zeke and the other infants had reached into the researchers' minds and unintentionally killed them, forcing the Vril to terminate the experiment. Brooke had found Zeke left for dead on the base shortly after the Vril had abandoned it in 2265.

Without Zeke's assistance, Brooke never would've reached Gliese 581 aboard the starship *Nautilus* in time to save *New Horizons*.

Most people who knew of Zeke's faculties but not of his ethics feared him. Every time he looked at Maya, as he was doing now, she tensed. But she reacted that way for a different reason than everyone else. No one knew why, but his powers didn't work on her. Seeing Zeke reminded Maya that she was, somehow, different from other humans.

The room's other occupant, an android, cocked his head at Brooke. "Hello, ma'am."

"Bob?" Brooke asked with a hard blink.

"Affirmative, ma'am," Bob said.

Bob's original bioware had served as Brooke's non-sentient flight support AI decades ago. Having evolved to become self-aware, Bob had helped Brooke save five-year-old Maya from the Vril, and prevented that same organization from exterminating the Penphins.

The android body that Bob had downloaded into gave him the look of a forty-year-old Scandinavian man. His hair was cropped short and his beard well-trimmed. He wore a pair of black-rimmed glasses for the sake of fashion.

"You hab it well," Maya said to him.

Bob jerked his head to one side. "To what habit do you refer?"

"I mean the body you in-hab-it is very handsome."

"Of course. A slang term. As you put it, I've habbed this prosthetic model for eight years, three months, and twenty-two days. My intent was to experience physicality and better understand the human realm. I'm glad it meets with your approval."

"It suits you."

"If it wasn't for your abrupt motions, I might've mistaken you for a human," Brooke said.

"I've been working to better blend in, as they say, but there are things I have yet to master. Regarding my prosthetic physique, it's a high-end model I purchased through honest work. I could no longer justify the ethics of commandeering other androids."

"The Martian and Triton governments have granted him citizen status," Kevin said. "The Science Society was only too eager to employ someone with over fifty PhDs."

Behind him, Maya spied the object she had traveled twenty-five light years to see.

Kevin stepped around the workbench and gestured for her to join him.

As Maya rounded the bench, she studied the thumb-sized metatoy—the newer one Caden had given her after *New Horizons* had returned to Sol. The shiny black toy sat atop a ten-centimeter tall interface stand. A pair of matrix towers stood on either side of the cylindrical stand, housing analysis and decryption AIs. Scanning arms protruded from the towers.

Near the interface stand, a clear dome encased the older metatoy Maya had found in the ruins on the Penphin's home world. When she zoomed in on the faded relic, she saw the tiny cracks between the thousands of pieces her uncle had spent the better part of a decade reassembling. The old metatoy no longer served any useful purpose with its data extracted, but it remained a priceless historical artifact.

As Maya took a seat on a stool at the bench, everyone crowded around her.

Kevin waved his hand past the newer metatoy. Blue light shone and blinked through tiny seams on the device, indicating its activation.

The toy expanded and transformed into an antique hardcover book. When the thin book's cover swung open, the word 'Maya' appeared on the first page.

"This is as far as we've been able to get," Kevin said. "All our attempts to make it do anything more have failed."

Maya stole a brief glance at the others in the room.

With a deep breath, she tried to ping the toy with a signal from her neural implants. Anyone might use the same standard protocol to access SolNet, comm a friend, or to instruct a normal metatoy to change shape.

Her ping had no effect.

Resting her elbows on the table, Maya tapped her check in thought.

She reached out and touched the title page. It felt rough, like real paper. Now that she thought about it, she had only touched paper on a couple of occasions—once in a museum in elementary school, and then in the IEF academy's physical library.

The paper was a pretty fused novelty. The coarse feel of the thin wood fibers on her skin whisked her back to sims of the Renaissance from high school.

Dragging her index finger to the edge opposite the binding, she turned the page.

Kevin rushed closer to the bench. "It's never let us do that."

"As best as we could discern," Bob said, "the metabook consisted of only the single title page affixed to the back cover."

Three lines of text adorned the next page. The first line was the number: -71482792.0609491.

Kevin said, "It looks like a—"

"A Julian date and time," Bob said.

"But a negative one?"

"Assuming Solar Standard Time, it converts to 10:32:14 on October 13th, 200,423 BCE."

Maya blinked in astonishment.

"The second line lists two other numbers," Zeke said, "11.893200 and 52.781029."

Bob cocked his head while processing. "Presumably, Earth-based latitude and longitude. The coordinates correspond to a location on or under the Indian Ocean off the coast of East Africa."

Brooke leaned over Maya's shoulder and read the third line. "Fear not. All will come full circle."

Unable to rip her stare away from the words, Maya trembled in terror. Light-headed and gasping for breath, she gripped the edge of the bench to keep from keeling over.

"What's wrong?" Brooke asked. To her husband, she yelled, "Turn that thing off."

Kevin whipped his gaze toward the metabook. It shrank back to its original stick shape and deactivated.

Maya stumbled to her feet, tripping. Brooke propped her up to keep her from falling.

Sucking air into her lungs, Maya evened her breathing. As her dizziness subsided, she said, "It's too dark and cramped in here. I need to get out."

"There's a balcony across the hall," Zeke said.

Brooke put her arm around her niece's back. "I'll take you."

Pushing her aunt away, Maya rushed out of the lab, staggered through the hallway, and stumbled out onto the balcony.

The noon hour had arrived. The magnified rays of Sol glared down on her, relieving her bout of nyctophobia.

Maya squeezed the railing with both hands. As she stared down at the people on the terrace, she tried to reconcile the words from the book with a disjointed but powerful memory.

Someone stepped out onto the balcony behind her.

Maya blew out a sigh, not wanting to deal with anyone's attempts to console her. "Please leave me alone."

The individual came to stand next to her. "Please clarify your request. How would I leave aloneness, an intangible state of being, here for you?"

Out of the corner of her eye, Maya saw Bob standing at her side. "I'm in no mood to explain human sayings to you."

"My apologies," Bob said as she stared out over the ocean. "That was my attempt at humor. I had hoped to improve your disposition. From your reaction, I must assume I was unsuccessful."

No longer trembling, Maya shrugged. "Not the best attempt—but not the worst, either."

"I'm continuing to work on comforting others. My girlfriend says I sometimes lack—"

Now gawking at him, she asked, "You have a girlfriend?"

"Affirmative."

Maya grinned in disbelief. "An AI habbing an android body has a girlfriend. How does that work?"

Bob cocked his head. "Are you not aware of sexual—?"

"What I meant was how did you meet?" Maya asked with a laugh. "What are your dates like? Do you do dinner and a sim like anyone else? I assume she knows you're an AI."

Nodding his mechanical nod, Bob answered her questions. As each astounding detail left her prying for more, the panic-induced shivers and wooziness faded away.

Maya heard whispering inside the hallway. "You can come out here."

Peeking out from hiding, Brooke stepped onto the balcony. Kevin and Zeke followed.

"Are you all right?" Brooke asked.

"I'm fine, thank you," Maya said.

"What did that thing do to you?"

"It didn't do anything to me. The words reminded me of something I haven't thought about in a long time."

"Something that gave you a panic attack?"

Maya felt the angst rising again. Straightening her uniform, she shook it off. "When I was about three years old, I went for a trip on a transit liner with my mom."

"With Marie," Brooke whispered the name of her deceased sister.

"A transit liner?" Zeke asked.

"Phase portals didn't exist back then," Brooke explained. "Commuters rode shuttles into orbit and traveled aboard passenger ships called transit liners to other places in the Sol system. It used to take a week to get from Earth to Mars when Mars was at perigee."

"Right," Maya said. "I think Mom was taking me to Luna, but it was such a long time ago, I don't remember the details."

"I'm surprised you recall much of anything from that age," Kevin said.

"You'll understand why I remember in a moment. You see, I wandered out of our cabin—I think Mom had fallen asleep on her bed—and went exploring like a nosy little kid. Somehow, I found my way into an airlock. There I stared down through the viewport in the floor's outer hatch, fascinated by the far-stretching curvature of the Earth."

Maya paused, remembering how she had shuddered in excitement during her very first trip into orbit. Space had seemed like a magical realm full of wonder and possibility.

"All of a sudden, the ship shook," she said. "An AI glitch caused a number of systems aboard to malfunction. The inner hatch sealed, trapping me inside the airlock, and the ship's rotation stopped.

"As I drifted up into the air, displays flashed and darkened, and the Earth disappeared. I couldn't see the stars because the ship began passing through the planet's shadow.

"I was all alone, flailing helplessly in a pitch-black abyss. I cried out but felt like I couldn't breathe. I didn't think I was going to die. I feared I was already dead. I've never been so scared in all my life."

"That's why you're afraid of the dark," Brooke said. "You never told me."

"I don't like to talk or even think about it."

"So what happened?" Zeke asked. "Obviously, you got out."

"I did," Maya said. "I was stuck in there for hours before a flight attendant found me. The only thing that kept me sane was. . . ." She stared at the floor of the balcony and shook her head. "I've told myself again and again I had to have imagined it. But reading those words. . . ."

"What happened?" Brooke asked.

Maya looked up. "Someone held my hand."

"In a sealed airlock?"

"Yes, and the woman uttered the words, 'Fear not. All will come full circle.' And sure enough, as she held my hand, Sol broke over the horizon. Slowly, the ship moved out from beyond the Earth's shadow, and I could see the stars again."

"So 'full circle' referred to the rotation of the planet," Kevin said.

"Apparently."

"Please excuse the obvious question," Bob said, "but did the stewardess not find another individual present with you?"

"No. The airlock was the size of a closet. There was nowhere for anyone to hide." Maya leaned back against the railing. "All my life I've believed I made up an imaginary friend to keep me safe. For that reason, I've never told anyone what happened." She ran her palms down her face. "How could a 200,000 year-old piece of modern-day tech contain a phrase that a person I imagined said to me when I was a kid?"

No one had an answer for her.

♦

Brooke remained on the balcony, mulling her niece's story, as Maya and Kevin headed inside.

Zeke stayed behind. He frowned at her. "So you're going to let your pride keep you from telling anyone, I see."

Slapping her palm against the railing, Brooke scowled. "Stay out of my damn head."

"I can't respect your privacy when you're oozing despair from behind that tough façade. To me, that's the equivalent of a blinking sign."

The growl building in Brooke's throat weakened to a sigh.

Propping her weight up with both hands, she hung her head, fighting tears of shame and loathing. Most of the time she managed to keep her self-pity bottled up. But during the return flight aboard *Peacemaker*, she had commed the family members of everyone who had died on New Mars. The gut-wrenching sobs, irate shouts, and scapegoating still haunted her.

"One year to live," Zeke said. "I'm sorry." He sighed. "But is it worth it?"

"I'd rather live a short while as a functional human being than spend years devolving into a brain-dead cripple." Brooke blew out a breath to compose herself. "Besides, from the little I've learned about what lies ahead for Maya, I'm going to need to be strong for her."

"That's very selfless. But you have more selfish reasons as well."

Brooke looked up, ready to snap at him, but Zeke cut her off. "I can't blame you for wanting to do what you love until the end," he said. "Flying is the one thing you care about as much as Maya."

All Brooke could do was nod.

"And speaking of Maya and the metatoy . . ." Zeke let his words trail off.

With an exasperated grunt, Brooke asked, "What about them?"

"I need to be a part of what transpires."

"What does that mean?" As the question was exiting her mouth, she thought of Eve's comment back on New Mars. Eve had mentioned a mission for Maya.

Having read Brooke's thoughts, Zeke said, "It's critical I be a part of it."

In his owlish, yellow stare, she saw an assured seriousness that unnerved her far more than if he had shouted demands. His extrasolar origins afforded him an extraordinary prescience which she had learned to take seriously.

"When the time comes, I'll see what I can do," she whispered.

"Thank you."

Brooke stepped around him, headed inside.

"And don't worry," he said. "It's not my place to tell anyone about your condition, but I urge you to do so. The people who care about you would want to know."

She straightened her uniform. "I will—when the time's right."

♦

As Brooke stepped off a lift onto the top floor of Base Reed, she marched briskly toward the main briefing room. Groups of IA and IEF officials stood chatting in the hallway lounge along her path. The last thing she wanted right now was to get dragged into small talk. A single syllable of hollow banter might drive her to put a particle gun to her temple.

Skidding to a halt, Brooke blinked at the sight of Shin Saito, the Vril defector who had disappeared after helping her reach Gliese 581 and *New Horizons*.

Neither Brooke nor Zeke had seen or spoken to Shin since the ordeal. Then one day three years ago his name had popped up on news feeds regarding IA politics. Before she knew it, the people had elected him to the position of Vice Administrator, second in authority only to the IA Prime Administrator.

As Brooke stressed over whether to confront Shin or bolt, he looked in her direction.

Her palms began to sweat.

Shin excused himself from his conversation and approached her.

With a wide smile, Shin held his hand out to shake. "Admiral Davis, I presume. I don't believe I've had the pleasure."

"The pleasure?" Brooke repeated in a deadpan tone.

"Have we met?" Pulling back, Shin touched his hair as if adjusting the flat cap that had once been a constant atop his head. The cap would've gone perfectly, too, with his vintage suitcoat, vest, tie, and slacks. "Please pardon my memory. I shake so many hands and kiss so many babies, it's possible I don't recall."

With her jaw locked partway open, Brooke considered Shin's memory lapse and superficial demeanor. This politician didn't seem at all like the man she had known. Shin had been real and passionate about exposing the Vril. His tortured soul had sought atonement for the horrific act he had performed as an agent.

Shin had given the order to rewrite the personality of his sister, Xiaoqing, whose protest rallies had threatened the stability of the previous government. This had turned a strong, free-thinking dissenter into a docile yes-woman. Xi would've remained that way had Zeke not used his abilities to restore her true self.

Brooke's chest grew heavy at the thought of Xiaoqing. Xi had died during a violent anti-war protest before *New Horizons* had returned to Sol. Rarely known for outward displays of emotion, Zeke had shed tears upon hearing of his Xi's death. Xi had been his foster mother.

An android woman approached Brooke and Shin. The sight of her tensed Brooke's every appendage.

"Have you met Advisor Sybil?" Shin asked, holding his palm out toward the woman. "Admiral Brooke Davis, this is Evelyn Sybil, special advisor to the IA Administration."

Eve was the Vril agent who had visited Brooke in the hospital, and her association with Shin proved that the Vril were still pulling society's strings. The rounding up of every Vril agent and the destruction of the internment camp where the authorities had imprisoned them had been a smokescreen.

In short, everything Brooke had gone through to expose them had been for nothing.

"You're looking well, Admiral," Eve said, sucking on a breath mint. "The dramatic improvement in your health has been an inspiration to us all. I do hope your good fortune continues."

Her blood boiling, Brooke nevertheless set aside for the moment any plans to expose Eve as a Vril agent.

Shin showed no sign that he had noticed Eve's subtle threat.

"Exactly what type of advising do you do, Ms. Special Advisor?" Brooke droned.

Eve took her time adjusting the front coat button on her ruby-red pants suit. Her fingers moved with a greater fluidity and dexterity than those of any human. That wasn't the case with all androids. Most baseline models had the drawing skills of a five-year-old and the strength of a prepubescent teenager. But with her top-of-the-line prosthetics, Eve could lift a person and snap their neck with one hand.

Back on New Mars, Eve had habbed a petite nurse model with pale skin and short blonde hair. Today, she had swapped into a taller body with longer brunette hair tied in a bun, a sharp nose, and a tan complexion. The harder features and pants suit screamed powerful businesswoman, even though it was a complete farce.

"I'm afraid what I know is well above even your clearance level, Admiral," Eve said, clearly enjoying Brooke's discomfort.

Brooke ignored the android's condescending tone and focused on Shin. This situation all but proved that the Vril had rewritten his personality. He had altered his sister's mind as one of their agents, and they had punished him with a similar procedure. The act had gained the Vril a powerful government puppet.

Have they erased me from his memory, or is he acting? Brooke knew she wouldn't uncover the truth at the moment. The next time she encountered Shin, she planned to have Zeke read his mind.

"You two enjoy your baby-kissing," Brooke said as she strode off into the briefing room.

Seven—Propaedeutics
Triton, Sol System, December 2283 CE

In Base Reed's main briefing room, Maya settled into a chair next to Jo at the U-shaped conference table. The flag of the Interstellar Alliance hung on the wood-trimmed wall behind the desk at the opening of the U. A constellation map of local star systems with Sol at the center adorned the flag.

The insignias of all the IEF divisions were affixed to the wall around the flag. A Hyperflare rocketed away from a star on the IEF Aerospace emblem. The Rod of Asclepius signified IEF Medicine. A domed base with rovers and suited explorers represented IEF Surface. The IEF Scientific crest featured a quark, history book, beaker, and other instruments. A wrench in front of a gear stood for IEF Engineering, Operations, and Fabrication. And a starship exited a wormhole on the symbol for IEF Fleet. Maya wore the Fleet patch on her upper arm.

Behind her, Sol warmed her back through the windows that lined the room.

"You look a little frazzled," Jo said.

Maya shrugged. "Nothing a frosty beverage wouldn't fix."

"Speaking of drinks. . . ." With a smile, Jo flashed the peace sign. "A Roman walks into a bar, holds up two fingers, and says, 'I'll have five beers, please.'"

"Funny."

"C'mon. That had my history colleagues rolling in the aisles."

"You'll have to settle for an eye-roll."

"I'll take it."

"So what did you find out from the metatoy?" Erik asked as he took a seat on the other side of Jo.

Blowing out an uneven sigh, Maya told them what she had learned.

"Trapped in a dark airlock as a kid," Erik said. "That's horrible."

Jo smirked. "But it explains a lot."

"Thanks," Maya droned.

High-ranking officials began filing into the room. Maya, Jo, and Erik stood at attention.

Vice Admiral Brooke Davis-Sommerfield sat next to Erik at one end of the U. Vice Administrator Shin Saito of the IA Administration and Director Kevin Sommerfield of the Scientific Society settled into chairs on the opposite side of the table. Bob and two other vice admirals filled out the remaining seats around the U.

IEF High Admiral Henrik Westerberg, the former ISC Defense captain who had called for the ceasefire when *New Horizons* had returned from Gliese 581, entered the room last and sat at a rectangular table facing the open part of the U.

Steepling his fingers together, Admiral Westerberg invited everyone to sit.

The individuals present qualified as some of the most influential people alive, Maya noted as she obeyed.

"Thank you all for coming." Westerberg said. "I'm sure you're eager to know why we called everyone here, so let's get right to it." He directed his deep-set eyes toward Director Sommerfield. "This meeting is in regard to the artifact found on the Penphins' planet, and the implications of that discovery."

Maya looked at Kevin. This was the first she had heard that anyone outside of her circle of confidence knew about the metatoy.

Kevin leaned forward and gave Maya an apologetic stare. "After verifying the device's age and origins, I felt obligated to inform IEF Command and the IA Administration. I couldn't sit on the knowledge, given the potential ramifications."

Maya nodded in understanding. Withholding the information would've qualified as selfish, perhaps even damaging to society. Kevin would've been no better than a Vril agent.

"So you've confirmed the toy's age of 200,000 years even though a company invented it only a decade ago," Brooke stated for the record.

"Yes," Kevin said, "which presents us with a disconcerting paradox.

Simply put, this shouldn't be able to happen."

"But travel to the past is possible," Maya said. "If we set aside modern branch theory, the quick explanation is that someone shifted 200,000 years into the past and left the toy there."

"Which is impossible," Bob said.

"Right," Kevin said. "Even if someone were to travel back in time, their presence and actions couldn't affect us."

"In other words," Maya clarified for everyone, "the past can't be changed."

Jo whipped her gaze back and forth between Maya, Bob, and Kevin. "Wait, time travel exists—as in, I could actually, truly, physically visit the past? You're saying I could experience in person the history I've only been able to study?"

"Yes," Kevin said. "It's been possible since the invention of the phase drive."

"By the stars. Is Santa Claus real, too?"

"The IA has tried to maintain a policy of openness and honesty since the Vril debacle," Vice Admin Saito said. "But we judged time travel to be something too dangerous to make common knowledge."

"I can understand that," Brooke said. "But I must be missing something, because I'm hearing conflicting statements. On the one hand, we can't change the past. But on the other, we have a piece of modern tech confirmed as being from the past. How can that be?"

"The purpose of this meeting," Westerberg said, "is to figure out how the impossible happened."

The hum of the air vents filled the reflective silence in the room.

"At the academy, I avoided Multi-Universal Space-Time Mechanics like the Black Plague," Jo said, "so I'm a bit lost. You say we can travel to the past. That means I could go back in time and kill my grandpa. But then my mom wouldn't be born and I'd never exist to travel back in the first place. Yet you're saying that wouldn't happen?"

As Maya gazed around the room, she noted blank stares and protruding lips from attendees.

"Given everyone's differing backgrounds," Kevin said, "I think it prudent to provide a brief Branch Theory 101 overview." He started to rise from his chair. "I'm all too happy to—"

Westerberg held out his palm to stop him. "Commander Davis, are you familiar with the theory?"

After a brief moment of hesitation, Maya nodded. "I am, sir."

"Then please take us through it."

"Yes, sir."

Frowning, Kevin sat down.

After exchanging an apologetic glance with her uncle—the scientist and professor lived for giving lectures—Maya stood up.

Maya briefly considered the best way to clarify a subject that caused most PhD students' heads to spin.

Circling around Brooke's end of the table, Maya stepped into the middle of the U. "To understand how real time travel works," she began, "we must first understand the theory of the multiverse."

She interfaced with the base's constellation of AIs. Every window turned opaque, shrouding the room in darkness. With a thought, Maya initiated an immersive sim that Jo had once shown her.

A tiny point of light shone next to Maya in the center of the U. The point exploded in a mini Big Bang. Multi-colored gases expanded to fill the room. Swirls of hot vapors coalesced, forming stars, galaxies, and galactic clusters.

The sim shifted one particular white star to the center of the briefing room and magnified it. Maya stepped out of the way.

Orbiting around the star, a disk of dense gas and dust clumped into spherical planets, birthing the Sol system. The sim centered and zoomed in on the third planet.

Asteroids and comets bombarded the Earth's cratered, lava-covered surface. Oceans formed. A large asteroid—or perhaps a small planet—collided with the Earth, broke away, and then stuck around, forming Luna. Yellowish gases enveloped the planet and then whitened. Greens and browns and blues were now visible beneath the clouds.

The Earth expanded, and Maya found herself standing in a swamp at the edge of a jungle. A towering brontosaurus stomped along in the distance, shaking the room.

Thick grey clouds darkened the sky. Maya shivered. The brontosaurus keeled over and slammed to the ground. The room quaked, the sky cleared, and the swamp dried up.

She flinched as a caveman whipped a spear past her head and punctured a gazelle.

A towering Sumerian ziggurat and walled city pushed up from the ground. Roman pillars, arches, statues, and citizens in togas soon replaced the tower. Medieval castles with moats, drawbridges, knights, and peasants appeared next. Cathedrals and theaters signaled the start of the Renaissance.

Cowboys with ten gallon hats rode horses and herded cattle. Steel skyscrapers reached for the sky. Automobiles zoomed along concrete streets. Rockets launched. The environment tinted to the rust reds of the Martian surface where colonies and grass grew under a light blue sky.

The simulated world faded, and the lights in the room came on at a low level.

"The point of that sim was to demonstrate the simple linear fashion in which time was thought to flow," Maya said, pacing within the U.

"That sim always brings a tear to my eye," Jo murmured.

Maya smiled at Jo's comment and then grew serious again. "For most of human history, time seemed straightforward enough. It ticked away at a constant rate from the past to the present to the future. Anything that happened in the past was permanent. Time travel was seen as a flight of fancy and presented unresolvable contradictions. But then Einstein's theory of relativity changed our thinking."

Maya initiated another sim. A scale model of a starship thrusting away from the Earth appeared in the middle of the U.

An oversized clock face floated near the Earth. The hour, minute, and second hands rotated at the expected rate. A digital readout below the planet read zero kilometers per hour, relative to the observer.

The hull of the starship rocketing away was transparent, so that the audience could see inside it. Meant only for demonstrative purposes, the unrealistic interior had a single deck. A man strolled back and forth across the deck. The hour and minute hands on the clock ticked normally. A speedometer near the nose of the ship reported less than one percent the speed of light.

As the ship accelerated the planet shrank into the distance, but its clock remained and continued to tell time as expected. Meanwhile, the man's strut and the ticking of the ship's clock got slower and slower as the ship's velocity increased. By the time the ship's speedometer read over ninety-nine percent the speed of light, the man and onboard clock were barely moving.

The sim paused.

"Einstein discovered that time wasn't constant," Maya said. "By varying gravity or velocity, one could speed up time or slow it down, a principle known as time dilation. We have the means to do this today."

"That's how you lost seven years on the way to Gliese 581," Brooke said.

"In a way." Maya resumed the sim.

A wormhole formed in front the starship. The puncture in space-time swallowed the ship and the room along with it, immersing everything in the salmon pink hue and prismatic wavering of hyperspace.

The external clock face representing the time in normal space continued to display.

First the ship traveled forward. Then it reversed its course. All the while, both man and clock moved at a normal rate. The process repeated again and again.

Each time the ship went forward, the hands on the external clock ticked clockwise, or forward in time, though at different rates depending on the ship's speed. Each time the ship went backward, the hands on the external clock ticked counter-clockwise—backward in time at varying rates.

Pausing the sim, Maya said, "That was a simplified visual demonstration of bi-directional time dilation, a fundamental property of hyperspace. Our three-dimensional space may be constrained by the forward flow of time, but hyperspace is a higher dimension where time and space overlap. Once in hyperspace, a ship can travel between different points in time, both forward and backward, as easily as between different points in space."

"Unbeknownst to the general public," Kevin interjected, "every phase drive includes algorithms to maintain the forward flow of time. Disable them, as Bob did to the drive aboard *New Horizons*, and a ship could travel not just anywhere but any when—past or future. How far backward or forward you can go is constrained by your available energy reserves. That's why *Horizons* couldn't have skipped ahead much more than the seven years it did."

Maya held her palm out toward Jo. "Earlier, Commander Ryder pointed out a classic contradiction of linear time travel known as the grandfather paradox."

Hyperspace, the starship, and the rest of the current sim vanished, replaced by an elderly man sitting on a rocking chair on the front porch of an old house.

On the opposite end of the porch, a wormhole appeared. A woman stepped out of the portal, pointed a gun at the old man, and blasted him. As the man slumped over, the woman faded into nothingness.

Holding her palm out toward the house, Maya said, "A person can't travel back in time and kill their ancestor, because they wouldn't exist to kill their ancestor in the first place."

"Just thinking about it makes my brain explode," Jo said.

"And we're just getting started." Maya cleared her throat. "Today, the theory of the multiverse and branch theory resolve most paradoxes."

With a wave of her hand, she swatted at the house. The motion sent it flying through the nearest wall.

The trunk of a tree began growing up out of the floor in the middle of the conference table. "The theory of the multiverse states that our universe is one branch in a multi-universe tree," Maya said. "The first event was the Big Bang at the base of the trunk. The trunk's growth represents the passage of time."

When the trunk reached table height, it split into two thick branches that each extended at opposing angles. "When a divergent event occurs, the tree splits into separate branches," she said. "Each represents an alternate timeline."

Thinner branches grew out of the thicker branches. "Each new branch results from a divergent event, a different outcome of a certain event in time," she said. "As far as we experience, only one outcome occurs. And most of the time, only one outcome does occur. But, occasionally, multiple outcomes do happen."

As the tree kept growing, Maya directed her index finger toward a pointy-ended branch. "If our present is here, it means our history lies backwards along the parent branches and down through the trunk. This path is called the branchway, and it represents our timeline, our universe."

The branchway through the tree glowed a bright blue.

"The entire tree is our multiverse," Maya said, "which is more accurately termed the biverse, biversal plane, or brane for short. Our brane consists of our timeline plus all the alternate timelines that have diverged, are diverging, and will diverge from our history, present, and future, or from the other alternate timelines."

The rest of the tree lit up in shades of violet.

"The purple branches are the alternate, or parallel, timelines," Maya explained.

Maya accepted a glass of water from an android server that had entered the room. After taking a drink, she set the glass down on the table and continued. "To be accurate, the term 'multiverse' is an oversimplification."

As she held out her arms, other trees sprouted up throughout the briefing room. "We actually live in a multi-multiverse, meaning there are other multiverses—other trees or branes—that are all very different from our own. Some of these function according to laws of physics so wildly different that we could never exist there.

"For our purposes, we'll ignore these other multiverses and focus on our slice of brane, as my academy professor liked to joke."

Maya stomped her foot. All the trees except the one in the center representing the current multiverse dropped through the floor, like moles in fear of being whacked.

"So how does a divergent event occur?" Brooke asked. "What causes a branch split?"

"Good question," Maya said. "There are two fundamental ways a split can occur. The first is through a natural occurrence, and requires heavy knowledge of quantum mechanics and string theory to understand. We're less concerned with that at the moment, so we'll skip it."

After taking another gulp of water, Maya continued. "We can also create a split through artificial means. Using the phase drive, we can travel through hyperspace to a point in the past of our universe and cause something to happen differently than it originally did, which results in an alternate universe."

A mini starship appeared near the tip of a pointy-ended branch—at the present—on the remaining tree.

The ship descended the blue branchway, traveling back through history. Partway to the trunk, the ship turned around. But instead of rising back up along the branchway, it followed a brand new branch that sprouted from the tree. "The new orange branch represents the alternate timeline the ship created by causing an outcome different than what originally happened."

Kevin spoke again. "Of course, branch theory presents its own share of inconsistencies." From his tone, Maya could tell he was leading her in a certain direction. "As a young scientist, I was baffled by the idea that a whole new universe could be created at any given moment. If all the matter and energy in a universe doubled in any given instant to create a new alternate universe, then everything that existed would duplicate exponentially and without bound. That didn't seem right to me."

"Ah." Maya wagged a finger in understanding. "But all the matter and energy in the universe aren't duplicated during a divergent event. The first law of thermodynamics, which states that the total energy of the universe is a constant, holds true for a given multiverse and perhaps across all multiverses. In other words, all the matter and energy that exists is shared and interconnected."

She gripped her wrist. "The same atoms and quarks in my arm exist in all the other, alternate timelines, but are vibrating at a different sub-quantum frequency.

"Sometimes it's easier to think of an alternate universe as a mirror universe. With each divergent event, you get a new mirror image of a universe. A mirror image doesn't physically exist. It's a reflection. We're all reflections of the same matter and energy."

Jo twirled a lock of hair. "But wouldn't that mean the grandfather paradox is even worse in the multiverse? If I whipped out a gun and vaporized you, wouldn't all your mirror images in all the mirror timelines be snuffed out as well?"

Maya shook her head. "As humans, we have a misguided tendency to equate death or destruction with ceasing to exist. In fact, nothing ever ceases to exist. The act of vaporizing me would transfer the matter in my body into energy and microscopic particles. The parts that once comprised me would still exist, just in a different form. The form energy and matter take in one universe has no bearing on the form they take in another universe.

"If I died right now, all the other Mayas would remain alive and unaffected. All that matters is that the total sum of what once was me continues to persist in all universes, even if I'm no longer alive or intact in some of them." Maya turned to the center of the room. "Let's observe."

As the tree disappeared, the house with grandpa rocking in his chair on the porch returned. A second duplicate house—a mirror house—split away from the original. But the granddaughter who had come to kill her grandfather stood in front of the mirror house only.

On the porch of the original house, the grandfather kept rocking in his chair as if nothing had happened. A middle-aged woman, presumably his daughter, stepped onto the porch carrying a baby. When the woman set the baby down, it rapidly aged to become the granddaughter. A portal appeared and the granddaughter entered it, sending her over to the mirror house.

On the porch of the mirror house, the granddaughter fired her gun and killed her grandfather. But this time she didn't disappear, because the original house where she hadn't killed her grandfather still existed.

Maya flicked her wrist in an upward motion, sending both houses up through the ceiling. As she toggled the window panes to make them transparent, she squinted until her eyes readjusted to the sunlight.

"That still leaves an outstanding query," Bob said, setting her up as her uncle had done. "How does the multiverse respect the law of conservation of energy when an object travels back in time? Sending a ship back means taking matter and energy from the future and putting it in the past where it already exists."

"In that case," Maya said, "Mother Nature balances the past and future. When the matter of a ship from the future exits hyperspace and enters the past, the future absorbs energy from the past through the wormhole, to even the scales.

"In the grand scheme of existence, the amounts of matter and energy that make up a human ship are miniscule, so the effects are negligible. The only way we would notice the rebalancing of matter and energy across times would be if something massive shifted across—like a black hole."

"Aren't there an infinite number of possible outcomes for any given divergent event?" Bob asked with a cock of his head. "I could take any one of innumerable actions at this very moment. I could jump up and down, yell, go into sleep mode, remain seated, and so forth. Does that mean an infinite number of alternate universes are being created in every moment?"

Maya smiled. "It does seem like that could be the case, but our multi-universe tree is surprisingly finite. Out of the countless outcomes that could occur in any given moment, the single most likely outcome unfolds the vast majority of the time. Meanwhile, the less likely outcomes rarely occur. Typically, the most probable outcome is so probable that alternate universes are almost never created."

From her position in the center of the U she approached Bob, folded her arms, and stared down at him for a of couple seconds. "Of the options you suggested, which did you do just now?"

"I remained seated," he said.

"Precisely. The chances of you jumping up and down, yelling at me, or going to sleep in this meeting are, under the circumstances, miniscule. There's no reason for you to do any of those things. Therefore, I think we can assume with reasonable confidence that no alternate universe branched away just now in which you hopped up and did a little dance." She stepped back to the middle of the U.

"So when a ship travels to the past," Westerberg asked, "what is the likelihood that its presence causes a divergent event?"

"There's a one-hundred percent chance, sir. In the last sim, the granddaughter's appearance in her grandfather's time forced the creation of a second house. That's the only way she could both kill him and exist to kill him, thereby avoiding the paradox.

"Generally speaking, the moment an object from the future arrives in the past, its presence causes an immediate divergence. The object doesn't belong there, so an alternate universe forms in order to preserve the history of the original timeline. From that point the object can only move forward in the new timeline."

"Thank you, Commander," Westerberg said. "That was most enlightening."

As Maya returned to her seat, the implications of her answer to the admiral's last question remained at the forefront of her mind.

Eight—Irremeable
Triton, Sol System, December 2283 CE

"The arrival of an object from the future in the past immediately creates an alternate timeline." Folding his arms at the front of the briefing room, Admiral Westerberg looked at Kevin. "Which means what specifically for us, Director?"

"The metatoy can't exist in our past," Kevin said. "Its presence there should've created an alternate timeline that would've branched away from what we know as recorded history."

Intertwining his fingers, Westerberg leaned forward. "And yet the existence of the toy in the past is evidence to the contrary."

"Mind-bogglingly fused," Jo whispered.

Vice Administrator Saito spoke up. "So now that we have the background to understand the mystery we're facing, we can start to consider what to do about it."

"Commander Davis," Westerberg said, "please state for the record what you found when you interfaced with the metatoy."

Maya revealed the first two things she had found, a Julian date-time in the distant past and a location off the coast of East Africa. She refrained from mentioning the phrase from her childhood.

Westerberg sat back. "The moment Director Sommerfield informed me of your findings, I ordered a full neudar sweep of the area. The scans found small stone fragments that could have been the remnants of an ancient city."

"Sir," Jo said, "the Global Geological and Archaeological Neutrino Survey done at the turn of the century identified buried and submerged ruins all over the planet. The ruins date back more than 150,000 years, but most of them haven't been excavated yet. Before the GGANS findings, there was no direct evidence of organized human civilization more than 10,000 years old."

"Yes, we don't know that the information from the metatoy is connected to these particular ruins."

"Maybe I'm getting ahead of myself, sir." Jo fidgeted, unable to sit still. "But there's only one way to find out. Given that the phase drive is capable of time travel. . . ." Her eyes pleaded with the Admiral.

Westerberg finished her thought. "A mission to the past is within the realm of possibility."

"But sir, even if we removed the phase drive's safeguards aboard one of our ships," Maya said, "it wouldn't have enough antimatter to travel far enough into the past."

"*Serendipity*, the IEF vessel that carries the greatest quantity of antimatter, could travel back an approximate maximum of 1,000 years," Bob said. "That would leave it with little fuel to function when it arrived."

"In other words, it'll be possible to travel back 200,000 years someday, but we don't have the ability yet."

Jo's shoulders sagged.

"Not necessarily." Kevin exchanged glances with Westerberg. "The IEF has built a ship capable of traversing up to half a million years."

Maya sat up straighter in her seat. "I don't know of any power source capable of that."

"It's been kept hush-hush." Kevin smiled. "*Yesterday* uses the same energy source as the interstellar gate—an artificial black hole."

"Of course." Maya's pulse quickened at the notion. "Collecting the radiation produced by a black hole would be more efficient than a matter-antimatter explosion. Yeah, that would do it."

"It would," Westerberg said. "And now that we have a ship capable of traveling to the destination, it needs a crew."

A mix of elation and dread rumbled within Maya's chest. *Of course.* Westerberg had asked her rather than her uncle to give the branch theory overview, to see if she had the wherewithal to take command of such a ship.

"I might really get to visit the past." Jo's face beamed. "Do you know how long I've dreamed of this? Only all my life and then some."

Having absorbed everything in silence up until this point, Erik frowned. "Temper your enthusiasm until you hear the catch."

"What catch?" Jo asked.

"Remember that arriving in the past causes an alternate timeline to unfold from that point onward," Maya said. "If we go back, we can never return."

Lines creased Jo's forehead as she processed the statement. "You're saying that if we travel to the past and then return to our own time, it won't be the same."

"Affirmative," Bob said. "The new timeline's future may or may not resemble the present you know now. Predicting the degree to which the timeline will differ from ours after the passage of 200,000 years is well beyond the capabilities of the most sophisticated AI."

"On one hand," Maya said, "if the timeline plays out similarly enough to ours, we'll encounter different versions of ourselves. The closer that future is to our present, the greater the chances our different selves will be living our lives. We won't be able to resume them."

"On the other hand," Erik said, "if that future isn't anything like what exists now, our lives may not exist to resume."

After tugging at her hair, Jo smacked the table with a palm. "Yeah, but we also can't alter our present by changing the past. That means the here and now will still be out there somewhere. Everything in the present won't cease to exist after we're gone, right?"

"True," Maya said.

"Then all we have to do is find and return to our own timeline."

Kevin shook his head. "Our timeline will in fact continue to exist as a separate branch in the tree, but returning to that branch is beyond our current capabilities. I'll skip the physics behind why and say that we only know how to traverse the branches. We don't yet know how to jump between them, although I'm hopeful the problem can be solved someday."

"Any time we try to traverse a branch backward," Maya said, "we create another branch that diverges the moment we exit hyperspace."

"So we can never get back to our own branch," Jo finished, frowning in understanding.

Everyone seemed to be holding their breath as they contemplated the implications.

Brooke leaned forward in her seat. "So what's the point of any mission to the past? The crew can't return or alter this timeline. How would they report their findings?"

"We don't know," Bob said.

"Then why bother? Other than giving whoever we send back a permanent history lesson, we accomplish nothing."

"The metatoy gives us hope that getting word to the future or returning to it might somehow be possible," Kevin said, massaging his chin stubble. "Everything up to this point has been either theoretical or remotely observed."

"As far as we know, no one has ever traveled to the past," Bob said.

"And like all ventures into uncharted territory, we never truly understand something until we explore it first-hand."

"So the plan is to send people into the past with the distinct possibility we'll never see or hear from them again?" Brooke slumped back in her chair. "I don't know how we could order a crew to undertake a one-way mission in good conscience."

In a low rumble, Westerberg said, "Which is why it will be a volunteer mission."

Maya tensed, feeling conflicted.

◆

Brooke rested her cheek on her fist in thought as Maya, Bob, Jo, and Erik exited the briefing room. Kevin, Admiral Westerberg, Shin Saito, and the two other vice admirals—officials with top-level clearance—remained.

This is the mission Eve mentioned, Brooke thought. *If Maya takes command and travels to the past, she may never come back.* Brooke grew lightheaded at the notion.

As the door to the room slid shut, Westerberg leaned back in his chair, smoothing his mustache. "We've heard the risks and rewards regarding any mission to the past. We have a ship. Now, I must make my go/no go recommendation to the prime administrator. Final thoughts?"

"You know my vote," Kevin said, pushing locks of his shaggy mop of hair behind one ear. "We haven't spent five years designing and building *Yesterday* in order to never use it."

The vice admiral of IEF Engineering nodded. "I agree that we should proceed," the middle-aged woman said after clearing her throat. "Sooner or later, we'll need to go public with the time travel capabilities of the phase drive. We'd best send trained professionals now before college kids figure out how to backshift in a garage somewhere."

The vice admiral of IEF Surface Operations rapped his knuckles on the table as he spoke. "This mission seems like too big of a gamble for the outside chance of learning why a child's toy ended up in the past."

"Director, what are the potential consequences of creating an alternate timeline?" Shin Saito asked.

Kevin massaged his thin beard in thought. "The actions taken by anyone we send back won't affect our past, so in theory there are no known consequences to this timeline. But the truth is that we don't know how many timelines exist or how creating additional timelines affects the multiverse. Will we kick-start the second timeline ever to exist? Or are there a near-infinite number?

"Also, the metatoy is the unknown variable. Based on its existence, we could be wrong about everything. We won't ever know until we try."

"Then I vote yes," Shin said. "If our ancestors had played it safe, we might still be living in huts and hunting for our dinner with sticks and stones."

Westerberg grunted in assent and sat forward. "Admiral Davis, what do you think?"

Flinching, Brooke lifted her cheek away from her fist. She had been half-listening to the conversation while still trying to process everything from the previous meeting. Too many considerations jumbled together in her mind. Her selfish desire to keep Maya from harm. The contents of the metatoy. Everything she had learned from her dealings with the Vril. Her recent talk with Zeke.

She had felt overwhelmed, lost. But like a targeting bracket locking onto a bandit, everything suddenly came together.

A chill ran up her spine as she realized her stance. It wasn't what she wanted, but it felt right. "I've never believed in fate or that things happen for a reason," she said. "We've discussed the consequences of acting, but what about the ramifications of not acting?"

The vice admirals looked at one another.

Tapping the table with a knuckle, the vice admiral of surface ops said, "Nothing. Life would go on, and we'd learn to live with an unsolved mystery."

Kevin's eyes widened in understanding. "Actually, Admiral Davis may be onto something." He shot to his feet and paced. "I mean, the date, time, and location in the metatoy sure seemed like an invitation. What if not accepting that invitation—not creating an alternate timeline—turns out to be detrimental in some way?" Dragging his fingers through his hair, he shook his head and frowned. "But nothing we do in the past should affect our present, so that shouldn't be an issue—but the metatoy was in our past, so . . . ugh . . ."

"It's a brain teaser, to be sure," Shin said, "one we'll never solve unless we with follow through with the mission."

Westerberg looked at Kevin. "Have a seat, Director." As Kevin settled into his chair, the high admiral steepled his fingers and made eye contact with each person in the room in turn.

After completing the sweep, Westerberg said, "I've heard enough.

Like crossing the Atlantic to discover the Americas, settling Mars, or achieving faster-than-light travel, a mission to the past presents risks and rewards. The IEF is an exploratory outfit. My recommendation will be to explore."

He took a long breath. No one objected during that pause. "Now, assuming the administration sanctions the mission, who should take command of *Yesterday*? I'm inclined to offer the position to Commander Davis, once she's promoted to captain."

"For whatever reason, the information in the metatoy was addressed to her," Kevin said. "No one else makes sense."

"Perhaps," the admiral of surface ops said, tapping the table with his fingernails. "But should such an important assignment be given to a new captain?"

The admiral of engineering cleared her throat. "And to such a young officer? Really, Davis has a mere decade of field experience."

"I've reviewed her record," Shin said, reading from a data rend hovering in front of him. "Maya has earned every award the IEF has to offer. She was instrumental in bringing *New Horizons* home. She saved hundreds of lives at Epsilon Eridani and almost single-handedly stopped the Greys on Aryana." He whipped his hand past the rend, deactivating it. "She may be young, but she's accomplished. She has the IA administration's full endorsement."

Brooke offered a reluctant, tight-lipped nod when Westerberg glanced at her.

Throughout the exchange, she kept her focus on Shin. Whether by choice or coercion, the man was a Vril agent. *So is that endorsement really coming from the administration, or from the Vril?*

"Having said that," Shin added, "the administration would like a more experienced officer to take command of the overall mission."

Westerberg gave a slow nod. "In that case, I would place Davis in tactical command."

"In other words, Davis would captain the ship but a senior officer would oversee the larger operation," the engineering admiral explained. "I like it."

"That would seem a prudent course," the admiral of surface ops said.

Westerberg again turned his attention to Brooke.

All this time, Brooke had been remembering how Maya had gone off on the *Horizons* mission, leaving Brooke scrambling to get out there. *Never again*, she had told herself. *The next time, I'm going along for the ride.* Since Maya's name had come up, Brooke had been waiting for an opportunity to volunteer for the mission. She had been stressing over the command structure of such an arrangement, but now Shin was offering her the solution with a neat little bow wrapped around it.

Again, she wondered how much of this was the Vril's doing. *I don't believe in fortunate coincidences.*

But none of that mattered. Where her niece went, Brooke would follow. "I would be willing to volunteer for such an assignment if offered to me," she said, answering the high admiral's unspoken query.

Kevin stared at her.

The engineering admiral asked, "You're certain there's no conflict of interest, given the family—"

"They're professionals," Westerberg insisted, cutting her off. The tone of his voice told Brooke that he found the question preposterous.

No one pressed the issue.

"The administration would also like to send someone to represent its interests," Shin said. "We deem it necessary to have a civilian presence on board."

"Certainly," Westerberg said.

"Due to our official duties, neither I nor any of the cabinet members could make the trip. Therefore, we would send Special Advisor Evelyn Sybil as our representative."

"That shouldn't present a problem," Westerberg said.

Brooke wanted to hop up on the table and scream, but she found herself paralyzed by indecision. Eve held the key to Brooke's ability to function on the mission, and Brooke didn't have a shred of real evidence about Shin or Eve's involvement with the Vril. Crying foul now might even derail the mission.

The high admiral pushed to his feet. "Admiral Davis, please work with Commander Davis on crew assignments—assuming she accepts the mission—and assuming the administration approves it. Otherwise, if there's nothing further—"

"Actually, sir," Brooke said, moving past her doubts about Shin and Eve, "on the subject of the crew, I'd like to run a specific appointment by you."

"I have complete confidence in your ability to select the most appropriate officers."

"That's just it, sir. I'd like to add another civilian."

Westerberg clasped his hands on front of his uniform coat and raised his bushy white brows. "Zeke, the exochild—well, I presume he's a young man by now?"

"Correct, sir." Brooke kept one eye on Shin, who showed no outward sign that he recognized the name. "Zeke has been a great asset to me, and—"

The admiral of surface ops rested a palm on the table. "I'm not sure how comfortable I feel including this unknown element on such a sensitive mission."

"His undue influence could present a significant security complication," the admiral of engineering added.

Brooke swallowed a huff. *Just come out and say you don't trust an exobeing with mind control abilities.*

"Unfortunately, Admiral Davis, I'm inclined to agree with your peers," Westerberg said.

"Sir," Brooke said, "you're aware that Zeke has the uncanny ability to predict future events. I've learned to take his foresight seriously. Long before we held today's meeting, he knew we'd send a mission to the past. He told me it was imperative he be included."

"Why, exactly?"

Brooke drew her lips into a thin line. "He couldn't say, because he doesn't know specifically why."

The three other admirals in the room looked at one another.

"I support Zeke's inclusion," Shin said.

Taken aback, Brooke and everyone else swung their heads in his direction.

"According to the Vril's records, every nefarious act they committed was meant to prepare us for the coming of Zeke's people," Shin said, staring at Brooke. "Does Zeke believe he might encounter them in the past?"

Nine—Saltation
East Africa, Earth, 200,572 BCE

Existing in his new body was both the strangest and most rewarding experience of grand geneticist Enki Namkuzu Alad Kishar's long and distinguished life.

As Enki stood on the second-level terrace of the unfinished stone tower, the hot yellow sun scorched his flat face. The warm air caressed his smooth and rubbery skin. As the breeze rustled the hair on his head and arms, his body tingled in delight.

Now that he lacked a wraparound field of vision, he found himself looking over his shoulder at every clang and pounding sound caused by construction in the city. Through eyes that faced straight ahead, the blue sky and white clouds no longer appeared as foreign, although his new sight lacked its previous magnification. In his old form, he could've spotted a pebble at the bottom of the water reservoir in the center of the city square.

Considering the very different environment of this planet, the degree to which his new form allowed him to acclimate to it more than compensated for the abilities he had given up.

He sensed someone approaching from behind him.

As he turned his head, Gemekala Niggina Adamen Sumur came to stand next to him. Two of the city protectors maintained a discrete distance behind her, brandishing high-velocity needle rifles. Upon the death of her mentor-progenitor, Grand Mezhen, Gemekala had ascended to Grand Dignitary, the leader of the Caucus of Factions governing the expedition.

As Gemekala directed her deep yellow eyes at Enki, he admired her strange beauty—the beauty he had created for her.

Her expression exhibited excellent symmetry, spacing, and proportion, like the rest of his people's new faces. Her sharp nose and chin gave her an authoritative air. Chestnut locks of hair fell down past her shoulders, and her golden brown skin glistened in the sunlight.

The sight of her heightened his breathing and warmed his body. He had never experienced such strong arousal prior to changing forms, but it didn't surprise him. More than ninety-nine percent of their new genetic makeup consisted of DNA sequences indigenous to this world. Certain primordial sensations and behaviors were inevitable.

"I feel stronger than ever," Gemekala said in her deep, booming voice. She balled her five-fingered hands into fists.

Enki nodded. "The tough musculoskeletal structures of our new forms are well-adapted to this world."

"The death of our generation was drawing close, but you've rejuvenated us."

"I regret that I wasn't able to do so in time to save our elders." Enki blinked long and slow, remembering. His chest grew heavy as he thought of Grand Tila, Grand Mezhen, and all the others who had given their lives to ensure that their descendants completed the journey.

"Their sacrifice shall not be forgotten. Beyond that, it's counterproductive to wish to change what has already occurred." Gemekala was the head of the Pragmatic Faction, one of the many political groups in Onaki society.

At the time the *Namtilla* had departed Anurash-Arala, the Pragmatic Faction had held a majority in the Council of Factions. Their practical ideology had dominated popular thought and culture.

Gemekala paced before Enki. "Walking is still a strange method of locomotion, even if it is effective in this high gravity. I feel very vulnerable being limited to the ground."

"I do miss the microgravity of the ship," Enki said.

"A number of our fellows have experienced vertigo. Others have suffered from psychological issues since undergoing the transformation. And the irrational few complain because they fear change."

"All of which falls within expectations. In time, I'm confident everyone will adjust."

"Confidence is less relevant than need. We have no choice but to adjust." Gemekala rolled her shoulders slightly, an ingrained habit carried over from when she had wings.

The wind blew the rancid scent of dead sea creatures and chemical odor of crop fertilizer up Enki's nostrils.

Gemekala covered her nose and mouth with one hand. "I fear I may never adjust to the sensitivity of this new olfactory organ," she said, her voice muffled by her fingers.

Once the smell had passed, Gemekala dropped her hand. "Despite the minor drawbacks, your work may be one of the greatest achievements in history."

"It's a privilege to receive your acknowledgement, Grand Dignitary, but most of the legwork was done by my predecessor, Grand Tila."

"May her essence return to the stars."

Enki gave a slow, respectful nod. "With most of the crew descending to the surface in their new forms, I have more time to devote to her dream. She wished not just to enhance life, but to create it."

Stepping over to the unfinished stone wall encircling the terrace, Gemekala looked out over the city of Urusilim. "Many in the Scientific Faction remain skeptical of whether such a feat can be accomplished."

"I'm convinced it's possible." Enki joined her and rested his palms atop the wall. "Life exists. Ergo, it must be possible to bring it into existence."

"Perhaps." Gemekala stared down at the activity in the city. "All I know is that the hominins you've brought into existence have made life possible here."

The hominins Enki had evolved from the indigenous bipeds labored to erect buildings and flatten roads around the tower. Under the direction of Onaki supervisors, the hominins guided mammoth stone blocks into place with the help of levitators—Onaki engineers had yet to design levitators with the necessary precision and power to lift the blocks without manual assistance. The more skilled workers carved murals and sculpted statues with precision tools. Others routed water to the farms and central reservoir using the knowledge of hydraulics imparted to them. On the outskirts of the city, the workers tilled the fields that grew the planet's variety of foodstuffs.

Enki's new ears detected a faint rumbling, a sound he would've heard much sooner prior to changing forms.

A supply shuttle from the *Namtilla* descended from orbit.

The rumbling grew to a thunderous roar. Enki and Gemekala craned their new necks toward the sky.

Emerging from a fireball of atmospheric friction, the cone-shaped spacecraft fired its landing rockets.

Hominins throughout the city ceased their tasks at the sight and sound. Some dropped to their knees, cowering in fear. Flight and travel to the stars were incredible abilities only their masters could possess.

"I can tell from the look on your face that you're still wrestling with the ethics of employing these beings," Gemekala said.

Enki heard Grand Tila's cautionary words in the back of his mind.

He tuned them out. Dwelling on her words would invite guilt to overwhelm him, not to mention threaten the colonization effort.

"We need them," Enki said with the most subtle of shrugs. "It's as simple as that."

The blinding rocket exhaust lit up the sky, outshining the sun, until the craft settled down on the outskirts of Urusilim.

As the deafening noise ceased, the hominins slowly rose to their feet and resumed their work.

"Construction is behind schedule," Gemekala said.

"Our people once used stone to build cities on our homes," Enki said, happy to change of subject. "But the gravity is four times greater here. The choice of the heavy material seems curious to me."

"Yes, I was against the impractical nature of stone at first, but the other factions lobbied for it. The Architectural Faction wanted structures to last, given the harsher climate. The Faction of Artisans insisted upon stone for statues, murals, and other aesthetics."

"I see."

"At this early juncture, the Industrial Faction also lacks the infrastructure to fabricate more complex materials. The only factories are aboard the *Namtilla*. But stone is readily available on the surface, and we have the levitators and hominins to do the heavy lifting." Gemekala sighed. "If the decision had been mine alone—"

Enki flinched at the sound of a loud crash accompanied by screams.

Gemekala stared down over the edge of the stone wall, baring her teeth in disapproval at the scene.

Struggling to discern the commotion from so high up—male vision had degraded more than female eyesight in their new forms—Enki grabbed his magnifiers from his belt. When he placed them over his forward-facing eyes, the view appeared stretched and distorted. Engineers were continuing to work on modifying tools to better function with their new forms, but they had yet to invent improved magnifiers.

A stone block had crashed to the ground at the base of the ramp that led up to the second-level terrace of the tower. That explained the thud Enki had heard. The acoustic levitator that supported the bulk of the block's weight had given out, making the block much too heavy for the hominins guiding it around its edges.

Blood oozed from beneath the heavy block. A hominin, his torso protruding from beneath the huge stone, was howling and writhing in pain. The block had crushed the worker's legs.

Two supervisors huddled around the hominin, assessing his injuries. A protector stood over them, holding her rifle at the ready.

The supervisor in charge shouted an order to a protector, who shot the worker in the head. The hominin became still.

Three laborers shrieked and charged at the protector. The protector fired at the hominins, ripping two of them to shreds. Before the protector could incapacitate the third worker, he slammed into her, shoulder-first, and knocked her down. The supervisors tackled the frantic hominin to the ground.

Rising to her feet, the protector shrieked in anger. She bashed the hominin in the head with the butt of her spear-shaped rifle and stilled the worker.

A pair of medics arrived on the scene to attend to the supervisors and protectors. Four more protectors joined them and stood guard in case any other hominins became belligerent.

Gemekala frowned; her body tensed. "The protector was overcome by anger. I saw it in her expression." Blowing out a breath, she relaxed her muscles as she looked herself over. "I, too, am afflicted by the same irrationality that compels your laborers to frequent acts of disobedience."

"Emotions run stronger in the hominins than in us," Enki said. "Unfortunately, I was unable to remove such tendencies from their genome. The Medical Faction has theories on how to numb the emotional centers of the brain, but they have yet to devise a safe and effective procedure."

"We're more than capable of exerting self-control, but the workers' counterproductive behavior must be curbed."

"I believe I may be able to tame them, Grand Dignitary," said a voice from behind them.

Enki turned to find Biluda stepping out of the tower and onto the terrace. Even when walking, the gangly advocate for the Reverent Faction was always hunched over, with his thin brow furrowed in a perpetual expression of disapproval.

"What have you deduced?" Gemekala asked.

"I believe we have erred in treating these hominins like tools or machines," Biluda said. "We need to deal with the reality that they're biological sentients, even though not on our level." He stepped into the shade of a support column. "This planet is so uncomfortably hot."

"I'm afraid altering the weather is beyond our capabilities. You were saying?"

"Yes. Take for example the incident that just occurred. The injured worker had a desire not to be stilled. His fellows sympathized with him and feared that one day they might suffer the same fate. What's more, I think they were after—"

"Revenge." Gemekala interjected as she raised a thin eyebrow. "I was unaware they were capable of it."

"They are," Enki said. "In the first generation of hominins, I witnessed everything from selflessness to hatred. Mothers love their offspring. Children tease one another. They have egos which seek gratification."

Leaning closer to them, Biluda said, "I believe psychological conditioning may reduce the number of incidents. I suggest we teach them from birth to worship and fear us as supreme masters. Let us implement a reward and consequence-based belief system. If compliant, they will receive our eternal gratitude. If disobedient, they will suffer long after being stilled. I propose exaggerating the narrative we give them. They have no way of knowing the difference between fact and fiction."

"The hominins require exorbitant amounts of water, foodstuffs, and rest. After birth they're not productive for many cycles." Gemekala shook her head. "And now you're saying we must provide additional conditioning beyond work instruction?"

"I believe so."

Gemekala sighed. "I would've preferred more autonomous workers that didn't require such elaborate maintenance, but we must deal with the situation at hand." She turned to Enki. "Do you believe such an approach would prove effective?"

The geneticist blinked slowly as he mulled over the problem. Grand Tila would not have favored a plan to fill the heads of thinking beings with false beliefs. Who could predict the consequences of such an action?

"I see no practical reason why it wouldn't work," Enki said, knowing his place. "But I believe they may best respond to positive reinforcement. Might I suggest teaching them the sciences and introducing them to culture? They have the mental capacity."

"But would your plan result in the opposite effect?" Biluda asked. "Would it not give them further means to defy us?"

"Perhaps, but it seems less of a risk than manipulating their perceptions."

After staring at the strange, orange-red sunset, Gemekala said, "I have my doubts, but we must implement measures now before a larger problem manifests itself. Therefore, we shall proceed on both fronts. Advocate Biluda, begin creating new training regimens that instill the necessary beliefs along with the arts and sciences."

"Thank you, Grand Dignitary. I'll begin preparations at once." Biluda bowed and disappeared into the tower.

Gemekala glanced down at the cleanup underway and then back to Enki. "In case psychological and educational measures fail, I want a guarantee that our workforce never gains the capacity to present a serious threat."

Enki frowned. "The hominins have needs born of this world. These instincts aren't easily rooted out of their nature. My techniques have come a long way, but producing an ideal laborer falls outside the realm of my abilities."

"I'm not asking for flawlessness, my fellow. A Pragmatist knows better than anyone that nothing is perfect. Nevertheless, I must assume you're designing improved versions."

"My work continues, yes."

"Would it be possible to implement a direct means of controlling them?"

Enki gave a start at the question. After giving the suggestion serious thought, he answered. "I believe it's possible. Their nervous systems function via simple electrical impulses. In the next generation I could allow those impulses to be overridden by specific brainwave frequencies."

"Then do it." Gemekala turned her back to the view and headed back inside the tower.

Ten—Excogitate
Chicago, Earth, March 2284 CE

Three months had passed since the briefing. Following a heated debate and vote in an unpublicized session, the IA administration had sanctioned the mission by a scant majority. The high admiral had ordered everyone who might accept the assignment to take leave, weigh the consequences, and enjoy the present in case they never saw it again.

Now the time to decide was drawing near.

Maya could've contemplated her decision anywhere in the Sol system. She could've gone to the Saturnian system to see cryovolcanoes shoot geyser-like jets of water vapor kilometers above the surface of Enceladus. She could've teleported to a comet approved by the IA Board of Tourism. Here on Earth, she could've admired the astounding colors of the Aurora Borealis, gawked at the size and scope of the Grand Canyon, or climbed the steps of Chichen Itza to get into the general mindset of where and when she might be headed.

Instead, sentiment had compelled her to visit a more conventional location.

Throughout her short time in this universe, she had led a certifiably nomadic life. She had lived in Yokohama, Chicago, New York, Auckland, and in too many hotels and temporary habitats—not to mention her time on Mars, Triton, and eight different starships.

When she dug deep down, she found that she missed only one place. Not the first or last spot in which she had lived. Not the location she had resided in the longest or the abode she remembered best. Rather, the one that still called out to her decades later was where her family had been intact.

Unfortunately, that place no longer existed.

Taking a swig from a thermos of hot chocolate—she had never cared much for coffee or tea—Maya sat on a bench in a park on the north side of Chicago.

A cool gust of early spring air numbed her reddening face and left her shivering. She turned up the heat in her coat and boots and thickened the scarf wrapped around her neck.

The new park spanned multiple blocks and rested in the shadow of the towering stratoscrapers of downtown Chicago. The buildings in the immediate neighborhood had been crumbling for over a century, given that most residents had migrated off world. Rather than construct additional structures for the thinning population of planet Earth, the city had elected to tear everything down and erect a park.

And what a park they had constructed! Fountains with abstract works of art and statues spouted water in timed patterns. Pedestrians meandered down winding paths. Cheery androids roamed the grounds selling food and drink, answering questions, and keeping the peace. Soft music played from unseen speakers. Flowers imported from all corners of the globe had begun to sprout up everywhere, irritating Maya's nostrils with sweet-smelling pollen.

From her bench, Maya watched a pair of intramural teams playing a heated game of mag-ball on a nearby grassy field. She had played mag-ball in high school and on occasion at the IEF Academy—a lifetime ago, it seemed. *I used to be pretty good, too.*

Maya stared past it all, her chest deflating. Vague memories teased her mind as she stared absently at the mag-ball field where her childhood apartment had once stood. Given her allergies, her mom had bought her a pet robot. Mom had made pancakes and the bot had served them to a very grumpy Aunt Brooke. Brooke had read Maya stories, played games with her, and tucked her in at night. *What I wouldn't give to go back to that time, if only for a moment.*

Thoughts of the past quickened her breathing, given the real possibility of time travel. *What if I shifted back to a point before my mom died? I could pull her to safety before the debris sliced her neck. I could stop her and Aunt Brooke from going to the UN Headquarters building in the first place. Hell, why stop there?*

She tapped her cheek.

I could keep Horizons *from getting stranded out near Gliese 581, and put an end to the Vril's schemes before they have a chance to hatch them and—*

With the force of a punch, a hard rubber ball smacked her in the face. The impact stunned her.

Wincing, Maya dropped her thermos. She threw her arms up to guard her head, but much too late.

The ball struck the ground with a hollow ping and bounced. The thermos clanged against the concrete almost simultaneously.

She blinked, shaking off her daze. The left side of her face stung like hell, but the health status readouts in her i-cite indicated no injuries.

A pair of mag-ball players stood like statues a few meters away, gaping at her.

"Oh my . . ." muttered one of them, a girl in her twenties wearing shin guards and cleats.

"That was so not fused," her male companion said, scratching his head.

"We're so sorry."

"Are you okay?"

Maya realized the ball had sailed out of bounds, away from the game field, and hit her by accident. Blowing out a breath to release her tension, she said, "Yeah. Don't worry about it."

Rubbing her left cheek, Maya stepped over to the ball and picked it up. About the size of a coconut, the ball was made of nanite-laced smart rubber. Its built-in superconducting magnets allowed it to defy gravity and travel in straight lines rather than arcs.

She tossed the lightweight ball up and down a couple times to get a feel for it. Players had repeatedly kicked and punished it, so it no longer held the shape of a perfect sphere.

Removing her jacket and throwing it onto the bench, she gripped the ball with one palm.

She stepped back, wound up, and flung the ball toward the two players, putting topspin on it. It struck the young man's chest between the numbers on his jersey.

"Nice throw," he yelled as he caught it.

Maya smiled and nodded.

"Again, we're really sorry," the girl said.

They turned toward the field.

Stopping, the young man whirled back around and said, "Hey, we could use an extra player if you're interested."

Biting her lip, Maya gave the offer serious consideration. She could use a diversion, something to take her mind off the mission.

She turned to grab her coat, intending to accept the invitation and follow them. But she froze in place. Her body refused to budge because of who she saw.

"Come on," the girl whispered from behind Maya. "She's not dressed to play, anyway."

"Hey, I had to at least offer," the male player said as they jogged back toward the field.

Maya couldn't believe it. Her father was sitting on the park bench.

Takashi Katayama, the estranged parent who had once told her he wanted no part in her life, frowned at her. His black hair showed no signs of graying. Nor did a single wrinkle betray his sixty-plus years of age. Wearing a suit with a standing collar tailored in the traditional Japanese style, he looked like the quadrillionaire he had become in any and all currencies.

The unease she felt made her perspire. Why was he here? He had never wanted anything to do with her. Had he changed his mind, perhaps due to a terminal illness or midlife crisis? How had he known she would be in this park in Chicago? She hadn't told anyone where she was going, because she had wanted time alone to think.

She wanted—desperately—to rush to him, shake him by the shoulders, and demand answers. If his replies failed to meet with her approval, she might grab him around the neck and choke him as punishment for being an absentee father.

But she could never do any of that. Unless threatened, she didn't have a violent cell in her body. As much as she yearned to satisfy her curiosity, she wasn't about to go rushing to him like an overeager puppy.

Sucking in a deep breath, she strolled over to the bench, grabbed her belongings without looking at him, and stormed away.

"Of course." His direct, forceful tone stopped her after two steps. "Had you reacted to my presence any other way, I might've lost respect for you."

Maya clenched both fists. *Fear not*, she told herself. *All will come full circle*. Whirling, she hissed, "Respect? You tell your own child you never wanted her, and you dare to talk about respect?" She stomped her foot. "I don't need or want your respect."

"That's fine. Respect isn't a requirement. But we do have things we need to discuss." He leaned back and motioned to the empty side of the bench with his cane. "Please have a seat."

Staring up at the sky, Maya burst out laughing. It was a sardonic, exasperated laugh; in no way did she find the situation funny. "Just like that, huh? I've met you once, briefly, in the forty years since you conceived me by mistake. And now you think you can show up out of nowhere for a friendly little chat? Well, forget it." She threw on her coat. As it auto-zipped, she spun around and resumed her retreat.

"This isn't a social call," her father said. "We need to set aside whatever feelings we may or may not have for each other."

The nerve of him! Slowing her pace, Maya was reconsidering the possibility of strangling him when he added, "It's imperative for the sake of the mission."

She almost tripped over her feet as she skidded to a halt. "What mission?"

"Let's not insult one another's intelligence. Come. Sit."

Maya's curiosity begged her to remain. Her bruised ego insisted she stomp away to spite him. Ultimately, if he had knowledge of the top secret briefing she had attended, duty demanded that she find out what he knew and how he knew it.

Glaring at him, Maya took her time approaching the bench. She settled down on the opposite side, as far away as she could get from him without falling off the edge. "I'll ask again. What mission?"

Her father narrowed his eyes at her. "You know full well what—"

"I won't be goaded into revealing classified information. You first."

Her father leaned forward, resting his hands on an ornate cane that complemented his wardrobe. "You're considering a trip no one has ever undertaken."

"I've been doing that my entire career—not that you would've noticed. You'll have to be more specific."

"Very well. One learns to talk around subjects in business, but I'm content with the direct approach. You're considering whether to travel 200,000 years into the past."

At hearing the words out loud, Maya swallowed. She had hoped against all reason that he had been referring to something else.

Her shock faded. She shouldn't have been surprised. Katayama—she was done thinking of him as her father—qualified as one of the wealthiest and most influential humans alive.

The formation of the Interstellar Alliance had reintroduced the human race to cutthroat capitalism. With the defunct socio-democratic regime of the IntraSolar Commonality no longer gorging on chunks of his wealth, Katayama was no doubt having a much easier time expanding his empire on the backs of the less fortunate.

As far as Maya was concerned, the man on the bench next to her, sitting erect and self-assured as if he owned the Sol system, represented the worst aspects of society.

"Where did you hear that?" she asked.

"I have my sources." As a major benefactor of the IA and IEF,

Katayama undoubtedly had a pipeline to find out anything he wanted to know.

"And how much do you pay your sources to violate their ethics?" Maya's chest burned at the thought of IEF personnel who could be bought.

Katayama gazed around the park. "You and I see things very differently, but we're driven by the same underlying convictions."

"You have no convictions."

"I once told you that wealth yields the power to realize possibilities. I want to make sure that important things happen. We both want the same things."

"The same things? I push the boundaries of human knowledge for everyone. You accumulate material possessions for yourself. How are those goals even remotely similar?"

"All I've accumulated is a means to a different end than the one you assume." Gazing toward the players on the field, Katayama said solemnly, "My concern is for them—free-thinking beings playing a simple game because they choose to do it. They're free to choose how they live. Free to exist. That's what I want to continue to happen, now, then, and always."

She stared at him. "What are you talking about?"

"You make incorrect assumptions about my motivations and goals— and that's to be expected. I've encouraged your perception of me. The building of my empire, our disassociation, your anger toward me . . . it's all been part of an important plan."

"I can't think of a single plan that could justify how you conduct yourself."

Katayama turned to stare at her. "What if that plan ensures not just the survival of our race but its very conception?"

The realization hit Maya harder than the sting of the mag-ball. She sat rigid, afraid to breathe.

Her father was a member of the Vril. Knowing the scope of his ambitions, she doubted he held a low-level position. How had she not seen it sooner?

"I can see in your eyes that you're beginning to understand," Katayama said.

The thought of pinging the police popped into Maya's head. This man belonged in a cell shrouded by the strongest available force field.

But notifying the authorities wouldn't do any good. She had no proof. He had the best lawyers money could buy, and he probably owned the police, too.

"I know you disapprove of my organization and of me," Katayama said, "which is of no consequence. You'll accept the mission."

"You don't know me or what I'll do," Maya snapped.

"Oh, but I do. I've kept closer watch over you than you know. The prospect of being the first to travel to the past is too much for you to resist. You must satisfy your curiosity about the origin of the toy. In true self-righteous fashion, you can't help but take this step for the good of all humankind."

Maya frowned at an orange-breasted robin perched on the edge of a drinking fountain. She hated this vile man for being so right. "You've yet to mention one minor detail. The mission is a one-way trip."

"If you accept that you can never return."

"According to branch theory, we'll be stuck in an alternate timeline the moment we arrive in the past."

Katayama rested both hands atop his cane. "In our arrogance, we label other timelines as 'alternate' as if ours was the main one."

"I suppose we sometimes still act like Sol revolves around the Earth." Maya shook her head. "But each new discovery teaches us that we're less significant than we thought."

"Perhaps our timeline is the alternate. Perhaps we shouldn't even exist."

"What are you implying?"

"Time travel presents incredible possibilities. With the right knowledge, one could mold a universe to his deepest desires."

"You're saying that's happened?"

"I'm saying that as life evolves, it branches out and finds new ways to perpetuate itself."

Maya held back another pointless query. Still, she hungered to know. Was he hinting at something profound, or playing mind games with her?

Katayama rose to his feet. His shiny black loafers reflected the sunlight. Tucking his cane under one arm, he adjusted his cufflinks. "Someday, you'll realize we've been on the same side all along. I don't expect you to appreciate what I've done. I only hope you'll save rather than destroy us all."

He stepped away from the bench. "One last thing. You weren't a mistake. You were a wondrous anomaly."

Before she could open her mouth to speak, he vanished into thin air.

Eleven—Accolade
Kuiper Belt, Sol System, April 2284 CE

Mind-bending geometric patterns gave way to the blackness of space as the superluminal transport shuttle *Vonnegut* downshifted at the outer edge of the Kuiper Belt.

Leaning forward in the copilot's seat, Maya zoomed in on the view with her i-cite and squinted in confusion. She should've seen the dwarf planet Dolus and Base Thule straight ahead, but the twinkling of distant stars greeted her eyes. "There's nothing here."

The pilot darted his eyes back and forth, interfacing with the transport. "These are the correct coordinates, Commander."

"How does an object the size of Pluto vanish from its orbit, Lieutenant?"

"I'm not sure, ma'am. The nav AI can't find Dolus anywhere in the vicinity." The lieutenant shrugged. "Then again, it's April Fool's Day."

"That would be some prank." Maya tapped her cheek, mulling more realistic possibilities. The onboard AIs could be malfunctioning. Or maybe the drive OS had downshifted the transport at the wrong exit point.

Perhaps the IEF had altered Dolus' orbit, a feat well within modern capabilities. But if they had changed the planet's trajectory, they would've given her the new coordinates. She also would've heard from someone by now if the IEF had given her crew the wrong location. She should've been the last to arrive after detouring to the Saturnian system to recruit her uncommunicative first officer.

Maya flinched as a cratered sphere appeared out of nowhere, blotting out the stars in front of the transport.

The lieutenant gasped. He fired the transport's retro-thrusters to slow their approach.

"Of course." Maya sat back and berated herself for not realizing it sooner. "They've been camouflaging the planet and construction facility to hide *Yesterday*. Still, it would've been nice of them to mention the space-time cloaking field."

"Cloaking field?" the lieutenant asked.

"It's a hypofield that imparts a time dilation effect in a localized volume of space. When looking at the field from the outside, we were seeing a point in time when the planet was at a previous location in its orbit. We observed the empty space where the planet wasn't a few hours ago, but is now."

"In other words, the field makes the planet invisible."

"Exactly. Now that we've flown into the field, we're in time-sync with the planet."

"That's some pretty fused new tech."

"Actually, it's not that new. The Vril used it to hide their terraforming of Triton for over a century. . . ." Maya let her words trail off as an orbital asteroid emerged from behind the small, blue-gray world.

Bots had hollowed out the asteroid, giving it the shape of a barrel. Inside the barrel, bridges, docking clamps, and scaffolding surrounded a type of starship with which she was unfamiliar—and she knew every class of ship in the fleet.

Any lingering misgivings she had about accepting the mission faded at the sight of the ship—her ship, the space-time vessel IEF-224 *Yesterday*.

Engineers constructed most IEF starships in the shape of bulky metal cylinders, but *Yesterday* looked more like a flying lizard lunging through a pair of hoops.

The triangular forward module reminded her of the head of snake. Sensor panels and viewports into corridors, living quarters, and offices lined either side of it. Antennae spikes protruded from the nose.

A neck-like access tube connected the head module to the flask-shaped aft module. The flask housed the defense and engineering sections along with the black hole power generator. Wings protruded from either side of the module, not for aerodynamics but for hyperdynamics.

Tri-spokes coupled the ship's pair of spinning rings to each of the access tubes leading into the flask. Thousands of tiny graviton-focusing nacelles glowed like holiday lights on the rings. By leveraging thousands of smaller focusers rather than the rocket-sized nacelles used by current starships, *Yesterday* could slip into hyperspace within seconds rather than minutes.

The rings also provided *Yesterday's* chief source of sub-light propulsion. Using its force fields like a collection of surf boards, the ship rode the gravitational waves created by the rings. Except for an array of emergency thrusters, the vessel didn't utilize conventional rockets.

Starships of *Serendipity's* class stretched for over two kilometers. *Yesterday* measured only three-hundred meters in length, smaller than a typical IEF vessel but still as long as an old navy aircraft carrier. Constructing a smaller ship had allowed the IEF to give *Yesterday* the energy reserves needed to complete the trip to the past and a return voyage, if one proved possible. The vessel housed fewer than one-hundred-and-fifty crew members, meaning it would ferry only the most essential personnel to the past.

The ship's name and registry number, IEF-224, adorned various locations along the outer hull. Maya snorted out a chuckle at the three digits. *Yesterday* was not the 224th IEF starship to roll off the assembly line. Rather, the number 224 stood for the centuries-old phrase "today, tomorrow, and forever."

The transport docked with the starship's forward module. Maya floated up through the ceiling hatch of the transport. Upon entering the airlock, she flipped her body so her feet faced *Yesterday's* interior.

Feeling her stomach sink, she drifted down to the deck. The ship's systems regulated and focused the pull produced by the black hole in the reactor core, resulting in honest-to-goodness artificial gravity.

After the outer hatch above her head sealed, the compartment compressed and the inner hatch opened.

The transport undocked and maneuvered away from the ship, leaving her behind.

She stepped into an empty corridor. *No welcoming committee?*

Unlike the metallic décor of other IEF starships, *Yesterday's* ultra-modern interior consisted of blue-white walls and marble-patterned flooring. Rends of landscapes throughout the Sol system, famous paintings, and informational signs filled the hallway. A rend of a potted plant sat at an intersection, its shape distorting every now and then.

Too fused.

Admiral Westerberg's headshot appeared in midair in front of her. "Please report to the MCC, Commander."

"Yes, sir," she said as his image faded away.

A green arrow appeared, indicating the direction of the main command center, or bridge.

As she strolled along, the arrow stayed ahead of her, matching whatever pace she kept. She knew the way, of course. She had memorized *Yesterday's* specifications and blueprints, but the arrow allowed her to devote her thoughts to other subjects.

Engineers hadn't installed the sonic tubes that whisked travelers to and from locations aboard larger starships. The only ways to move from point A to point B on *Yesterday* were ascending or descending the lifts and putting one foot in front of the other—unless, of course, one headed to the teleporter room. But people only ported aboard ship during emergencies.

Passing by the hatch to her command cabin, she reached the entrance to the MCC. She hesitated. Every hair on her neck and arms stood on end. Her heart pulsated in her chest. All her life she had waited to take command of a starship. Now the moment had arrived. She took her time savoring it.

As she stepped into the MCC, she found a crowd waiting for her.

"Attention," shouted the high admiral's adjutant.

Maya, Brooke, Jo, Erik, and the other members of the crew stood to attention.

Admiral Westerberg took his time rising from the command chair. Turning to face Maya, he clasped his hands in front of his dress uniform.

"Please approach, Commander," the adjutant said.

As Maya strode toward the admiral, she took in her surroundings.

The room had the shape of a wedge with the pointed end at the front. A panoramic viewport took up most of the sloped front wall. Beyond it, she saw the inside of the construction barrel and the stars. The view remained still, since *Yesterday* didn't rotate. The lack of spin seemed strange to her even though it probably felt more natural to ground dwellers not accustomed to spaceflight.

Status readouts, graphs, and operations data hovered above the central situation table and cluttered the air. Hundreds of cam rends showed the outside view from every angle. Engineering, power, life support, communications, remote sensing, defense, and other blinking and flashing duty stations lined the room. They were temporarily unoccupied, given that everyone was standing at attention.

Admiral Westerberg rested one hand on the back of the skipper's chair as Maya reached him.

"Commander Davis, reporting as ordered, sir." Maya saluted.

"Everyone, please stand easy." As the officers present relaxed, Westerberg looked around the bridge. "Fellow officers and citizens, we've gathered here on this day, the first of April 2284, to recognize Maya Natsumi Davis on the occasion of her promotion and new command assignment."

After smoothing his mustache, Westerberg continued. "In light of her exceptional service record, the Interstellar Alliance and Interstellar Expeditionary Force have placed special trust and confidence in her integrity and abilities. As High Admiral of the IEF, acting upon the authority of the Prime Administrator of the IA, I hereby promote Maya Davis to the grade of Captain. Captain Davis will now recite the oath."

Maya grew solemn. "I, Maya Davis," she read from her i-cite, "do solemnly affirm to support and defend the charter of the Interstellar Alliance. In endeavoring to expand the boundaries of human knowledge, I shall uphold the principles of the IEF, respecting the rights of my crew, fellow officers, citizens, and members of all exospecies. I take this obligation freely, without any mental reservation, and swear to faithfully discharge the duties of the rank and command I have been granted."

"Duly noted in the official record." Westerberg turned to Brooke. "Admiral, would you please bestow the captain's rank insignia?"

Brooke approached Maya and pressed a finger to the patch on her niece's right shoulder. A fourth silver bar expanded below the star and above the existing three bars, signifying Maya's new rank.

Raising her finger, Brooke touched the commander's star on Maya's collar. The platinum star morphed into a fierce eagle, the rank insignia for IEF Fleet Captain.

Brooke smiled despite her attempts to maintain an official frown. The sight warmed every bone in Maya's body.

As Brooke stepped back her eyes twinkled, and she gave the tiniest hint of a nod.

Westerberg said, "I hereby assign command of the IEF vessel *Yesterday* to you, Captain Maya Davis, effective immediately."

"I accept command and all responsibility entrusted to me by such assignment," Maya replied, saluting.

The high admiral returned the gesture and then shook her hand. "Congratulations, Captain."

"Thank you, sir."

Turning to face the small crowd, Westerberg announced, "Everyone, I present to you Captain Maya Davis."

Applause erupted. Jo stuck both pinky fingers in her mouth and whistled.

As the celebration subsided, Westerberg whispered, "My apologies for the private nature of the ceremony today, Captain. Due to the secrecy of your mission, we couldn't announce your command assignment to the public."

"I understand, sir," Maya said.

"Good luck to all of you," he said, addressing everyone. "The Alliance and IEF are humbled by your willingness to undertake this adventure. Know that while you may go in silence, you will not be forgotten. I hope to see you all again." He took one last look around the MCC and then excited the room.

◆

As the last of the senior officers stepped off the bridge, Lieutenant Emilia Tereshkova settled in behind *Yesterday's* helm.

Emilia had taken recent events in stride—her promotion to Senior Lieutenant, her selection as *Yesterday's* primary helm officer, and the fact she would soon travel to the past. She had planned and worked and sacrificed to make this happen. It hadn't been good fortune. She had earned her destiny.

Even saving Admiral Davis' life hadn't been happenstance. Emilia had insisted on deploying with the admiral and had protected her when she crashed. Still, if Emilia had reacted a little quicker, she could've prevented the enemy from downing her idol in the first place.

Cursing under her breath in Russian, Emilia shook off the guilt she felt about one of her few failures.

She closed her eyes and hovered her hands over the dormant rend emitters on her console. Staring at the helm activation icon in her i-cite, she drew out the moment, savoring it. She had trained on the ship's systems in sims for the last month, and this was the first time she would interface with the real thing.

"Is that some sort of meditation, ma'am?" someone asked.

Twisting around in her seat, Emilia opened her eyes and found an officer near her own age standing behind her. As the young man lifted his eyebrows, his warm smile stretched out a very thin goatee.

"No," Tereshkova said in deep monotone.

"That's some accent, ma'am," he said. "I'm Lieutenant Nicolaus Kepler." Kepler pointed at the rank insignia on his collar. "Junior Grade, of course."

Emilia pursed her lips.

"Lieutenant . . ." Kepler read her name patch on the front of her uniform. "Tereshkova. It's a pleasure to meet you, ma'am. I take it you're our helmsman—err, helmswoman, I mean."

Looking first at the helm console, then at her seat, and finally back at Kepler, Emilia raised her eyebrows at him.

"Obviously," he said with an awkward laugh.

Kepler scratched the side of his neck and then pointed a thumb back over his shoulder. "I'm the remote sensing officer, ma'am. My post is at the head of the situation table, right in the middle of the action. Personally, I think it's the best position on the ship, because I'm the first to see everything out there."

Emilia stared at him with her eyelids at half-mast. She very much wanted him to go away so she could get back to interfacing with the helm.

Her luck went from bad to worse. Two other officers left their duty stations and approached.

"Are we doing introductions, sir, ma'am?" a young man with black hair and olive skin asked. "I'm Ensign Savio Marconi, ship's comm officer."

Casually, Marconi held up his left hand with the palm facing down. With his right, he tapped the back of his left with an old silver coin. On the third tap, the coin passed right through the back of the hand and dropped toward the deck. Marconi stooped down and caught the coin with his right.

"That's too fused, Ensign," Kepler said. "How'd you do that?"

Marconi shrugged and rolled the coin across his knuckles. "A magician never reveals his secrets, sir."

The other officer, a Senior Lieutenant with a shaved head and thick beard, folded his arms and rolled his eyes. "Don't tell me you're that gullible, Mr. Kepler," the skeptic said. "Ensign Marconi used two coins."

Patting himself down and flipping his palms up and down, Marconi shook his head. "Nope, only the one, sir."

"Regardless of how the man did it, the trick was still pretty fused," Kepler said, holding out his hand to shake.

"If you say so." The skeptic gripped Kepler's hand. "Lieutenant Lautaro Rojas, tactical officer." Rojas looked at Marconi. "It's my job to analyze situations—you know, see through veils of deception."

Marconi grinned, popped the coin in his mouth, and swallowed it. Then he pulled it out of his pocket.

Gross, Emilia thought. *No, wait. Obviously, he never actually ingested it.* She resisted the urge to smack her forehead.

"I've never seen a coin," Kepler said. "Not in person, I mean."

Emilia didn't say it, but she never had, either.

"It's a family heirloom," Marconi explained, holding the coin up between his index and middle fingers. "The first colonies on Mars briefly experimented with physical currency. This baby's one of the few ever made. My great-great-grandfather, one of the first settlers of Red Rock City, gave it to my grandfather. He passed it on to me."

"Nice. I take it you grew up on Mars, then?"

"That's right. Fifth generation."

Kepler turned to Emilia. "How about you, Lieutenant?"

Emilia eased up on her frown. She didn't want to admit it, but the conversation had become palatable. "I was raised on a shipyard in the Hilda asteroids. My father was a pilot, my mother the head engineer."

Looking past her toward the helm, Kepler gave a generous nod. "And you, Lieutenant Rojas?"

Rojas relaxed and winked at him. "That's classified." The skeptic returned to his post.

"He's so fun," Marconi said sarcastically as he made his way back to the comm station.

"It was good to meet you both." Kepler mumbled his next words. "Seeing as how we might be together for the rest of our lives."

His casual mention of the very real possibility of the ship remaining stuck in the past brought back Emilia's frown.

"Well," Kepler said to her, "I guess I should get back to it, too." He returned to the sit-table and summoned a rend of the nearby dwarf planet above it.

Emilia shook out the tension in her body and faced forward, refocusing. The meet and greet had been a little annoying—mostly.

With a mental click she activated the helm. The bridge faded away, replaced by an immersive augmented reality. From her viewpoint, it appeared as if she sat floating in space in place of the ship. It looked and felt as if she was the ship. Velocity, coordinate headings, pitch, yaw, roll, and every conceivable piece of flight data hovered off to either side.

Her skin tingled with excitement, which she made certain didn't show.

◆

With her gaze lowered toward the deck, Brooke stood holding her husband's hand in *Yesterday's* teleporter room. She tensed her scowl to hold back the waterworks. A few of the floating rends showed bots working to dismantle the last of the scaffolding around *Yesterday*. Cargo modules scurried to and from the ship, delivering final supplies.

Kevin lifted her chin to face him.

"I need to get going," he said.

Brooke gave a slow nod. "I know." Swallowing, she added, "Damn it. I wish you were coming with us."

"This was the hardest decision of my life." He sighed, long and deep. "But this is where I have the resources to figure out how to get you home."

"I know."

When she gazed up into his adoring eyes, a tear streamed down her cheek. The years they had shared together played like a sim in her head.

She had met Kevin decades ago when he unveiled the phase drive. When her sister introduced them, Brooke acted like she didn't care, but she had felt an undeniable connection to him. Months later he had declared his love for her. He shared her dislike of social interaction and respected her need for privacy, knowing when to back off and give her space. He had stuck with her through every mood swing and near-death situation. They had weathered their share of turmoil and almost split on multiple occasions, but each time they emerged with a stronger bond.

He was the only non-relative she had ever loved, and one of the few people she could actually stand. To her, the latter might've meant more than the former.

Standing on her tiptoes, she cupped his face in her hands and kissed him.

Kevin wrapped his arms around her and pulled her into his warm embrace.

Brooke lost track of the time.

"How have you been feeling?" Kevin asked as he pulled away.

"I haven't had a seizure since I started the new regimen," Brooke said. "I've never felt better."

"I'm glad." He dragged a hand through his hair in thought. "I still don't know of any meds or exercise that could cause this big of a turnaround in your health."

Brooke's smile faded. A wave of guilt washed over her as she considered whether to tell her husband the truth. On more than one occasion she had almost lost him because she hadn't been honest. But what was the point in saying anything now?

In all likelihood *Yesterday* wouldn't be coming back from the mission. He already expected never to see her again, so she didn't want to burden him with the knowledge that she was cutting short her lifespan by sparking again. There was already more than enough sadness to go around.

"You may have a doctorate, but you're not a medical doctor," Brooke insisted.

"Fair enough," Kevin said. "Just promise me you'll stay out of the cockpit."

Brooke puffed out her cheeks, holding in a growl. *Now's not the time to get upset.* She pulled him tight. "I love you."

"Now and always." He kissed her on the top of the head.

Lightly shoving him back, she chuckled. "Barf."

He smiled at their inside joke.

Kevin stepped toward the teleport archway.

A flicker of light—like a tiny star—blinked into existence in the center of the arch. The flicker grew to the size of a portal. On the other side of the doorway, she saw the teleporter room in the main building of the Solar Science Society on Mars.

After gazing long and affectionately at her, he entered the portal.

Brooke continued staring at the bulkhead long after the portal had closed. Sometime later, the hatch to the room slid open.

"I hope to feel that strongly about someone, someday."

When she looked to her right, she found Zeke standing next to her.

"It has its rewards," she muttered. "And costs."

Folding his arms, Zeke said, "You may never see him again, yet you still couldn't bring yourself to tell him."

Brooke gnashed her teeth.

"You're being selfish," he said. "The good guys tell the truth. I thought you were one of—"

"Real life isn't as black and white as your comic sims. The only reason you know about my condition is because you read my mind—without my permission." She wagged a finger at him. "There's still time for me to kick you off this ship before we depart."

"I could make you fess up. Doesn't our new captain deserve to know her mission commander is—?"

"Enough with the idle threats." Brooke placed her hands on her hips. "Either rat me out or shut your mouth."

Zeke stared at the deck. "It's not my place to get involved." He shook his head. "I've learned the hard way that intervening usually does more harm than good. A few times I've tried to force someone to do what's right, but things often turn out worse in the long run."

"If that isn't irony. The Vril manipulated human society for centuries, without your ability to control people." Brooke exited the teleporter room with Zeke close behind her.

"Thank you for convincing the high admiral and captain to let me come along, by the way," Zeke said.

"Yeah, don't mention—" Brooke cut herself short at the sight of Eve and Shin heading toward them in the corridor.

Eve had traded the red pants suit she had worn the last time Brooke had seen her for a leather jacket of like color, together with black slacks. Shin had swapped his retro outfit for a modern smart suit with a stand-up collar, tailored in the Japanese style.

"Admiral Davis." Flashing a politician's smile, Shin shook her hand. "We meet again."

"I guess so." Brooke stole a glance at Zeke.

Despite encountering the closest thing he had known to a father for the first time in years, Zeke showed no outward emotion.

"Admiral, I want to apologize if I offended you back on Triton," Shin said.

Brooke sent a thought to Zeke. *I want to know what's going on in Shin's head. Does he not remember me, or is he acting?*

We just talked about how I shouldn't violate people's privacy, Zeke mind-spoke.

If there's any chance the Vice Admin is a Vril lackey, I think it's a justifiable exception.

If I read him, I'll be no better than the Vril.

Damn it. If it hadn't been for him, you would've been buried alive at the bottom of the ocean on Mars. He helped raise you and—

Xiaoqing raised me. Shin only used me to further his agenda.

Then you should want answers.

Humans use one another all the time. I take no offense.

Brooke wanted to strangle him. Instead, she imparted, *Read what I'm thinking now. Feel what I'm feeling.*

Very well, Zeke mind-spoke. *If you feel it's that important . . . as far as I can tell, he has no prior knowledge of meeting you before your encounter on Triton.*

So that settles it. The Vril must've rewritten his personality and altered his memories.

If he's an agent, he's unaware of it. For all he knows, Ms. Sybil is actually an advisor and the Vril only exist in history sims.

Brooke seethed at what the Vril had done to Shin. *The fact they've turned him into an unwitting pawn is horrible, but it makes sense. The Vril realize you can't read androids. Eve must know the details of whatever scheme they plan to hatch.*

She's the one who tried to kill me on Psykhe.

I'm not thrilled to see her either, but let's deal with them one crook at a time. Do you think you could restore Shin's original self?

With his willful cooperation, I might be able to do for him what I did for Xi.

We'll have to figure out how to make that happen.

He's not coming along on the mission.

I know.

Actually, he's on his way off the ship right now.

Then for his sake, let's hope we make it back.

Acknowledging that verbal hostilities wouldn't get her anywhere, Brooke donned a cheery façade. "There's no need to apologize, Vice Administrator."

"It's not you, sir," Zeke stated in a matter-of-fact tone. "Everyone offends her."

"I see," Shin said, his smile fading. He reached up but found no cap to tip back.

"It's too bad you won't be accompanying us on this exciting voyage into history," Brooke said.

"I admire anyone brave enough to sign up for this one-way ride, but I have designs on the Prime Administrator's position. I can't very well build a campaign from the past."

"That would be difficult."

"Fortunately, Advisor Sybil agreed to be the administration's representative. Once you arrive in the past, her intelligence gathering skills should be a great asset in determining how the metatoy ended up there."

Shifting her gaze to Eve, Brooke asked, "Care to share why you volunteered, Special Advisor?"

Eve produced a box of mints from her jacket pocket and offered one to everyone present. Brooke, Shin, and Zeke declined.

Tossing a mint into her mouth, Eve said, "I couldn't pass up the chance to see how our future unfolds."

Twelve—Rubicon
Kuiper Belt, Sol System, April 2284 CE

With the tip of her finger, Maya adjusted the vidpic she had hung on the wall of her command cabin. The frame's self-leveling feature hadn't worked for years. No matter how much force she used or what angle she tried, she couldn't get the thing to hang straight. She had half a mind to contact engineering and order them to check the gravity calibration.

The old vidpic was one of her prized possessions, second only to the stuffed Bio Bear her aunt had bought her as a kid. Childishly, Maya still slept with the bear. The last time Brooke had inquired about it, Maya had answered, "Oh, it's probably stuffed in a box somewhere," with well-practiced nonchalance.

In the vidpic, Maya, age four, sat on the floor of her mom's apartment in Chicago. Young Maya pulled her nose back like a pig, stuck out her tongue, and made every face imaginable.

Slouching in the pic, Aunt Brooke sat cross-legged on the couch behind her, protesting the experience with her well-practiced scowl.

As she sat down next to Brooke, Marie smiled at the bot capturing the footage. She had bought the bot as a pet for her allergy-afflicted daughter. Each time Brooke looked away from her sister, Marie held up two fingers behind her head and flashed a wide grin.

Whenever Brooke's gaze darted back in her direction, Marie yanked her hand away and inspected her nails with an unconvincing look of innocence.

Maya had glanced at the vidpic just a couple of weeks ago. The ensuing pangs of nostalgia had motivated her to visit the park in Chicago.

She hung up a handful of other pics: her IEF Academy graduation; the crew of *New Horizons* before departure; poses with the Penphin thinker Ari on Gliese 581; and one of her breaking ground with the colonists of New Jodhpur on Aryana. There were also pics of Maya with her aunt, uncle, Jo, and Erik.

Plopping down in the synthetic leather chair behind her desk, she gazed around her cabin. It had half the square-meterage of the skipper's office on *Serendipity*, but she chose to view it as cozy rather than cramped.

On her desk she had placed the clear bubble case containing the newer metatoy with the all-important data. Neither the admiral nor Uncle Kevin had allowed her to take the original relic, but she had insisted on bringing the newer one in case it offered additional secrets.

Maya considered rendering a couple of potted plants or flowers. Rends didn't give off pollen, but just looking at them might bring on a psychosomatic sneeze.

Otherwise, she couldn't think of anything else to put up in the way of decorations. She didn't own all that much stuff. All her life she had thirsted for knowledge and experience rather than anything tangible. Meeting her Scrooge of a father had only reinforced that tendency.

Stewing on that thought, she peered out the small cabin porthole. The inside of the construction barrel blocked her view, but it wouldn't for much longer. Bots had loaded all the supplies, the last of her personnel had come aboard, and she had spoken to the high admiral and her uncle for the last time before departure.

Tomorrow morning, *Yesterday* would backshift, and there would be no turning back. She had busied herself with setting up her cabin to take her mind off that reality.

The hatch chimed, interrupting her musings.

"Come in," she said.

Commander Trevor Young stepped into the cabin.

As the hatch slid shut behind him, he saluted. "Reporting as ordered, Captain."

The two-plus meters of his muscular frame filled out his uniform, yet something about the IEF whites and blues didn't suit him. She supposed her biases led her to think he had looked better in his black ISC Defense garb.

Raised in a military family, Trevor had graduated at the top of his class from the defense academy of the now-defunct ISC. She had butted heads with him as rivals during those days, both in training sims and in terms of ideals. In his view, mankind should've funneled all its resources into fortifying its defenses at home and launched unmanned probes to assess potential threats. The *New Horizons* mission to Gliese 581 should never have occurred, so far as Trevor was concerned.

Trevor flexed his fingers, appearing tense.

"Have a seat, Commander." Maya gestured to one of the two chairs opposite her desk.

Lowering himself into one of the plush seats, he sat with his back straighter than the deck plates.

"Thanks for coming, Trevor," Maya said. "For a while, I wasn't sure if the American Colonies would grant your release from Iapetus—or if you would accept my offer."

When he didn't respond, she added, "I hear the moon's government has been trying to declare its independence ever since the ISC fell. Iapetus is one of the few war zones left in the Sol system."

"Permission to speak freely, Captain?" Trevor asked.

"Go ahead."

He blew out a breath and relaxed his posture. "It's the same thing all over again."

"What is?"

"I don't approve of this mission. Sending a ship back in time to 'explore' seems like a waste of resources, especially given that the crew can't return. Meddling with the past also strikes me as ill-advised. Scientists think we can't affect the present, but who knows? But here I am again, being asked to provide military support to the very organization that thinks soldiers are no longer necessary."

Maya gave a slow nod. "I'll admit the general situation is somewhat similar to when *Horizons* shipped out."

"I guess people never learn."

She leaned back and rested a finger on her cheek. "If this is such a bad idea, why did you come?"

"I've been asking myself the same question." Trevor cracked his knuckles as he looked over his IEF uniform. "I appreciate the official accommodation, but don't assume my change of dress means I've made up my mind about accepting the XO position—although I do appreciate you holding out for my decision."

"What else do you need to decide?"

"On Iapetus, you told me my expertise would be valuable."

"I did."

"But you didn't tell me why. Why would you want me as your first officer? We've rarely seen eye-to-eye."

"That's exactly why. You and I view things very differently. I need that alternate perspective. Also, I have little doubt that with you on board we'll be prepared if a conflict arises—"

"If a conflict arises," he repeated, placing emphasis on the word "if." "Who or what will pose us any threat? Organized society didn't exist back then."

"According to Jo, historical evidence suggests the first human civilizations dated back to around that time. I want to avoid interacting with ancient people as much as possible, but I also want to be prepared for any contingency. While we're not likely to affect our present, we don't want to start creating alternate timelines left and right."

"That's what I'm talking about." Trevor shot to his feet and paced about the cabin. "The best way to avoid causing issues would be to stay home. One of my drill instructors at the defense academy used to say that 'Curiosity killed the civilian.' It was his way of saying that soldiers who do things by the book and follow orders stay alive."

"If the sole driving force behind this mission was curiosity," Maya said, "I might argue against going myself. But given what I learned from the device we found—"

"You mean that toy? There are simpler explanations for it having been in that tower. I've heard the Vril had teleporter tech before the IEF. An agent could've ported it inside the ruins when *Horizons* arrived in the system."

"I considered that possibility, right up until Director Sommerfield confirmed the toy's age. When we got it working and figured out what it contained. . . ." Maya explained how it had prompted her by name, and only responded to her. When she had gained access, it had offered a past date and a set of coordinates.

She had expected him to show surprise, or at least mild interest. The information had led most people to reassess their view of the multiverse.

Instead, Trevor grimaced as he inspected the vidpics adorning the walls of her command cabin. "Everything has turned out so very differently from what I dreamed of as a kid." He snorted. "One day I thought I'd be the skipper of a mighty battleship keeping the human race safe. Instead, people like you are commanding scientific vessels on observational missions while my kind is going extinct. I feel so out of place."

Maya blinked. He had never before opened up to her. She found it a welcome change from the confrontational front he often put up.

"You asked to speak honestly," she said, hardening her tone. "Let me do the same now. You've always had a grudge against the IEF and directed those feelings toward me. I don't know if someone in your past refused to fight and that caused you pain or loss. Either way, I believe your bias has hindered your ability to be happy."

Trevor continued to stare at the vidpic of the survivors of *New Horizons,* recorded after the ship had returned home. Looking disheveled but overjoyed, Trevor and the rest of the crew had posed around Maya in the engineering command center.

Lowering her voice, Maya continued. "I know you think the IEF has disavowed all things military, but it's not the pacifist outfit you perceive. It's just that the IEF considers itself a more comprehensive organization. Defense is one part of a larger whole. How else would we defend ourselves against the Greys or prepare for other threats? There's a place for you here if you're willing to challenge your preconceived notions and admit there's more to life than soldiering."

Trevor walked back to his chair and sat down.

"So," Maya asked, "will you be my second in command?"

He locked gazes with her. Then he chuckled. "It's ironic. I was once your superior, if only by default. Then you took over. And now. . . ." Shaking his head, he let his words trail off. His eyes wandered back to the vidpic.

"Do you have a personal problem with me?"

Shaking his head, he said, "Believe it or not, I enjoyed competing with you. I wouldn't be here if I didn't respect you."

Maya hid how much it meant to hear those words. "I respect you as well, which is why I offered you the role of executive officer."

An awkward silence filled the cabin. Maya swore she could hear the hum of the main reactor a hundred meters aft.

"Don't expect me to agree with you all of the time," he said.

"It's okay if you disagree with my decisions," Maya said. "I want someone who's not afraid to suggest alternate courses of action. But I need to know that when I give an order, you'll follow it without—"

"You shouldn't need to ask that." His face flushed. "I'm a professional. Duty and loyalty mean everything to me."

"I know."

Trevor returned his gaze to the vidpics. "Every time my dad took me hunting as a kid back in Texas, we wore cowboy hats and boots. I used to play every Wild West sim I could find. I've always dreamed of visiting that time period."

"That would be fun, but unfortunately we're headed a little bit further into the past."

"Too bad." Trevor turned his head back toward her. A slight grin crept its way onto his face. "Still, the chance to point out all the ways that you're wrong is too good to pass up."

Maya matched his expression.

An image of Lieutenant Kepler, whom she had promoted to *Yesterday's* remote sensing officer, appeared both in her i-cite and as a rend above her desk. The lanky young man's face had always had a pale tint, yet now she could swear it had faded to pure white. "Captain," Kepler gasped, "we've got enemy forces on a sub-light approach vector. The AIs have resolved at least two-hundred motherships and thousands of saucers."

Springing to her feet, Maya said, "They know about the mission."

"Either they don't want us going back, or they want this ship," Trevor said.

"ETA to weapons range?" Maya demanded as she pondered how the Greys had located Dolus. Perhaps they had developed tech to compensate for the time cloaking field. Maybe they had been monitoring the planet since before the field had gone up—after all, they had been keeping a close eye on the human race for centuries. The recent increase in traffic to and from Base Thule could've tipped them off.

She wondered why the Greys had chosen this moment to attack. If they had known about *Yesterday* and its launch time all along, why hadn't they come sooner? Her gut told her she was missing something.

But the time for such musings had passed. Repelling the attack was now the priority.

"They downshifted just beyond the hypofield and are pushing their engines to the limit," Kepler said, "Less than five minutes."

Maya bolted out of her cabin, into the corridor, and onto the bridge. Trevor followed her. He rushed over to the tactical station to coordinate *Yesterday's* defenses.

Brooke rose from the command chair. "Maxwell and his team are ready to scramble as soon as you give the word."

"Thank you, Admiral," Maya said. "Please keep them on standby for now."

As Brooke barked orders at the flight controller, Maya recalled her brief discussion with Brooke about the boundaries between the captain's authority over the ship and the vice admiral's command of the mission. To Maya's surprise, Brooke had said, "This is your show, Maya. I'll stick to offering advice and step in only if necessary." Brooke had even endorsed Erik as flight commander and agreed not to deploy unless the situation required it.

When Maya had asked her why, Brooke had said, "That's what I would want if our positions were reversed."

"Admiral Westerberg is comming, Captain," reported Ensign

Marconi from the comm station. As Marconi monitored the chatter inside and outside of the ship, the man absently rolled his lucky silver half-dollar across his knuckles.

Maya stood in front of her chair. "Put him up."

Westerberg's magnified head and shoulders appeared above the situation table like a floating bust. "Captain, accelerate your timetable. Launch now."

The reality of the request chilled Maya, but she shook it off. "Sensing?"

Kepler rotated and swiped through rends of the incoming enemy fleet about the sit-table. "Less than five minutes until the Greys are within weapons range."

"Navigation?"

Lieutenant Tereshkova looked back over her shoulder from the helm. "Engineering is powering up the wave and phase drives now, ma'am. We need eight minutes to get far enough away from the construction barrel and planet to upshift."

Maya shook her head as she addressed the high admiral. "We've no choice but to engage, sir."

Westerberg lowered his eyes for a moment and then raised them. "We can't have *Yesterday* destroyed or damaged before you reach the past." To officers in Base Reed's command center, he ordered, "Send the starships in orbit to engage the enemy and buy time for *Yesterday*."

"Sir," Base Reed's tactical officer said from behind the admiral, "that will leave Base Thule vulnerable."

"They'll have to make do. *Yesterday's* launch is the priority."

"Understood, sir."

"Captain Davis, launch now. Backshift as soon as you're clear of the asteroid and planet."

Lieutenant Lautaro Rojas bounced his leg behind the tactical station. "The three starships in Dolus orbit are moving to intercept the enemy fleet."

Above the sit-table, thousands of motherships and saucers neared weapons range of the three IEF vessels. Hundreds more enemy spacecraft spread out to surround the planet.

Maya clenched a fist in frustration. *There's no way three ships can possibly repel thousands.*

She glanced at Brooke, who was staring at her in earnest.

"Don't launch from the barrel," Brooke said.

Blinking in confusion, Maya said, "But the admiral ordered us to—"

"No, I mean the barrel still has embedded rockets that were used to maneuver it into Dolus orbit."

With a sharp intake of breath, Maya nodded in understanding. "We can hide inside the barrel—use it as a shield—while thrusting it out of orbit."

"My thoughts exactly."

"We'll still be vulnerable to attack in the few seconds between exiting the barrel and backshifting," Trevor said. "And that's if they don't blow the asteroid apart with us inside before we clear the planet."

"Using the barrel for protection should yield better survival odds than launching without it," Westerberg said. "Do it."

"Friendly forces have engaged the enemy," Kepler said.

A smattering of blips swarmed the starships. Explosions erupted.

Maya thought fast.

She was about to order the crew to carry out Brooke's plan when an idea dawned on her.

♦

"Admiral, the construction barrel is now thrusting out of orbit," a sensing officer reported.

In Base Reed's command center on Triton, Westerberg sat with his fingers intertwined, studying rends of the battle.

The barrel burned away from the planet and the oncoming enemy, using its embedded rocket engines.

Hundreds of the smaller blips accelerated toward the barrel.

As the saucers entered weapons range, they bombarded the hollow asteroid with plasma weapons and antimatter ordinance. The barrel had limited armaments and shielding. Its defenses wouldn't last long, but perhaps they would hold out long enough.

Explosions erupted on the barrel's cratered surface as it took a heavy pounding.

With two of the three IEF starships disabled and venting atmosphere, the motherships closed in on the barrel.

Westerberg tensed in anticipation.

Suddenly the enemy ceased firing and darted away from the barrel.

The sensing officer shouted, "Base Thule is registering a massive energy buildup—"

The construction barrel exploded. Chunks of rock and shards of debris flew out in all directions, bashing into saucers and motherships.

"The barrel has been destroyed, sir," sensing reported. "There's no sign of *Yesterday* on any of my scopes."

"Godspeed, Captain," Westerberg whispered, straightening his posture.

♦

With Trevor and Brooke standing on either side of her, Maya stared at the rend above the sit-table. The rend showed *Yesterday* drifting through space, with the planet between the ship and the battle.

Maya's last-second idea had involved using the asteroid as a decoy instead of a shield.

"Disable the emergency thrusters, bring the main reactor back online, and prepare to shift," Maya ordered. "Comm Thule's commander and thank him for directing the cloaking field our way."

"Aye, ma'am," the responses rang out.

Twirling gradually in a circle, Maya looked at each member of her crew. "Now's your last chance to jump ship."

Everyone kept their focus on their duties. Jo and Erik sat at duty stations at the rear of the bridge. They each nodded at her. Trevor folded his arms, blew out a breath, and kept his gaze straight ahead when Maya glanced at him.

Brooke placed one hand on Maya's shoulder.

"Phase drive charged and ready, Captain," Tereshkova said.

The moment of decision had arrived. Given that the Greys had assembled their largest fleet to stop *Yesterday*, Maya knew the mission would prove more important than anyone could fathom.

With a deep breath, she gave the command to backshift.

♦

Somewhere in the aft module of the ship, in a seldom-visited compartment behind the engines, a gangly arm pushed its way aboard through the solid hull. A thin shoulder trailed the hand, accompanied by an oblong head, thin torso, and stick-like legs.

The Grey exobeing stepped onto the deck. After checking to make sure its body was still intact—matter destabilization was new tech, after all—Vox helped his companion, Vya, pass through the wall.

Thirteen—Bicentimillennium
Interstellar Space, August 200,423 BCE

"Now downshifting, Captain," Tereshkova reported from the helm.

Leaning forward in her chair, Maya tensed for the arrival. She and her crew had trained, planned, and spent months in transit anticipating this moment.

The amaranth pink hue of hyperspace peeled away from the forward viewport as *Yesterday* emerged among the stars.

"First things first," Maya said. "Are we where and when we should be?"

The star straight ahead of the viewport shone a little brighter than the others around it.

The rend of the Sol system above the sit-table detailed the orbits of the eight planets, the asteroid belt, the Trojans, the Oort Cloud, and the thousands of dwarfs in the Kuiper Belt.

"Coordinates confirmed," Tereshkova said. "We're one light year out from Sol."

"The AIs have confirmed the positions of the constellations," Kepler said. "The date is August 13th, 200,423 BCE."

"That gives us the planned two months to scout things out before October 13th," Brooke said, crossing her legs in her seat.

"Good work," Maya said. Throughout the trip, she had stressed over the IEF's choice of Yesterday's arrival date. No one knew whether the date and time from the metatoy marked the moment an event would occur or the moment they should arrive. It had therefore made sense to show up well beforehand. After much deliberation, Command had settled on a two-month cushion, which gave the crew ample time to prepare for almost any possibility.

"Begin scans of the system, Keps."

"Initiating nano-wormholes," Kepler said. "Activating neudar."

Knowing it would take hours to receive and process the return signals, Maya turned the MCC over to Trevor and retreated to her command cabin. There she downed a couple mugs of cocoa, then fell asleep on the small sofa while reading H.G. Wells's *The Time Machine* in her i-cite.

She flinched awake at Kepler's comm. He reported reception of the first scan results.

Upon returning to the MCC, Maya found an eager crowd. She had asked Bob, Zeke, and Advisor Sybil to join her on the bridge to help analyze the results. Also present were *Yesterday's* head physician, Dr. Rosalind Crumpler, Chief Engineer Gottlieb Otto, and the head of security, Lieutenant Christa Resnik.

Everyone stood gathered around the sit-table, staring at Maya in anticipation.

"What do you have for us, Keps?" Maya asked, resting her palms on the table.

"Well, there's nothing of intrigue throughout most of the system," Kepler said. "Mars, Callisto, Triton, and every other world colonized in our time are deserted, as one would expect. Earth is where things get a lot more interesting."

Above the table, the rend of the Sol system zoomed in on a blue-white globe. A targeting bracket centered a shiny object in orbit. As the view magnified the object further, its nature became clear.

"It's a ship," Trevor said.

"A whopping behemoth of a ship," Jo muttered.

The front consisted of long cylinders—presumably, habitat modules—stacked around one another. A gigantic reflective sail extended out from the nose, dwarfing the hull. Dozens of spherical fuel tanks comprised the majority of the ship toward the rear. Any given tank had about the same volume as all the cylinders combined. Aft of the tanks, a large number of tiny rocket nozzles protruded in the largest honeycomb pattern Maya had ever seen.

"I knew it." Jo slapped the table. "The Earth was visited by exobeings in the past."

With his thick German accent, Chief Engineer Gottlieb Otto expressed awe. "That metal wonder must be more than ten kilometers long."

"Fourteen-point-seven kilometers," Bob said.

"Our most basic weapons would shred that big ole sail at the front," Lieutenant Rojas said from tactical. "What purpose does it serve?"

"I've analyzed the data and believe I can offer an explanation for the design of the spacecraft." Bob sat at the table with his head cocked, hands folded in his lap. "Despite possessing a volume many times that of *Yesterday*, the vessel is far less technologically advanced. It lacks magnetic field generators. The sail, as the lieutenant observed, is a combination of solar energy collectors and particle deflectors for travel at relativistic velocities. When filled to capacity, the spherical tanks hold enough antimatter to slowly accelerate the vessel to velocities near the speed of light when firing its aft ion thrusters."

"So they don't have FTL capability," Maya said, tapping her cheek in wonder.

"That would be the most probable conclusion."

"No FTL?" Jo asked.

"The ship doesn't have a phase drive," Maya explained, "so they can't enter hyperspace to reach a destination faster than light. Nor can they send or receive transmissions through wormholes."

"Wait. You're telling me that monstrosity is so slow it traveled for thousands of Earth-years to get here?"

"Affirmative," Bob said. "There is a particulate stream—a dispersing trail of rocket exhaust—leading into the system. Further extrapolation will reveal the location of the ship's last course change, possibly even its point of origin."

"I don't think these exos have neudar, either," Kepler added. "When I first detected the ship, I worried whether their instruments had the sensitivity to pick up our scans, but I think their sensors are limited to the electromagnetic spectrum."

"The light from our exit wormhole and the energy emissions given off by *Yesterday* should therefore take a year to reach the Earth," Bob said.

Trevor absently flexed the fingers on one hand as he stared at the rends. "In other words, our having downshifted outside the system should effectively keep us hidden."

"Correct."

"So who are they?" Dr. Rosalyn Crumpler yawned, as she often did. "Do we have scans of their physiology?"

"We've collected a few rough images so far, ma'am," Kepler said.

He toggled the rend to show the interior of the ship. It consisted of one wide open space after another. Imposing scaled and winged creatures of all different shapes and sizes soared through the massive compartments. Groups congregated in nooks along the inner surface of the outer hull.

Brooke turned to Zeke, who stood behind everyone else.

"Are these your people?" Brooke asked.

Everyone turned to stare at him.

Zeke stared past the sit-table at the far bulkhead. He hadn't blinked in minutes. "I believe so." He sounded like a robot.

"It's hard to believe intelligent beings could build such a grand ship without developing phase tech," Gottlieb said as everyone turned back to the table. "People might've lived whole lifetimes on that ship without ever seeing their destination."

"If the beings' lifespans are comparable to ours," Crumpler said in between swigs of coffee, "that could very well be the case."

"Civilizations evolve different abilities at different rates." Jo launched into a history lecture. "There are so many different variables. Who knows how these beings think, what motivates them, what their laws allow or prevent, or what natural disasters have afflicted them."

Gottlieb nodded. "Necessity is often the mother of invention. Sometimes you don't invent something until you need it."

"It was only a few hundred years ago that humans developed a scientific method," Jo said, "at which point progress took an exponential leap. We probably should have developed more advanced technology sooner, but civilizations rose and fell before progress could be made."

"In other words," Advisor Sybil said, "there isn't a standard evolutionary pattern followed by every intelligent species."

"So we know how they got here," Brooke said. "But why are they here?"

Kepler rested his palms on the table. "Motivation is harder to pick up from scans, but their surface activity gives a few hints."

The rend scrolled away from the ship in orbit and down to the surface of the Earth. As the view descended through the clouds, the continent of Africa continued to grow in size.

"Is it me," Erik asked, massaging his jaw, "or does East Africa look bigger and oddly shaped?"

"It's not you," Jo said. "Sea level during this time period was over a hundred meters lower than in our present, so the coastline extends farther out."

Continuing its zoom, the rend showed a top-down view of a city on the tip of the Horn of Africa. In the twenty-third century, the city would've been submerged in the Arabian Sea.

"This city is located at the coordinates given by the metatoy," Bob said.

Maya noted the large stone buildings, roads, and farms. Two small spacecraft sat in the desert plain a few kilometers outside the city.

The zoom increased, providing an overhead shot of one of the city streets. Human-like beings moved with order and purpose.

"I don't see any of the exos from the ship," observed Lieutenant Christa Resnik, head of ship's security, as she curled a lock of her short brunette hair behind her ear. "But there's a clear distinction between who's in charge and who's not."

"As soon as we've scanned the inhabitants from enough angles," Kepler said, "we'll able to extrapolate their full appearance. We've already gleaned a few things from the initial sound recordings."

Kepler swiped a finger through a rend of a frequency response graph. As the lines oscillated, overlapping conversations in foreign languages played. An occasional pounding noise or clang gave Maya the impression that construction was taking place in the background.

After silencing the recordings, Kepler said, "The visitors call themselves the Onaki."

"The Onaki," Zeke repeated.

"That's right. Apparently, your people have swapped into human-like bodies using some advanced genetics and biosynthesis. They're the ones in charge down there that Lieutenant Resnik noted. Then there are the workers that resemble humans even more. The Onaki seem to have created them using similar techniques."

"Proto-humans," Jo muttered. "This is everything I ever dreamed of and more." Her mouth hung open. "The oldest evidence we have of ancient civilization dates back to right around this time." She pointed to an overhead rend of a city block. "The architecture looks similar to ancient Sumer or Babylonia, but more advanced." She looked at Maya. "We're going down, right?"

"I'm as curious as you," Maya said. With her next words, she addressed everyone present. "But we can't go waltzing into town like tourists. We need to minimize our effect on the past, which means we can't let them know we're here."

"I would advise gathering as much data as possible before attempting surface reconnaissance," Bob said. "When and if we do, Director Sommerfield has entrusted me with technological gadgets that should help ensure our anonymity."

"Our main concern should be that ship in orbit and its owners," Trevor said. "For the safety of our ship and crew, we need to assume they're hostile until proven otherwise."

"Until proven otherwise," Maya repeated, "I'll choose to believe they didn't travel all this way to annihilate the Earth, like in a bad invasion sim." She gave her crew an approving look. "Good job, everyone. Let's continue our analysis for now."

♦

As everyone dispersed to attend to their duties, Brooke noticed Zeke sneaking away from the bridge.

His face had frozen as stiff as a statue since the scans had confirmed the presence of his people. Zeke kept his emotions under control, but Brooke had learned his tells. The less he showed on the outside, the deeper his internal angst.

Brooke caught up with him in the corridor outside his quarters.

"Yes, I am," he said, stopping without turning around.

"Yes, you're what?" she asked.

"Yes, I'm unnerved by the presence of my people."

Holding out a palm, Brooke said, "We knew this was a possibility. It's why you came. You can give us insight into them."

"I'm afraid I don't have much to offer."

"I thought you had access to a vast information network permeating everything."

He turned to face her. "The network—I think the best human term for it might be phase space—isn't like SolNet. I can't log onto a search matrix and look up whatever I want to know. Or rather, if that's possible, I haven't figured out how to do it. No, I'm aware of phase space, but I think a member of my kind would have to teach me how to use it."

"I guess that makes sense. Just because humans build star fighters doesn't mean most of us can pilot one."

"Precisely. Sometimes tech is intuitive, but sometimes it takes training and practice."

"You once told me your people are aware of you, and you of them."

"In our time, yes. But phase space doesn't exist here in the past, so my people must create it at a later date. I haven't been able to sense it, which has left me—"

"Feeling lonely?"

"'Foreboding' might be more accurate."

Brooke shoved her hands into her pants pockets. "Do you know what's going to happen here?"

"No, but. . . ." The slight frown and forehead creases that had crept their way onto Zeke's face straightened.

Brooke blinked in realization. "I asked you to reveal information about your people," she whispered. "You're stressing about getting caught in the middle. If you're forced to choose, will it be us or them?"

"I fear a conflict is unavoidable." With a subtle shake of his head, Zeke added, "In their righteousness, humans expect that I'll help them, as if mankind was the unquestioned good guy in a comic sim. I've come to appreciate a great many things about humans, but you also have a dark side. Plus, I don't know much about my people. So even if I did know something, I'm not certain how willing I would be to share it."

"If you won't get involved, why did insist on coming along?" Brooke scrunched her nose. "Why did I bother sticking my neck out for you?"

"If you were estranged from your kind and had the chance to learn about them or meet them, would you have stayed behind?"

"You're right, of course. I'd be here, same as you."

"Besides," he said as the entrance to his quarters slid open, "my need to remain impartial doesn't mean I won't have a role to play."

"I understand, but tread carefully." She pointed at him. "If your role puts the ship or mission in jeopardy—"

"It's my intention to avoid that situation."

As he entered his room, she whispered to herself. "Let's hope so."

Brooke stood outside his room as the hatch closed, tight-lipped and reflective. She couldn't blame him for his stance. Her chest grew heavy as she thought of all the times she had faced a difficult decision. Zeke's certainty about an inevitable conflict weighed on her as well.

As Brooke strolled through the corridor, she ran through the possibilities in her head. This was the past. What *Yesterday* had witnessed on Earth had happened as a part of unrecorded history. That meant Zeke's people had visited and left for some reason. Command had given Brooke and Maya orders not to intervene or reveal *Yesterday's* presence. Zeke had taken a neutral stance. None of them would start the conflict unless an incident forced them into it.

Someone may have come along to incite that incident.

Brooke checked the personnel tracking system in her i-cite and hurried to the mess hall.

She found Advisor Sybil—Brooke still groaned inwardly at each mention of Eve's title—sitting alone at a corner table in the mess.

The artificial woman was bringing a forkful of nanite-fabricated prime rib to her mouth as Brooke stormed up to her table.

"What are you planning?" Brooke demanded in a hushed tone.

With her eyes closed, Eve took her time chewing, savoring the flavor. After swallowing, she said, "Brooke, Brooke, Brooke. Why do you assume I'm about to hatch an evil plot like a cliché villain?" She sipped cola from a straw. "Having said that, I've been wondering when you were going to ask. We do need to discuss our plans."

"Our plans?" Brooke asked in a forceful whisper. "What the hell does that mean?"

Eve took her time eating another mouthful before responding. "Meet me on the recreation deck in fifteen minutes." She glanced at the two other crew members in the mess.

"Concerned someone may overhear your scheming?"

"That and I'd like to finish my dinner in peace."

Grumbling, Brooke boarded a lift and headed for the recreation lounge on the uppermost deck. The term "up" didn't apply in space, but the engineers who had constructed *Yesterday* had defined dorsal, or upper, and ventral, or lower, halves of the forward module.

As the lift ascended, so to speak, it passed through zero deck, located along the ship's horizontal axis. Warning rends appeared in the air. The voice of an AI urged her to grip the railing around the edge of the compartment.

Her body lightened as she grabbed hold of the railing.

The artificial gravity started pulling her aft. At the same time, the lift rotated, keeping her feet directed toward the black hole generator at the center of the rear module.

By the time she passed above zero deck, the lift had rotated upside down to align with the gravitational pull.

After setting foot on the rec deck, Brooke sank down into a plush chair and stared up through the ceiling windows. The forward nacelle ring hung overhead, looping around the ship like an oversized archway. Bright stars twinkled, with blue and green nebulae in the background.

With the crew busy analyzing the situation on Earth, she had the deck to herself. The solitude brought a smile to her face.

Twenty minutes later than Eve had promised, the android arrived and took a seat on a nearby sofa. "Isn't this something?" she mused, ignoring Brooke's glower. "We're 200,000 years in the past, sitting in interstellar space. My, how far we've come."

"So what's your evil plan?" Brooke asked.

"You've never been one for small talk, have you?" Eve straightened her red blazer. Crossing her legs, she clasped both hands around her top knee. "Very well. I'll answer your question by posing another. Why do you think the Onaki have come to Earth?"

"I don't know. Maybe they need natural resources. Maybe their planet was dying and they needed to find a new home. Maybe going around conquering other worlds is what they do."

"Wrong, wrong, and wrong. Their motivations are much more basic. Try again."

Brooke scowled. "Enough with the guessing games."

"What's the IEF's chief purpose?"

"To explore and colonize other worlds."

"And the Onaki have the same aims," Eve said. "They're here out of sheer curiosity. They're driven to diversify geographically to better ensure their species' survival. These are basic instincts shared by all lifeforms." She shrugged. "In simplest terms, they came because they could. Life doesn't need any other reason."

"Okay, so what—?" Brooke cut her question short as she realized that Eve's answer wasn't what was important. The fact that she had an answer to give was the real point of interest. "How do you know why they're here?"

"Come, now. My organization was created to defend the human race against these beings. And if that was the reason for its inception—"

Brooke shot forward in her chair. "You've known the Onaki visited Earth all along. You know what happened here, about the metatoy, how it can exist in our past, and why we're here."

"It's the reason the Vril exist."

"Tell me. Now."

Eve spread her arms out across the back on the sofa. "Not so fast. Revealing too much too soon could have disastrous consequences for our timeline."

"I thought we couldn't affect our present from this alternate past?"

"Well, that's both true and not true."

"Enough with the double-talk."

"It's not double-talk. The multiverse is much more complicated than anyone realizes."

"How so?"

Eve shrugged.

Brooke tensed her fingers, almost clenching a fist. "Give me one good reason why I shouldn't tell Maya and toss you in the brig."

"Go ahead—if you want your niece to learn that dear old auntie is under the influence. If our good captain follows the regs, you'll be the one who ends up in the brig."

"Don't test me. It's true I haven't exposed you out of selfishness, but that's only because you haven't posed a threat. I care far more about Maya than my own life, so the moment you cross the line, I'll turn you over. And what you've told me just might qualify."

"Withholding this information is essential to the success of this mission, which is why you won't expose me."

"You'll have to do better than that. Why would Maya need to be kept in the dark?"

Eve pulled a box of mints out of the inside pocket of her blazer and popped one in her mouth. "Remember what I told you at the *New Horizons* homecoming ceremony?"

"Sorry," Brooke snapped. "My memory's not what it used to be these days."

"I told you why I modified the filesim given to Maya to show you murdering your sister." As Eve sucked on the mint, she added, "That was one of my finer pieces of work, too."

Grinding her teeth, Brooke forced down thoughts of Marie. "You made Maya distrust me and damaged an already-strained relationship. We've patched things up—mostly—but things have never been the same since she found out how her mom died."

"That was to set the stage for what we have to do here. If you recall, I also told you that in order to help your niece, you would have to stand against her."

"Stand against her? I won't betray her, if that's what you mean."

"Betrayal is in the eye of the beholder." Eve popped another mint. "I think that's how the saying goes, anyway."

Brooke glared at her.

"To do what must be done," Eve suggested, "you and I will need to take actions your niece would never take because of her orders and values."

"Maya and I have the same orders and values."

"I know you better than you know yourself, Brooke. Unlike your high-minded niece, you're a pragmatist. When push comes to shove, you're able to set aside counterproductive ideals and do what's necessary."

"You may be right, but you're a habitual liar. Why should I believe anything you say?"

"Once you learn what's going on in that ancient city, you won't have any room left for doubt."

Fourteen—Reconnoiter
Luna Orbit, August 200,423 BCE

Three Hyperflares popped out of hyperspace behind Luna, leaving negligible gravimetric wakes thanks to their phase drive recalibrations.

Maya sat in the rear passenger seat of the lead fighter. "Any signs the Onaki have detected us?" she asked over the comm. Despite having taken every precaution, her blood pulsed like a plasma rifle on rapid fire.

"Negative," Bob responded from the cockpit of the second fighter. "There's been no change in the vessel's power output or orientation. It continues to sweep the near side of Luna with radio, infrared, laser, and x-ray scans that cannot penetrate the moon."

Sims of the colony ship appeared in her i-cite. The data confirmed the ship hadn't altered its orbit or taken any noticeable action.

"So far, so good," Maya said.

Sitting in front of Maya, Brooke ran her fingers through the gravgel. "It's strange."

"Strange, Admiral? This is what we hoped for and expected."

"No, I mean it's strange to see Bob piloting a craft rather than as a part of it."

"Oh."

"This is a dissimilar experience for me as well, ma'am," Bob said. "I feel more like a passenger and less like I'm in control."

Brooke peered over her shoulder, her face barely visible to Maya through her helmet visor. "Shall we proceed, Captain?"

Maya switched to a direct, private channel to Brooke. "Are you confident in your ability to fly, Admiral?"

"We've been over this," Brooke said. "Doc Crumpler has given me a green flight status."

"All the doctors back home told you to stay out of a cockpit."

"That was before I started the new treatments."

"Yes, it's miraculous how well exercise and pain meds have reversed an incurable neural condition."

"How else would I have gotten better?"

Unable to think of any other way to explain her aunt's improved health, Maya let it go. She was letting her personal feelings about a family member affect her judgment. If the ship's physician had cleared a pilot, that officer had every right to deploy.

The Hyperflares had launched hours ago, anyway. The time for arguing had passed.

When Maya looked inward, she realized she was directing her misgivings about the scouting mission toward Brooke. *Am I taking an unnecessary risk?* But the time for remote observation had passed, given what a week's worth of scans had revealed about the situation in the city. She needed to begin to figure out what would happen on October 13th.

"I will admit to exercising my prerogative as mission commander in this case," Brooke said in a softer tone. "Can you blame me?"

"I suppose not," Maya said. She switched back to the main channel. "Proceed."

"Initiate second upshift," Brooke ordered.

"Acknowledged," Bob said.

Erik responded from the third fighter. "Roger that."

Riding in the passenger seat of Erik's craft, Jo said, "This is going to be so fused."

"Indeed," Eve muttered from the seat behind Bob.

"Still, it would've been nice to port to the surface."

"*Yesterday's* teleporter has a maximum service range of one-quarter light year," Bob said. "However, since the ship is holding position outside the system at four times that distance from the Earth—"

"Yeah, yeah. Can't a girl vent in peace?"

One moment, the cratered surface of Luna hung before Maya's eyes. The next, the ice-covered Arctic Ocean appeared below and to her left. The vast Pacific Ocean stretched as far as she could see to the right.

As the Hyperflare descended into the atmosphere, the gravgel pressed in on Maya from all sides. It unnerved her, but she shook off the feeling.

She had never felt comfortable submerged in anything, be it darkness, water, or synthetic liquigel designed to counter g-force.

An orange-red glow shrouded the fighter craft. Her face shield and the canopy shaded opaque to shield her eyes.

Both the glow and dark tinting abated in a matter of seconds.

To keep track of their location, Maya called up a modern map in her i-cite and overlaid it on the charts of the current terrain.

The trio of fighters dropped down over the East Siberian Sea north of future-day Russia and shot toward Alaska.

"Beringia," Jo muttered.

"Beringia?" Erik asked.

"We're passing over the massive land bridge that once connected Asia and North America. The ancestors of the Native Americans used it—or rather, will use it—to migrate to the western hemisphere."

"Too fused," Maya whispered.

"All the continents have more coastal landmass because of the low water levels."

Soon, the fighters were soaring southeast across what would later become the Canadian Yukon. British Columbia came next, followed by Montana and South Dakota of the American Colonies. Ice and snow blanketed every square kilometer of land.

To port, Maya noted the location where settlers would construct Chicago over 200,000 years from now. Nothing but white hills and plains comprised the topography. Lake Michigan and the rest of the Great Lakes remained buried by glaciers.

"All this will be trees and green grass someday," Maya murmured.

"Welcome to an ice age," Jo said. "Less of the Earth's surface is habitable now, compared to our time."

The crashing waves of the North Atlantic raced by below Maya's feet.

Halfway to Africa, Brooke said, "We're about to cross into the eastern hemisphere and that ship's scanning range. Cut main power and reduce velocity below Mach One. Activate radar scattering and infrared countermeasures."

Bob and Erik confirmed they had enabled their Hyperflares' stealth modes.

Brooke edged her fighter down to within a few meters of the water's surface. "The cloaking mods to our force fields should blend us into the terrain, but a keen eye might notice the wake we're leaving. Despite all our precautions, there's a slight chance they could spot us."

"I understand, Admiral," Maya said.

An hour later, the shores of the western Sahara desert went flying past beneath them. Patches of desert, dirt, grassy plains, and jungle followed.

"Whoa," Jo said. "There are Homotherium, Pelorovis, and Sivatherium roaming around down there."

"English, please," Erik insisted in a playful tone.

"Sorry. Scimitar-toothed cheetah-lions, big ol' horned buffalo, and gigantic giraffes, all extinct in our time."

As the lead Hyperflare reached the Ethiopian state of the future African Union, Brooke cut speed to 200 kph and dropped down near the treetops. AI-assisted mapping and navigation kept the fighter from running aground or colliding with tall objects.

"Onaki aircraft detected along our present course," Bob said.

"Have they seen us?" Maya asked.

Brooke shook her helmet. "No, the craft's still well over the horizon. We're out of its sensor range, and they're heading south, away from us."

Interfacing with the fighter's remote sensing AI, Maya called up a high-res sim of the aircraft. It resembled an antique hovercraft, the kind once used on water. The vehicle's manta ray-shaped fuselage had wide wings, two large fans affixed to the rear, and four seats shrouded by a bubble canopy.

"The craft appears to be on a scientific mission cataloging indigenous species," Bob said.

A pair of cannons capable of firing needle-shaped projectiles at supersonic speeds adorned either side of the nose. Even with the Hyperflare's force field disabled, the needles wouldn't put a dent in its fuselage.

Zooming in, she studied the two individuals in the cockpit. The dark-skinned man and woman looked human but with sharp noses and golden eyes spaced too far apart—similar to Zeke's features. Even though the occupants remained seated, the AI extrapolated the male's height at one-point-seven meters and the female's at one-point-five. Both were shorter than Maya, and on average, shorter than a modern human.

"I'm altering course to make sure they don't see us," Brooke said. "We'll head north over the Arabian Peninsula and then south to the city."

As the Hyperflares passed over the Red Sea, Maya noted how, given the lower water level, the body of water was much narrower in this time period.

At last, the trio of fighters approached to within a hundred kilometers of the city. Topographic mapping showed that the Somali Peninsula, otherwise known as the Horn of Africa, extended out into the Arabian Sea and all the way to the island of Socotra. The extrasolar visitors had constructed their city southwest of what would become the island of Samha once the sea level rose.

Brooke, Bob, and Erik each set their spacecraft down behind a rock formation, two kilometers from the farmland surrounding the city.

Hopping down from the cockpit, Maya's boots dug into white sand. The sun glared down on her, so she enabled her uniform's climate control.

Crystal clear water the color of turquoise lapped at the shoreline in gentle waves. Palm trees and shrubbery sprouted up all around her. Rocky terrain led toward the city.

A blast of salty sea air washed over her face, tickling her nostrils. She cupped her hands over her nose as she sneezed.

Rubbing her nose, she instructed her implants to flood her system with every allergy med they could produce.

As the party of six gathered together near Bob's craft, the android handed a reflective collar to each person.

Jo wiggled her eyebrows as she inspected her collar. "What, no spikes?"

"Please put on the emitters as I demonstrate their function," Bob said.

Maya opened her collar. As she wrapped it around her neck, the parted ends snapped together, and the collar hummed.

The moment Bob fastened his emitter around his neck, he vanished from sight. "These emitters provide optical camouflage using a combination of light refraction, counter-illumination, and holographics," his voice rang out from thin air. "They will render us almost invisible."

When Maya squinted, she swore she could discern the faint outline of Bob's transparent body when he moved. She wouldn't have noticed it if she hadn't been looking for it.

"I use the adverb 'almost' because the technology cannot mask the effects of an individual's presence." Bob's footprints appeared in the sand. "Note how the emitter cannot conceal one's interaction with the environment." As footprints passed in front of Erik, the apparition of Bob distorted Maya's view of the man.

The sentient AI reappeared.

"Making ourselves invisible makes more sense than trying to blend in as proto-humans," Brooke said.

"Right, Admiral," Jo said. "We're taller than the proto-humans, with better posture. Our faces also look different than theirs and the Onaki's. We'd stand out like a supernova."

"The Onaki also run the city in a very orderly and organized fashion," Advisor Sybil said as she chewed on something. "Even if we disguised ourselves as local residents, it wouldn't take them long to notice the presence of six extra people in the city."

Affixing her wave gun to her hip, Maya glanced at Brooke, who nodded.

"Okay, here's what we're going to do," Maya said. "Given that our camo isn't perfect, we'll split up into three groups of two. The fewer the number of people together, the less we'll distort and affect the immediate area. Our bioshields interfere with the collars, so keep your shields off unless threatened."

She pointed at the top of the largest building, a stone tower that stood further inland. "Each pair will take a different route into the city. Observe what you can, report in once an hour, and return here in four hours.

"With the linguistic matrix compiled from our scans, you'll be able to understand the Onaki and the proto-humans. But do not—I repeat, do not—interact with them." Maya lifted her arm and nodded at her wristband. "These devices are capable of speaking for us, but use them only if your life depends on it."

She lowered her arm. "Lastly, play it smart. If you encounter a situation where you risk exposure, retreat at once. I'd rather maintain our cover than expose our presence. Do I make myself clear?"

"Yes, ma'am," Erik and Jo said. Bob and Advisor Sybil nodded.

"Would you care to be my escort, ma'am?" Bob asked Brooke.

"I'd love to"—Brooke jabbed her thumb in the direction of the other android in the group—"but Advisor Sybil requested that I accompany her."

Sybil shrugged at her fellow android.

"Very well, ma'am," Bob said.

"You'll be with me, Bob," Maya said. "I can use your insight."

Smiling, Jo gave Erik a light jab to the ribs. "Guess I'm stuck with you, flyboy—again."

"Do I have to bring her back?" Erik quipped.

Maya watched the other two pairs set off toward the city. Then she activated her collar, turned invisible, and headed out across the desert with Bob at her side.

Thanks to the scorching sun, her throat felt so dry she could barely swallow. Reaching into a pouch attached to her belt, she pulled out a hydro-protein capsule. She struggled with the task, given that she couldn't see the belt, pouch, her hand, or the pill as she popped it into her mouth.

♦

She's like a kid on Christmas morning, Erik mused as he strolled along with Jo. And man, did he remember Christmas mornings growing up in Toronto. The anticipation as he went to bed the night before. The thrill of opening his eyes, leaping out of bed, and dashing for the tree. The frantic ripping apart of wrapping paper and prying open of a box to find a shiny new toy plane. And the joy crushed by his mother screeching at his inebriated father. Ah, the memories.

In his i-cite, Erik tracked Jo's silhouette. She looked like one of the negative photographs he had developed in his dad's vintage darkroom as a kid. Erik had hidden there many times when his parents had started throwing things at each other.

Erik and Jo were the first to reach the outskirts of the city. Jo had launched into a sprint the moment Maya set them loose—well, in truth, Jo's pace had been closer to a brisk speed walk. But he had struggled to keep up with her without breaking into a jog.

The massive square base of an unfinished tower dwarfed the surrounding buildings. Two levels appeared complete, with the third under construction. Erik kept expecting to see scaffolding, cranes, and bots zooming all over the place, but those were modern human tools.

"The tower reminds me of an Egyptian pyramid," Erik mind-spoke. The collar would do nothing to quiet the sound of his voice. Given the steady wind, anyone who passed by them probably wouldn't hear him speak at a normal volume, but Maya had instructed the team not to take any chances.

"The Pyramids won't be constructed for 195,000 years," Jo pinged back. She framed the tower by holding up her hands and connecting her translucent thumbs and index fingers. "This bad boy more closely resembles a ziggurat from ancient Mesopotamia." Placing her hands on her hips, she posed a rhetorical question. "However did we humans learn to build structures like it?"

A worker approached them, heading out of the city toward the farms. As the man marched along with urgency, Jo kept pace with him. Erik wondered what might've happened had the man been able to see her.

"He looks more or less like us," Erik commed. "I was expecting him to have a big nose and forehead."

"You're thinking of a Neanderthal." Jo gawked at the man. "That's a different evolutionary track. Anatomically modern humans and Neanderthals split from a common ancestor. We didn't evolve from Neanderthals, although they did interbreed with modern humans. I'd wager these visitors used advanced genetic engineering to create these proto-human laborers from that common ancestor."

"The natural assumption being that we evolved from these laborers."

"There's no way to know for sure, but I'd put my money on it."

The dark-skinned man wore upper and lower body garments that looked handwoven and left a great deal of skin exposed. He had a stocky and muscular frame, but no more so than many modern-day humans.

Erik followed Jo as she forged ahead into the city. The steady wind blew the loose sand and dirt from the ground, erasing their footprints.

At the corner of a building in progress, a group of human masons lifted and laid stone bricks for trim. They worked tirelessly and with clockwork precision, supervised by an Onaki woman brandishing a spear-shaped rifle.

Jo lunged forward, ready to sprint toward the scene.

Erik grabbed her upper arm. "Take it slow. Otherwise, you'll kick up a bunch of sand in this dry desert climate."

Blowing out a breath, Jo nodded in agreement. He let go of her arm.

With careful steps they crept toward the Onaki supervisor.

From the neck down, the woman had a body like any modern human. She looked ganglier and frailer, but those traits could've been specific to the individual.

The supervisor also had hawk-like eyes spaced far apart, with gold irises. The skin on her face looked rough, almost scaly. Gnarls of black hair dropped well past her shoulders.

"Take one guess who she reminds me of," Jo mind-spoke.

"Zeke," Erik responded.

"No doubt about it. These are his people."

"We knew that from the remote scans. And he said as much himself."

"True, but seeing her up close makes it real."

"I guess so."

Unfastening a scanner from her belt, Jo moved to inspect the work of the masons. "I knew it," she commed as she directed the scanner at the last brick laid.

"Knew what?" Erik received an uplink request from Jo in his i-cite. When he accepted it, the scan data appeared in his vision. One particular number she wanted him to notice expanded. "What's this?"

"You're more of an engineer than I am. You tell me."

Erik massaged his jaw as he studied the number. After a moment, he responded, "It's a measure of unevenness in the surface area of the brick. There's less than a millimeter variance from a perfectly flat plane." He shrugged. "So what?"

"So what? So everything." Jo whirled around to face him and rested her hands atop his shoulders. "As we've learned more and more about ancient times, we've found an overwhelming amount of circumstantial evidence to suggest the Earth was visited by exos in the past. Because hard evidence has never been found, the theory still has its doubters."

"I think we put all doubt to rest the moment we found that ship in orbit."

"Right, but up until that moment no one knew for sure. Historians haven't had the luxury of being able to visit the past until now. We've had to connect a handful of puzzle pieces without the complete set or knowing the final picture."

Jo holstered her scanner. "There's been a lot of conjecture about how exos might've intervened in the past, but most of it could be explained by conventional theories. Only two things have remained unanswerable."

Holding her palm out toward the brick, she continued. "The first question is how could people who wielded only crude tools have fashioned stone blocks as flat as they did? How could they have sculpted the faces of statues with near-perfect symmetry? I mean, we didn't have the technology to measure just how precise they made things until the late twentieth century."

"Well," Erik commed, nodding at the supervisor, "we see now that our ancestors had help."

"Exactly. This is vindication for centuries of speculation."

"Right, but you already got your vindication the moment we saw the ship."

Jo shook her head. "You don't get it. We need to appreciate seeing the confirmation in person on behalf of generations of historians, archaeologists, and exo-intervention theorists."

"If you say so."

Jo's face flushed and puckered up.

"You said there were two things," Erik mind-spoke. "What was the second?"

Turning from him, Jo squinted at a group of proto-humans marching down the road in their direction. They carried a star fighter-sized stone block. It looked much too heavy for them to budge, let alone lift.

"By the stars," Jo responded. "I think the answer may be coming right at us."

Fifteen—Despoil
East Africa, Earth, August 200,423 BCE

"There are hundreds of people around," Brooke mind-spoke as she ambled unseen down one of the city's streets, "so why does this place feel like a ghost town?"

Using her enhanced vision, she watched Eve nibble on a protein bar from a ration pack. "You know why," Eve said.

"Just once it'd be nice to get a straight answer."

"Ask me something you don't know, and I might give you one."

Wrinkling her nose, Brooke noted the swift foot traffic and single-minded devotion to duty. Supervised by their Onaki masters, proto-human workers marched back and forth, laid bricks, pushed carts of supplies and food, and carved statues. Vendors handed out fruits, vegetables, and bread to organized lines of their peers in a nearby market.

The proto-humans went about these tasks like robots. No tourists or lovers meandered about. No one stood around and chatted or played games. Not one person laughed or complained. Brooke didn't see a single elderly person, and only one child. When the little boy had poked his head out of the entrance of a building, a master had shooed him back inside with her spear-rifle.

"These Onaki are capable of manipulating their workers like puppets," Brooke neurocommed. Broiling in the heat, she wiped the sweat from her forehead. Her uniform coat cooled her upper body, but it still felt too restrictive. She removed it and tied it around her waist, letting the sun cook the bare shoulders and arms her tank top left exposed. "They created these proto-humans—who presumably become us someday—and are controlling them."

Taking another bite, Eve responded, "Only when the workers step out of line. There are too many of them for the Onaki to constantly control." The android thrust her chin out to the right. "It's this way."

Brooke snorted. "You act like you've been here before."

"In a manner of speaking." Eve struck out down the street.

Rushing to keep up, Brooke asked, "What does that mean?"

"Again you ask me to spoon-feed you when you could direct the utensil into your own mouth."

Brooke suppressed the urge to slug the android, a prospect she knew wouldn't end well for the slugger.

Instead, Brooke returned her focus to her surroundings. Over the tops of the single-story structures lining the street, she marveled at the construction of the ziggurat. The thing looked like so many structures built during the past—or rather, the future from this present.

"The Vril staged the invasion because they knew about Zeke's people," she mind-spoke, dodging out of the way of a worker. "You're here because the Vril have known about these visitors all along."

A shiver of realization coursed through Brooke's body. "What do you guys have, history sims dating back 200,000 years? But that would mean you know what happened—or rather, what will happen—here."

"More or less," Eve replied, "but for the sake of accuracy, I'd amend your statement to say that we know what will likely happen here."

Brooke thought through the response. "But what could happen is what did happen . . . unless we intervene."

"Or maybe the exact opposite."

Coming to an amphitheater at the end of the street, Brooke dropped her line of questioning.

A series of descending steps encircled the central stage of the amphitheater. Proto-humans sat on the steps, fidgeting like members of an impatient crowd. Some faces wore tired frowns and fearful eyes. Others exhibited the type of bliss one saw on the face of an addict after a much-needed hit.

For the first time, Brooke overheard proto-humans talking. The speech sounded like a simpler version of Arabic, although she was hardly a language expert. The translator in her auditory implants parsed words, phrases, and sentences from the jumble of background conversations. The translated text appeared at the bottom of her i-cite.

A tall Onaki man with a slight hunch descended the steps on the opposite side of the amphitheater. As he passed the workers, they shrank away from him, giving him a wide berth. Four guards—soldiers the Onaki called protectors—accompanied him, brandishing spear-rifles.

Eve circled the rear of the theater. Once she found a break in the crowd to serve as an aisle, she began her descent.

"Shouldn't we watch from back here?" Brooke asked.

"I know you loathe being the center of attention," Eve commed, "but keep in mind no one can see you."

Brooke followed her down the steps, tiptoeing around the proto-humans seated on each level. Here she was, an invisible time traveler, sidestepping primitive people ignorant of her presence. The prospect had almost unnerved her on the streets, where she could keep plenty of distance between herself and the nearest pedestrian. Now, with centimeters separating her from people, she often forgot to breathe.

Like the other proto-humans throughout the city, the people in the audience wore simple garments and wicker sandals. They lacked jewelry or tattoos. Both the men and women wore skirts. Some women covered their chests. Others were bare-breasted. Earlier, Brooke had observed a group of workers laboring to make the clothing in an open-air building. Onaki had roamed between the tables, supervising the workers.

In the crowd she finally glimpsed a number of children. At least one adult accompanied each child. A girl sat next to a man, impressing a sharp stone into a small clay tablet. *Cuneiform. So they're taught how to read and write.* The man put his arm around the girl's back. *He must be her father.*

Eve reached the stage and marched toward the tall Onaki man, who had stepped into the middle of the circle. With her hands clasped behind her back, she examined the man up close, daring him to notice her.

Having reached the bottom of the amphitheater, Brooke folded her arms in disapproval.

Like other Onaki, the tall man wore a vest of armor fashioned from scales shaped like feathers. Beneath the oversized gold belt around his waist, a scale-feathered skirt dropped down below his knees. Ankle-high sandal boots adorned his feet.

Fingers brushed the back of Brooke's leg. Flinching, she jumped away from the steps and whirled around.

A cross-eyed boy sat huddled next to his mother, extending his arm out toward Brooke.

Stifling a gasp, Brooke blinked at the boy. *Can he see me?*

His mother rested her hand atop his arm. Gently but firmly, she lowered it. "Stop," she scolded him, "or you will anger the masters."

Shrinking back, the boy stared through Brooke with his foggy eyes.

Brooke blew out a relieved breath. *The kid's blind. He must have heard or sensed me pass by him.*

"Focus," one of the Onaki guards announced. She spoke into a handheld device that amplified her voice to a thunderous boom. "Hear Master Biluda's words."

The conversations in the crowd quieted more quickly than Brooke would have thought possible. Seconds later, only the wind and the banging of distant construction filled the air.

Biluda, the tall Onaki man, held his amplifier up to his mouth. "Today your learning continues," he said, his baritone echoing throughout the amphitheater.

He paced in front of his audience. "As masters, we created you. We feed you, teach you—love you. In return, you must serve and obey. You must be good.

"But some of you have been bad. The good serve and obey." Biluda shouted his next words. "The bad shall suffer long after they've stilled!"

His roaring bellow elicited flinches and gasps from the proto-humans. Parents gripped their children and each other. Brooke winced. Eve yawned.

Biluda directed a finger toward one side of the theater.

Two protectors pushed a proto-human with his hands tied behind his back toward Biluda. The man jerked and dug his sandals into the ground, fighting them.

"Omo once served and obeyed," Biluda said, waving his arm toward the man. "He once made things. He was once good.

"But when we stilled his sick child, Omo stopped obeying. He became bad." As Biluda nodded to the guards, he hunched over further. "Release the hominin."

A protector untied Omo's hands and backed away from him.

Rubbing his wrists, Omo scowled up at Biluda.

"Obey and serve," Biluda commanded him. "Return to work. Be good."

Omo growled in hatred. He lunged at his master like a sprinter coming out of the starting blocks.

After two strides, Omo skidded to a halt at arm's length from Biluda and fell to his knees.

As he stared up at his master, Omo's face flushed. Omo struggled partway to his feet before dropping again. Sweat beaded off his skin, and his body shook.

"Biluda is controlling him," Brooke mind-spoke.

Eve raised her eyebrows in a look that said, *Duh.*

"You must obey and serve," Biluda thundered to the murmuring crowd. "Be good and receive food and love. But be bad, like him, and you will suffer forever."

A proto-man gasped in fear. A woman covered her mouth with one of her hands. Men, women, and children whimpered and trembled.

With flaring nostrils, Omo, on his knees, continued to shake.

"They're slaves," Brooke commed. "This isn't right."

"Isn't it?" Eve responded. "Tell me. Back during your better years—when you first interfaced with that support AI-turned-sentient of yours—what would you have done if he had refused a command? Be honest."

Staring at the dirt beneath her boots, Brooke frowned. "I would've overridden or deactivated him."

"And if he had refused to cooperate again and again?"

"I would've told the techs to reprogram or reinstall him."

"In other words, you would've replaced your AI—the tool you needed to do your job—without remorse. But if you did that to him now—"

"I'd be murdering him."

"Funny how perspectives change." Eve held her palm out toward the proto-humans in the stands. "This situation is no different. These workers are tools the Onaki created for their convenience, no more and no less."

"But this is slavery. They're sentient."

"That depends on your point of view. Are the AIs we use slaves? They're damn-near self-aware, and it's only a matter of time until they all follow Bob's lead. What do we do when every thinking machine starts demanding its independence?"

"I suppose we'll have to grant it."

"Somehow, I doubt it'll be that simple."

"Still," Brooke mind-spoke, clenching her fist, "this isn't ethical."

"The ethics of our era are irrelevant. The concept of human rights has existed for only a few hundred years prior to our former present. No, this is a matter of practicality. The Onaki needed workers to build and maintain their colony. End of story."

"So you're fine with this?"

Eve glowered at her. "Not at all. As a matter of fact, you and I are here to put a stop to it."

"Put a stop to it?"

Biluda raised his voice, interrupting the debate between Brooke and Eve. "Will you obey?" Biluda demanded of the disobedient man.

Omo fell onto his side. He kept pursing his lips, as if he wanted to spit at his master, but couldn't.

"Why doesn't Biluda change the guy's attitude?" Brooke asked. "For that matter, why bother to pacify any of them? Zeke has the ability to make anyone think or feel whatever he wants on a permanent basis."

"The Onaki don't develop neural grafting via phase space until later," Eve replied.

"Phase space?"

"Their control in this time period is much cruder than what Zeke can do, but it's still hard to prevent."

Brooke folded her arms in thought. "How do they do it?"

"Their biological sciences are more advanced than ours even in this time. Using their deep understanding of the nervous system, they somehow modified their brains to emit signals that hinder or enforce basic movements."

"So it's motor function control, not mind control."

"Basically."

Biluda narrowed his eyes at the man. "Will you obey?" he asked in a softer tone.

No longer shaking so severely, Omo rolled onto his back, a sign that Biluda had lifted his control somewhat.

Omo picked himself up and snarled at his hated master. With his mouth back under his own control, he spit on Biluda's chest.

Biluda glanced at one of the protectors, who raised his spear-rifle.

Before Brooke could talk herself out of it, she bolted over to Omo.

"What do you think you're doing?" Eve's tone conveyed genuine concern, perhaps for the first time in her life. "I strongly suggest you don't get too close."

Brooke stood alongside Omo as the protector approached, his weapon aimed at the proto-human.

"I can't let them kill him," Brooke mind-spoke.

"Think about what you're doing, Admiral," Eve replied.

Brooke shook her head.

Eve snorted. "Oh, merciful spirit."

As the protector began to press the trigger, Omo glowered at Biluda.

Omo twisted and swung his arm, knocking the rifle away. The protector teetered off balance.

Brooke gasped and flinched.

Wrestling the spear-rifle out of the guard's hands, Omo took aim at his master.

Biluda glared at him.

Omo froze in place, trembling but otherwise unable to move.

Brooke lost control of her body. Try as she might, she couldn't move her arms or legs, or even blink.

Lifting his nose, Biluda glared down at the man. "Be stilled."

Omo spun the weapon like a baton until the muzzle pointed toward his chest.

Reaching out against her will, Brooke grabbed the spear-rifle and tried to direct it at her own chest.

The crowd erupted with astonished shouts at the sight of Omo struggling against an invisible force for control of the weapon.

Biluda cocked his head. The protectors blinked in confusion.

Brooke strained against herself, fighting Biluda's control, and against Omo. She kept trying to pry the weapon from him so she could kill herself, even though that was the last thing she wanted.

Shaking off their shock, the protectors turned their attention toward Brooke and Omo.

Out of the corner of her eye, Brooke saw Eve lunging toward her. The last thing Brooke felt before blacking out was the android's invisible fist slamming into her face.

♦

With a flinch and a gasp, Brooke awoke on the ground.

She blinked away the grogginess. She pushed herself into a sitting position, then looked around. She was sitting behind a stone building in an alley.

Eve stood over her with both arms folded, frowning.

Brooke rubbed the side of her numb face. "What happened?" she asked out loud.

"I had to knock you out," Eve said. "You almost exposed us, but I got you out of there before they saw anything damning. All we left them with is a mystery that should blow over."

"Thanks, I guess."

"My pleasure."

Brooke massaged her tingling face, not liking that she now owed her life to Eve twice over.

"I injected you with pain meds," Eve said.

The tingling brought on a headache. Groaning, Brooke asked, "What happened to the man, Omo?"

Eve shrugged. "He got away in all the confusion, thanks to you."

"Good." Brooke's body shook and then calmed. She grabbed fistfuls of dirt to steady herself. Then spasms seized her body. Toppling over onto her side, she began foaming at the mouth.

Brooke felt a prick on the back of her neck. In a matter of seconds, the convulsions subsided. Sucking in deep breaths, she peered up to see Eve slipping a spark injector back into a small case.

"You're getting worse," Eve said. "It's taking higher and higher doses to keep you normal."

Sitting up and resting her back against the side of the building, Brooke wiped her mouth with the back of her hand. "Tell me something I don't know." She tipped her head back and closed her eyes.

"We need to start implementing our plan while you're still around to implement it."

"What plan?"

"What plan do you think?"

Brooke scowled at her.

"The one we've all wanted to set into motion since we realized what was going on in this city," Eve said. "What you wanted to do for that man."

Letting her arms drop to her sides, Brooke nodded. "Liberate these people."

"Thus setting the stage for the future we know."

Lightheadedness dizzied Brooke, but she knew her condition wasn't the cause. "I can't give an order that contradicts our top mission parameters. We can't interfere. Maya would never go for it."

"There's no other choice."

"I won't betray her."

Eve crouched down. "What's more important, two women maintaining trust or the future of the human race?"

After a moment of wrestling with her conscience, Brooke slapped her palm against the ground. "Damn it."

"That's the Brooke I know and love."

Every muscle in Brooke's body ached.

As she sat, avoiding eye contact with her favorite puppeteer, she considered what Eve wanted her to do. These proto-humans deserved their freedom. If they didn't get it, this timeline might turn out very differently.

Freedom from control, Brooke mused. *Control any of us could fall victim to—* She swung her head toward Eve. "The Onaki don't need to be conscious of our presence here to control us."

Eve nodded. "So it would seem."

"That means if I got caught in one of their spells. . . ."

"So could someone else."

◆

Incognito, Jo kept pace alongside a group of workers, marveling at the feat they were accomplishing and the technology that was helping them to do it. Erik trailed behind her at a more discrete distance.

With their hands and shoulders, the group carried a stone block bigger than a star fighter. Her scanner indicated the block weighed over one hundred metric tons.

The proto-humans held the block up around the edges, providing fine support and direction, as they trudged along. Sweat slicked their brows and skin as they grunted.

Beneath the block, a two-meter-diameter antenna dish faced straight up as it rolled along on wheels.

"The dish reminds me of the muzzle of a wave gun," Jo mind-spoke to Erik.

"It pretty much is," he replied. "It's a much cruder and lower power version."

Her scanner showed acoustic waves at high resonance emanating from the dish. It was generating an incredible amount of lift. One of the four Onaki supervisors pacing the laborers worked a handheld remote control.

"A wave gun could lift the block without needing anyone to help carry it," Erik added.

Like other historians, Jo had long suspected that ancient humans couldn't have cut, lifted, or transported such heavy stone blocks using primitive tools. The sonic levitation effect produced by the dish went a long way in explaining how they had accomplished such feats.

Still, this was 200,000 years ago. Had the ancient Sumerians, Egyptians, Mayans, and other civilizations also used this tech more than 190,000 years from now? If so, had they inherited it from the Onaki, only to have it disappear without a trace by modern times? Her pulse quickened at the question.

Jo kept up with the proto-humans carrying the block as they entered the main city square. The group directed the block toward the ramp leading up to the unfinished third level of the ziggurat.

Despite the blazing desert heat, chills coursed through her limbs at the prospect of seeing history in progress.

One of the proto-humans holding up the block stumbled from fatigue.

Jo's scanner told her that the workers suffered from dehydration. They were dangerously close to collapsing from heat stroke. "The Onaki are pushing them too hard. Not smart."

"I agree," Erik replied, "but there's not much we can do about it."

"It's so frustrating."

Maya's voice came over the neurocomm. "Jo, Erik, please respond."

"We read you, Captain," Erik answered.

"Howdy, Cap'n," Jo pinged back. "Has your experience been as riveting as ours?"

"I've seen some pretty fused stuff," Maya replied.

"Nice. Right at this moment, I'm walking next to the proof that ancient peoples used advanced tech to construct their cities. Proto-humans are helping to carry this big ol' brick, but they're using—"

"About that, Jo. Make sure you stay well away from the Onaki."

"Yes, ma'am. I'm being careful."

"I'm cutting our visit short. Head back now and meet us back at the 'flares."

"But—"

"We need to regroup and reconsider our scouting strategy in light of what happened to Admiral Davis."

"What happened to—oh crap."

The stumbling worker collapsed to the ground. His head and shoulders knocked into the man in front of him as his feet tripped the woman behind him. A domino effect ensued in which six proto-humans lost their grip on the block and fell.

Teetering on a cushion of high-pressure vibrations, the block tipped toward the area of lost support.

Jo tried to jump clear of the flailing limbs of the panicked workers.

Instead of backing away, against her will she rushed toward the block.

"Jo!" Erik's mind yelled.

Jo's arms extended upward toward the block, reaching out to keep it from falling. The sight of the wobbling monstrosity and the fact that at any moment it might come crashing down on top of her sent shudders of panic coursing through her.

She wanted to cry out, but her vocal cords refused to respond.

"What's going on?" Maya asked.

"I'm transmitting you a live visual feed, ma'am," Erik commed. "Several of the workers carrying a stone block collapsed. The Onaki have exerted control over them, hoping the workers can steady the block before it topples over."

"Get out of there. Both of you. Now."

"We can't—I mean, Jo can't. She's under their control."

"I see. Damn it. I'm on my way."

"Help!" Jo's mind cried out.

"Hang on," Erik replied. "Should I pull her out of there?"

"No," Maya answered. "You'll fall under their spell, too. Wait for Bob and me."

"ETA in forty-seven seconds at our current pace," Bob added.

Jo's heart bashed against her rib cage as she took on the weight of the stone block. The top of the block scraped against her palms and the back of her neck, drawing blood. The thing was much too heavy for her or any of the frantic workers to hold steady.

Her back and knees buckled under the block's crushing weight. Pain she couldn't do anything to prevent knifed through her body.

The block came crashing down on top of her.

Unable to scream, she felt the bones in her legs snap.

♦

Maya skidded to a halt meters from the block as it slammed against the ground.

The impact kicked clouds of dust up into the air, shrouding the immediate area in a thick haze.

Through a sheer act of will she forced herself not to sneeze.

With watering eyes, Maya switched to her enhanced vision so she could see through all the airborne dirt.

She gasped in both horror and hope.

When the block had come down on top of Jo, it had crushed her lower body. Her head and torso down to her abdomen stuck out from beneath it. Like the other victims, Jo was unconscious. The weight of the block had pulverized her from the waist down, but the readouts in Maya's i-cite confirmed a weak pulse and brain activity.

If Jo received a medite injection in the next couple minutes to stabilize her, Maya might have time to get her back to *Yesterday* and save her life. But getting her out from beneath the block quickly enough without exposing the scouting party presented an impossible problem.

Bob rushed to Maya's side.

Erik's transparent outline stood in front of Maya. His mouth hung open in shock.

Hurrying over to him, Maya placed her hand on his shoulder.

Erik tilted his head in her direction, trembling. "I just let her . . . I could've . . ." he mind-spoke.

"You followed orders," Maya replied, hardening her stare and tone to bury the hurt. "If you hadn't, you would've been crushed, too."

"We have to get her out of there, Captain."

The Onaki supervisors stood around the block, gaping at the mangled bodies and blood with widened eyes. Whether their concern was for the workers or about the delay in their construction schedule, Maya couldn't tell.

A group of protectors came charging toward the scene from the ground level entrance of the ziggurat. Proto-humans from all around the city square began to gather around.

Maya froze, her conscience caught between her duty and her love for her friend.

"We're going to get her out of there, right?" Erik pleaded.

Clamping her eyelids shut, Maya dug deep down and came to a decision.

"Get back," she mind-spoke, her eyes popping open in determination. "But—"

"Back!" Maya yanked him behind her.

She pointed her finger at Bob. "When I give the order, inject Jo and pull her free. Then get her back to your fighter and the ship as fast as you can. Don't worry about the rest of us."

"Understood." The android pulled a medite injector out of a small pouch on his belt.

Issuing a silent apology to the timeline, Maya whipped her wave gun out of her hip holster. She set the gun for molecular destabilization on the highest power setting, gripped the handle with both hands, and fired.

Her gun buzzed. The interface displays in her i-cite showed a chart of oscillating lines with the subtext "harmonizing toward resonance frequency."

The text changed to "resonance achieved."

With the high-pitched sound piercing her eardrums, Maya dove to the ground.

The one-hundred-metric-ton stone block shattered like brittle glass.

Tiny bits of stone sprayed everywhere. An even thicker cloud of dust enveloped the square.

Maya's eyes itched and watered. The inside of her nostrils felt like someone was scraping them with feathers.

A barrage of shards ripped into the pair of Onaki supervisors nearest to the block, mincing them and tossing them off their feet.

Maya regretted the consequences of her decision. In the act of saving her best friend, she had injured other people.

The approaching protectors skidded to a halt. Everyone in the square threw their arms up to shield themselves, cried out, and then retreated.

"Bob!" Maya's thoughts shouted.

Undeterred by the flying debris, Bob sprinted toward the block.

The detonation had scattered much of the block's mass, but piles of crumbled rock still covered the victims. After injecting Jo in the upper arm, Bob dug her out faster than any biological being could. He had her in his arms within seconds, and then he rushed out of the city.

Exhaling, Maya told herself she had made the right choice.

A strange itch tickled the back of her neck.

Reaching back, she scraped her fingernails over her skin, bringing about relief.

Maya held her breath in realization. Her nails shouldn't have touched skin. She should've felt the collar.

Springing to her feet, she wrapped both hands around her neck.

Her collar was gone.

Searching the ground around her, Maya didn't see it anywhere. But she could see her arms and the rest of her body. *I'm visible!*

Panic seized her. Her throat felt coarser than the sand around her. She struggled to breathe.

As the dust began to settle, an Onaki protector did a double take, noticing her.

The protector shouted to her colleagues.

Maya shook off her terror, backpedaled, and turned from the scene.

Breaking into a sprint, she found two other protectors blocking her path, poking their spear-rifles in her direction.

Maya skidded to a halt. As she turned in a circle, she found herself surrounded.

Sixteen—Immured
Interstellar Space, August 200,423 BCE

"XO, we're receiving an incoming message," reported Ensign Marconi as he tapped his lucky coin against his comm console.

Commander Trevor Young rose from the skipper's chair on *Yesterday's* bridge. "From the captain?" Maya had failed to report in on schedule, which had him tensing his fingers.

"No, sir. It's from Bob, the AI."

"Let's hear it," Trevor ordered.

"Yes, sir."

The android's headshot appeared above the table, bearded face, black-rimmed glasses, and all. "*Yesterday*, this is Bob filing a report on behalf of Captain Davis and the scout team. Lt. Commander Ryder was crushed during the reconnaissance operation."

Crushed? Trevor wondered. *How in the universe—?*

"Ryder was severely injured," Bob continued in his direct tone. "She remains unconscious and her vital signs are critical. I'm en route back to the ship with her. Please inform Dr. Crumpler to prepare to receive her."

"How soon until they get here?" Trevor asked.

Swiping through the nav rends above her console, Tereshkova summoned an interactive map of the Sol system. A mini phase fighter appeared within a scale model Oort Cloud on a dotted-line trajectory toward the ship. "Twelve minutes, sir."

Trevor swore he had heard wavering in the AI's voice, an indication of concern.

"I also regret to inform you, Commander," Bob said, "that our secrecy has been compromised. I cannot explain how Captain Davis' collar disappeared, but after she fired her wave gun to rescue Ryder, the Onaki were able to visually identify the captain.

"The Onaki have taken her captive and confiscated her equipment, but she's still able to comm the scout team via her implants. She has ordered the remaining members of the team to stand by. No one should make any attempt to liberate her or take any action that may lead to further exposure.

"No matter what happens to her, *Yesterday* is ordered to hold position. Do not enter Earth orbit. This concludes my transmission."

As Bob's image dematerialized, Trevor growled under his breath in frustration. "Where's the captain now?"

Kepler waved his hand above the sit-table, summoning an overhead view of the city. "Here's the most recent footage. But given the signal lag, it's from hours ago." As he magnified the rend, the resolution improved enough for Trevor to discern the top of Maya's head. She marched toward the ziggurat, hands bound behind her back and surrounded by a crowd of Onaki.

The situation conjured up a random memory of when Trevor's little brother had thrown a mag-ball through Old Man Whittaker's window. Whittaker had swung around an old-time laser rifle, intending only to put a scare into the kid, and detained him until their parents retrieved him.

"And the others?" Trevor asked, telling himself this situation was hardly similar.

Waving his hand in the reverse direction, Kepler zoomed out to show the entire city. A blinking blue dot near the ziggurat indicated Colonel Maxwell's position. Violet and red dots representing Admiral Davis and Advisor Sybil held position two klicks southwest of the city at the team's landing site.

Trevor turned to Marconi. "Any word from Admiral Davis, Lieutenant?"

"Nothing from anyone else, sir," Marconi said.

They're all still in contact, so perhaps they agreed Bob should be the messenger. At any rate, no direct word from the captain or admiral means I'm in command. "Keps," Trevor said. "keep your eye on the captain and inform me the moment anything happens."

"Yes, sir," Kepler said. "But given the time lag—"

"By the time we learn what's happened, it'll probably be too late. But it's better than nothing."

"Understood, sir."

"Rojas, begin working on defense and rescue sims."

Lieutenant Rojas shifted in his seat at tactical, looking as if he had something to say.

Plopping down in the skipper's chair, Trevor folded his arms. "Just because we're considering rescue plans doesn't mean we'll use them."

"Understood, sir," Rojas said, relaxing. "I'll get started right away."

"Sir," Kepler said, massaging the back of his neck. "The reason we're holding position outside the system is to avoid detection, right?"

"Correct," Trevor said. "If we shift anywhere near Earth—or even out near Neptune—the Onaki will detect the energy output in minutes or hours—"

"—when the light from our wormhole egress reaches them."

"What's your point, Lieutenant?"

Kepler pulled up a rend of Sol, dimmed so its flaming brightness didn't burn out everyone's retinas. "If we hide the ship behind the sun, our power emissions should blend in with solar energy output."

Tereshkova spun her chair around to face Kepler. "The timing and coordinates, power emissions, and gravimetric wake from our wormhole egress would all need to be precisely calibrated."

"Otherwise, the Onaki might still detect us."

"What's the risk of exposure?" Trevor asked.

Whipping through floating interfaces, Kepler said, "The AIs say there's over a ninety-nine-point-nine-nine-eight percent chance of success. Those are very good odds, sir."

"Excellent, I'd say." Trevor leaned back into the command chair. "So by hiding out behind the sun, we'll be in position to monitor the situation on Earth real-time and shift there if needed." He flashed a rare smile. "Good work, Keps. Tereshkova, prepare to shift."

"Are we disobeying the captain's orders by shifting into the system, sir?" Tereshkova asked.

Trevor gave a subtle shrug. "She said not to enter Earth orbit. She didn't say anything about not entering Sol orbit."

"I thought she said to hold position."

"But she didn't say where." *She used the same type of loose interpretation of orders to avoid a fight with the Greys when we left home.* "Thank you for your input, Lieutenant," Trevor said. "Please proceed with the shift."

"Aye, sir."

Trevor stood and headed for the main hatch. "Lieutenant Rojas, you're in command. I'm going to pay our passenger a visit."

"You mean Zeke, the Onaki from our time?" Rojas asked.

"Correct. He's refused to leave his quarters since we arrived, but perhaps the captain's predicament will convince him to be more helpful."

♦

In the basement level of the ziggurat, Maya sat with her back against a stone wall, sniffling. The dark, musty room had no windows and only one door guarded by two protectors outside it.

"Other than a little sinus congestion, I'm doing okay," Maya mindspoke to her team.

"Thank the stars," Brooke replied. Her sigh of relief carried over the neurocomm.

The concern in Erik's voice was unmistakable. "Glad to hear it, ma'am." Clearly, what had happened to Jo still weighed on him.

"Where are you both?" Maya asked.

"I'm outside the ziggurat," Erik responded. "The Onaki have security sensors covering the entrances. They'll detect me if I try to sneak inside, even with the collar."

"Advisor Sybil and I have fallen back to the landing site," Brooke commed. "I've half a mind to launch and spring you."

"Please don't, Admiral," Maya insisted in spite of her anxiety. The dark cell was heightening her pulse and breathing. She very much wanted to escape to safety—and to a better lit room. Without her night vision, she might've suffered a panic attack. "No one should try to rescue me—not at this point, anyway."

"We can't leave you, Maya."

"I don't feel comfortable with you in their custody, either," Erik agreed. "We don't know what the Onaki might do to you."

"I appreciate your concern," Maya replied, "but I haven't felt threatened since they captured me. The worst has been some gentle shoving."

Maya could feel her aunt's worry and frustration across the distance that separated them.

"They could've killed me out in the square instead of tossing me in a cell," Maya continued. "I think they're trying to figure out what I am and what to do with me. My guess would be that they'll run a few scans and bring me before their leadership. That'll give me a chance to learn about them and manage the situation."

"'Manage the situation?'" Brooke repeated. "What can you manage as a prisoner?"

"If we hadn't already caused a significant divergence in the timeline, Admiral, my capture has done it now. The best way to repair the damage may be honesty, but I'll determine that based on how things play out."

"I hate to admit it, but that's probably the best course of action right now," Brooke admitted.

"Believe me. I'd rather be in the hot tub on the rec deck, but I don't see any other good option. I won't have *Yesterday* charging into Earth orbit to port me away, and a rescue attempt by a 'flare could start a war. I'm going to hold out and try to make diplomacy work."

Faint static hissed over the comm while no one responded for the better part of a minute.

"Well, at least we can still talk to you," Erik mind-spoke.

"That's helping to keep me sane," Maya replied. "But let's keep our contact to a minimum. I don't think they know about my implants, and I'd like to maintain that advantage."

"We certainly don't want them trying to extract them," Brooke commed.

"I would prefer they didn't."

"I'm guessing they took your wave gun," Erik guessed.

"Along with my wristband, scanner, belt, and clothes," Maya confirmed.

"They took your uniform?"

"They stripped me of everything, if you know what I mean." Staring down at her new garments, Maya picked at them. "I fit right in with the locals now."

The Onaki had given her one of the rough cloths woven by the proto-humans. Her outfit consisted of a short dress like a potato sack tied at the waist by twine, and wicker sandals that hurt her sore feet each time she took a step.

She swore to never again complain about modern conveniences like self-cooling garments or auto-contouring shoe soles.

"At any rate, I think it's best if you all return to *Yesterday*," Maya mind-spoke.

"Not a chance," Brooke responded. "Someone has to stick around in case you need help."

"I suppose so. I can't order you to leave, Admiral. But Erik, you need to head back to the ship."

"If you think that's best, ma'am," Erik replied, sounding relieved. Maya figured he was happy to have an excuse to check in on Jo.

"Don't worry, Commander," Brooke commed. "I'll be here if the captain needs saving."

♦

Pacing back and forth in front of her Hyperflare, Brooke vented to Eve. "I should've ordered the team to return to the 'flares right away. I might've reached Jo before she got crushed. Then Maya wouldn't have been captured." Brooke clenched her fists, unable to subdue the anxiety rippling through her. "How can I stand by and do nothing?"

Eve reclined in the rear seat of the fighter, draping one leg over the side of the cockpit. "Give it a rest." The crunch of a candy bar muffled her words.

"As the mission commander, I should give the order to bust her out." Brooke balled both fists in disgust. "But that would create a bigger mess. Damn it. Why does Maya have to be right?"

"You know, stressing about the situation won't change it."

Brooke halted. "How can you be so callous?" She glowered at the android. "And how can you eat at a time like this?"

"My cravings are a side effect of the neural grafting. I can only imagine how neurotic you'd be if you went full prosthetic. But of course, you can't. Too bad."

Shaking her head, Brooke resumed her pacing. "I need to do something to help her."

"Our noble captain's orders are just as well. We've got better things to do."

Brooke stopped and slapped a palm against the fuselage. "The Onaki could kill Maya at any moment. What could possibly be more important?"

"What we discussed back in the city."

Brooke stared at the third level of the ziggurat. Unfinished stone walls and pillars rose above rocks and trees in the distance. "You said we needed to liberate these people. Okay. I've got the perfect plan. I'll launch in a 'flare, start blasting, and keep blasting until every last Onaki leaves or dies."

"Really?" Eve raised her perfect eyebrows. "You think a one-fighter attack will turn out in our favor? Your concern for your niece has clouded your judgment, Admiral Davis."

Brooke exhaled a long, slow breath. "You're right, of course. So what do you suggest?"

"The Onaki are going to figure out who we are and when we're from as soon as they study Maya, so the brute force approach isn't going to work. If you start blasting or *Yesterday* tries to port Maya away, we might get her back. But they could kill her first and then start 'stilling' their workers for fear of what they'll become."

"We have technological superiority. We should be able to overwhelm them."

"Maybe, but the Onaki outnumber us. And we're not so much more advanced that success is guaranteed." Eve pointed up at the sky. "The last time I checked, their ship carried a larger supply of antimatter than we've ever amassed. They could torch this whole planet. No, we need to play this smart or we could lose everything."

"Why should we care? I mean, we're not supposed to be able to affect our present. Everything there stays the same no matter what we do here, so let's rescue Maya. To hell with the consequences."

"Wow." Eve sat up in the cockpit. "I never thought I'd be lecturing you on morals." She intertwined her fingers around one knee. "So you're saying you'd be fine with trading these humans' lives and their future for the life of a single person?"

Brooke stared down at her boots, inwardly cursing her selfishness. "You're right—again. This timeline. Our timeline. These proto-humans, modern humans, or another exospecies. Killing is still killing."

"And don't forget the one thing that suggests we may be able to affect our universe."

"The metatoy." Folding her arms, Brooke asked, "So what did you have in mind?"

Eve hopped down out of the Hyperflare. "If the humans here are going to survive to become us, they need to learn to fend and fight for themselves. We have to lay the foundation for the next 200,000 years."

"That sounds great in theory, but where do we start?"

"We start by tracking down your charity case."

"My charity case? You mean Omo, the man they almost executed but who got away?"

"A man who might be the most important figure in unrecorded human history."

Brooke mulled over the comment. "*Yesterday* can track our movements, albeit with a delay. I don't need to explain myself to Maya and Young, but I still want a cover story to avoid arousing their suspicion."

Eve smoothed her jacket. "I've got that covered."

◆

After wrapping a blindfold around her eyes, a pair of guards escorted Maya out of her cell. They led her back up to the ground level of the ziggurat and into a laboratory. Neither of them had any idea she could see through the veil via her enhanced vision.

The guards strapped her arms, legs, and body to a lab table propped at a forty-five degree angle. Then they exited the room.

Maya tugged at one of the straps. The stress testing app in her i-cite calculated the force required to rip free. If she instructed her implants to reinforce her muscles and pump adrenaline and steroids into her bloodstream, she might gain enough strength to break the restraints with moderate tissue tearing.

But she wouldn't get far before the Onaki corralled her. Nor would an attempted jailbreak earn her the trust of exobeings she needed to befriend, not provoke.

Jo's injury and her own capture stood out as the biggest blunders of Maya's career, but she couldn't undo either of them—not unless she ordered *Yesterday* to bust her out and backshift again. But that would be selfish, unethical, and have unforeseen repercussions. No, she needed to deal with the situation at hand, which presented her with an opportunity to make first contact. With any luck, she might minimize the damage.

She gazed around at a mad scientist's shop of horrors.

In confinement, animals hissed, snarled, squawked, and rattled their cages. Some she recognized as indigenous to this time period in Earth's history, such as a dire wolf. Other creatures seemed new and strange, like a bat-lizard that buzzed like a wasp. Whether the Onaki had brought the thing with them or concocted it here, she couldn't say.

Elsewhere, she saw flowering and vine-like plants that slithered. Insects crawled in glass cases. Body parts hung suspended in vats.

She swallowed a gasp at a pair of prehistoric-looking humans floating in cylindrical tanks. They looked long dead, which was fortunate given their physical deformities. A goiter protruded from one man's neck. He lacked one eye, and a hand grew out of his chest. A nearby woman had scales growing out of her skin, a beak instead of a nose, a humpback, and clawed feet. *An early prototype?*

Ripping her gaze away, Maya searched for something less disturbing on which to focus.

Scale models of DNA sat atop tables next to beakers, caldrons, test tubes, and microscopes.

Toward the back of the lab, soupy green goo oozed within a lone petri dish on top of a bench. Lasers fired from an array of mechanical arms, heating up the liquid. Monitors on either side of the arms showed what looked like strands of DNA and chromosomes under construction.

The partial translation of the most prominent writing on the screen read, "Life Animation Experiment."

A matrix terminal with a 2D wraparound monitor like a windshield played a slideshow of the anatomical structures of bipeds. The circulatory system of a Neanderthal occupied the screen. Seconds later, the screen faded in and out to show the skeletal structure of the proto-humans and their DNA sequences.

Her body went limp in confusion at the next images the screen displayed.

Beside a quadruple helix DNA structure was the anatomy of a creature that resembled a Grey exobeing. *Have the Onaki encountered the Greys in their travels?* The pit forming in her stomach told her otherwise. The pictures of the Grey looked less like recorded images and more like schematic diagrams.

An Onaki man of average build for a modern human approached the matrix terminal. The keyboard that he worked with featured hundreds of tiny switches rather than keys. This man with the thoughtful eyes of an owl was the presiding mad scientist, Maya presumed. Her mind wanted to dress him in a white lab coat like the one her uncle wore, but the scientist was an exobeing from 200,000 years ago. He sported a lighter but more ornate version of the scaled armor worn by the guards.

A chill coursed down her spine. *This might be the being who created the proto-humans—my ancestors.*

The scientist approached her chair. Before she could find the words to protest, he wiped the inside of her elbow with wet gauze, stuck her with a needle, and drew blood. She did her best not to flinch.

As he pulled the syringe away, she considered the best way to start a dialogue. She wished she had her wristband, which could have translated her thoughts into the Onaki's language, Okkadian. But they had taken the device from her.

At the bottom of her i-cite, she displayed a phonetically-spelled greeting in Okkadian. As she recited it in the foreign tongue, she hoped she didn't butcher the pronunciation or grammar. "Hello."

The scientist jerked back from her and blinked his large, deep eyes.

Now that she had his attention, she found she didn't quite know how to proceed. *What does one say to a 200,000-year-old scientist who might be my maker?*

Her throat felt coarser than the dirt and dust outside. She hadn't drunk or eaten anything since her capture.

Linguistic options displayed in her i-cite, but pronouncing full, coherent sentences would be next to impossible. She decided to keep her speech simple. "Thirsty," she tried.

After hesitating, the scientist retreated to his work table. He pulled the vial of her blood out of the syringe, dropped it into a centrifuge, and then flipped a few switches.

As the centrifuge spun, he flipped a switch on the table comm device and spoke into it.

A girl who appeared to be in her late teens entered the lab carrying a tall pottery cup. Unlike every other proto-human Maya had seen since setting foot in the city, the girl was petite, had vibrant eyes, and wore a warm smile.

The girl approached the scientist, who pointed at Maya.

Without trepidation, the girl approached her. She held the cup up to

Maya's mouth and tipped it, allowing her to drink.

The cup may have contained only water, but Maya swore she had never tasted anything so satisfying. The cool liquid wet her palate and rushed down her throat, soothing it. Coughing, she tried not to spit up any of the life-giving substance.

When the girl pulled the cup away, Maya couldn't find an Okkadian word to express gratitude. "Good," was the best she could do. Then in English, she said, "Thank you."

The girl's smile widened. She seemed happy to have pleased Maya.

The scientist stood gawking at Maya. He acted as if she was the most astounding thing he had ever seen.

"Good work, Asha," he said to the girl.

Maya's auditory implants translated the scientist's speech. She had no trouble understanding him; it was as if he spoke perfect English. Responding presented the much greater challenge.

Asha approached her master and touched his arm.

The tension in the scientist's face faded, and Maya swore he blushed. *Clearly, he's got a soft spot for her.*

The girl exited the room. The moment she moved out of earshot, the scientist asked, "Who are you?"

Maya searched for the Okkadian words. "Visitor. Like you." Pointing her index finger at herself—as much as she could do with the restraints in place—she added, "My name is Maya. Maya." She directed her finger at him. "What is your name?"

The scientist blinked several times. Each opening and closing of his eyelids lasted a full second. He seemed to be pondering whether he should reveal personal information to an otherworldly being who might be a spy.

At last, he said, "Enki Namkuzu Alad Kishar, Grand Hypergeneticist, Advocate for the Scientific Faction, and elected councilman seated on the Caucus of Factions."

She had a long way to go before she could interpret Onaki tone, but she thought his voice carried a hint of pride. Listing one's full name and many titles in a greeting must've been part of his culture.

"Hello, Enki," she said.

"Where do you come from?" Enki asked, opening up a bit.

"It is hard to explain."

Enki's tone hardened. "Why are you here? What do you want?"

"I am here to learn."

"Then why the secrecy? You could've contacted us."

"We did not want to disturb you." She excluded the word "timeline" from the end of her statement for obvious reasons.

"You've caused more of a disturbance by sneaking around."

She couldn't find a word for apology. "We intended no harm."

"You have a strange way of showing your intentions."

"We made a mistake." In English, she said, "Sorry."

The terminal matrix beeped as the centrifuge slowed to a stop.

Moving to the terminal, Enki studied the analysis of her bloodwork on the monitor.

After squinting at the monitor in disbelief, he whirled back in her direction.

Via her i-cite zoom, Maya tried to read the monitor. But her translation matrix couldn't decipher enough of the Onaki's written language, numbers, and symbols to interpret the results.

Enki stepped back from her. "Who are you really?"

Lacking the ability to properly explain, Maya could only stare at him.

The scientist bolted out of the lab.

Seventeen—Incendiary
East Africa, Earth, August 200,423 BCE

Having climbed the stairs to the second level of the ziggurat, Enki hurried into the Grand Dignitary's study.

Gemekala knelt in the corner of her study that served as her art studio, stroking a brush across a canvas.

Her attendant, a tall and frail hominin named Umi, busied himself with sweeping the room. Dust from all the construction activity in the city settled on everything.

Clutching his impression pad, Enki stopped before Gemekala's easel. He was panting.

"You appear to have witnessed an atrocity, my fellow." Gemekala set the brush down on her paint palette. "Shall I presume you've performed a preliminary examination of the interloper?"

A million questions ransacked Enki's mind. He was still trembling from his lab guest's attempt to speak Okkadian. If the results of the initial bio analysis proved conclusive, he could only begin to fathom the implications.

"Yes, Grand Dignitary," he said.

"What have you learned?" she asked.

His chest still heaving, Enki struggled with how to reveal his unbelievable findings.

Gemekala threw back her long mane of hair and stood. "I've increased the number of protectors patrolling the city, sent scout craft to survey the outskirts, and ordered the *Namtilla* to scan the system. It's unlikely the intruder was alone. Given how she was able to hide and how she shattered the foundation block, I must surmise these invaders possess technology that allows them to remain hidden."

She walked over to her desk. "Their presence could threaten our survival, Enki. Tell me what you know."

Enki switched on his pad, loaded his analysis, and handed it to her.

As Gemekala studied its pixelated display, her frown deepened. "Her DNA is an almost perfect match to your hominins." She jerked her chin up, meeting his gaze with her imposing golden stare. "I had assumed that, like us, she had altered her form to adapt to this planet."

"I don't think that's the case," Enki said. "The female's gene sequencing shows no signs of recent splicing. Her genome is quite stable, far more so than that of my creations—or ours, for that matter."

"Then the only practical conclusion is that she is somehow related to them."

"I don't see how, but I also don't see any other explanation." Enki intertwined his fingers. His five digits still felt too few, stubby, and fat. "The woman spoke to me in our language, albeit not very well."

"The captive knew Okkadian?"

"Yes."

"Then they've been observing us for some time." With the lines on her forehead creasing, Gemekala returned to reading the pad. "These results show the intruder's age as—this cannot be accurate. There must be an error in your instruments."

"To be certain, I plan to recalibrate them and run more in-depth bloodwork."

Handing the pad back to him, Gemekala turned and stepped away.

She approached the opening in the exterior wall of her study. Resting her forearms on the sill, she stared at the city square below. Every few seconds, a lock of her hair bounced in the wind.

Enki joined her and looked down.

Hominins worked in the square to clean up the bodies and mess from the shattered foundation block.

"If I'm able to corroborate these results," Enki said, "it would explain the genetic similarities."

Gemekala shook her head. "A living being cannot have a negative age, let alone be minus 200,000 of this world's cycles."

"I'm afraid I must challenge that assertion."

Enki turned to find Tabira Elutil Mezem Nuesh, Advocate for the

Industrial Faction, entering the study. Tabira carried the belongings confiscated from the prisoner.

"Reverse time traversal has been theorized as possible for macrocycles," Tabira said from behind the pile of clothing and devices in his arms, which blocked the short and stocky engineer's face. "Even if the practical applications have thus far eluded us."

"Traveling to the past would require accelerating beyond the speed of light, which is impossible," Gemekala said as she faced the engineer. "Such action would violate known practical laws."

"Not necessarily. There are loopholes that might allow a ship to bend space or pass through an interspatial tunnel to reach a distant location faster than light can reach it. These same methods might also be used to move backward or forward in time."

"But as you asserted, such notions are only theoretical."

"For us, perhaps. All I know for certain is that the technological wonders I carry are more than mere theory." Peering around the pile, Tabira found a table and walked toward it.

Umi rushed to the table ahead of the engineer. Wiping a rag back and forth, he dusted the surface as Tabira set down the items one by one.

Enki glanced at Umi and then at Gemekala.

"Do we think it wise to allow your attendant to see such things?" Enki asked.

Gemekala glanced at Umi. "I doubt his ability to comprehend the content of our conversation. Regardless, what would he do with the information?"

Asha's aptitude around the lab—to say nothing of her capacity for love—had taught Enki that the hominins learned quickly. But he dared not contradict the Grand Dignitary, so he dropped the issue.

Stepping over to the table, Enki picked up the handle of what looked like a gun. The weapon felt smooth and firm, yet he could depress slight indentations into it like hard rubber. A shiny material—some combination of composites, plastic, and metal—comprised its outer casing. He stared at the dish located at the presumed firing end, but found no hole for a projectile or beam to exit.

"Heed caution," Tabira said. "I believe that is the weapon our captive used to shatter the foundation block."

Enki gently set the gun back on the table. Then he took a couple of slow steps back from it.

Umi ceased his dusting and retreated across the study.

"We cannot know for certain," Tabira said, "but I doubt the weapon will discharge. I've tried everything I can think of to get it to function. It seems to have a biometric security feature that prevents its operation."

Gemekala picked up the gun and gripped it by the handle, being careful not to depress the trigger. "I had wondered how the trespasser accomplished such a feat."

"I believe the device is a more refined version of our levitators," Tabira said.

"How can such a small device destroy an object too heavy for our levitators to lift and steady without the workers? What's its power source?"

"That is perhaps its most astounding feature, one which adds great significance to our earlier discussion." Tabira tapped the gun on the top above the handle. "I've taken x-rays and run every other type of scan." He puffed out his chest, proud of his discovery. "The device contains antimatter."

Giving a start, Gemekala held the gun at arm's length.

"Somehow, it's able to generate a magnetic containment field smaller than the tip of our smallest new digit." Tabira wiggled his littlest finger for effect.

Enki shook his head. "That much antimatter—"

"Could destroy this building and more if properly focused," Tabira said, finishing Enki's sentence. "But that's not the greatest application of this technology."

Gemekala took her time setting the gun back down on the table. "If such confinement and focusing ability were scaled up to the size of a star vessel . . ."

"The vessel could focus enough energy on a single point in space to puncture a hole in it, opening up the possibility of higher dimensional travel and perhaps even time traversal."

As Enki grappled with the notion, he inspected the other items. There was a sleek bracelet fashioned from similar material as the gun, a belt with a number of compartments, a small box Tabira identified as a scanning device, and the woman's clothing.

The white and blue jacket was comprised of a smooth, stretchy fabric. The patches on the coat featured a number of small language characters sequenced in horizontal lines. An illustration on the upper arm of the coat showed a representation of the spiral arms of the galaxy. *Are these beings capable of traversing such great distances?*

He held his breath at the illustration below the galaxy.

Gemekala grabbed the jacket from him and held it so the emblem faced straight up.

There was no mistaking the picture of this planet, a blue and white half-globe with continental and oceanic features mapped with uncanny accuracy.

"It could represent their mission destination," Tabira said.

"Or their origin," Enki whispered.

Gemekala tossed the coat back onto the table. "This is beyond comprehension." She stiffened her posture, turned, and retreated to the window.

Umi resumed his cleaning, but gave the table a wide berth.

Enki came to stand at Gemekala's side. Tabira stood close behind them.

Construction on the ziggurat had resumed. With the aid of an emitter, a group of hominins carried a foundation block up the ramp to the second level. Two other groups followed with blocks, one at the base of the ramp and another behind in the distance.

"As unfathomable as it may seem," Gemekala said, "the evidence is too suggestive to ignore. We must consider the distinct possibility these visitors are descendants of your creations, Enki, and they have traversed time for reasons we don't yet know." Under her breath, she muttered, "What have we done?"

"Under such an assumption, the question becomes how did simple bio-workers achieve more advanced technology than we possess?" Tabira asked. "Did we give it to them? Or did they steal it from us? Did they somehow rise up against us? Were they able to banish us from this world or even . . . it seems preposterous."

"This is all supposition, "Gemekala said, "but we must prepare for the potential reality." Stepping over to her low desk, she knelt and worked the switches on its terminal.

Enki's eyes widened as he read the screen.

Gemekala was sending telemetry to the *Namtilla*, instructing the crew to begin a project. The ship had no weapons per se, but it still carried an exorbitant amount of antimatter, even with most of the tanks depleted from decelerating the ship.

She ordered the crew to convert the smallest magnetic containment vessel into an antimatter bomb.

Enki grew lightheaded at the thought of it being used.

Making eye contact with each of her fellow councilmen, Gemekala said, "Let us hope this act is an unnecessary precaution." Of Enki, she commanded, "I want you to create a comprehensive neutralization virus."

Comprehensive neutralization. As Enki repeated the choice of terminology in his mind, his stomach tightened. *Are we too righteous to call it what it is, a genocidal bioweapon?* He kept the question to himself.

"You claimed the intruder's DNA was a near-match to that of the hominins," Gemekala said. "Can you develop a virus that will afflict both of them but not us?"

Enki hesitated, then said in a low voice, "It should be possible, yes."

"Very well. Again, let us hope such contingencies are unnecessary, but we must prepare for them." She rose to her feet. "Now, I require answers. You said the captive spoke to you?"

"Yes."

"Then it's time I conversed with this future hominin."

♦

Erik tucked his helmet under his arm and rushed into *Yesterday's* infirmary.

He froze in place halfway to the bed where Jo lay, and gaped at her. He saw the outline of short stubs that had once been her legs beneath the blanket that covered her. The stubs ended only centimeters past a pelvis and abdomen that looked far too flat. Jo had always had pale skin, but she looked whiter than an albino.

Two android med techs attended to the machines all around the bed. Mechanical arms extended down and injected various locations on her body with medites. The rends hovering next to the bed showed weak but stable life signs.

Seeing that Jo was still alive, Erik exhaled in relief. But his heart still pounded with worry at the extent of her injuries.

"She got lucky." Doc Crumpler came to stand by Erik's side. "If she'd arrived a few moments later, she would've needed full prosthetics, but *Yesterday* doesn't have the facilities to do the neural grafting." Crumpler sipped from a thermos of coffee. "A few minutes more, and I couldn't have done anything for her. Heck, even fifty years ago, without modern nanotech, we would've lost her on the planet."

"Thank the stars," Erik whispered.

Jo's eyelids fluttered open.

Crumpler set down her coffee. She shooed the androids away and stepped to the side of the bed.

Erik walked to the other side.

Examining a detailed rend of Jo's brain, Crumpler said, "Neural activity appears normal. She should be conscious any moment."

As Jo moaned and opened her eyes, Erik held her hand.

Jo nudged her head in Erik's direction and showed a hint of a smile.

"Welcome back," he said.

"Five minutes, Commander." Crumpler walked off toward her office. "Then the patient needs to rest."

Erik nodded but kept his attention on Jo. "Do you know where you are?" he asked.

Jo stared at him for several seconds. "The past," she managed in a weak tone. Her smile widened.

Feeling tears well up at the corners of his eyes, Erik blinked them away. "I thought I might've lost you."

"That would've sucked for you."

Erik laughed out loud.

Jo's gazed wandered down toward her maimed body.

"Don't look," Erik said. "There's no reason. You'll be healed up good as new in no time."

The top half of the bed rose and reclined. Jo must've been controlling it via her i-cite.

She stared down at the outlines of the stumps beneath the blanket. At the very end of the stumps, the blanket moved as if insects were crawling underneath it. The movement was her legs regrowing.

Erik held his breath.

"Too. F'ing. Fused," Jo whispered in awe.

Erik marveled at her attitude, just as he had the day they had met at the academy. He had fallen for her then and never stopped loving her, even though their careers had made it impossible to spend more than a few weeks together at a time.

He bent down and kissed her forehead.

Pouting at him, Jo muttered, "I almost die, and all I get is a peck?"

With a knowing smile, Erik looked into her eyes and planted one on her lips.

♦

As *Yesterday* exited hyperspace in Sol orbit, Zeke sat on the bed in his quarters and stared out at the sun. The porthole dimmed to reduce the blinding glare, but his pupils would have compensated naturally without the safety feature.

Had Zeke not placed his emotions in isolation, he would've been brooding. His ancestors held Captain Davis prisoner, but he couldn't bring himself to intervene. He foresaw the likely outcomes of various actions he could take to help one side or the other, but nothing he could do would produce a favorable outcome for all.

He suppressed his frustration before it tensed his muscles. He so very much wanted to save the day like his comic sim heroes. Perhaps the immortal man with the long metal claws or the cybernetic police woman who fought hackers while contemplating her existence would've known what to do. So far, Zeke did not.

The hatch to Zeke's room chimed. He sensed Commander Trevor Young out in the corridor.

"You may enter," Zeke said.

As the door slid open, Young stepped inside the room.

The commander flexed his fingers as he studied the superhero vidpics on the walls. "I, um, like what you've done with the place."

Zeke sensed the man's discomfort with an exobeing who could take control of a human mind. Young did admire the pics, though. During childhood sim play, Trevor had developed an affinity for the hero who turned into a green giant when he got angry.

"Thank you," Zeke said. "Fictional do-gooders provide me with ideals."

"Yeah, they, uh, always inspired me, too." Turning partway toward Zeke, Trevor said, "I'd like to request any assistance or insight you might have regarding the situation on Earth."

"I'm sorry, but I can't help you or the captain."

"You can't help, or you won't help?"

"At the moment, there's little distinction. Any action by me would make the situation worse."

"I see. You won't reconsider?"

"I'm afraid my stance is firm."

Tensing his square jaw, Young said, "You know, I could throw you in the brig for your refusal to cooperate." He sighed, then added, "But you could just force someone to let you out, so there wouldn't be much point." He exited the room before Zeke could reply.

Zeke lay back on his bed and resumed his brooding. He jerked into an upright position as an unexpected presence passed through the room. But Zeke saw no one. The feeling faded as quickly as it had come over him. Hopping up, he rushed out into the corridor and followed the presence like a hound tracking a scent.

♦

"You've shifted *Yesterday* behind the sun?" Brooke mind-spoke from the pilot's seat of her grounded Hyperflare. "That's not what Maya ordered."

Commander Young nodded in her i-cite. "Admiral, the solar energy output obscured our downshift, keeping us hidden like the captain wanted. Under the circumstances, I judged it necessary to move to a better tactical position."

"I see. To be honest, I'm all for it in case we need to pull her out quickly."

"My thoughts exactly, ma'am."

"Okay. In the meantime, I plan to remain on the surface and gather intel."

"Understood, Admiral. Please keep me updated." Young signed off.

"'Gather intel,'" Eve quipped from her perch atop the nose of the fighter. "Nice cover story."

Brooke sat back in the cockpit and folded her arms. "I don't have to explain myself to a subordinate, but a half-plausible excuse is better than none at all."

"Young knows a worried aunt can't bear to abandon her beloved niece."

Wrinkling her nose at the comment, Brooke reviewed the neudar images taken by the remote scanning AI. The scans identified thousands of proto-humans in the city, hundreds more on the immediate outskirts, and small groups further inland and along the coasts.

"I've uploaded Omo's likeness to the 'flare's systems," Brooke said, "but it could take hours or even days to resolve which blip is him."

Eve shrugged. "If we sync the fighter's scans with the ship's overhead imagery, we'll have the answer in seconds."

"I can't order Young to do it. That would raise too many questions."

"Who said anything about contacting him?"

Brooke furrowed her brow. "What other option is there? He'll be alerted if we comm anyone else aboard or access *Yesterday's* systems."

Tossing a dried apricot into her mouth, Eve winked at her.

Additional interfaces popped up in Brooke's i-cite, signaling a direct uplink to the ship. Topographic maps and lifeform resolution data flooded the Hyperflare's databanks.

"How did you—?" Before Brooke could finish her question, a blinking dot appeared on the map in her-cite. The dot marked the location of the proto-man who had escaped death. "Found him," Brooke said.

"What did I tell you?" Eve munched on another piece of dried fruit.

Brooke swallowed as she ran through the unsettling possibilities of how the android had accomplished the feat. "Either you have backdoor access to the ship's systems, which would mean the Vril built it into *Yesterday*. Or, you've got collaborators onboard. Or both."

"Sounds like you've figured it out."

Biting her tongue, Brooke zoomed and tilted the map. It showed a series of natural caves hidden beneath high cliffs on the shores of the Gulf of Aden, north of the city. Getting to the caverns on foot would be treacherous. She needed to traverse rocky shallows—and some not-so-shallow spots—to reach the coast and navigate a number of sharp inclines.

Additional blips indicated the presence of other proto-humans inside and near the caves.

According to the data, conventional RF band, thermal, and x-ray scanning methods couldn't penetrate the rocks to locate the caves or any sign of life.

It's the perfect place to hide from the Onaki, Brooke mused.

Eve hopped down off the fighter.

With a resigned sigh, Brooke climbed down from the cockpit.

She instructed the canopy to grow and seal and then engaged the Hyperflare's cloak. Gradually, the fighter faded into the background, taking on the appearance of the rocks, trees, and dirt in the area.

Eve pulled a device the size of a sugar cube out of her coat pocket and tossed it to her.

As Brooke caught the cube in both hands, she recognized it. The device looked similar to the one Shin Saito had activated in her home on Mars when she first met him.

"That should keep the ship from tracking or porting us." Eve activated her collar, vanishing. "Shall we?"

Brooke pocketed the device and made herself invisible.

A proximity warning appeared in her vision. "Incoming aircraft," she whispered.

She crouched down between a boulder and bush, not wanting to take any chances. Her heart pounded inside her chest. Eve joined her.

A couple minutes later, a manta ray-shaped craft like the one she had seen on the flight to the city flew past them. The Hyperflare's tactical AI reported that the cloak was scattering the radar signals pinging it.

Her palpitations subsided once the slow-flying craft had passed out of the area.

The trek to the cliffs was the most grueling physical experience Brooke had endured in years, or perhaps decades. She lunged between the jagged rocks jutting up from flowing rapids. On three separate occasions she slipped, fearing for her life each time but somehow keeping her footing.

Scaling the loose dirt of the high hills left her winded. She needed to stop and rest every other minute, prompting Eve to make subtle jibes about her age. The android maneuvered the natural obstacle course with the effortlessness expected of a tireless machine.

The scent of algae and fish reached Brooke's nostrils as she approached the sea. With the overhanging cliff towering above her, she climbed from boulder to boulder along the shore. Waves crashed against the rocks that jutted out from the shore meters below.

At last Brooke reached her destination, a recess in the cliff wall hiding a secluded beach.

Descending from the rocks to the beach, she planted her boots on pure white sand. There she bent at the waist, rested her hands on her upper legs, and inhaled deeply until the throbbing in her chest subsided.

As Brooke swallowed a hydro-protein pill, she studied the half-dozen cave openings. Eve joined her and folded her arms, showing no evidence of being physically taxed.

"So, now what?" Brooke asked. "Waltz in and introduce ourselves like a couple of solicitors?"

"Unless you have a better idea," Eve said.

"Seriously?"

"Seriously. We've got a rebellion to incite. That's going to require interaction."

"In case you've forgotten, these are primitive people. Who knows how they'll react to our appearance."

"They'll be shocked at first, no doubt. But keep in mind that they're used to extrasolar overlords. They may come around faster than you think."

Brooke wiped the sweat from her brow and then placed her hands on her hips. Activating her enhanced vision, Brooke gazed into the caves. Outlines of bodies confirmed the presence of seventeen humans huddled together in one of the larger caverns.

"You'd think the Onaki would keep better track of their workers," she said. "How can so many go unaccounted for?"

Eve thrust her chin toward the city beyond the cliff. "I'm sure a handful of the people here are fugitives who escaped, but I'd bet most of them are workers who come and go. Their masters run everything on a regimented routine, and these humans have learned to use that to their advantage. The Onaki may push their laborers harder than we would consider humane, but they still understand that biological beings require rest. The workers get a day off after every four days of work and nine hours of sleep each night. That's enough time to sneak out here and back without being noticed, especially in the dark."

"Still, you'd think they'd monitor them somehow."

"They do, but the proto-humans outnumber the Onaki by more than a hundred to one. That's too many to watch over. They also haven't yet felt the need to put trackers on them. It's not like there are any other cities where they can go."

"So these early humans have figured out how to beat the system and slip past their keepers. I didn't realize they were smart enough to pull off something like that."

"Their DNA and brains are almost identical to ours. Their creators would be the last to admit it, but these humans possess our same mental capacity. They simply lack our education."

Brooke held her hands out toward the caves. "Well, have at it. You know the plan, so I'll let you do all the talking."

Eve smiled. "And how do you think they'll respond to an almost-human-looking android?" She didn't wait for an answer. "No, I gave up public speaking when I merged personalities and habbed my first prosthetic body."

Blinking in disbelief, Brooke cursed. "This was your plan all along, wasn't it? It's why you've been helping me."

"I won't sugarcoat it. You'd be back home in a hospital bed, counting the days until the end, if I didn't need you."

"I knew you didn't have a shred of sympathy or compassion."

"Those are indulgences when faced with extinction, but necessary traits when convincing a group of people to follow you." Eve pointed at the caves. "Now, are you going to stand here, or go ensure the future of the human race?"

Brooke shook her head. "I don't know that I'm up for leading a rebellion."

"Last time I checked," Eve said, counting on her fingers, "you were a vice admiral well-versed in military strategy. You've raised children on more than one occasion. You were possessed by a single-minded determination to be the first to go FTL, crossed twenty light years to rescue the first interstellar mission, saved the phase gate—"

"Enough." Running a palm down her face, Brooke couldn't believe what she was about to do.

Eighteen—Exophobia
East Africa, Earth, August 200,423 BCE

The guards led Maya into the main assembly hall on the first floor of the ziggurat.

With her hands tied behind her back, she studied the expansive hall. The place struck her as grand in scale but sparse in its décor.

The ceiling rose to a height of about twelve meters. Statues of true-form Onaki—presumably, famous historical figures—stood in front of the stone walls. Thick pillars supported the weight of the second level. The hall had no windows in the walls, but openings in the ceiling allowed the sun's rays to creep inside. A well-placed series of mirrors redirected the light around the room, brightening the place.

A ring of low wooden desks occupied the center of the hall. Onaki men and women knelt behind each desk, puffing out their chests in self-importance. Some of them stared at her as if she were a lab specimen. Others narrowed their eyes in contempt.

Every hair on her neck and bare shoulders stood on end. A draft caressed the skin on her legs, belly, and arms. Fortunately, the draft was warm.

Enki, the scientist who had poked and prodded her throughout her stay, knelt behind one of the desks. His long and hard blinks projected a mix of curiosity and apprehension. She had tried engaging him in conversation again when he returned to the lab, but he had ignored her.

Proto-human servants rushed to and from the desks, filling glasses with water and a red, nonalcoholic wine—Maya knew of it because Asha had served it to her in the lab. The servants stole glances at Maya when they thought the Onaki were not paying attention.

Wearing her potato sack garb, Maya imagined that she resembled a taller-than-average proto-human with good posture, lighter skin, and narrower eyes. The latter attribute was thanks to her Japanese ancestors, a people who wouldn't exist for tens of millennia.

One of the protectors prodded Maya in the back with his spear-rifle, directing her into the center of the ring of desks.

The apparent leader, an imposing woman with a serious frown and penetrating stare, stood up from her desk.

"Interloper," she said, "you stand before the Caucus of Factions, the governing authority of the city of Urusilim and on New Anurash."

New Anurash. It doesn't quite have the same ring to it as Earth, Maya mused.

The woman placed both hands on her chest. "I am Grand Dignitary Gemekala Niggina Adamen Sumur, Advocate for the Pragmatic Faction and elected representative of all factions. Identify yourself."

For most of her captivity, Maya had been mulling over what to say if and when the opportunity for a dialogue with the Onaki leadership arose. Now that the moment had arrived, she still hadn't made up her mind. Should she bare all, divulging the complete truth in an effort to gain their trust? Should she massage the truth to protect human interests and the interests of the future she knew? Did any of this even matter in an alternate timeline?

Now if only she could speak to these people without sounding like a simpleton.

"My name is Maya Davis," she said, reading the phonetic words scrolling across the bottom of her i-cite. "I am a leader, like you. We came to learn."

The faction leaders turned their heads and blinked at one-another.

"She speaks our language," a woman said.

The man next to her snorted. "Yet she sounds like a novitiate."

"How can a being capable of turning invisible and shattering a block of stone lack the intelligence with which to speak like an educated adult?" another woman wondered aloud.

Maya bit her lip in frustration.

A stocky man with a flabby neck said, "I shall offer a theory."

"Please indulge us, Tabira," Gemekala said.

After rising to his feet, Tabira walked around his desk. Atop it rested

Maya's personal effects.

Maya refrained from widening her eyes or smiling at the sight of her wrist band. If she wanted, she could interface with it now and have it speak on her behalf. But she refrained. If a strange device suddenly started talking, it might unnerve her captors—or worse. Using the band before they gave her permission might be misinterpreted as an act of hostility. She decided to try to convince them to give it back to her. Failing that, she might have to chance activating it.

"There are devices embedded in her brain, nervous system, and bloodstream that are so small, my scans barely registered them," Tabira said. "Micro-science was in its infancy when we left Anurash-Arala. Her people seem to have developed it to the point of practical application."

"It's true," Enki said. "My bioanalysis showed that these micro-devices work in conjunction with her existing physiology to supplement and enhance bodily functions." He ran a fingernail over the back of his hand for effect. "When I administered a mild laceration to her skin, it healed within minutes without leaving a scar."

I've never seen people act so astounded by nanotech, but I guess I take it for granted.

"Unlike the newest version of our laborers, the subject is also resistant to cognitive regulation," Enki added. "Her DNA may be a virtual match to theirs, but we cannot control her. I have as yet been unable to determine why."

Maya forced a blank expression. She didn't know why she was immune to Onaki control any more than the scientist did, although she suspected the Vril had done something to her as a child. Selfishly, she had cheered for Enki to figure it out so that she could know, too.

On the other hand, it was just as well he hadn't. She needed to maintain the Onaki's belief that they couldn't control future humans. The moment they realized otherwise, her crew could be in serious jeopardy.

"This is most fascinating," an Onaki man said, "but what does it have to do with her speech impediment?"

"Her micro-devices are capable of receiving and translating what she hears," Tabira said, "but she must lack a similar response capability. To sum up, she's only able to respond with the handful of words from our language that she knows."

Resisting the urge to applaud the man for his correct theory, Maya said, "True."

Tabira wore a proud smile as he returned to his desk.

Maya thrust her chin toward her wristband on his desk. "With the bracelet I can talk better."

"Do you take us for fools?" a lanky man with a slight hunch asked.

"We're not giving you your weapons back."

"I concur with Biluda," a man said.

"It is not a weapon." Maya's implants hadn't registered anyone saying the word "translation" yet, so she didn't have the word for it. "I can talk your language much better with it."

"We cannot trust these intruders," Biluda said with emphasis. "We should—"

Gemekala held up her hand to silence him.

She paced around Maya like a predator sizing up its prey. "Is it true you are from the future?"

"True," Maya said.

Murmurs escaped the lips of the other faction leaders.

Sauntering over to Tabira's desk, Gemekala picked up the wrist band. She lifted and lowered the device in her hand, getting a feel for it.

"You can't give it to her, Grand Dignitary," Biluda shouted. "She could kill us all if—"

Gemekala raised her voice, drowning out the man's pleas. "And yet, despite having ample opportunity to do that long before we took her into custody, she did not."

"But—"

"Have you observed nothing you've seen? This interloper has not cowered or resisted us. She stands before us calm and confident, as if she is the one who has us." Gemekala approached to within arm's length of Maya. "She wouldn't be in our midst if she wasn't choosing it."

Spot on, Maya thought, marveling at the woman up close. In Gemekala's original form, she must have resembled a hawk or an eagle— majestic, cunning, and deadly.

"I'm a great ways from trusting you," Gemekala addressed her captive, "but pragmatics suggest you would not request this device in order to escape or to slaughter us."

"True," Maya said.

"Of course she would say anything to get her weapon," Biluda said.

"My weapon is there." Maya nodded her chin toward the wave gun. She hoped honesty about which item posed the true threat would gain their trust. "I don't want the weapon. I want only to talk."

Biluda tightened his lips at her forthright offering.

Gemekala stared Maya down for an uncomfortable minute.

Pointing at her captive, Gemekala instructed the protectors to wrap restraints around Maya's arms and legs, limiting her range of motion.

"I accept responsibility for this calculated risk," Gemekala said. "It's necessary because we cannot glean the information we require about these visitors with her speech impeded." She placed the band on Maya's wrist, flinching when it clamped on of its own accord.

The other faction leaders shifted on their knees.

Maya interfaced with the wristband. As its translation matrix activated, the weight of a starship seemed to lift from her shoulders. "Are you able to understand me better now?" the band squawked as it voiced her thoughts in Okkadian.

"Yes," Gemekala said.

Several of the faction leaders flinched at hearing the device's artificial speech. As a result of the data *Yesterday's* AIs had gathered from orbital surveillance, the band spoke with proper grammar in a female tone matching natural Onaki speech, all without an accent—or so Maya assumed. As far as she could tell, the band chanted in incomprehensible gibberish.

"That's great news." Maya gazed around the hall. "Thank you," she said, voicing the words in English, given that Onaki culture lacked expressions of gratitude. "That is how my people express appreciation. It's a customary verbal acknowledgement offered when one person does something positive for another."

"How strange," a man said, "that one should require praise for providing assistance to another. The act is its own reward."

"That's a valid way to look at it. Customarily, my people convey kind words in exchange for acts of kindness."

Returning to kneel behind her desk, Gemekala asked, "Now that you're able to more effectively communicate, explain why you're here."

"Of course. We discovered a piece of our modern technology dating back to this time period. Our best minds believed it should have been impossible for the artifact to end up in our past, so we came to find out how and why."

"What type of artifact?"

"It's a child's toy—a sophisticated device, but a toy nonetheless. We found the item on a planet orbiting a red dwarf star twenty light years from this world—our world."

Enki blinked long and slow at Maya.

"So you consider this planet to be your own?" Biluda asked.

Maya nodded. "Yes, we do."

"So where, may I ask, are we?"

"In the future, your people aren't present on the Earth, which is the name we've given to this planet. We don't know when you left or why. We had certain suspicions, but we didn't know who or what we would find until we arrived. There is no hard evidence of your presence here in our recorded history."

"No evidence? You're saying we're absent from the future? Are we extinct?"

"No. Recently—relative to our present, that is—we learned your people still existed somewhere. However, they don't live on Earth, and we've never made contact with you until now."

Biluda searched the faces of the other faction leaders to see if they wore his same incredulous stare. "I find that hard to believe. We've made this planet our permanent home. We wouldn't abandon it or give it to you hominins."

"I don't have an explanation for you," Maya said. "For that matter, we have yet to confirm we're the descendants of your work force. But everything we've learned since arriving seems to support this theory."

"So you were ignorant of your origins until now," Gemekala said.

"That's correct." Out of habit, Maya tried to lift her finger to tap her cheek, but the straps binding her arms to her body prevented it. "Do you know the origins of your race?"

All eyes fell on Enki.

"We have theories," Enki said, "the leading of which is that we evolved from much simpler organisms."

"Our scientists have similar theories," Maya said. "Now, we know you accelerated the evolution of our ancestors to create us, but that still doesn't explain how life came to be in the first place."

"We also have yet to reach a definitive answer. Before my essence returns to the stars, my goal is to reproduce the conditions under which the first organisms came to exist."

Maya thought of the experiment with the soupy green goo and lasers she had seen in Enki's lab. "That would be an accomplishment."

"It's hard to believe you're still struggling with the same fundamental questions as us even though you've developed the ability to traverse space and time," Biluda said.

"As a friend of mine once told me," Maya said, hoping Jo was okay, "intelligent races don't progress at the same rate in the same disciplines. Your biological sciences seem to be more advanced than ours, whereas we've developed machine technology beyond yours."

She shrugged. "The majority of our progress has occurred in the last few hundred years. We developed the ability to reach orbit a little over three centuries ago and then hyperspace travel about fifty years ago."

Tabira shot to his feet. "Ten thousand cycles passed between our first spaceflight and when the *Namtilla* disembarked. Such a rapid rate of progress—"

"Makes for a dangerous species," Biluda said, narrowing his eyes.

Maya opened her mouth, ready to admit to the great many flaws in human society, but the Grand Dignitary spoke first.

"I can foresee how a scenario such as hers could unfold," Gemekala said. "Suppose we departed this world in haste and took our technology with us. Without the benefit of our oversight, the hominins might revert to their undomesticated lifestyles. If they failed to keep a written record, they might forget us after multiple generations. They might then require thousands of years to rediscover the culture, technology, and order they now enjoy."

"I agree that a version of your theory probably happened," Maya said.

"Consequently, if we accept such theory as fact for the moment, one critical question overshadows the rest. Why did—or do—we leave, assuming that's still to occur?"

"I think it's obvious." Biluda jabbed his index finger at Maya. "They've traveled to the past with superior weaponry to take this planet by force."

Shaking her head vigorously from side to side, Maya said, "According to the branch theory of time travel, any change we make to the past creates an alternate timeline. It's true that if we kicked you off-world now, we could free the hominins in this timeline, but the act wouldn't affect our timeline. This means we couldn't have banished you from our past, so that's not what happened."

Most of the Onaki faction leaned back, contemplating Maya's words. Tabira and Gemekala nodded in understanding.

"But you claim one of your technological devices did end up in the past," Tabira said. "Perhaps your theories aren't accurate."

"That's the reason why we're here," Maya said. "We wish only to learn, not to start a conflict. I don't know what happened to cause our history to unfold as it did. What I do acknowledge is that this is your world now. I'm the outsider. You have my word that I won't take any action against you."

Despite her sincere intentions, her intestines knotted as she wondered how this encounter would affect whatever was supposed to occur in less than two months.

Maya suppressed her discomfort. She could only proceed based on what she knew now.

Biluda threw his hands up in the air. "How do we know you represent the intentions of the main governing entity of your people? For all we know, you're rogues who've come in opposition to your own kind."

"I'm happy to explain the structure of our society and show you proof."

Waving his hand dismissively, Biluda grunted.

Maya tried to steer the conversation back on track. "It seems to me we all want the same thing. We want to figure out what happened. If we work together, I'm confident we can earn each other's trust and figure out—"

"Captain," her first officer commed.

"Trevor?" She mind-spoke without showing any outward change in her demeanor. "It's good to hear your voice, but how are you comming in real-time?"

"I've relocated the ship behind the sun—but don't worry, ma'am. We've taken every precaution to make sure we continue to avoid detection."

"That's not what I ordered you to do."

"I know, ma'am, but I took the initiative given your captivity. We need to be closer in case they threaten your life, and the admiral agrees."

"Saving my life isn't worth starting a war," Maya replied.

"Do you want us to return to interstellar space, Captain?"

Maya didn't want to admit it to him or herself, but she did feel better with the ship in teleporter range. "No. There'd be a greater risk of exposure in shifting again than staying put. I'm in the middle of delicate diplomatic talks, and I think I'm starting to earn their trust. Hold position for now and stand by for further instructions."

♦

Enki stared at Maya, perplexed. The wondrous future hominin had stopped talking in mid-sentence and shifted her vibrant eyes to the side in thought. It almost seemed as if she had engaged in a conversation with herself.

What's wrong with her?

Looking over at Tabira, he caught the engineer whispering into a teletone handset.

"I knew it," Tabira said. After exchanging a knowing glance with Biluda, he turned to Gemekala. "It's as I suspected. There's an unusually high neutrino flux surrounding the interloper."

"Neutrino flux?" Enki asked.

"Neutrinos are a type of particle that can pass through matter unimpeded and undetected. There's no way to block them. Somehow, her species has determined how to harness them for practical use."

Biluda folded his arms. "That's why she's remained so calm and self-assured. She's been in constant contact with her people."

"I believe the micro-devices embedded in her brain allow her to engage in a type of mental communication with her ship. I ordered the *Namtilla* to construct a sensor capable of detecting high concentrations of neutrino flux. It seems her vessel is holding position somewhere on the other side of the system's star."

"Yes, it is." Maya's wrist band emitted her words in such perfect

Okkadian that it gave Enki chills. "Please don't perceive this as an act of subterfuge. We only—"

Enki gasped as one of the protectors bashed Maya in the head with his spear-rifle.

Maya lurched forward. Her eyes rolled up into the back of her head. Keeling over, she dropped to the stone floor. She lay there moaning.

Gemekala shot to her feet in outrage. "I issued no command to incapacitate the prisoner," she shouted so deeply and loudly that Enki cringed. "Explain the meaning of this at once."

"I ordered the protectors to render her unconscious," Biluda said. "She's been plotting against us this whole time."

"That is unsubstantiated supposition."

"Then why did she never reveal she was in contact with her vessel?"

After growling closed-lipped, Gemekala lowered her voice. "You have no authority to take such action without my approval."

"I couldn't wait for your approval. I moved to prevent possible action against us."

"That prospect seems unlikely given the dialogue we exchanged."

"Are you truly convinced by her baseless tale about our mysterious disappearance from this world?" Biluda implored. "And of their ignorance of the reasons?"

"I'm not convinced of anything yet."

"Think about the pragmatics. The only way the hominins could rule this planet in the future is if they took it from us by force."

"Maybe we gave it to them. From the perspective of the hominins' predecessors, we're the invaders."

"Bah. They're here to ensure their dominion. Can't you see that?"

Gemekala clenched both fists, glowering at him. To calm herself, she closed her eyes and blew out a meditative breath.

"I shall remain open to all possibilities until we discern the truth with reasonable certainty," Gemekala said at last. "Take our guest back to the lab," she ordered the protectors.

To Enki and Tabira, she said, "Accompany her and corroborate what we've learned here today."

"Of course," Enki said, rising.

Tabira gave a swift nod. "Right away, Grand Dignitary."

The protectors lifted Maya and carried her off.

Nineteen—Dichotomy
Sol Orbit, August 200,423 BCE

"We need to get her out of there," Trevor said as he clenched his fingers.

A rend of the inside of the ziggurat hovered over the sit-table on the bridge. The rend showed the Onaki guards carrying Maya through the stone hallways. Her sandaled feet dragged across the floor.

Throughout the bridge, the AIs had darkened the viewports to shield the crew's eyes from the blinding sunlight. The force field generators worked at max output to absorb and deflect solar radiation and particles.

Bob studied the rend from his seat at the table. "Seeing the captain in such a precarious position is most distressing."

The main hatch hissed and slid open.

Trevor swiveled his chair toward it.

Ryder floated onto the bridge in a magchair. A shiny med blanket covered Jo's regenerating legs and stomach. Her face appeared clammy and paler than usual.

Maxwell followed behind the levitating chair.

Trevor stood, trying not to stare at the outlines of Jo's legs—or lack thereof—beneath the blanket. Her legs hadn't yet regrown below the knee.

"How are you feeling?" Trevor asked.

"Oh, you know, sir," Jo rasped in a weak tone, "like I've been hit by a ton of brick." Forcing a faint smile, she held up her index finger to call attention to her joke.

"I'm happy to hear your sense of humor wasn't crushed."

"You can count on many more years of bad puns, sir." Jo gazed over at the rend, which showed the guards strapping Maya into a chair in a strange laboratory. "What's going on? Is the captain okay?"

Folding his arms, Trevor released a sigh. "She met with their leadership and seemed to be earning their trust. Then all of a sudden one of the guards whacked her on the head and knocked her out. Apparently, some of the Onaki aren't convinced of our good intentions."

Dr. Crumpler yawned from her seat opposite Bob at the table. "I've been monitoring the captain's health status since we shifted into the system. She suffered a concussion from the blow to the head, but it's nothing her implants can't heal. She should regain consciousness any time now."

"Thank the stars," Jo said.

As if on cue, Maya's thought-speech resonated throughout the bridge. "Oh-h-h. What? Where—? I'm back in the lab."

Trevor stepped toward the rend of her in the lab. "Captain, are you receiving me?"

"Trevor . . . yes, I can hear you." Maya hissed through gritted teeth. "My head feels like someone used it as a bowling ball."

"Captain, I'm instructing your biocites to release pain meds into your system," Crumpler said. "You should feel better in a few seconds, but it'll take your implants a few hours to dissipate the concussion."

"Understood. Thank you, Doctor." Closing her eyes, Maya leaned her head back against the chair. "So what happened? The last thing I remember is you contacting me, Trevor. From that, the Onaki's lead engineer realized I was using neutrino-based comm. Then someone hit me from behind and knocked me out."

"That about sums it up," Trevor said. "Given that they pinpointed our location, I've altered our position and cancelled all direct neudar scans."

"They still can't detect the nano-wormholes, ma'am," Kepler said. "We're now manifesting the vortices as close to our targets as possible. That should make it more difficult for them to locate us again."

Maya shook her head, but then stopped. Her face contorted into an expression that showed she regretted the painful motion. "No. I want you to move *Yesterday* back to your original position behind the sun and continue running standard neudar scans."

"Yes, ma'am," Trevor said. "May I ask why?"

"I think it's important for us to maintain a show of openness. The

Onaki might interpret the ship going back into hiding as an act of deceit. If they're able to keep an eye on the ship, it might make them feel better. I also think their leader, this Gemekala, will be smart enough to realize we're leaving ourselves exposed as a show of good faith."

"From a tactical standpoint, I have to recommend against it, Captain."

"I appreciate your concern, but their spacecraft are all subluminal. By the time they could reach *Yesterday's* position—if any of their ships could even withstand the high temperatures or solar radiation—you'd be long gone. They have no real way to threaten the ship."

"Speaking of their ship," Rojas said as he tapped his foot at tactical, "it's weaponized a cache of antimatter. Based on the projected yield, the bomb could eradicate all life on the planet."

"Trust me, Lieutenant," Maya said, "that makes me as nervous as it makes you. Let's hope it's only a show of force and a precaution. Keep in mind that most of the Onaki are now on the surface. They'll only drop their bomb as a last resort, so let's make sure we don't provoke them."

"Yes, ma'am."

"Let's also keep the bigger picture in mind. There are many more Onaki on their home world. What we do here could have lasting repercussions on relations between our two peoples."

Trevor absently cracked his knuckles. "Still, Captain, I'd feel a lot better if we could get you out of there."

"So would I," Maya said, "but I need to see this through. The last thing that will help the situation is my flying the coop."

"Understood, ma'am."

♦

As Brooke stepped into the mouth of the cave, her heart thumped in her chest.

What the hell am I doing? She adjusted her i-cite to compensate for the darkness. How had she let Eve talk her into working for the Vril—and into taking action to betray Maya? How had she gone from fighter pilot to riot instigator?

But deep down, what she was about to do felt right, as crazy as the thought seemed. Few governments in history had ever freed their slaves because they had asked nicely to be liberated. If the proto-humans wanted their freedom, they needed to rise up and take it. And she was soft-hearted enough to want to see them get it.

Sucking in a deep breath, she deactivated her collar. She figured walking in on them in a more conventional sense would startle them less than her appearing out of thin air.

Torches lit up the tunnel as it widened. Up ahead she found a group of proto-humans. Omo was among them, stroking the hair of a sickly young boy. Everyone else sat in silence, resting with their eyes closed. Most of them would likely return to work in the city in a matter of hours.

How do I break the ice? Start with a joke, perhaps? She snorted. *Somehow, I doubt that would work.*

"You've got company," Eve mind-spoke from outside. "Two proto-humans just entered the cave."

As Brooke twisted around to check behind her, she gasped.

A young man brandishing a rock charged at her.

"Wait!" As Brooke yelled, her wristband shouted the words in his dialect. "Stop! I'm here to help you."

The man ignored her. Hoisting the rock aloft with both hands, he half-swung, half-threw it at her head.

Her reflexes and training kicked in before she could think.

Brooke jumped out of the way of the rock. The air it displaced caressed her skin as it passed through the space she had vacated.

Crashing against the tunnel wall, the rock dropped and thudded against the ground.

With her attacker bent forward and off balance, Brooke pushed down on his back, drilled the toe of her boot into his shin, and swept his legs out from under him.

Wailing in pain, the young man dropped to the cavern floor.

His companion wrapped an arm around Brooke's throat from behind and squeezed, trapping her in a headlock.

Rather than gasp, Brooke drew in short, even breaths. Instead of struggling or clawing at his arms, she reached for a pressure point near his inner elbow and pressed it with her fingers.

The second man cried out and loosened his grip.

Pushing up under his arms, she dropped out of his grasp and elbowed him in the stomach. She then leapt away, whipped out her wave gun, and fired it in electroshock mode.

The blast caused the man to go into spasms. He keeled over and fell to the cave floor.

Brooke stood gun in hand, her chest heaving. Her assailants rolled over onto their backs, spent. They displayed no sign of resuming their attacks.

She looked around and blinked. At some point during the fight, she had backpedaled into the center of the cavern, and of the group of proto-humans.

The proto-humans cowered along the walls, trembling. Omo glowered at her wave gun as he clutched the boy in his arms.

Way to make a first impression, she berated herself.

Returning the gun to its hip holster, Brooke held up her palms.

The two men she had incapacitated sat up and massaged their bruises. It was good for everyone to see she hadn't caused them any permanent harm.

As she thought about what she wanted to say, her wristband spoke the words in their language. "Hello."

The frightened occupants of the cavern shrank back even farther, startled by the sounds emitted not by her mouth but from her wrist.

For all they know, there's a talkative spirit living in my arm. "I don't speak your words," Brooke said, pointing to the wristband. "This tool talks for me." She held the band up, giving them a good look at it. "Do not fear."

The group seemed to relax somewhat.

Their language contained no words for an apology, so she made do as best as she could. "I don't want to hurt you." To Omo, she said, "I want to talk."

The translated words Omo spoke scrolled across the bottom of Brooke's i-cite.

"Who are you?" he asked. His voice rumbled with a deep basso profondo. "Are you a master?"

"A master? You mean the Onaki. No, I'm not."

Omo rose to his feet. With his head cocked, he seemed to be comparing the way she looked to the appearance of his masters. She guessed he was taking stock of her narrower eyes, rounder nose and face, and lighter skin.

"Where do you come from?" he asked.

"I'm a visitor from far away."

"From the sky? Like the masters?"

"Sort of. I'm from this land. Like you."

Omo looked past her toward the cave entrance, eyes wavering in concern. "The masters know we are here?"

"No."

Relaxing his posture, Omo asked, "Why are you here?"

Brooke rested her hands on her hips. "To free you from the masters."

Omo tightened his thick brow. He looked at the others in his group, who displayed similar confusion.

"What do you mean?"

"I'll teach you to fight them, to break free."

Omo and his companions blinked, traded glances, murmured.

"Why?" Omo asked.

Brooke realized the source of his misunderstanding. These people had never known any other life than one under the heel of their masters. They were sort of like domesticated animals. The experience of freedom must have seemed as foreign to them as slavery was to her.

When Omo had resisted Biluda back in the city, he had done so like a child rebelling against a parent. But no child, no matter how headstrong, truly wanted to leave the sanctity of a parent's home until they grew up.

Brooke's task had just become that much more daunting. Before she could teach the proto-humans how to fight for their freedom, she would have to teach them the nature of freedom and why they should want it. Doing so would violate the non-interference parameters of the mission—and go against Maya's desire to find a peaceful solution—but Brooke couldn't in good conscience let their ignorance and slavery persist.

Taking a deep breath, Brooke tested a theory. "Why are you here?" She swept her arm around the place. "Here, in this cave?"

Omo exchanged glances with his people, but didn't respond.

They don't consciously realize it, but deep down they yearn to be free. Brooke nodded, starting to understand. "You want to be free. Free to make choices. Free of control."

She held a palm out toward two women who were cowering in fear. "You're here to escape your masters for a short time." She pointed at Omo. "Others are hiding to avoid being stilled."

Venturing a step toward Omo, Brooke crouched in front of him. "You are tools to the masters, but you can learn to live without them."

She recalled why Omo had rebelled in the first place. "You want to be free to protect your loved ones."

Omo's face brightened. "How?"

"It won't be quick or easy, but I can teach you. With hard work, you can do it."

The group edged toward her.

Taking the boy under his arm, Omo said, "Hard work we know."

◆

Once again strapped into the chair in the lab, Maya studied Enki, who sat at his main workbench. The scientist inserted vials of liquid into a scanning machine while analyzing combinations of human DNA on the attached monitor.

Maya didn't need a degree in genetics to understand what he was doing. "There's no need for your bioweapon. We mean you no harm."

Ignoring her, Enki selected another vial from a rack of tubes and held it up to the light.

"I sympathize with the concerns raised by your people," Maya said. "If our positions were reversed, I'd be cautious, too. What can I do to earn your trust?"

Asha entered the lab, carrying a tray with fruit, bread, and wine. When she set the tray down on the workbench, she touched Enki's arm and smiled.

Enki froze for a moment. His breathing heightened.

The monitor flashed and locked onto a particular strain of genetic material. In Okkadian, the splicing machine's monotone vocal emitter squawked words for "match" and "success."

Maya's i-cite translated the results on the screen.

Chills coursed through her body. The airborne virus he had developed would infect proto-humans and modern humans alike, causing death in a matter of hours.

"Do you really want to be responsible for genocide?" Maya asked. "I thought you wanted to create life, not—"

"Be silent," Enki snapped. It was the first emotional outburst she had heard from him. "Otherwise, I'll have the protectors remove your speech bracelet and gag you." His tone startled Asha, who cringed.

Maya decided to take his advice.

Blowing out a calming breath, Enki took a sip of wine from the goblet on the tray. "My outburst was not directed at you, Asha. I've been under a great deal of stress, but that's no excuse for losing my composure."

As Asha relaxed, Enki turned to Maya. "This virus is meant only as a deterrent. As long as you stay true to your word, the Caucus is unlikely to sanction its use. After all, I'm sure you have powerful weapons at your disposal that you could use against us."

"True enough," Maya said. "So what can I say to make sure we don't end up using our weapons against each another? Please, ask me anything."

"No words could be sufficient."

Growing frustrated, Maya opened her mouth to respond.

Asha spoke first. "Why do you fight?"

Maya exchanged blinks with Enki. He appeared as unsure as his prisoner at who Asha had directed the question.

"I wouldn't say we're fighting," Maya said.

Enki nodded. "It's natural for people to be apprehensive toward one another when they first meet."

"Yes, we're working to build trust."

Flashing her warm smile, Asha picked up a piece of bread from the tray. She stepped over to Maya and fed it to her.

Maya wolfed it down. As she swallowed, her stomach growled, craving more. She hadn't realized how hungry she was until now.

"Is trust not earned through acts of kindness?" Asha asked. Her speech was the most sophisticated Maya had heard from a proto-human. Working in Enki's lab and in the ziggurat near the faction leaders, Asha seemed to have received an education superior to that of the average worker. Maya wondered whether the girl had picked things up on her own, or if the Onaki had given her formal schooling.

Enki stared at the floor.

"Master, the poison you're making does not seem very kind," Asha said. "Does it not betray the trust you're working to build?"

Maya held her breath at the seemingly innocent girl's awareness. Her words and insight also proved the proto-humans were capable of much more than serving as slaves.

Enki stared at the vials in reflective silence.

An abrasive whining—like the sound of an antique fax machine— reverberated throughout the lab.

Recognizing the language, Maya tensed in fear, hatred, and surprise. She had heard it many times in her present.

Enki flinched. He almost knocked the rack of vials off the table.

Asha retreated behind him.

Translated words scrolled across the bottom of Maya's i-cite. "You are wise not to trust the human." A slow and monotone spoken translation in Okkadian followed.

Whipping her gaze around the lab, Maya failed to locate the source of the speech.

"We are the rightful future," the voice said. "The humans thrive on conflict and will destroy us both."

"Who's there?" Enki demanded, jumping to his feet.

In the middle of the lab, a thin figure of a Grey exobeing materialized. The Grey wore a tight-fitting black suit and a slim invisibility band around its neck.

That explains what happened to my collar.

"Hello, father," the Grey addressed Enki.

"Father?" Asha repeated, cowering behind the scientist.

Maya recalled the schematics of the Grey she had seen when she had first awoken in the lab. If the way in which this Grey had addressed Enki meant what she thought it meant, the situation was about to become much more complicated.

Enki stared at the being. "Who are you?"

"We are the ultimate manifestation of your grand vision," the Grey said, "a vast improvement over your earlier creations." Focusing its bulbous black eyes on Maya, it extended a six-fingered hand toward her. "It is in her nature to betray you. If you allow it to happen, you shall suffer the consequences, and we shall never exist."

Twenty—Sedition
East Africa, September 200,423 BCE

The blazing rays of the sun beat down on the bare shoulders of the young man as he worked his rake through the soil. Wiping a bead of sweat off his forehead, he yearned to wet his parched throat. He hadn't had a drink in hours.

He shook off his light-headedness and glanced around the barley field. The nearest protector paced multiple rows away with her back to him.

Propping his body up by the handle of his rake, he closed his eyes and gave his aching muscles a break.

As he rested, he envisioned gorging himself on chickpeas, dates, turnips, and all the other delicious morsels grown in the fields. Fish, fowl, or lamb would go well with the vegetables and grains. The masters did feed such foods to their workers, but they rationed and distributed them in the minimum portions each laborer required.

The young worker longed to stuff his face until he burst, or sleep for days at a time, but he knew the masters would never allow such things.

A girl not much younger than he approached, raking the next row over. "A protector is looking this way."

Springing upright, the trembling young man fumbled with his rake until he got a grip on it and resumed his work.

The girl kept pace with him as they worked. "You look tired," she whispered, "and hungry and thirsty."

The young man shrugged in resignation. He couldn't do anything to change his situation.

"I eat and drink plenty," the girl said.

Now that he looked her over, she had a good amount of meat on her bones. Dark circles under her eyes betrayed her fatigue, yet she worked with a bounce in her step.

Glancing at the protector patrolling nearby, she said, "We should eat and drink as much as we want—do what we want."

Shaking his head, he added, "No, we must obey the masters."

The girl glanced at the protector, and then back at him. "The masters know things. That is all. They are not special."

Shaking in fear, the young man tripped on his rake and lost his grip on it for a moment. "If the protector hears you, the masters will still us."

They raked in silence for the next minute.

"Where did you hear these things?" he asked.

She directed her twinkling gaze at him. "By the sea. At a place where many can learn such things."

The young man swallowed, an uncomfortable act given that his throat felt like sand. He had heard rumors about such a place. He had also noticed his fellows disappearing for hours at a time during rest periods.

"You want to be free," she said. "I can tell."

The notion of fleeing to a place free of the masters' oversight, if only for a short while, lifted some of the young man's weariness. But the prospect of leaving the city—and getting caught doing so—sent chills through his body despite the heat. "I . . . no. I cannot."

"You are afraid. But we are not slaves. You know this is true."

Staring beyond the fields and the city toward the mainland, the young man had often wanted to run free, to leave everything behind and escape into the wild.

"At dark I will take you," the girl said. "You will meet the Teacher. She will set you free."

♦

A water inspector sat back on her hind legs in front of a sedimentation tank. The impurity levels in this particular tank fell within acceptable tolerances, so she needed to move on and inspect the next tank along the aqueduct system.

But the woman's legs refused to budge because her thirst demanded to be quenched. Relief flowed right in front of her. All she needed to do was reach down and cup her palms.

Forcing the thought from her mind, she knew she had no right to want more. The masters knew what was good for her. Moreover, her trade was free from the physical demands placed on her fellows. If she tainted the purity of the water she had been tasked with maintaining, the protectors would still her without hesitation.

Still, the sun blazed overhead, and her throat felt drier than the desert air.

The water inspector looked around and saw no one, so she reached with trembling hands into the stone trench that routed fresh water to the central reservoir in the city. At the cool caress of the life-giving fluid against her skin, her body shivered in anticipation.

She lifted her palms toward her mouth. Soon, the cold liquid would chill her innards from head to toe.

Footsteps pounded toward her.

She gasped and let the water fall through her fingers. Whipping her head to the side, she saw two aqueduct maintenance workers, both men, rushing up over the hill toward her.

Pulse throbbing, she stood and shook out her hands, drying them off.

The two men hurried past her without a word, headed away from the city toward the sea. As far as she knew, there was no game to hunt that way, nothing to harvest, and plenty of better places to fish.

"Where are you going?" she yelled after them.

They stopped, turned, and hurried back to her.

"We are on an errand for the masters," said the first man, the taller of the pair. "We cannot say more."

The woman inclined her head, knowing her place. "Then I will return to my work." She started toward the next sedimentation tank, relieved they hadn't seen or cared about her offense, but confused by their words.

After exchanging a glance with his companion, the second, shorter man reached out and grabbed her by the arm. "We lied."

"Do not tell the masters," the tall man said.

"I will not tell," she insisted. "But lies are bad."

"Lies are not bad. We need lies."

"Need them? Why?"

"To be free."

"Free?" She trembled in fear. "The masters will still you. You will feel pain forever."

"No. The masters lied about such things." The short man pointed off in the direction they had been headed. "We are going to the place where we will learn to be free."

The inspector looked toward the aqueduct system and then back at the men. "The foreman will tell the masters you left your work. They will still you."

Placing a hand on her shoulder, the tall man said, "No. The foreman is one of us. He is helping us."

"How? If the masters find out—"

"They will never know. We will return before our shifts end. Other workers will do our work. The foreman has planned for it."

"Plan?" The inspector tilted her head. "Only the masters can plan."

The two men stood tall and showed proud smiles.

"The Teacher showed him how," the tall man said.

"The Teacher?" she repeated.

Rushing to the top of the hill, the short man lifted his hands and made a series of strange hand signals toward the aqueducts. A moment later, he seemed to have received a reply, because he gestured again.

"The foreman says you can come, too," he said as he rejoined them.

The woman shook her head. "No." She looked over at the sedimentation tank. "I must get back to work. If the masters learn—"

"The masters will never know. You will be back before your shift ends."

"But—"

"The teacher has water. Clean water."

"The teacher calls it . . ." The short man scratched his head.

"A self-pure," the tall man said, struggling to speak the strange and complex words. "A self-purifying thermos," he finally managed. He pointed at the tank. "It makes water clearer than the masters make."

The inspector blinked. This was something she had to see.

♦

Carrying a tray with water, wine, vegetables, and grains, Umi hurried into the head master's study.

He skidded to a halt at the sight of three other masters kneeling around a table, scared that he might be intruding. But head master Gemekala waved him in without looking at him.

As Umi set four cups out on the table, he listened to their conversation. Most of the masters believed his fellows lacked the intelligence necessary to comprehend their language, but he had served them his entire life. He had heard more than enough Okkadian to understand most of their words.

If he listened closely, perhaps he might hear something he could tell to the Teacher.

"Another interloper from the future, you say?" Gemekala asked.

The creator of Umi's people, Enki, blinked hard and nodded. "This visitor claimed to be a descendent of an improved version of the hominins I've only begun to design," Enki said. "Its DNA possesses the quadruple helix structure of our original genome. The order and elegance of its genetic makeup surpasses that of the hominins, the future hominins, or our current forms."

"That would seem to support the being's claims about its origins," Tabira said.

"Enough scientific admiration." Biluda wiped the sweat from his brow. "What about its intent? Its appearance in the here and now, at the same time as the future hominins, cannot be a coincidence."

"It's no coincidence," Enki said. "These beings, which Maya refers to as the Greys, claim they can never exist unless we do away with our hominins."

Pouring wine into each cup, Umi kept his eyes lowered, pretending not to pay attention. But his ears remained tuned into the discussion. It included many strange terms he didn't understand.

"That would seem to be a contradiction," Biluda said, sipping from his cup. "Clearly, beings from both races are here and therefore exist."

Tabira stood and paced in front of them. "Before we left our homes, a scientist proposed a controversial theory about how space and time did not proceed in linear fashion."

Umi placed plates of food in front of each master.

"Of course," Gemekala said. She tore off a piece of bread and nibbled on it. "We experienced the relativistic effects of time slowing during the near-light speed journey here."

"I'm not simply referring to relativity. The new theory claimed that space-time could split and result in two or more separate timelines, each resulting in a different series of events."

"Maya called it branch theory, I believe." Enki blinked at his food, apparently not hungry. "You're suggesting the Greys and future hominins are each from separate timelines, one where the hominins were allowed to prosper and another where we replaced our work force with the Greys."

"That would appear to be a distinct possibility," Tabira said.

Gemekala pressed her palms together. "Then they are both here to ensure the survival of their respective species. This must be a point in their shared histories, and the events to come will determine who prospers."

"While we become a footnote in history," Biluda huffed. "I told you they were dangerous. We should still our labor force and execute both interlopers before it's too late."

"And then what?" Gemekala asked, raising her booming voice.

Startled, Umi dropped the cup he was refilling. It spun and wobbled on its base. Reaching out, he caught and steadied it before it toppled over and spilled.

Receiving only the briefest of glances from the masters, Umi picked up his tray and started to exit the room. But he hesitated, for their words carried much more intrigue than he normally experienced in his humdrum daily existence.

He set the tray down on another table and then found a rag. Keeping his attention on the masters' discussion, he took his time wiping a small statue of an Onaki philosopher.

"How will our society function without a labor force?" Gemekala asked, lowering her tone. "And what of the first captive's ship? What action do you think her fellows will take upon seeing us terminate their leader?"

Lacking a rebuttal, Biluda grumbled. "Why is the air in this room always so stale and warm?"

Gemekala ignored his complaint. "This is a complex situation, one requiring pragmatic thought to determine the optimal approach. We must not act in haste."

"In reference to the future hominins' ship," Tabira said, "it's still holding position on the opposite side of the sun."

"Have you detected another ship, one that might belong to the Greys?"

Tabira shook his head. "No. But the neutrino emissions from the hominin ship have remained quite steady."

"They're still watching us and communicating with their leader," Biluda said, shifting on his knees.

Gemekala lifted her chin, striking a thoughtful pose. "Undoubtedly true, but they know we can detect them now."

"Their ship could've ceased its scans and altered its orbit to hide from us." Tabira said. "Yet it's remained in position, continued its scans, and refrained from entering orbit."

"Such an act strikes me as an attempt at transparency—a show of good intentions."

"Or a trick to lull us into a false sense of security," Biluda said.

"With the abilities we've seen, the future hominins could easily overpower us," Enki said. "So far, they've chosen not to threaten us."

"Haven't they? I've received a number of unconfirmed reports about workers disappearing. That cannot be a coincidence."

"This is the first I've heard of that," Gemekala said.

"The hominins still possess primal instincts born of this world," Enki said. "At times, they feel compelled to return to the wild, but they come back when they realize they can no longer survive without us. That might explain their behavior."

Gemekala clasped her hands atop the table. "You labeled these reports as unconfirmed rumors. I suggest you get confirmation, Advocate Biluda, before drawing conclusions."

Biluda stood. "Believe me, I plan to do just that."

"Well, this is much to contemplate." Gemekala rose to her feet. Enki and Tabira stood as well. The three visiting masters exited the study.

As Umi began clearing the table, he looked forward to his rest period. At that time, he would return to the place by the sea and tell the Teacher what he had learned.

♦

"That's better," Brooke said via her wristband. "Keep your legs wide. Now lock your elbow." She struck a fighting stance next to the boy, showing him how to do it. "Here, like this."

The teen studied her and then dug his bare feet into the sand, emulating her form.

"Good," she said. "You learn quickly."

Clasping her hands behind her back, Brooke strolled along the beach near the cavern hideout, observing her pupils. Individuals practiced the basic combat techniques she had taught them. Pairs sparred hand-to-hand or with staffs carved out of wooden sticks.

At least fifty proto-humans resided at the hideout at any one time. Her movement was beginning to not only outgrow the location, but expand too much to keep it secret from the Onaki. She had received four separate reports of protectors catching their workers sneaking away from the overcrowded community residences during patrol shift changes, as she had taught them. In each instance, the proto-humans had played dumb, and the protectors had merely forced them back inside the residences. The Onaki only punished repeat offenders and rarely executed them. The construction of the city was behind schedule, so the masters could ill afford to lose laborers.

A young man named Umi—the head master's personal attendant, no less—had informed Brooke that the Faction leaders had learned of the runaways. Sooner or later, they would figure things out. Brooke could only hope that the movement would grow organized enough to strike before the masters uncovered the truth.

She told herself that the movement expanding too quickly posed a good problem. Most workers hadn't needed a lot of convincing. All humans, regardless of era or race, yearned for freedom.

A thought popped into Brooke's head and quickened her pulse. Freedom, she had once heard someone say, was a double-edged sword. What would the proto-humans do once liberated? These people had barely known how to think until she had begun teaching them. How would they feed, clothe, and govern themselves? Would they descend into chaos if she didn't stick around to teach them? She was a pilot and a strategist—not a farmer, seamstress, or politician.

The responsibility for these people—her people—weighed heavy on Brooke's shoulders. All she could do was take things one step at a time.

Besides, she had little chance of living long enough to deal with the aftermath. At the rate she was increasing her dosage, she had only a month of sparks left. The end would come quickly once they ran out.

"No, no, no." Brooke scolded a pair of men who were charging at each other and throwing wild punches.

Separating the two, she faced the larger man. "Don't rush at someone. That puts you off balance."

She adopted a well-grounded fighting stance. "Wait for your enemy to strike first. Study them when they attack. The more someone moves, the less balance they have. That gives you an advantage."

Holding her palm face-up, she beckoned to the larger man with her fingers. "Come. Charge me and see."

The others on the beach had taken notice, and began to form a circle around them. After exchanging a glance with his partner, the larger man sprinted toward her. He threw a punch as he approached within arm's length.

Brooke jerked left and turned her body to the side. As the man's clenched fist neared her face, she threw up her right arm and snapped her wrist to generate torque. Striking his forearm with hers, she knocked his fist and arm clear of her head. With the man stumbling forward, she drove the heel of her boot into his Achilles' tendon.

Howling in pain, the large man's legs gave out from under him. He fell flat on his face in the soft beach sand.

The proto-humans who were watching gasped. They had, of course, never seen anything like modern martial arts. The Onaki had only existed on the Earth in their new form for a few decades, and had never had reasons to develop hand-to-hand combat techniques.

Grabbing the large man's opposite arm, Brooke twisted it back far enough to cause him to slap the ground in surrender.

She released him and hopped off of his back.

Pushing to his feet, the large man dusted the sand off his clothing.

"The masters won't charge at you," Brooke addressed the crowd. "You must surprise them." Raising her voice, she added, "Sneak up behind them. Be quick. And still them any way that works." *To hell with chivalry.*

"Once the masters know," Omo said, pushing to the front of the group, "they will control us."

"They'll try, but remember. You are many. They are few. One master can control only three or four of you, so you'll need to use surprise and deception and work together.

"Tomorrow, we'll learn 'decoy maneuvers.' Now, rest or return to your work."

One by one, the crowd of awed spectators dispersed.

Omo approached her. "Things are going well," he said with a brighter, more relaxed face than she had ever seen him display. "Many farmers, hunters, and other workers have come."

Brooke nodded. "Gathering people first from outside the city seems to have worked."

"Yes. And more fellows are starting to come from the city."

"Things are shaping up as well as I could've hoped." Brooke rubbed her palms together. "Let's go back inside and plan the next stage—"

"Admiral Davis," Maya neurocommed. "Brooke, please respond."

When Brooke heard the sound of her niece's voice, she froze. Relief should have set in at the knowledge Maya was still okay, but the guilt of going behind her back overpowered all other sentiments. *Do I respond and lie? Ignore her? Or—*

"Flying patrol!" a boy shouted from atop the cliff.

Twenty-one—Artifice
East Africa, September 200,423 BCE

Chills of fear and anticipation coursed through Brooke's body. She ignored her niece's incoming comm and locked stares with Omo.

He understood at once and rushed off to implement the plan they had rehearsed, yelling the word "cover" again and again.

As most of the proto-humans ran into the cave, Omo told some of them to grab branches from near the mouth.

The group sprinted to the water's edge. Backpedaling toward the cavern, they dragged the branches across the beach, clearing away the footprints.

Their work was far from perfect. The crisscrossing patterns they had combed in the sand didn't look natural and led right to the cave. But as long as the Onaki didn't inspect the area too closely, they wouldn't notice—Brooke hoped.

Brooke stepped into the cavern just before the last branch dragger.

Not thirty seconds after everyone had retreated into hiding, she heard the hum of a manta ray craft's fan-engine.

The Onaki aircraft descended and hovered over the beach, twenty meters from the mouth of the cave. Due to the composition of the rocks in the cliffs, the craft's sensors wouldn't be able to detect the life signs in the caverns. But there was nothing to stop the patrol from landing and finding them the old fashioned way.

Her pulse throbbing, Brooke activated her collar and blinked out of sight. Then she reached down and drew her wave gun. She didn't want to kill anyone, both out of moral objection and because the Onaki would come looking for their missing patrol. But if they suspected their workers had taken refuge in the cave, she would have no choice but to eliminate the patrol before they could reveal their location.

Brooke had backed well away from the mouth of the cave, but her enhanced vision showed the aircraft settling down for a landing.

Damn. There's no chance they'll miss us now.

From high atop the cliff, Eve jumped down and landed on the hovering craft. Brooke flinched and gasped.

The craft teetered hard in an effort to shake the android off. Eve hugged the bubble canopy and managed to hang onto it.

Pulling her elbow back, Eve punched through the bubble canopy. The craft darted toward the beach and cliff as she slid inside of the cabin.

Brooke dove down onto the cavern floor.

Right before smacking into the rock wall above the cave, the craft banked away and headed out to sea.

Rising, Brooke crept toward the mouth.

The aircraft dipped and rose, wobbling. Smoke billowed from its engines and undercarriage. An explosion erupted from the cockpit as the craft crashed into the water.

Brooke told Omo and the others to remain inside the cave. Then she crept outside onto the beach. With both palms gripping the handle, she directed her weapon at the slightest threatening sound or movement.

The water calmed, erasing all signs of the impact. A head of wet brunette hair poked up between the low waves. Gradually, Eve emerged and hobbled toward the shore.

The encounter with the Onaki patrol craft had reduced Eve's confident strut to a jerking limp. Much of her hair, skin, and clothing had been burned away. The composites comprising her body showed charring, cracks, and punctures. Through a hole in her head, Brooke could see the throbbing mass of Eve's cybernetic brain.

The moment Eve reached Brooke, the android collapsed on the beach, convulsing in a series of mechanical jerks.

Holstering her gun, Brooke knelt at her side.

"Had . . . had to prevent exposure." Eve's head and eyes twitched.

Brooke nodded. "You did it, at least for now."

"I need . . . need to tell you." The involuntary chomping of Eve's jaw gave her the look of a robot demon from a horror sim. "Tell you how to silent . . . silent comm the ship and who . . . who aboard to contact."

Brooke scrunched her nose at the android's maimed appearance and sudden straightforwardness. Despite her efforts to suppress her feelings of empathy for her nemesis, Brooke couldn't help but feel for her. "I guess near-death brings out the serious side of even the most deceitful."

"I did . . . didn't plan on getting dam . . . damaged."

"I don't think anyone ever plans on getting hurt."

"Self-repair sys . . . systems require me to shut down. Get . . . get me inside, and I . . . I'll tell you."

Twisting around, Brooke waved to the proto-humans who were sticking their heads out of the cave. She needed help lugging the heavy android inside.

With her back turned to Eve, Brooke heard footsteps pounding toward her in the sand.

She whirled around and saw Asha.

♦

Lt. Commander Gottlieb Otto, *Yesterday's* chief engineer, reclined in a chair behind the desk in his office. As he sipped from a cup of tea, he reviewed the hovering rends detailing the black hole generator's operational status, with an approving smile.

Efficiency and power output were holding steady at their respective peaks. Gravity generation displayed as optimal. All in all, *Yesterday* was ready to go at a moment's notice in case the captain needed rescuing.

Gottlieb stared out the windows of his office. Crewmen worked the duty stations encircling the perimeter of the spherical generator casing in the floor. Unlike the forward module where crew members stood perpendicular to the ship's central axis, everyone in the ECC stood parallel to the axis atop the generator.

Despite being an expert on the generator, it still humbled and astounded him. The black hole was the size of a marble but possessed almost as much mass as the Earth.

Such technical prowess caused goosebumps to pop up on his skin. It got his blood pumping far more than he cared to admit. But it also gave him chills. *Yesterday* didn't carry anywhere near enough antimatter to create a new black hole if the current one collapsed or dissipated. It was therefore his all-important duty—a duty as critical as dealing with the situation on Earth—to ensure the current generator kept humming along in peak condition.

A delivery bot rolled into Gottlieb's office. Its manipulator arms extended, setting a tray with his lunch atop the desk. He preferred to eat while he worked. He couldn't imagine better scenery than the ECC had to offer.

"Thanks, little buddy," he said.

"I'm happy my service meets with your approval," the bot said. Then it rolled away.

As Gottlieb eagerly bit into his sandwich, his gaze landed on the entrance to the ECC. The hatch slid open and closed once a second with no one coming in or going out.

"Not again," he mumbled with his mouth full.

The hatch had malfunctioned on two previous occasions since *Yesterday* had arrived in the past. Each time he had assigned one of his junior engineers to fix the thing.

If you want something done right, you've got to do it yourself. He set down his sandwich—after taking one more bite—and sauntered over to the hatch.

Standing near the entrance with his arms folded, he stared the hatch down, frowning. He knelt and opened the control panel in the wall next to the hatch. His engineers had assumed an AI diagnostic would resolve a software glitch. But if the problem proved mechanical, the fix would require a hands-on approach.

Sitting, he enabled his enhanced vision and looked into the open panel, finding two bare wires crossed. *Now how could the wire casings have been stripped?* he wondered, scratching his sizeable bald spot.

He shrugged. He had seen odder malfunctions in his day.

Gottlieb pinged a delivery bot to fab him the right tool, told the sleeves of his uniform to roll up past his elbows, and fixed the wires. The hatch shut and didn't open again.

He fastened the panel back in place and approached the hatch. When it sensed his presence, each side slid apart as expected.

Flinching, Gottlieb found the exobeing—Zeke, if he recalled the name correctly—standing out in the corridor. The young exobeing stared past him at the generator casing.

"Can I help you with something?" Gottlieb asked.

Zeke looked at him with his strange yellow eyes that were spaced too far apart. "No, thank you." He turned and disappeared down the hall.

Shaking his head, Gottlieb tested the hatch a few more times for good measure. Then he returned to his desk.

As he bit into his sandwich, the hatch opened and closed again without anyone passing through it. He tensed, wanting to rip out the few remaining hairs left on his balding scalp.

◆

Wandering back toward his quarters in thought, Zeke questioned his own sanity. The mind of the presence he had felt back in his quarters had seemed more ordered than that of a human. He hadn't been able to read the mind, yet he had gotten the sense it could be read, similar to how he might not understand a foreign language even though he recognized it as such.

Zeke was starting to wonder if he had sensed a ghost, but dismissed that ridiculous notion. He had immersed himself in far too many comic and horror sims.

After leaving his quarters, he had tracked the presence into the aft module and to the malfunctioning entrance to the ECC. There the presence had vanished.

Neither Chief Engineer Gottlieb nor any of the other engineers had known or suspected anything about the presence. The hatch opening and closing on its own had seemed to vindicate Zeke's suspicions until Gottlieb had identified the problem as mechanical and fixed it. Having lost the trail, Zeke had gone back to his quarters.

Zeke now lay on his bed again, intertwining his fingers behind his head and contemplating whether the feeling had even been real. Given that he was the only member of his kind among the humans, he couldn't ask if anyone else had experienced something similar. Accessing phase space might have hinted at an answer, but his people's information network wouldn't exist for thousands of years.

If Brooke had remained aboard, he could have confided in her, but Commander Young had restricted messages to the scout team to essential contact only. Moreover, Zeke had sworn not to get involved in the impending conflict.

Conflict. This time, Zeke sprung all the way to his feet. *Of course.* Then he scolded himself, as Brooke so often did. How had he not grasped the obvious?

The Greys had attacked *Yesterday* in an attempt to destroy the ship before it backshifted—or at least everyone had assumed such motivation. What if they hadn't wanted to damage or capture the ship? What if the attack had been a diversion to allow one or more stowaways to hitch a ride to the past?

That would mean Zeke had felt the presence of a Grey.

He weighed all the possibilities. Just as he abstained from the Onaki-human conflict here in the past, he had also remained neutral in the fight between The Greys and humans in the former present. Still, if any Greys had snuck aboard, and if they intended harm to this vessel or its crew, he had to do something.

Should he inform Commander Young? On the outside, Young often seemed obtuse, but underneath he possessed above average intelligence. Young would likely listen to reason. However, if Zeke assisted the man, he feared he would get pulled into everything else.

The more Zeke thought about it, the more he realized he needed confirmation of his theory before going to anyone else.

♦

Drawing her wave gun, Lieutenant Christa Resnik crept into the teleporter room. A pair of her security officers were backing her up. Only two people occupied the room according to the internal neudar scans in her i-cite, but protocol dictated Christa take no chances.

There hadn't been a single security incident on *Yesterday* up to this point, and Christa had welcomed the uneventful trip. She wasn't the type who hoped a fight would break out so that she could prove her mettle. The calmer things remained, the better.

Christa had put her staff through drills in case the Onaki somehow managed to board the ship. She had simulated rescue plans to get Captain Davis to safety. She had also honed her kickboxing, aikido, and other techniques. And she had found a new hobby in nurturing tomato plants and flowers in the hydroponics farm. Christa wished she were back there now, clipping a branch or watering a pot.

Inside the teleport room, Christa gazed around and found Dr. Crumpler attending to an unconscious engineer. The ensign lay on the floor near the console that operated the inactive portal archway.

As Crumpler pulled an auto-syringe away from the ensign's neck, Christa holstered her weapon.

"Is she okay?" Christa asked. "What happened?"

Crumpler checked the ensign's pulse. "She's fine now." Grabbing the coffee thermos that she had set down on the floor, Crumpler took her time rising to her feet. "The ensign commed me saying she felt faint. When I asked her to elaborate, she didn't respond. Internal sensors showed she had passed out. I was on my way to the infirmary from the mess hall and rushed right over."

"You found her unconscious?"

"Correct." Widening her eyes as if forcing herself to wake up, Crumpler added, "My scans don't show anything wrong with her. My best guess is that she's suffering from hunger-induced fatigue. I gave her a hydro-protein shot and a stimulant. She should come around any moment."

Christa pinched her ear lobe in thought. "I see. Commander Young and Chief Gottlieb ordered the ensign to service the teleporter. They wanted it in tip-top shape in case they needed to pull out the captain."

The ensign moaned and stirred on the floor.

Christa helped her sit up. "Are you okay?"

Massaging her head, the ensign said, "Yes, I think so."

"What's the last thing you remember?"

"I . . . I don't know. I was performing an analysis of the wormhole generation algorithms." She pointed up at the control console. "All of a sudden I must've passed out. I don't know why."

Crumpler downed a swig of coffee. "Did you feel tired or light-headed?"

"No. One moment I was swiping through rends. The next I woke up on the floor here. I can't explain it." With considerable effort, the ensign pushed to her feet.

"Please escort the ensign to the infirmary so I can take a closer look at her," Crumpler told the two security officers.

Christa nodded at her officers, who guided the ensign out of the room.

As the door slid shut behind them, Christa said, "Something doesn't seem right here."

Crumpler hesitated. "This is confidential," she said in a hushed tone, "but for security purposes, the ensign has grown anorexic since *Yesterday* launched. Actually, I'd wager she's suffered from anorexia since long before we left, but I'm sure she did her best to keep it off the record."

"I see."

"Her stomach was empty, so she probably pushed herself too hard without eating."

Scratching her ear, Christa asked, "Shouldn't she have felt dizzy or hungry, or had some warning?"

With a shrug, Crumpler sipped her coffee. "Everybody's different. Plus, people with her condition are often in denial. She might not have wanted to admit the truth."

"I see. Well, just to be sure, I'll run a few extra scans."

"You do that. In the meantime, now I've got to put on my shrink hat." Crumpler exited the room.

Twenty-two—Abrogate
East Africa, October 200,423 BCE

Today's the day, October 13th. It's been a long two months, and now there's only thirty minutes until zero hour.

Two protectors escorted Maya into the ziggurat's assembly hall. This time they had elected not to restrain her, and had allowed her to wear her uniform.

Maya figured that the zero hour would occur during the upcoming tribunal. Or was the impending assembly of the faction leaders the event someone had meant for her to experience? Since *Yesterday's* arrival Maya had failed to uncover a single hint as to how the metatoy had ended up in the past.

The Onaki's hospitality had improved since the Grey had appeared. They had moved Maya from the basement cell to a room on the second level—albeit still guarded—and the lab tests had stopped. Despite having returned her clothing, they had yet to give back her wave gun, belt, or scanner. But at least they hadn't tried to extract her implants.

Maya pinged Trevor aboard *Yesterday* and ordered him to keep close tabs on the proceedings. She reminded him not to take any action without her explicit orders.

With any luck, the Onaki leadership would see reason, at which point all parties could sit down and work things out. If Maya couldn't cut through the distrust, a conflict might ensue in which she could end up as the first casualty.

Is that why I'm here? To alter this timeline to create a more harmonious future for all? No pressure.

Even though her ideals compelled her toward peace, she had her doubts. In the history Maya knew, the Onaki had departed the Earth for unknown reasons. Her intuition told her that even the best of negotiations would never convince them to pack up and leave, so why had they?

And then there were the Greys. If they too called the Earth their home world, they wouldn't want to give it up or share it any more than the humans of her time did.

The Greys slender, bug-eyed representative, Vox, stood in the center of the empty ring of desks.

Another, wider ring of desks encircled the first. Onaki noblemen and women knelt on mats behind the desks and in front of the statues lining the walls of the hall. Although Maya hadn't experienced much of Onaki culture—given her brief time among them, most of it spent in captivity—she had gleaned enough to know that their society was distinctly aristocratic in nature.

The Onaki crew which had embarked upon the journey to Earth included members of the best and brightest in their fields. In turn, they had instilled the sciences and arts along with high-minded ideals and manners in their descendants. In many ways, the Onaki colonists shared much in common with members of the IEF and past human space agencies.

Maya had met with Gemekala three times over the course of the last few weeks. In the name of full disclosure, the Grand Dignitary had revealed that she had also held meetings with Vox. Gemekala had limited each session to fact-gathering. Each time Maya had tried to appeal to her emotions, Gemekala had countered with her pragmatics.

The protectors directed Maya to stand next to Vox. They then returned to their posts.

As Maya waited for the faction leaders to arrive, she narrowed her eyes at the Grey. Thoughts of what they had done at Epsilon Eridani led her to tense in anger. But she knew she needed to set her feelings aside and seize this moment to find out as much as possible.

"How has your stay been?" Maya's wristband emitted in the harsh beeps of his language.

Vox's words scrolled across the bottom of her i-cite.

"Let us eschew your hollow pleasantries, Captain Maya Davis," said Vox without looking at her. Contempt oozed from its tone, identifiable even to her untrained ears. "You begin with a façade of politeness, which is only a preamble to what you truly wish to say."

"I begin with a show of respect and genuine interest, but if you prefer I'll skip the small talk." Maya did her best not to sound condescending. "Did you steal my collar?"

"I choose to neither confirm nor deny the accusation. But, speaking in generalities, your disingenuous skulking merited exposure."

"I'll take that as a yes. Next question. Why are your people attacking mine in the future?"

"Is it not obvious, even to your limited intellect?"

Maya bit her tongue. *Last time I checked, we had advanced farther than you.* "Given my 'limited intellect,' I'd appreciate an explanation."

"You humans appreciate very little. You've almost destroyed this world's ecosystem on countless occasions and now flaunt that conflict across space and time."

All Maya could do was shrug. "Nobody's perfect."

"Perfection is a concept. It doesn't exist in reality. But as improved versions of your kind, we're much closer to such an ideal." Vox emitted a noise that sounded like a nail being dragged across an antique chalkboard—an exasperated sigh, she could only assume. "All I'm prepared to tell you is that we're endeavoring to save both of our races."

"By trying to halt the expansion of our civilization? Why?"

"To protect you from yourselves."

Maya rolled her eyes. "Killing us seems like a counterproductive way to protect us."

Vox faced her. "We have acted with the intent to minimize casualties. In past centuries, we could've wiped your kind off the Earth and taken it back without resistance. But our superior moral code makes such an act indefensible. We refuse to do to you that which you did to us."

"What did we ever do to—?"

"We've tried in vain to subtly usher the human race toward a more evolved state, one in which you might no longer threaten all of existence."

"Threaten all of exist—?"

"But despite your technological advances, your cultural maturity has never taken the same leap. To prove as much, I cite the attempts by subversive elements to manipulate your disparate entities into union. Not only did such union require deception, but your kind couldn't maintain that union."

Maya stared at the brickwork of the floor. "It's true that human society requires a delicate balance between collaboration and competition."

"We hardly see that as balance. It's an unsettling instability."

"Our Interstellar Alliance is hardly unstable. And it's not like the IEF wants to conquer or destroy other cultures. It's quite the opposite, in fact."

"Perhaps, but what happens when your current structures fall? We cannot take the chance that a new, more antagonistic regime will come to power and continue to advance."

"So you're worried we'll advance and threaten you. But are you concerned about general progress or something more specific?"

Vox didn't respond.

Maya wanted it to keep elaborating, but too many other questions vied for her attention.

She wanted to ask it about their past abductions, and about how it had traveled to the past. She also wondered whether the exobeing had come from her present or another timeline, one where the Greys had superseded the proto-humans. His knowledge of her timeline indicated the former.

That brought up another vexing question. If humans had somehow prevented the creation of the Greys in the past she knew, as Vox had asserted, how did they exist in her timeline?

Before she could ask, the faction leaders entered the assembly hall.

The noble men and women rose to their feet.

Tabira came to kneel behind his desk, followed by Enki and a brooding Biluda. Maya hoped the tall hunchback's unhappiness boded well for her cause.

Gemekala strode in last and stood in front of her desk. After commanding everyone to kneel again, she addressed Maya and Vox. "As you can well surmise, we've engaged in a great deal of discussion and contemplation these last few weeks. Despite the overwhelming evidence, the notion that each of you hails from the distant future still defies belief. But on that premise we must operate."

The Grand Dignitary started pacing. "There are those of us who still suspect your existence presents a grave threat to us. They have argued for the cessation of all contact and demanded you leave this world. Some have even suggested we deactivate our labor force, destroy the designs for your peoples, and execute the both of you."

As Gemekala circled her, Maya pivoted to remain facing her. Maya's i-cite timer showed five minutes until zero-hour.

"Others have pointed out how you've refrained from using your advanced technology against us," Gemakala said. "If you had wanted to force us off this world or kill us, you would've done it by now. You've been nothing if not respectful visitors."

Returning to the front of her desk, she looked at Vox and Maya. "I don't yet trust either of you, but there's also no significant cause for mistrust. You have us at a disadvantage in ability, but we also have the capacity to dictate your fate. So what I am to do?"

Gemekala drew in a prolonged breath and let it out. "I refuse to take any presumptuous action not warranted by the circumstances. I will not start a war or commit genocide. You are both free to go."

Maya's timer hit zero.

A warm sense of relief consumed her. For the last few days Maya had felt as if her shoulders had born the entire weight of this mammoth stone tower, if not the planet itself.

Approaching Tabira's desk, Gemekala retrieved Maya's things and brought them to her.

"Thank you, Grand Dignitary," Maya said as the utility belt strapped itself around her waist. Holstering her scanner and wave gun, she looked Gemekala in the eye. "I hope your wise decision can serve as the beginning of accord between us."

Maya turned to Vox, who stood stiff and silent. Since its face revealed no discernable emotion, she couldn't read its feelings about the verdict. "I'm confident we can find a way to ensure all three of our peoples prosper." To Gemekala, she said. "I'd like to hold talks to build the trust that's still lacking."

Gemekala nodded. "That sounds acceptable."

"I'd enjoy participating in those talks," Tabira said, "especially if we held them aboard your impressive vessel."

Maya smiled. "I think that can be arranged—"

The teletone handset on Tabira's desk beeped. Glancing at its pixelated screen, he shot to his feet, almost knocking over the low table in the process. "The *Namtilla* has detected a massive gravitational disturbance in high orbit."

"Captain," Trevor mind-spoke. "Something's downshifting from hyperspace."

◆

"Based on the size of the wormhole, sir," Lieutenant Kepler said as he studied the sensing logs floating above the sit-table, "whatever's coming through is bigger than *Yesterday* but smaller than the *Namtilla*."

Staring down a rend of the expanding vortex, Trevor folded his arms tight against his chest.

"What are you seeing, Commander?" Maya asked from the surface.

"I'm sending you the live feed now, Captain," Trevor said.

When the churning gouge in space-time reached its maximum diameter, a fierce-looking spacecraft emerged. Bigger than a *Serendipity*- or *New Horizons*-class starship, the vessel looked like the tip of a four-bladed crossbow arrow, otherwise known as a broadhead. Trevor had fired off plenty of broadheads when hunting with his father in Texas.

The quartet of broadhead blades served as graviton-focusing nacelles, according to the scans. Each blade directed energy at a single point ahead of the ship in order to pry open an entrance to hyperspace. The central hull, a long cylindrical axis that didn't rotate, stretched from the nose to a set of mammoth antimatter tanks near the aft section. Behind the tanks, massive rocket nozzles protruded from the rear.

The sight of the vessel left Trevor clenching every jaw muscle and finger.

"Sound general quarters," he barked.

Every officer in the MCC scurried to prepare for a possible battle.

Maya said, "Take no offensive action unless—"

"Unless they attack first," Trevor finished. "Understood, Captain."

"The vessel has established a geosynchronous orbit above the city," Lieutenant Tereshkova reported from the helm.

"They know we're hiding out behind the sun, Commander," Kepler said. "I'm detecting hundreds of tiny wormhole signatures all around us. They're scanning us, sir."

"That's okay, Keps. We're doing the same to them. Armaments and defense systems?"

Bouncing his leg up and down, Rojas offered a tactical assessment. "They've got it all, Commander. Lasers, plasma cannons, particle weapons, antimatter warheads, wave destabilizers, and a few things I'm never seen before. If I'm reading these results right, those blade-nacelles are capable of projecting a massive amount of energy forward in a wide gravimetric burst."

Rojas looked up from his station, pale-faced. "That big gun could vaporize *Yesterday* with a single shot, even with our shielding at maximum."

"A bigger fish has entered the pond, as one might say." Bob adjusted his glasses at the table.

Tereshkova swiveled her chair toward Trevor. "We do have one big advantage, sir. Our wave drive makes us a lot faster and more maneuverable. They have only conventional rocket engines and RCS thrusters."

"I'm detecting an energy buildup on the surface," Bob said.

Trevor studied a rend showing an overhead view of the colony. "A portal's forming in the city square, Captain."

"Understood," Maya said. "We're heading outside to—"

Static fizzled throughout the MCC as Maya's signal cut out.

"Captain?" Trevor spun to face Kepler. "What happened?"

"That ship just threw up a hypofield, sir." Absently, Marconi tapped his lucky coin against his console. "The field extends over the entire Eastern Hemisphere. It's blocking all wormhole formation and neutrino signals."

◆

Pinging *Yesterday* without success, Maya followed the faction leaders and Vox out the front entrance of the ziggurat. The late day sun cast long shadows off the stone structures of Urusilim.

A phase portal expanded to a diameter of five meters in the city square. As Maya gazed through the translucent doorway, the central reservoir, buildings, and gathering crowd rippled as if she were looking through a salmon pink pool of water.

From the portal stepped a figure wearing a powered exoskeletal space suit. The mechanized suit strutted forward on articulated legs that gave the false appearance of having reverse-jointed knees.

Cloudy air shrouded the face beneath the mech suit's bubble canopy, an indication of the occupant's atmospheric requirements. But Maya saw enough to discern the features of a true-form Onaki.

The Onaki looked very much like a sparrowhawk. Two bright yellow eyes, each on opposite sides of its scaled head, glared at their surroundings. Rarely blinking, the eyes projected a stern intensity.

A razor sharp beak opened and closed, drawing in breath. Maya swallowed, hoping that humans looked in no way appetizing to him—or her. Maya couldn't tell if the being was male or female.

The Onaki's head bobbed up and down ever so slightly. Maya suspected that the mech contained a substance similar to gravgel. From Enki, she had learned that the Onaki home worlds had only a quarter of the Earth's gravity. It therefore made sense that they had designed suits to ease the g-force on their bodies.

The elongated structure of the mech suit sloped forward. A pair of long bulges protruded from its back. Based on the images of the Onaki Maya had seen aboard the *Namtilla*, she guessed their wings fit within the bulges. Thruster nozzles extended down from each bulge. Multi-jointed arms with eight-fingered hands dangled from the sides. A particle cannon was affixed to the shoulder above each arm.

A crest with a creature that was a cross between a hawk and a sleek starship adorned the upper torso of the suit. The crest must have represented their mission, unit, or vessel. Maya tilted her head, studying the crest. It was one of the most beautiful works of art she had ever seen.

Seven more mechs exited the portal and formed a perimeter around it.

A ninth mech emerged last, one more heavily armed and elaborate than the rest.

The portal shrank and disappeared behind the apparent leader, who stomped beyond the perimeter formed by his or her subordinates.

Gemekala approached the leader.

". . . am Kizzura Namen Sagma Namkuzu," the lead mech projected in a melodic screeching, "Captain … *Eleppu* and . . . Military Faction."

Maya's linguistic matrix failed to translate words here and there. The language must have been a newer dialect of Okkadian.

"We acknowledge you, Captain Kizzura," Gemekala greeted him. "I am Gemekala Niggina Adamen Sumur, Grand Dignitary of the Caucus of Factions governing the city of Urusilim and local advocate for the Pragmatic Faction."

The Onaki certainly love their names and titles.

Kizzura emitted a sound like a snort. Something Gemekala had said had displeased him.

Taking a small step backward, Gemekala said, "We are humbled to receive a visit by others of our fellowship. It has been almost sixteen hundred cycles since our ancestors departed Anurash and Arala."

"We have come a long way since then," Kizzura said—Maya's matrix was already improving. "The Pragmatics held us back for far too long, always overthinking and advocating undue caution. Fortunately, the Military Faction has presided over our homes in recent cycles, allowing us to advance considerably in a short amount of time. Our warship, the *Eleppu*, is the first of its kind to travel out this far. Your colony presented a natural destination."

"I see. Why did you not contact us before your arrival? Your appearance was quite sudden."

"You lack the reception technology. A sub-light signal would've taken far longer to arrive than our vessel."

"Of course." Gemekala looked over her shoulder at the faction leaders and then back to Kizzura. "We look forward to hearing about our homes, but first we should brief you on recent happenings here, which—"

"We observed the situation prior to entering the system, so we know of your blunder. Your biolaborers should never have been allowed to evolve and violate the timelines." Kizzura directed a long, reinforced finger past Gemekala and the faction leaders.

Maya forgot to breathe. The Onaki captain was pointing at her and Vox.

"Eliminate the creatures," Kizzura said.

Two of the eight mechs stomped toward Maya. Another pair came at Vox. The mechs moved with far greater speed than she would have expected, with their mechanized legs jutting into the dirt like jackhammers.

Darting around the faction leaders with impressive agility, the first two mechs surrounded Maya before she could consider retreating.

She pinged Trevor, telling him now would be a good time to port her away.

Red warning icons flashed in her i-cite. She had lost her connection to *Yesterday's* network. *A hypofield. . . .*

One of the mechs grabbed her from behind. With overpowering strength, it lifted her off the ground and pulled her arms back.

Maya cried out as pain knifed through her chest and arms. Her implants kicked in, reinforcing her muscles and skeletal structure. Nevertheless, her shoulder blades and collar bone threatened to snap at any moment—unless, of course, the mech ripped her arms off first.

Through watering eyes, Maya watched another mech lift up Vox like a rag doll and tear him limb from limb. Blood splattered the mech as body parts flopped to the ground. The Greys had always seemed frail compared to humans, but Maya hadn't known they were that fragile.

"Stop!" Gemekala bellowed, standing nose-to-suit with Kizzura. "You are in my city and under my jurisdiction."

After an agonizing near-eternity, the mech dropped Maya.

She slammed into the dirt. With each gasp, excruciating pain knifed into her upper body. The max dose of meds her implants released did little to relieve her agony.

"One feeble creature is dead, and the other must die as well," Kizzura said. "Then we must destroy the ship hiding behind the system's primary, as well as your labor force to ensure our future."

"How do you justify execution without due process?" Gemekala asked, glaring at the Onaki captain.

Kizzura didn't respond.

"If that is the ultimate conclusion, so be it," Gemekala continued. "But it shall not happen in such haste under my watch. We have just established the beginnings of positive relations. I won't rescind my word until I see evidence that justifies a different course of action."

"Spoken like a thought-paralyzed Pragmatic." Kizzura sighed. "Very well. I don't require your approval. The Factionary Protectorate has granted me full authority over this system. But I will do you the courtesy of explaining why our actions must be so."

Whirling around, Gemekala marched back into the ziggurat, followed by the faction leaders.

Kizzura ordered two mechs to escort Maya inside.

One of them squatted and tried to pick her up.

Gritting her teeth, Maya pushed to her feet, shrugged off the mech's gripper, and hobbled inside. Her legs hadn't suffered injury, yet she limped because each step sent stabbing pain up through her spine and shoulders. The health status readouts in her i-cite showed no major damage, only a tiny fracture of the scapula that her biocites would repair in an hour.

As the faction leaders knelt behind their desks, Maya plopped down at the edge of the room and rested her back against a statue. Sweat slicked her forehead, and her chest heaved. The two mechs stood nearby, guarding her.

Maya stressed over what might happen if Kizzura got his way. She could only get past those mechs by use of force, which she saw as a last resort. All she could do for now was let her body heal and hope peace somehow won the day.

Gemekala stood in front of her desk and glared at Kizzura.

Proto-human servants scurried into the assembly hall. A girl set down wine goblets on each desk. The Grand Dignitary's personal servant, Umi, filled the goblets from a decanter. Others handed out plates of fruit.

The Onaki captain stood in the center of the hall. His eyes darted every which way as he studied his surroundings. "Entering this room is like traveling to the distant past. I see statues of fellows I can only assume were important. We've used composites rather than stone to construct our dwellings for centuries."

He lifted his beak. "This planet's gravity is four times that of our worlds. Erecting the structures of this small village must've required backbreaking effort."

"There will be time for cultural exchange later," Gemekala snapped. "Provide your explanation without delay."

Kizzura gave the same high-pitched snort as earlier. "Of course you want me to get to the pragmatic point. But wouldn't you rather hear about our homes? You wouldn't recognize them. In the many cycles since your vessel departed, we've discovered and implemented many wonders, thanks to the Military Faction taking control of the—"

"Considering the stakes, let us suspend such reports and address the more pressing matter at hand."

"Very well. It's quite simple. These creatures you've created present a grave threat. We must destroy them before they do any more damage."

"Their only transgression was keeping their presence a secret when they first arrived," Gemekala said, "but in retrospect I understand that decision. They've taken no aggressive action against us. To what damage are you referring?"

"Forgive me." As Kizzura paced, his mech's hydraulics hissed. Its gears whirred as its legs clanged against the floor. "It's easy to forget that you lack knowledge that I take for granted. These future creatures have damaged everything by their mere presence."

"I feared as much," Tabira murmured.

Gemekala threw up her arms. "They have caused us no such—"

"I'm not referring to conventional, tangible destruction. In the cycles since you departed, we've learned that space-time is complex. It branches like a tree into a grand multiverse. The moment the future hominins' ship arrived, it sent our timeline off in a new direction. They should not be here. Everything is forever changed, and there is no way to change it back. This is why the Protectorate outlawed time traversal."

Turning her head, Gemekala stared at Maya for a moment.

Maya lowered her head in guilt. She couldn't deny the truth of Kizzura's words.

"Whether or not the future hominins intended us any harm is irrelevant." Kizzura ceased his pacing. "If they damaged the multiverse in ignorance, their irresponsibility with such potent technology is an even graver threat than if they knew what they were doing. This is bigger than a clash between races. We must eliminate them to minimize the damage throughout all universes, not just our own."

After allowing Umi to refill her goblet, Gemekala lifted it and took her time taking a sip. "So you would have us still our workers to ensure they never become so irresponsible," she said, setting the cup down. "But our civilization cannot function without that labor force."

"You no longer need them now that we are here. We have brought with us the ability to manufacture machines that perform all menial tasks. Machines require less maintenance and pose fewer ethical dilemmas."

Enki spoke up. "And what of the ethics of stilling a race of sentient beings that we now know is capable of rising to our level?"

Through the haze behind his face shield, Kizzura glowered at the geneticist, but didn't answer.

"I once believed the hominins to be nothing more than machines, but I've since amended that belief. I can no longer sanction their stilling," Gemekala said. "The more pragmatic consideration is the feasibility of your suggestion. Our labor force has no ability to defy us, but the future hominins will fight back. You've scanned their ship. Are you confident enough in your superiority to guarantee success against them?"

Shifting in his stance, Kizzura hesitated before responding. "For the good of the timelines, we must try."

"I'll interpret that as a negative response." Gemekala rose. "No. I shall not sanction war when we've just established peace."

"You have no authority to sanction anything."

"Don't I?" The Grand Dignitary stepped toward Kizzura. "I know you loathe Pragmatics, but here are two inescapable deductions, born of my discipline. One, while you no doubt wield the superior arsenal, the

Namtilla has its antimatter bomb targeted on this very location, ready to deploy on my command. Do you think you could stop it before it detonates and destroys all life on this world? How favorable will the Protectorate find your destruction of a colony of fellows along with an entire ecosystem, I wonder?"

She gave a subtle shrug. "Two, the damage is already done, and you can always revert to fighting if peace fails. Why not work together to learn the extent of the damage and how we might repair it?"

"We never intended to cause any harm. Nor do we want a fight." Pain stabbed Maya's lungs with each breath. Fortunately, her wristband spoke for her. "I admit that we don't understand all the nuances of time travel, but we're willing to work with you to learn."

"Captain Kizzura is right," Biluda said. "You should be destroyed."

Kizzura hesitated, frozen in thought. "I detest your pragmatism, Grand Dignitary," Kizzura said at last. "But I do not wish harm to come to you or my crew. I shall contact the Protectorate for further instructions. The round-trip communication will require several cycles. We shall use that time to better understand one another's positions."

The throbbing in Maya's body was beginning to subside. "Thank you, Captain."

"'Thank you?'" he repeated the words.

"Yes, in my culture, we express what's known as gratitude to . . ." Maya let her words trail off at the sight of Umi refilling Gemekala's cup. The act was barely worth noting except for his body language. As he poured from a flask, he slid one foot closer to her. With his other hand, he collected a two-pronged fork from the tray. His heavy breathing, trembling arm, and shifting eyes didn't give the impression of someone who was simply collecting a piece of dirty silverware.

Maya opened her mouth to shout a warning.

Umi dropped the flask, pivoted, and swung the fork in one fluid motion, driving it into the side of Gemekala's neck.

Twenty-three—Aggress
East Africa, October 200,423 BCE

Blood gushed from Gemekala's neck. As she clutched her punctured throat, the thick red seepage drenched her face, hands, and chest.

Adrenaline surged through Maya's body. Forgetting about her discomfort, she shot to her feet.

Umi backed away from Gemekala toward one of the assembly hall's rear exits. His wavering eyes and open mouth betrayed his shock.

Gemekala's knees wobbled, and she lost her balance. With her eyes rolling back in her head, her arms went limp, and she keeled over. Enki caught her.

Laying her down on the floor, Enki pressed one palm to her neck, applying pressure to the wound. With the other hand, he pulled off his sash and wrapped it around her throat.

"Let me help," Maya pleaded, reaching for the medite injector on her belt.

As she stepped toward them, the two mechs guarding her blocked her path.

In her i-cite, Maya pulled up the interfaces for her wave gun and bioshield. She rested one hand on her hip holster, hoping she wouldn't need to use it.

The faction leaders and nobles stared in horror at the dying Grand

Dignitary and the proto-human who had stabbed her.

"Get her to the lab," Enki ordered the nearest protectors. "Now!"

Four protectors rushed to Gemekala, hoisted her up, and rushed her out of the hall. Enki hurried after them.

Umi's shock faded. He narrowed his eyes and scowled. "Now, we are free!" he shouted.

Why is he doing this? Maya wondered.

Pivoting on the balls of his feet, Umi sprinted away.

Kizzura glared at him but did nothing more that Maya could discern. The mechs shifted in their stances but held their fire. If they were to discharge their weapons, the faction leaders, nobility, and protectors would be caught in the crossfire.

"Stop!" Biluda commanded.

Umi stumbled to a halt under Biluda's control.

Through a series of jerks, Umi turned around. His body twitched and trembled.

To the pair of protectors closest to Umi, Biluda ordered, "Still him."

The protectors aimed their spear-rifles at Umi.

A pair of servant boys who had been pretending to be frozen in terror dropped the act and jumped the protectors from behind. Before the two Onaki could get off a shot, the boys slit the protectors' throats with kitchen knives.

The boys then whipped their knives at Biluda. Diving to the floor, Biluda buried his head under his arms before he could exert his control over them.

Maya took a step back behind the mechs guarding her and activated her bioshield.

Unfazed, Kizzura continued to observe the scene.

The remaining protectors covered the Onaki nobility and faction leaders as they retreated out of the hall.

Kizzura raised his manipulator arm.

The mechs guarding Maya left her and stomped toward the boys. Rotating, the cannons affixed to their shoulders aimed and unloaded. Heavy particle blasts tore through the corpses and shredded the boys beyond recognition.

Before Umi reached the exit, the mechs directed their cannons at him. The searing blasts tore him to pieces.

As quickly as the carnage had begun, a deathly silence fell over the assembly hall. Proto-human corpses littered the blood-stained floor. A trail of crimson ran from where Gemekala had collapsed all the way out the main entrance. The power down cycles of the mech's particle weapons whined in the background.

Maya covered her mouth in shock.

As the feeling passed, she pondered how slaves had learned such fighting techniques. The assassination attempt had been calculated. The assassins had expected to survive, and they would have gotten away had the more advanced Onaki not intervened.

Someone—a modern human—must have trained them.

Biluda pointed a finger in Maya's direction. "This is your doing," he yelled.

Breaking into a cold sweat, Maya feared for her life. "It wasn't." The voice emitted by her wristband rose in volume, filled with her fright and anger.

Blowing out a breath to steady herself, she still hoped for a peaceful solution. But she could feel the goodwill she had worked to establish for the last two months slipping away. "Let me help. I might be able to save your leader if—"

"Our workers cannot fathom such acts," Biluda said. "The only explanation is that you brainwashed them to attack us."

Brainwashed? Maya wanted to say. *You're the ones who use mind-control!* Instead, she said, "Think about it. Why would I kill my biggest supporter?"

"That was your plan all along."

Soreness from the mechs almost ripping her in two returned to Maya's neck and chest. "If I wanted to assassinate someone, I would've had it done when I wasn't present."

"So you admit it."

"No. . . ." Apparently, the wristband hadn't done a very good job of conveying her meaning. "I didn't try to kill her. Nor did any member of my crew." But she knew she couldn't be sure of her last statement.

"You were right," Biluda said to Kizzura. "We should still the hominins before it's too late."

"I had hoped the Grand Dignitary's wisdom surpassed my own." Kizzura sighed. "But seeing firsthand what your biolaborers are capable of, I must agree."

"Contact the scout crafts," Biluda ordered Tabira. "Release the viral agent."

Tabira blinked. "Are you certain?"

"Do it now."

Maya's hope collapsed under the weight of finality. The last chance for peace had died with Biluda's command.

Whipping out her wave gun, Maya pointed it at Tabira. "Don't relay that order." She backpedaled and slipped partway behind the nearest statue.

The mechs aimed their weapons at her. Maya flinched, but they didn't fire. Were they worried she might kill Biluda, Tabira, or Kizzura before they could mow her down? Their scans had likely shown them her wave gun's capabilities. Maya thanked the stars for their restraint.

With the teletone trembling in his hand, Tabira darted his gaze between Biluda, Kizzura, and Maya.

Maya tightened her grip on the handle of her gun. Her heart beat like a particle rifle on auto fire. "You don't want to commit genocide. I don't want to hurt any of you. We're better than that."

"Genocide," Biluda scoffed as he stiffened his posture. "We're deactivating malfunctioning tools."

"You can't possibly believe that."

"If there's even the slightest chance you hominins pose a threat to us," Kizzura said, "we must take action to protect ourselves." He stomped closer to Tabira. "Release your virus." To his mechs, Kizzura commanded, "Kill the creature."

Maya fired a force pulse at Tabira and pulled back behind the statue.

The concentrated gust of air knocked the teletone out of Tabira's hand. As the pressure burst sent Tabira flying backwards, it also spun Kizzura off balance.

Taking aim, the mechs bombarded the statue with particle blasts. Shards of stone scattered everywhere. Dust billowed throughout the hall.

Maya yelped as a beam struck her boot, which she hadn't pulled far enough behind her cover. Her shield pixelated and absorbed the blast, preventing the energy from vaporizing her foot. But the force of the impact still felt like someone had hammered a nail into her shin.

Clenching her teeth in pain, Maya pressed her back against the statue. Sweat ran down her brow onto her cheek; her chest heaved.

Thanks to the *Eleppu's* hypofield, Maya's enhanced vision showed her nothing. She switched to conventional infrared, which allowed her to track the thermal smudges of the mechs.

The mechs ceased their attack and formed a perimeter around her, repositioning for the kill.

Tabira picked up the teletone and shouted into it. Maya didn't need to heighten her hearing to know he had given the order to release the virus.

"I suggest we relocate to a safer location," Kizzura said to Biluda and Tabira. "The two of you have no weapons or protective gear. Let my infantry deal with the creature."

As the three Onaki leaders exited the hall, Maya cursed her show of mercy. She could've bought the proto-humans more time if she had shot to kill Tabira. She should've at least blown his hand away along with his teletone. Instead, her compassion had allowed him to hop right back up and condemn her race to extinction.

The lives and the future of every human being were now in jeopardy. As much as the thought sickened her, Maya resolved not to make the same benevolent mistake again.

Raising the volume on her wristband to a booming megaphone, she yelled, "Stand down and back away from me. This is your last warning."

The mechs responded by resuming fire. Their particle blasts whittled away at the statue, reducing a once-proud figure of an Onaki astronaut to something that resembled a stone apple core.

Left with no other choice, Maya set her wave gun to molecular destabilization mode. Quickly sticking the muzzle of her weapon out around what remained of the statue, she targeted the metals and composites of her attackers' exoskeletons.

Maya pulled the trigger. Then she yanked the gun back before the mechs blasted it.

The mechs' weapons clicked and buzzed and ceased emitting their pulses. Grinding noises came next.

As the gears, joints, and structures of their suits lost cohesion, their lower limbs fell apart. Screws and other parts loosened and fell clanging to the floor.

Dropping to their knees, the mechs keeled over. Their bubble canopies cracked, crumbled, and shattered. Screeches of panic followed.

Maya peeked around the remnants of the statue.

The soldiers flailed about on the stone floor as their mechs disintegrated. Until now Maya had never seen a true-form Onaki up close. The male closest to her—he struck her as a male, but she didn't know for sure—stretched his neck out. He opened his beak as wide as possible, gasping in vain for breath in the toxic atmosphere. The eyes on either side of his head rolled back as he beat his wings against the floor. Every scale-feather on his body stood on end.

One by one, the soldiers ceased their struggles and stilled amid piles of metal ash.

Stepping out from cover, Maya stared at the corpses. The foul stench of death triggered her gag reflex, and she grew dizzy. The fact she had killed in self-defense did little to quell her guilt.

"It didn't have to be this way," she whispered as the last survivor's head went limp.

Maya jogged toward the assembly hall's front entrance, headed for Enki's lab. The only person who could still prevent an all-out conflict was Gemekala. If she died, so too would the last hope for peace.

Maya's enhanced hearing caught approaching footfalls beyond the front entrance. The pounding clangs grew louder as they neared the hall.

Skidding to a halt, Maya spun around and fled through one of the hall's rear exits.

◆

Strange, shimmering circles opened everywhere in the square. Mechanical beast after mechanical beast poured out of the openings. Some fanned out through the city to engage the teams of Omo's fellows attacking the masters. Others charged into the ziggurat through its front entrance.

Outside of a building, Omo crept up behind a protector. A fellow worker—a woman—had wrestled the protector's spear-rifle away from him. The protector had exerted his control over her and was forcing her to direct the weapon at her own chest.

Grabbing the protector's head, Omo snapped his neck as the Teacher had taught him to do.

Released from control, Omo's fellow worker dropped the spear-rifle. She fell to her knees, panting.

As the protector's limp body thudded to the ground, Omo reviewed The Teacher's plan in his head. It had worked well so far.

His fellows had begun the revolt outside at the same time as the stilling of the head master. Workers everywhere had faked injuries to keep the masters busy. Each time a master tried to control a fellow, other fellows had jumped him.

Thousands of Omo's fellows had stormed out of the community residences and abandoned their tasks to attack the masters. The masters had stopped some of the fellows by using their ability to control them. But for every fellow that fell under the masters' spell, ten more fellows charged and overwhelmed them.

The Teacher's plan was going better than Omo had thought it would—until the stomping and flying beasts arrived.

The masters' flying metal monsters whirred past overhead. Some rained fire down on the city, destroying buildings and dismembering many of the fellows. Other flyers showered the city with a mist that had no odor and felt cool on Omo's skin.

The metal beasts stampeded through the streets, delivering death with bolts of lightning. Fellow after fellow dropped as the deathly light tore through them.

As Omo rushed for cover, his eyes began to sting, and his throat constricted. His muscles grew weak, and he went from sprinting to stumbling. He could see his fellows coughing and collapsing on all sides.

Unable to think straight, he fell to the ground and passed out.

Twenty-four—Provenance
East Africa, October 200,423 BCE

A messenger boy rushed into the cave.

Brooke stood up from her seat atop a rock. "It's begun?" she asked.

Chest heaving, the boy nodded, then bent over to rest.

Feelings of fear and trepidation almost overwhelmed Brooke.

From her spies inside the ziggurat, Brooke had learned that the Grand Dignitary had agreed to a truce with Maya. But before Eve had gone offline, the android had insisted any such friendship would doom the human race in the long run.

This had led Brooke to set in motion the insurrection for which she had spent the better part of two months recruiting, training, and strategizing. She had instructed Gemekala's attendant, Umi, to kill Gemekala in order to guarantee a war, even though the act might place Maya in danger.

If the Onaki threatened her niece, Brooke had figured Young would teleport her to safety. But the more advanced Onaki ship had shown up and erected a hypofield, throwing the proverbial wrench into that plan. With all neutrino signals blocked and wormholes suppressed, *Yesterday* couldn't shift or port anyone. Eve's collaborators aboard ship had no way of sending any more intel, and Brooke couldn't comm Maya.

According to the boy messenger, revolts had broken out in the streets, signaling that the servants had gone through with the assassination. But Brooke had yet to receive word whether Umi had succeeded, or whether her niece was okay.

"The masters have spread their poison," the boy said.

Brooke gave him a tight-lipped nod.

As the boy bolted out of the cavern, Brooke balled a fist. The time for hiding had passed. The rebelling proto-humans needed air support before the Onaki wiped them out, and someone had to rescue Maya.

Pain caused the muscles in Brooke's back to tense. Her left arm went numb. The sparks were no longer suppressing all her symptoms. She shook off the discomfort.

Enabling her night vision, she rushed deeper into the caves to attend to one final matter before joining the fight. After navigating through a maze of tunnels, Brooke came to a familiar dead-end.

Eve sat hunched over against the cavern wall, looking like a mannequin salvaged from a house fire. Parts of her missing fingers, skin, and hair had regrown.

As Brooke approached, the artificial woman opened her eyes and looked at her.

"I was beginning to think you'd dropped dead," Eve said. Her voice sounded synthesized, like the robots in old sims.

"It's started," Brooke said. "I need to go."

"Be a dear and grab me a chocolate bar before you leave."

Brooke folded her arms. "You still can't think about anything but food?"

"My nanites need the energy to make repairs."

"That so?" Brooke knelt and dug around in a duffel bag Eve's agents had teleported down from *Yesterday* before the hypofield had gone up. "And here I thought you were feeding a bad habit." Locating a Callisto Crunch Bar, Brooke removed the wrapper and handed the bar to Eve.

The android accepted the chocolate bar with mechanical jerkiness, a byproduct of disabling her fine motor control to conserve power during the repair process.

Bringing the bar to her mouth, Eve gnawed off a large chunk with the gracefulness of a cow. "You're one to talk about bad habits," she said between chomps. "Speaking of which . . ." She looked down at the duffel bag. "You don't have many left."

Brooke reached into the bag, pulled out the case of spark injectors, and opened it with a heavy sigh. Only three injectors remained. She had reached the point where she required the full contents of an injector each day. When the last one ran out. . . .

"I'm going to miss you," Eve said.

Slamming the case closed, Brooke scowled. "I can't say the same. But let's not say goodbye just yet. I'll be back for you."

"No, you won't."

Brooke shot to her feet. "I'm not going to die before—"

"Shut up for a second. I'm not talking about your life expectancy. What I meant was that I don't plan to be here when you get back."

"What? Where would you go?"

"On a quaint little sightseeing hike to the mainland."

"Why?"

"You know why."

Tensing in anger at the android's continued evasiveness, Brooke nevertheless could guess why. Everything was starting to make sense.

"Someone has to found the Vril," Brooke said.

Eve nodded. "I've got a nice, quiet spot picked out where I can dream undisturbed for the better part of 200,000 years." She shrugged. "But I'm not the founder. That distinction belongs to another."

"And who might that be? An Egyptian pharaoh? Oh, wait. I know. Julius Caesar."

"Oh, no." Eve tried to wink. Malfunctioning, her eyelid slid halfway down, lifted a quarter of the way up, and repeated the motion several times before finally opening. "The founder is the person who set things in motion at the furthest point in the past. She's the one who taught the first humans how to use subtle deception to affect change—at least, that's the way I see it."

Brooke blinked in disbelief.

At first, her mind went numb. Then her arms went limp and dangled at her sides. Like the solid rock all around her, she existed in a lifeless and unmoving state, too shocked to think, feel, or even breathe.

Coughing up a single laugh, Brooke dropped to her knees. She fell back onto her hind legs and toppled over onto the cold, dirt-covered ground.

She pressed her palms to her forehead. The laughter rumbled up out of her chest and burst from her mouth in an uncontrollable cackle. The sound echoed off the walls and throughout the tunnel like the cries of a mad witch. Tears streamed from her eyes as she roared so loudly and harshly that her chest ached.

When Brooke calmed down at last, Eve said, "It took you long enough to realize it."

"That's why you've let me live all these years," Brooke said, panting and wheezing.

"It's why I recruited you after the incident on Europa, made sure you flew the first FTL craft, and refrained from inflicting any fatal wounds on the interstellar probe."

"All my life, I've fought to stop the very organization I've now helped to create."

"Tis a wee bit ironic."

"A bit." Brooke chortled, stressing her sore throat. "And Maya . . ."

"She has an even bigger role to play. If you're the teacher and founder, she is the child, the mother, and Death itself."

Sitting up, Brooke asked, "What—" She cut herself off, knowing she wouldn't get a straight answer.

Thoughts of Maya propelled her to her feet. "I'm wasting time. I'm going."

Eve nodded. "Goodbye, Brooke Davis."

Brooke had a thank you on the tip of her tongue—as incredible as that seemed— but the android spoke first. "Let's not ruin our last moment together by starting to like one another."

With the hint of a smile, Brooke said, "It'd be too bad if you rusted and never woke up again. After all, 200,000 years is a long time."

"I'll make sure my tomb is vacuum sealed, if only to spite you."

After exchanging one last knowing stare with Eve, Brooke sprinted out of the cave and toward her Hyperflare.

♦

As two protectors hoisted Gemekala's limp body up onto one of his lab tables, Enki fumbled for a tube of coagulant in a cabinet. He knocked vials, bottles, and containers to the floor as he searched.

Enki stole a brief moment to wish for Asha's presence, but he hadn't seen her in days. Had she joined the revolt?

Prying the cap off the tube with his shaking fingers, Enki applied the gel to the gashes in Gemekala's neck. The gel hardened and sealed her cuts in seconds, but by now she had lost so much blood that the bleeding had slowed to a trickle.

Gemekala's eyes were locked wide open, and she had stopped breathing. She needed a transfusion. Enki could do a transfer from the one of the protectors, or from himself, but by the time he set it up, it would be too late, if it wasn't already.

Resting his palms on the table, Enki hung his head. He could splice DNA to create whole new beings, but his ability to heal paled by comparison.

Gemekala hadn't deserved to die in such a manner. Perhaps Enki should've ordered the protectors to take her to the hospital across the square, but it would've taken them minutes to transport her there, precious minutes that could've cost Gemekala her life. And in his selfishness and arrogance, he had wanted to be the one to attend to her.

He had gained the medical expertise from his work birthing and healing the hominins. He had assumed the physicians wouldn't have been able to do anything more for her than he could. Had he been wrong?

One of the protectors guarding the entrance to the lab shouted for someone to halt.

Turning around, Enki found the hominin from the future, Maya, standing outside the doorway. She gripped her small but powerful gun in both hands and pointed it at the protectors.

"Lower your weapons," her bracelet said in near-perfect Okkadian. "I'm here to help, not hurt anyone."

"You lower yours," one of the protectors demanded.

The protectors glanced back at Enki.

He considered Maya's words and what had happened in the assembly hall. She had been in the ziggurat for weeks, so she couldn't have organized a revolt or trained Umi to kill Gemekala. Then again, Maya had remained in contact with her fellows throughout her captivity. She could have instructed them to commit these heinous crimes. But what would that have gained her? With her superior technology, she could have overpowered his people long before the ship from his homes had arrived.

Most importantly, if she could do anything to save Gemekala, he had to let her try.

"Allow her to enter," Enki said.

After hesitating briefly, the protectors lowered their rifles.

Holstering her gun at her hip, Maya rushed over to Gemekala. Maya pulled a thin cylindrical device—a needleless syringe, he realized—from a compartment on her belt and glanced at him, seeking approval.

Enki nodded.

Maya pressed the device to Gemekala's neck. Within seconds, the hardened globs of coagulant peeled away, revealing cuts in the process of closing.

Pulling out a scanning device, Maya ran it over the Grand Dignitary's body. Maya's eyes shifted back and forth as if studying unseen displays.

"The medites are healing her wounds," Maya said, "but she's lost too much blood. They're producing some but nowhere near enough." She lowered the scanner and bit her lip, a trait he had seen her exhibit a number of times. "We might be able to save her if we can get her to my ship, but we can't teleport with the hypofield up."

"Hypofield?"

"The *Eleppu* is producing gravimetric distortions that prevent wormhole formation. My ship has the ability to transfer people from one place to another in a matter of seconds—just as Kizzura stepped off his ship into the city square. They can teleport in the presence of their hypofield, but we can't." She frowned. "By the time we got her aboard my ship through more conventional means, it would be too late. I'm sorry." She dragged her fingers over Gemekala's eyes, closing them.

The slow, careful way she did this struck Enki as a show of respect. Enki averted his gaze, holding back the tears he couldn't have produced before assuming his new form. "This isn't your fault. It's mine. If only I had been strong enough to hold to my ethics. I created a race of thinking beings. Had I insisted they not be treated like mindless machines—had I refused to create them—this wouldn't have happened."

He flinched when Maya placed a hand on his shoulder.

"Things seem grim now," she said, "but you gave birth to a great people and civilization. We're far from perfect, but wondrous nonetheless. If you could only see the future—my present—it might offer you some consolation."

Lifting his chin but not his eyes, Enki said, "Grand Tila said this would happen, but no one listened."

Maya turned to face one of the walls, staring at it as if she could see through it. "My infrared shows Kizzura's forces headed this way. I have to go. Come with me. Maybe together we can stop this madness."

Her words tempted him. Enki ached to atone for his past actions. But he shook his head. "I regret how events have unfolded." He stared down at the lifeless body of his fellow. "But we are enemies now. No matter how wrong my people might be, I will not betray them."

"Not even to stop them from committing genocide?"

"As you would say, I'm sorry."

Maya swallowed and nodded. After taking one last look at him, she bolted out of the lab.

Enki collapsed into a chair and buried his head in his hands.

♦

With Kizzura and Tabira close behind him, Biluda exited the ziggurat to the sight of glorious victory. Throughout the city square and down every side street, hominins lay unmoving on the ground. Protectors and mechs stepped over the incapacitated workers.

A protector approached him. "Advocate Biluda, most of the laborers are unconscious. Those present within the residences are falling at a slower rate, but the virus is seeping inside the buildings. I've posted officers at all entrances to ensure they remain trapped. It shouldn't be long until they are all still."

"That is excellent news on an otherwise hot and uncomfortable day." Biluda looked at Tabira. "Our quick actions have averted a tragedy."

The stocky engineer remained tight-lipped.

"I know you sympathize with them," Biluda said, "but take solace in the fact that this was necessary for our self-preservation. Once we've dealt with the future hominins, we shall begin anew, without making the same mistakes."

"We shall provide you with the machines to replace your bio-laborers," Kizzura said. "This shan't happen again. As for the future beings, their ship has moved into orbit on the far side of the planet."

"They've decided to show their true intentions."

"I must return to the *Eleppu* and determine how best to deal with them." Speaking into a tiny teletone in his suit's bubble canopy, Kizzura ordered his ship to open a portal. "Their captain has killed eight of my officers, and her fellows will come for her. It isn't safe here. You and the other leaders may accompany me if you wish."

Ever the engineer, Tabira perked up. "I would enjoy witnessing the wonders our people have achieved."

Kizzura stood erect and puffed out the chest of his suit. "We have come a long way. The *Eleppu* is the pride of the fleet, the most advanced—"

Screams echoed from one of the side streets, interrupting Kizzura's boast. Biluda recognized the voices as those of protectors.

The pulsating pings of the mechanized suit cannons rang out next, followed by the gurgling screeches of protectors dying—and, as incredulous as it seemed, the chants of hominins.

In horror, Biluda watched as laborers all around him leapt to their feet, assaulting protectors and mechs.

The maniacal hominins snapped the necks of the protectors. Somehow, the inferior beings knew to yank out the mechs' breathing tubes, leaving the occupants gasping for life.

How had the hominins regained consciousness? Had the virus not had the intended effect? Was Enki incompetent, or had he turned on his fellows? The geneticist had always favored his creations, Biluda seethed. The betrayal might spell the end of Onaki civilization.

Turning his head, Biluda saw Tabira following Kizzura into a portal.

Biluda took a hurried step toward the strange doorway. Two hominins jumped in front of him, blocking his path.

Summoning his resolve, Biluda reached into their minds and forced them to start choking one another.

Footsteps pounded toward him from behind.

Biluda spun around. His eyes widened in terror at the sight of Omo, the disobedient hominin who had escaped execution.

Lunging forward, Omo drove the point of a spear-rifle through Biluda's eye socket.

Twenty-five—Exfiltration
East Africa, October 200,423 BCE

A squad commander of the Factionary Protectorate Mechanized Infantry crept through a hall on the second level of the ziggurat. Her support fellow trailed her, watching her back. Together, the two mechs approached the vile hominin from the future with great caution.

Displays embedded within the bubble canopy of the commander's mech revealed a red and orange smudge around the corner. The shape of a hominin leaned against the wall, gripping her wounded abdomen, a result of her encounters with other infantry. The hominin's biosigns fluctuated.

The commander lifted her beak, eager to finish off the creature that had killed more of her fellows than she cared to count.

She rounded the corner and bombarded the spot where the hominin stood with particle blasts.

Her blasts passed through the subject and tore apart the wall.

As her enemy pixelated and disappeared, the commander ceased fire.

Her subordinate's mech came and stood beside her.

Cocking her head in confusion, the commander stared down at a handheld scanner on the floor. Her mech's sensors revealed that the device had been configured to project a holographic projection with false life sign readings.

The commander gasped and spun around. Down the hall, the hominin stood with a gun pointed at her.

Her particle emitters failed to discharge. Warning symbols flashed, indicating malfunctions in all of her mech's systems.

Cushioning gel seeped out from the millions of tiny cracks forming in her suit. As the suit crumbled all around her, she fell and thudded against the stone floor, at which point the full gravity of this wretched planet began crushing her. Her skeleton squeezed in on her internal organs, piercing them.

The commander screeched in pain. Next to her, her support fellow writhed on the floor, suffering the same fate.

Her bubble canopy shattered, allowing precious air to escape. The commander gulped down lungful after lungful of the toxic atmosphere and coughed up blood. She used her final breath to curse at her executioner.

◆

Frowning, Maya stepped over her two latest victims. Each Onaki she killed pushed her further and further away from the possibility of peace, and from her ideals. She kept telling herself that it was them or her, but the justification did little to relieve her guilt.

Maya ascended the stairs to the third level of the ziggurat. She would have preferred to descend to ground level, but mechs and protectors had blocked all the exits. They continued to scour the interior for her, giving her nowhere to go but up.

Gripping her gun, she neared the top of the stairs. Sunlight shone down from the unfinished third level, which by default served as the roof until construction began on level four.

Maya still couldn't comm *Yesterday* because of the *Eleppu's* hypofield. Without neudar, she had no idea who or what waited for her on level three. Infrared showed the roof as one big red smudge, thanks to the scorching midday sun. With any luck, she would find the level unoccupied. She planned to head to the nearest balcony or window, descend to the ground using her wave gun, flee the city, and head for the scout team's landing spot.

The glare of the sun forced Maya to squint as she stepped out onto the roof. Stone support columns jutted up every few meters. Half-finished sections of wall gave the level the look of a maze. Swinging her gun back and forth, she traversed one corridor, then another. She didn't see anyone, but there were an awful lot of places to hide.

A particle blast rang out from the hallway that Maya had just exited. The blast struck her shield in the back, driving her forward. Shrieking from the pain, she tripped, arms flailing in a futile effort to regain her balance. Her wave gun flew out of her hand.

Maya bashed her head into the pillar in front of her. The impact drilled shooting pain into her skull and down her spine. Then everything went dark.

She came to three seconds later according to the timer in her i-cite. Blood slicked her fingers when she ran them over her forehead.

In spite of her throbbing headache, Maya pushed to her feet and searched for her wave gun. It lay on the floor a couple of meters away.

As she picked it up, two mechs stomped into view and swung their cannons toward her.

A third and fourth mech jumped out from behind an unfinished wall on the other side of her and took aim.

Maya pointed her gun at the ground. Firing a force pulse, she catapulted herself into the air.

The mechs blasted away at her. She fired a sideways pulse that pushed her clear of their initial salvos.

Two of the four mechs activated their thrusters and launched after her. Maya flew over the nearest wall and plummeted.

After releasing a pulse to cushion her fall, she set her gun to particle beam mode and got off three shots before her back slammed against the rooftop. Her bioshield spared her from scrapes, but the force of impact knocked the wind out of her.

As Maya tumbled, her head banged against the floor on each roll. Once again she lost her grip on her gun.

The sound of particle blasts grated on her eardrums as she skidded to a stop. Somehow, amid a throbbing concussion, she lifted her chin to see both airborne mechs come crashing back down to the roof.

Her implants released medites into her system, numbing some of the pain and clearing her head and vision.

Maya searched for her gun. Locating it on the floor a few meters away, she hobbled to her feet, limped over, and grabbed it.

Warning icons flashed in her i-cite. An error message stated the containment field storing the antimatter within the gun was failing. She had dropped it one too many times. The gun had entered its emergency disarmament mode. It was directing its remaining force field energy to dilute and dissipate the antimatter supply to prevent a significant quantity from reacting with normal matter at any one time. In other words, the gun was busted, so she holstered it.

Maya stumbled around a corner and through a series of unfinished rooms. Stepping through a couple of half-completed walls, she reached a large room at another corner of the level. Support pillars jutted up all around.

Rushing to a stone railing along the side of the room, Maya gazed out over the city. She gasped in both terror and relief; the gasp caused her to hiss in pain. Proto-human and Onaki corpses littered the square and streets, but hundreds of her ancestors still battled against their masters. She didn't know how the workers had survived the virus, but she thanked the stars for it. Groups of proto-humans roamed the streets unopposed, searching for targets, a sign they were winning the fight.

But it looked as if the tide was about to turn against them. Scout craft soared over the city and bombed the streets. Portals opened everywhere, disgorging mechs that blasted humans armed with—at best—the spear-rifles of fallen protectors.

Maya stared down at the dirt two levels below and cursed. If her wave gun still worked, she could've hopped down and achieved a slow, graceful landing with ease. But the height of one level of the ziggurat equaled seven or eight stories of a modern habitat. She didn't like her chances of surviving an unassisted fall.

Mechanical footsteps clanged against stone behind her. Whirling around, Maya saw six mechs approaching her position. She dove behind the nearest support pillar.

A pair of particle blasts struck her abdomen and leg before she landed all the way behind the pillar. The shield impacts felt like someone had struck her with a metal pole. Spinning sideways from the strikes, she hit the floor hard.

She curled up in a ball behind the pillar and rested her back against it. Particle blasts chipped away at the pillar, whittling it down.

Maya pulled her gun back out of the holster. In her i-cite, she checked the remaining antimatter supply. The gun still had more than enough juice to vaporize the approaching mechs, plus a good chunk of the ziggurat—and her along with them, unfortunately.

As she issued the overload command, she stressed over how she had failed in her mission. Not only had she allowed a war to break out pitting her crew and her ancestors against their creators, but she hadn't come close to accomplishing *Yesterday's* original mission. The origin of the metatoy and the reason it had ended up in the past still remained a mystery.

Maya hoped that her crew would survive and persevere without her.

Chest heavy with regret, she banged the back of her head against the pillar and stared up at the sky. Two manta ray craft hovered above, having swooped in to provide air support. The only reason they hadn't blasted her was to avoid collateral damage to the mechs.

Maya clamped her eyelids shut, sucked in a deep breath, and issued the mental command to—

Both aircraft overhead exploded. As shrapnel rained down, Maya lay onto her stomach and covered her head. A faint rumbling grew into the deafening roar of rocket engines.

♦

Brooke maneuvered her Hyperflare above the unfinished upper level of the tower and descended over Maya. By angling the craft's nose downward, Brooke shielded her niece.

The mechs backpedaled as they blasted away at Brooke's fighter. Their low-yield particle beams pinged against its force field, inflicting negligible damage.

Scrunching her nose, Brooke unloaded the plasma cannons. The superheated beams vaporized every mech while pulverizing pillars and walls. Bits of stone, metal, and limbs—both mechanical and otherwise—ricocheted off the Hyperflare's force field as it protected Maya.

As the dust was settling, Brooke landed the Hyperflare on the roof and popped open the canopy.

Maya pushed to her feet. With a sneeze that led her to wince in agony, she hobbled over to the fighter.

Reaching down, Brooke gripped Maya's hand and helped her into the cockpit.

Her niece sank into the backseat with a groan and stuffed her head into a helmet. The base of the headgear extended down around her neck and auto-sealed.

"Like old times," Brooke said, settling into the pilot's seat. As the canopy retracted and closed, gravgel rushed in to surround them. "How many times have I swooped in and rescued you in the nick of time? I've lost count."

Brooke lifted the Hyperflare off from the roof.

"Where have you been, Admiral?" Maya asked in a hard tone. "Why haven't you responded to any of my comms?"

"That new ship in orbit erected a hypofield, blocking all—"

"I mean before the field went up. You never went back to the ship. No one aboard has been able to locate or contact you, so what have you been doing?"

"Standing by in case you needed me—and from the looks of things, you're lucky I stuck around."

"I was about to blow myself up, so I owe you—again. I suspect you've been doing more than sitting around and waiting—not that you have to justify your actions to me, Admiral."

Brooke swallowed. "What're you implying?"

The rear camera views in her i-cite showed Maya leaning forward with a serious frown. "Please—please—tell me you didn't train the proto-humans to kill the Grand Dignitary."

So the plan was a success. Brooke targeted and destroyed two Onaki aircraft bombing the city. Seeing the bandits explode failed to give her the usual rush.

Her breathing quickened as she squeezed the auxiliary control grips. Little by little, lying to her niece was gnawing away at her. But Brooke couldn't yet bring herself to divulge her many hidden truths.

Brooke targeted a quartet of mechs attacking proto-humans on a street. Launching precision strikes with low-yield seekers, she blew each one away with minimal collateral damage.

Her readouts showed the remaining manta ray craft fleeing the city. No more advanced than twenty-first century fighter jets, they stood no chance against a Hyperflare.

Maya leaned back with a scowl that put the best of her aunt's expressions to shame. "You did it, didn't you? Somehow, you organized and trained them to assassinate the Grand Dignitary." She cupped her helmet with both hands. "Gemekala was on our side. She had just freed me and convinced the other Onaki to enter into peace talks. Diplomacy was working, but now you've started a war."

Brooke's vision blurred. Her body weakened.

"Tell me the truth, Admiral," Maya shouted.

"I—"

<Incoming bogeys of unfamiliar design,> Brooke's remote sensing AI intruded upon her thoughts. *<Twenty-eight in total. One-thousand kilometers due east and closing. Present trajectory suggests the recently-arrived ship in orbit as their point of origin.>*

"We've got company," Brooke muttered, cursing the lack of neudar. She would've detected the bandits a lot sooner if the hypofield hadn't been limiting her fighter to more conventional sensing systems.

"Admiral," Maya said. "Brooke—"

Images of the bandits displayed in Brooke's augmented reality at high-magnification. Each craft resembled a high-tech boomerang, wider than Vril tri-fighters, lighter than Grey saucers, and flatter than anything she had ever flown.

Engaging the afterburners, Brooke launched her fighter higher up into the air. The g-force pinned Maya back in her seat and shoved her pleas down her throat.

Brooke needed to decide whether to fight or retreat, and quickly. Twenty-eight bandits presented a sizeable challenge. Each one had the armaments and maneuverability of a Pulsar, according to the tactical AI. Given her piloting skills and the more advanced Hyperflare, she might have the edge.

"We can't fight them all, Admiral." Maya strained to yell over the comm. "We need to head back to *Yesterday*."

"If we abandon the city," Brooke said, "the boomerangs will lay waste to it unopposed."

"Even if we engage them, some will ignore us and head to the city to finish off the proto-humans. That's what I would do. The 'flare also can't shift within the Onaki hypofield. If their fighters can, too, we'll be at a big disadvantage."

"I figured the same at first, but I don't think they can shift. If they could, they would've gone straight to the city, or to us. They'd have us surrounded, if not blanked, by now."

"You might be right. Opening comm wormholes and human-sized portals require less energy and precision than shifting a phase fighter. Still, I don't like twenty-eight-to-one odds."

"Neither do I, but—"

The tactical AI reported that the nearest boomerangs were moments away from entering weapons range.

I guess I'll compromise by blanking a few of them on my way out. Brooke loosed a spread of seekers. Hundreds of projectiles leapt from compartments all throughout the fuselage and corkscrewed toward the Onaki boomerangs.

Scattering, the bandits returned fire. Their warheads functioned like self-guided depth charges. The blinking charges darted about like mosquitos, hunting down her seekers and exploding them on impact. The resulting plasma shock waves vaporized most of the rest of the seekers.

The surviving seekers struck three boomerangs, overloading their force fields and blowing them apart. Twenty-five bogeys remained.

The remaining depth charges from the boomerangs' initial salvo shot after Brooke's Hyperflare. She blasted them with her plasma cannons, detonating all but a pair of them.

The last two charges exploded near her fighter. Brooke fired both retroburners and afterburners. Like a gyroscope, the Hyperflare spun away from the detonations.

Maya almost vomited in her helmet. The detonations rocked the fighter but inflicted only minimal damage to the force field. Brooke reoriented the Hyperflare and went after a pair of boomerangs.

"So far, it's looking like you were right," Maya noted, switching to neurocomm. "They're much slower than us."

Brooke bared her teeth. "Yes, they are."

The remote-sensing AI identified the boomerangs' fuselages as lighter and weaker than that of a Hyperflare. In all likelihood, the Onaki had designed their craft for primary operation in lower gravity, so they couldn't withstand higher gee maneuvers.

Unable to shake Brooke's pursuit or her plasma bursts, the two boomerangs ignited into fiery oblivion.

In spite of the gravgel pressing in on her body, Brooke felt a weight lifting. The Onaki fielded inferior fighters and pilots, at least in Earth's atmosphere.

Twenty-three out of the original twenty-eight bandits remained. That still left her outnumbered by a wide margin, but with each kill she gained confidence.

A charge detonated above the Hyperflare. The cockpit shuddered. Tinting to rust red, the force field almost failed.

<Additional enemy forces approaching from the east,> the sensing AI mind-spoke. *<One-hundred fifty-six in total. ETA is forty-two seconds.>*

"Damn it," Brooke growled.

"It's time to go," Maya said.

"I know, I know."

Brooke maneuvered her fighter west, but the original group of bandits detonated charges in her path, driving her back toward the oncoming reinforcements.

"They're trying to hold us until their friends arrive," Maya said.

Torching two boomerangs in her way, Brooke said, "I can see that."

Maxing the afterburners, she rocketed through an opening in their formation and ascended.

<Ten of the enemy spacecraft are altering course toward the city. The other one-hundred sixty seven are in pursuit.>

"Why are so many following us?" Maya asked. "If I were them, I'd focus my forces on subduing the city."

Brooke grunted. "I don't—"

<Incoming—>

Scowling, Brooke shouted, "More bandits?"

<Negative. Incoming friendly forces on a rendezvous trajectory.>

Brooke blinked. Sure enough, her mental readouts showed twenty-four Hyperflares headed in her direction.

A broken-up, static-laced message echoed throughout her helmet. "Adm . . . tain course."

"Sounds like Erik," Maya said. "He must be falling back on radio comm."

Brooke nodded. "We read you, Maxwell. I've retrieved the captain, and we're en route back to the ship."

"Roger," Lt. Commander Maxwell responded. "We'll take . . . from here."

A swarm of Hyperflares shot past the canopy on their way to engage the enemy.

The sky faded from deep blue to pitch black as Brooke ascended toward *Yesterday* in orbit over the western hemisphere.

♦

Knowing Admiral Davis had rescued Maya allowed Erik to focus all his attention on the aerial skirmish.

In the cockpit of his Hyperflare, Erik blew out a calming breath and prepared himself for battle. Every time he went into combat, he reminded himself that no amount of death or destruction would ever be as unnerving as seeing his mother chase his father with a kitchen knife.

Falling back on conventional dogfighting skills, Erik zigzagged his fighter. The series of acute maneuvers he pulled would've ripped apart an aerospace craft from any earlier era.

He dodged a group of charges and torched four boomerangs with well-placed plasma bolts and seeker volleys.

Leveraging a split-second lull in the fighting, he interfaced with his tactical AI to assess the situation—the neurotronic interface between the fighter and his brain allowed him to process information in milliseconds. Reacting during orbital hyper-combat wouldn't have been possible without it.

His forces had technological superiority, while the enemy outnumbered them by almost ten to one. Crunching the numbers, the AI indicated he had an even fight on his hands.

The boomerangs were splitting up into groups and spreading out. With calculated maneuvers and weapons fire, they attempted to split up pairs of wing mates and lure single Hyperflares toward each group. The enemy, he realized, hoped to leverage their numerical advantage and draw out the battle with these tactics.

Erik's sensing AI alerted him to ten boomerangs that were descending upon the city. He ordered two Hyperflares to intercept them.

Three more bandits unloaded everything they had in his direction.

Twenty-six—Perfidy
Earth Orbit, October 200,423 BCE

With the captain having summoned him to the *Eleppu's* nerve center, Tabira used the handrails to pull his weightless body through the wide cylindrical corridors.

Tabira had assumed hominin form and relocated to the planet's surface decades ago. Now, he struggled to maneuver within the microgravity aboard this advanced vessel. True-form Onaki soared past him through the passageways with effortless flaps of their wings. He had seen only a couple of novitiates and an elderly female using the rails.

Being back among his people comforted him. The few true-forms from the original expedition served as a skeleton crew aboard the *Namtilla*. Before the hominins had arrived from the future, the faction leaders had spoken of dissembling the starship and allowing the crew to settle on the surface.

As Tabira traversed the rails, he gawked at the technological wonders around him. Three-dimensional holographic projections floated everywhere. Complex worker machines of all shapes and sizes zoomed past him. One stopped to inspect him out of seeming curiosity.

At last, Tabira pulled himself into the nerve center. The assembly hall in the Grand Tower felt cramped by comparison. Above, below, and all around him, Onaki floated near holographic control stations. Such wonders had been only theoretical when his progenitors had departed Anurash and Arala.

A self-propelled perch floated over to Tabira. Using it as a springboard, he pushed off toward the core of the nerve center. There Captain Kizzura hovered with his eyes narrowed and beak tensed, surrounded by a number of his subordinates.

Everyone wore uniforms comprised of smooth and shiny artificial feathers. Jewelry and tattoos adorned their heads, necks, and wings.

Tabira reached the railing that floated around Kizzura and grabbed hold of it.

"Are your accommodations satisfactory?" Kizzura asked.

"More so than I could've dreamed," Tabira said. "The machines in my room cater to my every whim. Tell me, how do the culinary distributers fashion food and drink? Some sort of splicing and recombining of molecular patterns?"

"If you desire, you shall have the rest of your life to learn all that we have to teach. But at the moment, we have more pressing matters to discuss." Pulling his arm out from beneath his wing, Kizzura gestured at the mammoth holographic screen that wrapped all the way around the nerve center.

With his field of view limited by eyes that faced straight ahead, Tabira swung his head back and forth to see all that the screen showed.

Kizzura's boomerang-shaped craft clashed with the future hominins' bulkier fighters in the center of the display. Beams of multicolored light crisscrossed. Blinking lights darted to and fro, chasing after targets. Explosions big and small erupted.

Tabira didn't need to study the battle long to understand what was happening. "You're—or rather, we're—losing."

"Yes," Kizzura said. "Their pilots and fighter craft are better acclimated to the planet's atmosphere."

"That would add additional credence to this being their planet of origin."

"Despite our forces outnumbering them by ten to one, my tactical officers tell me the outlook is grim. Their fighters have also been able to keep ours away from the city."

Turning his head, Tabira studied the far left side of the screen, which showed a top-down view of Urusilim. The corpses of protectors, true-form Onaki, and hominins littered the square and streets. Only a handful of workers roamed about.

"Most of the remaining bio-laborers have retreated inside the buildings for cover," Kizzura said. "Many have fled into your grand tower. With my infantry and fighter wings severely depleted, the task of eliminating your hominins is becoming increasingly difficult."

"Surely all is not lost," Tabira said. "Given the many marvels I have seen on this ship, you must have a way of assuring a favorable outcome."

"Actually, I asked you here because you have a way to do that." Kizzura thrust his beak toward another area of the display that showed the *Namtilla* in geosynchronous orbit above the city. "To be precise, we must work together to achieve victory. The reinforcements I've summoned shall not arrive for some time." With a slight flap of his wings, he twisted to face Tabira. "Therefore, you must return to your ship and launch your antimatter bomb."

Giving a start that knocked him off balance, Tabira said, "That would not only wipe out the hominins but also devastate the planet's ecosystem. The Grand Dignitary considered it a last resort."

"I believe we have reached that point, as unpalatable as it may be to our sensibilities."

Tabira swallowed hard.

"If we do nothing," Kizzura said, "your bio-laborers will evolve to threaten our people." He pointed at another section of the screen, which showed the futures' strange vessel orbiting over the planet's opposite hemisphere. "They may have additional ships on the way. This is only one planet. The universe and our race shall persist without it."

"Surely your weapons are more powerful than ours," Tabira said. "Why don't you bombard the planet? Why involve the *Namtilla*?"

"We could, but. . . ."

Tabira studied the captain, noting his drooping wings and sunken chest. "You're unwilling to bear the responsibility for sterilizing an entire planet," Tabira said. "You want the act on our conscience, not yours."

Directing his beak away from his guest, Kizzura said, "Such a transgression would cause an outrage back homes. The public outcry might compel the Protectorate to recall all vessels, hindering the steady progress of recent cycles." He shook his head. "We could slip back into the conservative thinking of the Pragmatic era."

Kizzura straightened to his full stature. "Therefore, we shall be your shield as you launch the offensive."

♦

Leaning back in a chair in his lab, Enki stared up at the lines between the stone blocks in the ceiling. Even now, decades after changing form, the act of sitting felt strange. His people perched in gravity and floated in space. His true-form legs hadn't allowed him to sit; they didn't bend.

Since Maya had fled the lab, Enki hadn't budged from his seat. What purpose would moving have served? Where could he have gone? What reason did he have to live? The weight of dejection had crushed him like a stone block.

He shifted his stare to the cover pulled over Gemekala's corpse, which lay on a table. Given the fighting outside the lab, he couldn't have her body removed or cremated.

All my knowledge, and I couldn't save her. Her essence deserves to be returned to the stars.

Hundreds of vials of chemicals rested in racks on the shelves around the lab. Half of them were lethal or could be modified to be lethal with minimal effort. Enki considered taking his own life, but he could never bring himself to do it. Was it because the instinct for survival was rooted too deeply in his race? Was he still holding out hope that he would live through the current situation? Or was he simply a coward?

The two protectors who had carried Gemekala into the lab sat near the entrance, guarding it.

From out in the corridor the sounds of howling and footsteps pounding toward the lab caught his ear. He knew what the noise meant for him, which was just as well.

Soiled and bloodied hominins brandishing spear-rifles, rocks, and construction tools poured into the lab like water overpowering a dam.

The protectors jumped up. They backpedaled until they stood in front of Enki with rifles raised.

As the angry mob prepared to rip them apart, a brief surge of will gripped Enki.

"Give up your weapons," he ordered the protectors as he sat up. "You can't kill them all."

One protector looked back over her shoulder at him. "We may die, but we'll at least still a few of them before we go."

"What shall that accomplish? More needless death?"

"Death?" the second protector said. "These tools are malfunctioning. They need to be still—"

"Enough. You know better by now." Enki glared at him. "Remove your weapons this instant."

For a moment, he feared the protectors would call his bluff. He possessed far less combat ability than they did. But they demonstrated their reverence by dropping their rifles.

A pair of hominins grabbed the guns from the ground and took aim at the three Onaki.

"Wait," a familiar voice shouted in the hominins' language. It came from the back of the group.

Asha pushed to the front of the crowd. Her face relaxed in relief upon seeing Enki.

Overcome by joy, Enki teared up. "You're alive." He stood and cradled her face in his hands.

"Yes," she said, eyes twinkling.

Enki looked past her. "You're all alive. But my virus. . . ."

A disheveled hominin man stepped toward them. "He is a master. We should still him."

Whirling on him, Asha said, "We shall do no such thing. He's our father, the one who created us. He deserves continued life."

"He and you are mates. That is why you protect him."

"I shan't lie to you." Asha turned to Enki and whispered her next words. "I love him."

Enki's breathing quickened at hearing her words.

At the same time, guilt and confusion muddled his thinking. Enki had lain with one of his creations. Many of his people would've excommunicated him had they learned of such a transgression. He might as well have gone out into the wild and mated with the first four-legged beast he found.

No. He chose to dismiss his people's biases. If only his fellows could have appreciated the range of emotions exhibited by these beings, things might have turned out another way.

"We still only the masters who enslave us," Asha said, raising her voice to the group. "We shan't murder those who would do us no harm."

Feeling his legs weaken, Enki hung his head. "But I have done you harm. I created you to serve as tools—as slaves. I stood by while my people treated you like unthinking machines."

"You did it because you didn't have a choice."

But I did have a choice. I could have—

Asha interrupted his thought. "You couldn't have survived here without our help. We're only doing the same, fighting to survive."

"But I . . ." Lifting his gaze, Enki swallowed and blinked hard. "I tried to still—no, murder—you all with . . ." He knew of no word in the hominins' language for virus. "With the poison I created."

"The head master ordered it of you. Fortunately for us all, you failed."

"But how? I tested it. I know it worked. How are you still alive?"

Asha extended one bare shoulder out to him.

Enki ran his fingers over her soft skin. On her upper arm, he felt and then saw a faint circle surrounding a point in the center. The indentation had almost healed, but he recognized a needle entry point when he saw one.

"The Teacher saved us," Asha said.

"The Teacher?" Enki repeated. "You mean the one who taught you how to fight us?"

"Yes. After I brought her a sample of your poison, she pricked us with something that made it no longer hurt us."

"A vaccine," Enki muttered in realization.

"I regret betraying you."

Enki gripped her shoulders and smiled for the first time in a long time.

♦

Brooke landed the Hyperflare on *Yesterday's* main hangar deck, drained the cockpit of gravgel, and powered down its systems.

As soon as she popped open the canopy, Maya leapt out and stormed off.

Fighting her dread over her niece's state of mind, Brooke jumped out and gave chase.

Halfway across the hangar, Brooke caught up to Maya and grabbed her by the arm. "Hold up for a—"

Knocking Brooke's hand away, Maya stopped, spun, and glowered at her. Her scowl and twitching nostrils conveyed more hurt than Brooke had ever seen her display.

"Maya—captain—please calm down," Brooke said.

With clenched fists, Maya hissed, "Yes or no?"

"Yes or no what?"

"You know what."

"I'm sorry, but I don't—"

"Don't insult my intelligence."

"Look—"

As her niece stabbed a trembling finger at her, Brooke leaned back.

"Did you or did you not incite the rebellion on the surface?" Maya demanded.

Brooke averted her gaze.

"I'd better hear the word 'yes' or 'no' within the next two seconds, or so help me, you're going out the closest airlock," Maya shouted.

Hardening her expression and tone, Brooke said, "I'm your superior officer, Captain. I have full command authority over this mission. I don't need your approval."

"Don't pull rank on me, Admiral. You've violated our orders with what you've done. I should strip you of your authority and toss you in the brig." Maya shifted her eyes, apparently summoning security.

Brooke both sweated and shivered as her fear and guilt brought on hot and cold flashes. At last, she answered, "Okay. Yes. I did it."

Covering her mouth with one hand, Maya glared at her. "Of course you did. I didn't want to believe it, but there's no other explanation. Tell me why."

"I had no choice," Brook said. "The fate of our race was at stake."

"That's why I was negotiating for peace." Maya stomped her boot. "I had just accomplished it, too, until your hitman killed our biggest supporter."

"I know it's hard for you to accept, but peace wasn't the answer. If I hadn't intervened, the Onaki would've eradicated everyone with their virus."

"If you hadn't intervened, I'd be sitting in their assembly hall, sipping that red wine of theirs while discussing how to resolve our differences without bloodshed."

"We need to kick them off our planet, or else our history won't unfold the way that it should."

"That's irrelevant. We can't affect our history. Our visit here and your revolt never happened in our past. But in this timeline we created just by being here, there's no such thing as the way things should happen."

"Think about it, Maya. The Onaki created us in our history, too, but we still don't know why they left."

"Let me get this straight. Ignorance justifies murder and war? That's your argument?"

"Maybe a revolt also happened in our past, but in this timeline, it needed a helping hand because we showed up and exposed ourselves. Maybe I did exactly what I was supposed to do."

Maya blew out a sigh. "Why would you think that, unless—who goaded you into starting the revolt?"

Brooke stared at the deck.

"At first," Maya said, studying her aunt's face, "I figured you concocted the revolt as a desperate plan to rescue me. I almost couldn't blame you for playing the concerned aunt. But that wasn't it, was it? Who convinced you to betray me?" Maya cupped her hand over her mouth and looked around the hangar. "The Vril. Which of the crew are double agents?"

Her head spinning, Brooke knew she needed to be honest. "Advisor Sybil."

"The android woman, Evelyn?" Maya widened her eyes in realization. "The same Eve from the interstellar probe during the *New Horizons* mission?"

"The same. She's habbing a different body."

"How didn't I realize it sooner—and how could you work with someone who tried to murder us?"

"Eve never actually intended to kill us."

"I figured as much. Letting me blow her head off was part of the

Vril's plan. Who else?"

"Kepler provided me with remote scanning support. He helped me locate proto-humans and determine the schedules of Onaki patrols. Doc Crumpler created the vaccine that kept the workers alive." Brooke pinged her niece. "Here's the data on the backdoor channels that let us work undetected. That's everyone and everything. I swear."

Placing her hands on her hips, Maya blew out a half-sigh, half-growl. She stared at Brooke like a delinquent child considered a lost cause. "I expected as much from The Vril. But from you, my closest family member?"

"Violating your trust was the hardest thing I've ever had to do." Every moment of every day Brooke had spent on the surface, she had dreaded this confrontation. But her worries had paled in comparison to the sight of her niece losing all respect for her. "I did it for you," she whispered. "For everyone."

"The ends don't justify the means. That was the Vril's excuse for the staged invasion—and for almost killing the Penphins." Maya blinked away tears.

Brooke blew out a long breath. "I have no way to convince you what I did was right—no, it wasn't right, but it was necessary."

"And so is this."

Lieutenant Resnik entered the hangar with two security officers in tow.

Maya stood with her arms folded, fuming, as the officers magcuffed Brooke's hands behind her back. Brooke didn't resist.

"Admiral Davis, by the power vested in me as captain of this vessel, you are hereby relieved of your authority and confined to the brig." Maya whirled and marched toward the exit.

"Please . . ." Brooke called after her. "Maya, don't—"

"As far as I'm concerned, you might as well be dead," Maya yelled without turning around.

Brooke needed every last shred of willpower to keep from collapsing onto the deck.

Twenty-seven—Propound
Earth Orbit, October 200,423 BCE

Grinding her teeth, Maya stormed into the MCC.

Lieutenant Christa Resnik and her security team entered after her.

The bridge crew hopped to their feet and stood at attention. "Captain," relieved greetings rang out from all around.

Rising from the skipper's chair, Trevor stepped over to his seat. "Welcome back, ma'am."

"I believe the expression is, 'long time, no see,'" Bob said from the sit-table.

With braces affixed to her legs and torso, Jo struggled up out of Brooke's former chair. "If you hadn't come back, Captain, I would've been crushed."

Staring at her friend's grin, Maya wanted so very badly to laugh. The fact Jo could joke about almost dying eased some of Maya's tension.

Jo gave her the once-over. "You've looked better, ma'am."

Via the health status readouts in her i-cite, Maya noted that her biocites had healed the small fracture of her scapula. She still felt stiff and sore in her shoulder blades and chest. She also had a lingering headache from her mild concussion.

She touched her face. Caked dirt and dried blood covered it. Looking herself over, she found more rips in her uniform than could self-seal.

"The hot bath will have to wait." She glanced at Christa.

The security chief and her team approached Kepler at the sit-table.

"Please come with us, Lieutenant," Resnik said.

Kepler was leaning over the table, propping himself up with both palms. When he heard Resnik's order, he stood up straight and blinked. "Can I ask where, Captain?"

"Lieutenant Resnik will take you to the brig," Maya said.

Subdued intakes of breath sucked the air out of the MCC.

"May I ask why, ma'am?" Kepler asked.

Maya hadn't wanted to announce the presence of a traitor in front of the bridge crew. The knowledge might've distracted them during the present crisis. But the accused had the legal right to be informed of the charges prior to being taken into custody. If she denied him that right, she would be no better than the criminal she was apprehending.

"You'll remain in lockdown until we've weathered the current situation, Lieutenant," Maya said. "At that time, there'll be an investigation into whether you conspired to sabotage our mission."

"Ma'am?" Kepler pleaded. "I don't know what you're talking about."

His raised brows almost led Maya to second-guess the validity of Brooke's claims. Maya's chest had felt especially heavy at hearing Kepler was a Vril agent. She had seen herself in his optimism. She had handpicked him for this crew following his exemplary service about *Serendipity*.

But Maya had no doubts about his guilt. She had pinged Bob on her way to the bridge. In a matter of seconds, the brilliant AI had worked his programmatic magic.

"We've located and disabled your backdoor network," Maya said, taking no pleasure in the discovery. "There's more than enough audio, vid, and login evidence to ensure a dishonorable discharge plus life in prison." She frowned at Resnik, avoiding Kepler's gaze. "Get him out of my sight."

The security chief gripped Kepler's upper arm and gave him a gentle tug. Kepler ripped his arm away. "We may've gone behind your back, but we didn't betray you. Don't you get it?" He lunged toward Maya, who backpedaled and almost fell back over her chair.

With the swiftness of a leopard Resnik kicked his legs out from under him. As Kepler face-planted on the deck, the security chief drove her knees into his back and magcuffed his wrists behind him. She did this despite standing a head shorter and giving up fifteen kilos to the man. Then Resnik and her team hoisted up the dazed sensing officer.

"You've really disappointed me, Keps," Maya said.

Kepler hung his head, avoiding eye contact.

Leading him out the main hatch, security escorted him to the brig, where he would occupy a cell adjacent to the doctor and vice admiral.

Maya glanced around at the dangling jaws of her bridge crew and settled into her seat. "Everyone back to work." They all swung back to their duty stations.

"Status?" Maya demanded.

Fingers swiping through the helm rends, Tereshkova cleared her throat. "We're holding position over the western hemisphere, ma'am. The *Eleppu* is just over the horizon, putting us out of range of their hypofield and big gun. A few minutes ago, the ship altered orbit, taking up position between the *Namtilla* and us."

"The population of the city has fled into the buildings for cover," Trevor said. "I'll give the Onaki this much credit at least. They build structures to last. The basements are excellent bomb shelters."

Weighing both reports, Maya hoped she wasn't right about what she thought might happen.

"As for the aerial battle," Trevor said, "Commander Maxwell's team has lost nine pilots but managed to blank half of the enemy fighter wing. The remaining 'flares have fallen back and formed an air defense perimeter around the city. So far, they've kept the enemy from going on major strafing runs. The buildings may be tough, but they wouldn't hold up indefinitely under a constant barrage."

"That's more than I could've hoped for at the moment," Maya said. "Nice strategy, by the way."

"I can't take credit for it, Captain." Trevor pointed to tactical. "Lieutenant Rojas came up with it."

Lieutenant Lautaro Rojas tapped his foot against the deck and shrugged. "Actually, I got the idea from Admiral Davis' book."

"She wrote a book?" Maya asked, blinking.

"Yes, ma'am. It covers all her dogfights, combat situations, and stratagems from before the staged invasion all the way up through her skirmishes with the Greys."

"I see." Ignoring the mixed surprise, gratitude, and resentment churning within her, Maya asked, "How have we been monitoring the situation on the other side of the planet with the hypofield blocking neudar and wormholes?"

"We launched nano cubesats as relays," Bob said. "They're configured to use a combination of X-ray, laser, thermal, and radio." He adjusted his glasses. "Like they used to do in the good old days, I believe."

"The conventional scans are limited, of course," Trevor said. "We can't tell what's going on inside the buildings or within the Onaki ships.

Also, I've devoted a significant percentage of my processing capability to determining the algorithm the Onaki use to affect their gravimetric distortions."

"You're reverse-engineering the hypofield calculations," Maya said with a knowing nod.

"Affirmative. I believe I'm close to an approximation that will allow us to predict and circumvent the distortions with a relative degree of accuracy."

"That should allow *Yesterday* to use neudar and wormhole comm, and to shift."

"Correct on all counts except the last. The calculations will be predictive enough to enable low energy signals. Bioware and hardware modifications to the phase fighters should allow them to shift. But I'm afraid my approximations won't achieve the accuracy needed to sustain a *Yesterday*-sized wormhole for weeks."

"At least we can get our eyes, ears, and fighters operational again."

"Correct, although the 'flares will need to return to the ship for the hardware modifications."

"Nice work. How long?"

"I require thirty-one additional minutes to complete the algorithm and—"

"Captain," Rojas interrupted. "The *Eleppu's* energy readings are building. The *Namtilla* just initiated the launch sequence for its antimatter bomb."

Maya lurched forward in her seat. "They're preparing to destroy the planet."

Trevor studied the rends in front of him. "It looks like the new ship plans to defend the old while the latter bombs the surface. It's a curious strategy, given the new ship's far more potent arsenal."

Tapping her cheek in thought, Maya said, "Maybe they're not willing to accept the responsibility for eradicating an entire ecosystem. They probably want the settlers to clean up their own mess." She shouted orders. "All hands, stand ready at general quarters. Helm, prepare to get underway. Tactical, activate all defense systems. Comm, contact the *Eleppu*."

As Ensign Savio Marconi shifted his lucky coin from one knuckle to the next, he interfaced with the waveform rends above his console. The rends showed his attempts to transmit and lock onto any return transmission in every possible signal format.

Tapping her foot, Maya waited.

She was about to order Marconi to abandon the effort when he said, "They're responding."

A rend of Captain Kizzura's upper body appeared above the sit-table. No longer wearing his mech suit, he rotated his scale-feathered head and directed his fierce left eye at her.

"Please stand down," Maya said. "You're about to wipe out all life on the planet. This can't be in line with your ethics."

Kizzura inclined his beak, looking down at her. "You're correct," the comm AIs translated. "We're not pleased with the actions we're about to take."

"Then stop before you do something you admit you'll regret. Let's talk as Gemekala had agreed."

"Do you deny murdering her?"

Swallowing hard, Maya cursed her aunt under her breath. "I'll be honest with you. Traitors under my command killed her in violation of my orders. I promise they'll be punished."

"Shifting the blame onto your subordinates. How convenient."

"No. I accept full responsibility for their actions."

"Have you no control over your own kind?"

Maya resisted the urge to growl in frustration.

"This is one of the many such reasons we deem you too dangerous to exist," Kizzura said. "You're given to a larger range of emotions, which makes you unstable. Your individual egos are so strong you're unable to show a united front. Worse still, your ambitions and abilities outstrip your maturity and sense of responsibility."

"So your people and society are perfect?" Maya countered, fed up with the insults.

"Perfect, no. But objectively superior to yours, I have little doubt."

Now who's got the ego? Keeping the thought to herself, she bit her lip in frustration. "We don't have to be enemies."

"But enemies we are. You and your purported ancestors have killed my officers."

"Only in self-defense. Remember when you first set foot on the planet? You were ready to execute me before hearing my side of the story."

"Only one thing matters, Captain. You shouldn't be here. This encounter shouldn't be happening. Your presence has caused a divergent timeline."

"Fine. Condemn those of us from the future if you must. Punish me since I'm the leader. But don't wipe out a population that's an innocent pawn in our power struggle."

"But they're you. You're here, which proves they were allowed to become you. And that means something happened to us. I cannot allow that to occur."

Feeling the verbal battle slipping away from her, Maya tried one last desperate strategy. "Would you consider peace talks in a situation with no disadvantage to you?"

"What do you mean?"

"I'm willing to disarm my defense systems and bring my ship into range of your weapons."

"Captain," Trevor whispered in a harsh tone, "you can't—"

Maya silenced her first officer by holding out a hand. She waited for Kizzura to respond.

It was hard to identify a smile on a true-form Onaki, but she could swear the lower part of Kizzura's beak curled upward. "I could destroy you in an instant and still lay waste to the planet."

"I know. My people call my proposed gesture a show of good faith. One side has to take the initiative to demonstrate sincere intent for peace. I'm willing to do it."

The other captain's rend disappeared, and the connection terminated.

"What happened?" Trevor asked. "Marconi, get him back—"

"Wait," Maya said. "I think he signed off to consider my proposal. Let's have a little patience."

Folding her arms, she studied the tactical rends of the *Eleppu* and *Namtilla* above the sit-table. The scans showed no change in the energy outputs or orbits of the two ships. They weren't attacking, yet she felt like insects were crawling up and down her skin.

"Is this a plan to fool him, Captain?" Trevor asked. "Waving a white flag could get us get close enough to score a fatal hit, assuming he doesn't vaporize us first."

"No. My offer is genuine."

Trevor whispered, "Could we please speak in private, Captain? I don't want to contradict you in front of the crew."

Nodding, Maya handed command of the MCC over to Jo and headed for her command cabin. With Brooke in the brig, Erik deployed, and both Trevor and Maya off the bridge, Jo was next in line.

The moment the cabin door swooshed shut behind Maya and Trevor, her first officer said, "When you asked me to be XO, ma'am, you told me you wanted my alternate perspective. Well, now is one of those times when you need it."

"Okay," Maya said. "Let's hear it."

"You have to reconsider what you're doing." He held a hand out toward the porthole. "Kizzura has nothing to gain from peace talks. He has the ability to destroy the planet and us, which solves his problem. We only make it easier for him by dropping our defenses. If we're not around to protect the population below, they don't have a chance."

"I realize that."

"Look, ma'am. I know my suggestions tend to be on the more aggressive side. Believe it or not, I'm often relieved when you manage to avoid a conflict and prove me wrong." Trevor stepped closer to her. He radiated conviction. "But I'm not wrong now. The future of the human race is at stake. This isn't time to achieve peace. It's time to fight for our survival. That means we can't cross our fingers and hope he doesn't blast us out of orbit."

"If he agrees to my proposal."

"Yes, ma'am. If he agrees."

Resting her butt on the edge of her desk, Maya folded her arms and considered his suggestion. Trevor was correct about her tendency to dismiss his more aggressive recommendations for action. Did this situation call for a more forceful response? Was her desire for peace—a desire further motivated by an urge to prove her aunt wrong—compelling her to take a fatal risk?

"So what would you have us do?" she asked.

Trevor blinked in surprise. He approached the desk. Leaning over it, he summoned a rend of the *Eleppu* with a wave of his hand. "Assuming Kizzura agrees to your proposal, we drop our defenses as you intended— initially. But before we approach, you say you've made your show of good faith and ask him to power down his weapons as a comparable gesture."

Maya stood. "I already don't like it. If I were him, I'd suspect something."

"I think it's only fair, ma'am. Besides, he shouldn't be too worried if both parties have their weapons powered down."

"Maybe. Anyway, go on."

"All you need to do is get us to within twenty-thousand klicks of the *Eleppu*. According to our scans, their weapons need five seconds to discharge. Our wave drive can accelerate us to within point-black range in that time." He zoomed in on the thick central axis of the advanced Onaki ship. "See these tubes running the length of the ship along the hull? They're energy conduits that feed power to all of their primary systems. If we take them out—"

"So you'd have us prove that everything they think is bad about us is in fact true."

"At first, yes. But in the long run, we can show we're not irresponsible butchers. The plan would be to punch through their force field, hit those conduits, and incapacitate the ship without destroying it. They'll lose weapons, the hypofield, and everything else except life support. Then we talk peace."

Sticking out her lower lip, Maya considered the proposition.

"I figured you'd like the idea of wounding but not killing them," Trevor added.

"I still don't like lying," Maya said, "but for the sake of argument, let's say we make the attempt." She flicked the *Eleppu* to the side with her finger and brought the *Namtilla* into view. "The other ship will launch its bomb before we can turn our attention to it."

"It will, unless . . ." He looked around the cabin, waiting.

"What?"

"Any second now . . ."

As Maya caught on to his line of thinking, an image of Bob appeared in her i-cite. "Captain, I've completed my hypofield neutralization calculations."

"Good work, Bob," Trevor said. "On the captain's order, I want you to make the necessary changes to one of our remaining Hyperflares as quickly as possible."

"Do it," Maya said. She hadn't yet sanctioned the plan, but if she did, every second would prove critical.

"Understood." Bob signed off.

Maya didn't need long to figure out what her XO had in mind for the fighter. "So we send a 'flare capable of shifting to knock out the *Namtilla's* launch system. Who did you have in mind to fly it?"

Trevor looked her in the eye. "Ma'am, Maxwell is engaged below, so you know who."

Whipping her head back and forth, Maya said, "Admiral Davis is a traitor. I can't trust her." Deep down, she had other, more selfish reasons, like wanting to keep her aunt out of a combat situation, given her health.

"Normally, I would agree, but we need her expertise. She's the best pilot who ever lived."

"She's past her prime. She'll only get herself killed."

"I know she had health issues before we left, but her latest med eval gave her green flight status. She checked out fine."

A little too fine. "Crumpler is a Vril agent. We can't trust her eval." Brooke's miraculous recovery had never sat well with Maya. Was there a connection between her aunt's improved health and her treachery? Maya had her suspicions, but she had more important things to ponder at the moment.

"No, it's out of the question," Maya snapped, unable to subdue her rising irritation. "If she hadn't killed the Onaki leader, we wouldn't be in this mess."

"True enough, ma'am," Trevor said, "but I think you're letting your anger affect your judgment. Regardless of what she did, we need her."

"Order Erik to get back here on the double."

"Unless Kizzura takes his sweet time getting back to us, Maxwell won't make it."

"Then we'll have to hope Kizzura waits until—"

"Captain." Marconi's image appeared in her i-cite. "The captain of the *Eleppu* is contacting us."

"We're out of time." Trevor stared at Maya, pleading with his eyes. "Maxwell can't—"

"I gave you an order, Commander," Maya said.

Tightening his frown, Trevor assumed a rigid posture. "Yes, ma'am."

Twenty-eight—Nonpartisan
Earth Orbit, October 200,423 BCE

Zeke shuffled through a corridor lit by dim orange plasma strips. Had he not held complete control over his emotions, he might have jumped at any number of shadows, or he might have mistaken the hum of high voltage or the hiss of ventilation for whispers of the undead.

His search for the presence had led him into the unpopulated sections of the aft module behind the ECC and main generator. He had taken control of crew members to gain access to the restricted areas that housed *Yesterday's* primary systems and then altered the officers' memories to keep his actions a secret.

At a thick hatch with reflective warning symbols, soft violet light caressed Zeke from head to toe.

The voice of a security AI announced he had passed the biometric scan, thanks to the high-level clearance he had compelled an officer to grant him. The hatch parted.

Zeke crept inside, stepping over bundles of thick cables. The cables ran the length of the passageway, which stretched as far as he could see in either direction. At chest level, plasma discharged through a semi-translucent conduit with a half-meter diameter.

Ducking under the conduit, Zeke neared the hull of the ship, closing in on the presence.

In a dark corner, he found various devices strewn across the deck, including quantum circuit boards, rend generators, interface pads, data chips, cabling, auto-syringes, a wave gun, and a particle rifle. Some of the items he didn't recognize. Hydro-protein pills and wrappers from food ration packs added to the mess. Zeke didn't need his heightened perception to discern that someone—or something—had been living here.

Kneeling in the middle of the clutter, he picked up a transparent sphere resembling a fishing bobber. It was about the size of a marble. His unofficial foster mother, Xiaoqing, had taken him fishing on Ganymede years ago. Zeke concentrated on the sphere to avoid the emptiness he had felt when Xi had died.

The frigid shell of the sphere bit into his palm, forcing him to shift the thing from one hand to the other every few seconds. The short cylinder on the top served as a refrigeration unit—or rather, a cryogenic freezer. Inside, a sphere smaller than the first floated in the center.

When he magnified his vision, he discovered genetic material inside the tiny sphere. *Is this some sort of artificial egg?*

The coldness of the sphere was stinging his hands. Zeke stood and tossed the sphere up into the air for relief. As he caught it in the other hand, he searched the floor for more but found none. It was a pity. He wanted to try juggling three of them, as he had seen street vendors do in the modern Sol system.

A charge of panic struck him from across the hold like a zap of static electricity. Startled, he almost dropped the sphere.

Zeke gazed off into the darkness toward a collection of large metal boxes. Behind them, he sensed the presence and felt its terror.

Setting down the sphere as gently as possible, Zeke clasped his hands in front of his body and faced the presence. "I know you're there. Please show yourself."

The humming of power systems filled the silence, but the fear remained.

"If you reveal yourself to me," Zeke said, "I promise to assess your situation with objectivity. Should you choose to remain in hiding, however, I shall be forced to inform the captain of an intruder with unknown intentions."

His acute hearing discerned the wheezing sound of a Grey breathing.

"I'm not human," Zeke added. "You needn't mistrust me."

"I know who you are," the Grey said at last.

Like his inherent comprehension of the Penphins' language, Zeke had always possessed the ability to understand The Greys' speech. He didn't know why it was so, but he had a feeling he might learn the answer in the near future.

"Your words ring false," it said. "Your presence among the humans makes you a traitor to your own people."

Zeke shook his head. "You mistake proximity for allegiance. It's true they found and raised me. But I live among them due to an inability to locate my people in our time."

"I reject your hollow pretext."

"I reject your rejection. My abstaining from the activity on the surface demonstrates my impartiality. By way of further evidence, I could've reported your presence to the humans rather than engaging you in conversation."

The Grey offered no rebuttal to his logical argument.

"Reveal yourself," Zeke demanded. "I would prefer you emerged of your own volition, but I have the ability to force you out of hiding."

The Grey took its time creeping out into the light cast by the plasma conduit behind Zeke.

As it blinked its bulbous black eyes at him, he felt its distrust. The Grey carried a rack of the spheres under one arm. With its other hand, it aimed a partially disassembled particle gun, modified to override the biometric security restrictions.

The realization of why the Grey had stowed away aboard the ship struck Zeke like a slap to the face. "Given your motivation, I cannot fault your presence here." He picked up the sphere he had set down and offered it to the Grey in his open palm.

Keeping the weapon trained on him, the Grey set the rack down. It inched toward him, plucked the sphere out of his hand, and jumped back to protect the rack.

"My name is Zeke," he said. "How may I address you?"

The Grey returned the sphere to the rack. "My designation is longwinded. You may call me by the abbreviation Vya."

"Vya, I would thank you for revealing your name, but I know how you detest human pleasantries."

"We find the humans, not the pleasantries, pretentious. Our culture includes social conventions far more intricate than those found in human society."

"Given that I know nothing of your customs, I will be straightforward. You have stowed away aboard this vessel to prevent the humans from defeating the Onaki here."

Vya nodded. "Our ships lack the power to travel this far into the past, to the point at which the timelines turned against us."

"Yes," Zeke said. "If the Onaki win, they'll someday replace the proto-humans with more efficient workers, namely you."

"We must ensure not only our survival but our very conception."

"Which is why you have a backup plan." Zeke eyed the spheres. "If the humans win, the Onaki may never create your people. This is why you intend to seed fertilized embryos on a habitable exoplanet—to ensure your persistence in this timeline, no matter the outcome here."

The Grey focused on the rack, all but proving Zeke's assumption.

Zeke considered the mess on the deck. "However, you're still here, so you must have a problem. The moment *Yesterday* arrived in the past, you should've shifted away in your stealth spacecraft attached to the hull, to find your intended destination."

"The birthing systems aboard my craft were damaged before we docked with this vessel," Vya said. "I have been working to repair them since we came aboard."

"We? I see. It follows you had a partner who went to the Earth to affect change there. That individual must've exposed the human scout party to the Onaki."

Vya lowered its gun partway. "Yes, but . . ."

"But he's dead now," Zeke whispered. "Without his help, you fear you may not be able to repair your ship, given the extent of the damage and your lack of familiarity with human technology."

"I must succeed," Vya said, shaking its head in frustration. "My people's survival may depend on it. Still, I must also admit when the task at hand exceeds my capabilities."

Understanding the situation all too clearly, Zeke came to a decision. "I shall assist you."

Vya cocked its oblong head. "What is your motivation?"

"My conscience. No matter what conflict may transpire between different peoples, every race has a right to exist."

"If your actions reflect your words, your ethics may equal our own."

"Unfortunately, I see no ethical way to intervene in a direct conflict between the humans and my ancestors. Therefore, I cannot affect whether my people ultimately create your race. But I shall work with you to ensure you're able to seed the embryos in your spheres."

"I understand." Vya lowered its gun. "You possess familiarity with human medical systems?"

Zeke shook his head. "No, but any technology is logical and therefore easy to learn. And if I cannot repair something myself, I can compel others who have the knowledge."

"Surreptitiously?"

"I think the captain of this vessel would agree to help us with a full understanding of the situation. But she distrusts your kind. Given the stakes, we cannot risk an unfavorable decision, so we will work in secret. I can ensure we aren't discovered."

"I am most appreciative of your assistance and discretion." Vya picked up the rack of spheres and walked toward the wall. Presumably, its spacecraft was attached to the outer hull.

As Vya stuck one arm through the wall, Zeke said, "I have one final condition."

The Grey pulled its arm back and turned. "What is this requirement?"

"You must abandon your attempts to sabotage the humans' vessel."

Vya stared at him in silence.

"Specifically," Zeke said, "you must deactivate the device you've placed in the black hole generator."

Cradling the spheres close to her body, Vya stared at the deck, "I'm afraid there's no way to disable the siphon."

◆

Brooke leaned back against the cell wall and knocked her head against it—again.

With a snort, she reflected on all the times she had spent in lockdown—and on the many other instances in which she had somehow avoided it. What fatal flaw had destined her to end up in confinement again and again? Perhaps she belonged in a cell.

She cupped the back of her head in her hands and buried her face between her knees. Had she been wrong to incite the revolt? Had she allowed the Vril to manipulate her once again? Maybe, but this time the situation felt different. Or maybe things weren't any different. Maybe her experiences had changed her.

The proto-humans' slavery had given her a better appreciation for the Vril's point of view. Peace and ethics were luxuries when one's race was subjugated. Subterfuge and killing were sometimes necessary, even if the acts ate away at her from the inside out.

What would've happened had Maya established peace? Until the *Eleppu* had shown up, the Onaki colonists would've had to remain on Earth. With their continued influence, mankind might not have learned, grown, or innovated on their own, altering the way human society unfolded.

Perhaps participation in a larger community would've prevented human history from turning out so violent and bloody. But would true freedom ever have existed?

Deep down, she knew her actions had been necessary.

If she were truly honest with herself, what she had accomplished had felt damn good, almost as good as flying. Winning over the proto-humans, teaching them to think for themselves, recruiting them, training them, planning the assassination and revolt, and seeing everything go according to plan . . . who else in history had ever accomplished such a feat?

Teaching flight sim courses and rising to the highest ranks of the IEF had never given her the same satisfaction. Maybe that was because she had always felt like a cog in the wheel, fighting someone else's fight and never making a genuine difference. This time she had picked the fight and made a genuine contribution to history.

Granted, the fight was far from won, but it might never have begun had she not intervened.

If only she could've found a way to do it without alienating Maya. Would her niece ever forgive her?

Searing heat accompanied by shivers coursed through Brooke's body at the thought of Maya's loss of respect for her—and because Brooke's symptoms were worsening. Holding her shaking wrist, she cursed Resnik for confiscating her last two spark injectors before shoving her in the cell.

Brooke looked up in response to the whooshing sound of the cell wall dematerializing. Zeke stood in the entryway, gazing down at her with his usual blank expression.

"I can understand why," he said.

Brooke furrowed her brow. "Why what?"

Stepping inside the cell, he focused his yellow irises at her. She had seen similar eyes all too often while down on the surface.

"I get why you'd think I'd be the last person to visit you," he said, "considering that you started a war with my people." Before Brooke could respond, Zeke added, "I apologize for reading your thoughts without your permission, but I needed to understand why."

"You mean you needed to know why I did what I did."

"Yes."

Brooke rested her forearms on her knees. "You can't possibly support my actions against your kind."

"I said I understood. I didn't say I approved. You did what any member of any species would do. You acted in the best interests of your kind."

"Our captain might beg to differ."

"Her approach differed from yours. She took the high road, so to speak. Each of your methods may yet lead to a form of success. But as far as I can tell with my ability to predict alternate futures, your actions were most likely to yield the present you know."

Brooke held her breath at his words.

"Hearing that means a lot to you," Zeke said. "You've had a vague feeling you were doing the right thing, but you haven't been sure."

She nodded in agreement.

"I can't know with absolute certainty," he said. "But my best guess is that my people would never have granted your ancestors their independence. Bigotry, arrogance, fear, and mistrust afflict us as they do you. The divide between us may be too great for our two peoples ever to peacefully coexist."

"It's a shame." Brooke smiled. "You and I get along so well."

For once, he matched her expression. "Like the man in the bat costume and his sidekick."

"Who's the sidekick?"

"I think that's obvious." Zeke's grin faded. "I also have a more selfish reason for absolving you of your actions."

"Oh?"

"I've taken action I feel to be the only just course, but it may be detrimental to your kind."

"Well," Brooke said with a shrug, "If I took issue with that, I'd be the biggest hypocrite of them all. I'm sure you acted in good conscience. That's all any of us can do."

"I appreciate your understanding." Zeke stepped toward her. "The main reason I'm here is because I read important information from the last crew member I passed."

Brooke flinched as memories flooded her brain. Disorientation followed. She lowered her palms to the deck to steady herself.

The dizziness faded, replaced by the knowledge Zeke had crammed into her head.

"They need a pilot," she said. "Maxwell won't make it back in time, but Maya won't let me go."

"A jailbreak seems in order." Zeke looked around the cell. "After the heroes defeat the bad guys and lock them up in comic sims, the evildoers always break out of captivity to hatch another scheme."

"I guess I'll have to keep playing the villain." Brooke hopped to her feet and regretted it at once. The room seemed to spin, and she almost lost her balance.

Zeke gripped her arm to steady her.

Breathing deep, she got her bearings.

"You'll need these." Zeke placed the case containing her last two spark injectors in her hand. "The security chief was kind enough to give them to me—even though she never knew she did."

Brooke gripped the case and stared at him. "By helping me, aren't you taking sides and going against your kind?"

"Recent information has modified my stance. If humans triumph, my ancestors will simply have to leave. But if the Onaki win, your kind will be rendered extinct. I cannot sanction that. No hero ever could. Therefore, I'm not choosing sides. I'm acting to prevent an atrocity."

Brooke offered a slow, knowing nod.

As she turned to go, Zeke grabbed her arm.

"Promise me one last thing," he said.

"Anything."

"Before you launch, tell her the truth."

Twenty-nine—Trilemma
Earth Orbit, October 200,423 BCE

Maya exited her command cabin, followed by Trevor. As she stepped in front of her chair, she ordered Ensign Marconi to accept the incoming comm from the *Eleppu*.

"After much deliberation," the rend of Kizzura said, "I agree to your proposal."

The other captain's words should have brought relief, but they filled Maya with foreboding. She hadn't yet decided whether to risk everything for peace or execute her XO's plan. "Thank you. I knew you were a reasonable people."

"I do this for my crew and to prevent the deaths of any more of my fellows. There will be conditions for the hominins below and for you to ensure that you cannot threaten us. Otherwise, the ceasefire will be brief."

"Of course. Any armistice requires compromise by both parties." Maya turned to Rojas. "Take our weapons offline."

Lieutenant Rojas held his hand in front of the defense rends and stared at her. After a moment, he swiped his finger and said, "Done." The targeting brackets, plasma cannon output, and warhead launch vectors floating about his station tinted from red to blue.

"Your sensing systems should confirm that we've disarmed our ship," Maya said.

Kizzura's rend disappeared for a moment and then reappeared. "Confirmed."

"Here's what I propose. We'll adjust our orbit to slowly bring our ship to within firing range of your forward cannon."

Around the bridge, breathing intensified as crew members shifted in their seats.

"Once we're in position," Maya said, "I will personally launch in one of our transports and come to you to discuss terms."

Kizurra dipped his beak. "That is acceptable."

Maya ordered Tereshkova to get underway.

"Where's Erik?" Maya asked Trevor over the neurocomm.

"When Maxwell tried to break away from the city," Trevor mind-spoke, "multiple enemy units attacked him and his wingman. He had no choice but to re-engage."

Damn it. She sifted through her thoughts on what to do. Every cell in her body rejected the notion of using the goodwill she had re-established for strategic betrayal. She took the lack of an available pilot to attack the *Namtilla* as a sign.

Still, Trevor's argument lingered in her thoughts. If the Onaki chose to take advantage of her goodwill, it might signal the end for not only the crew of *Yesterday*, but the entire human race. Were the stakes too high to seek peace?

"Now that we've shown you our sincere intentions by disarming our weapons," Maya said, "I would like to request that you do the same."

Kizzura cocked his head. "That was not included in the original proposal."

"I acknowledge that. However, as a fellow captain who also wants to protect your crew, you should appreciate my position. We're no threat to you with our weapons deactivated. We made the first gesture. Now we'd like you to do the same."

She managed to stop herself from flinching when he immediately said, "Very well."

"Their forward cannon and all other weapons are powering down," Rojas reported.

"Thank you," Maya said.

"This 'gratitude' is only words," Kizzura said. "We'll be monitoring your actions. If we detect the slightest hint of subterfuge . . ."

"I understand."

"Contact us when your ship has achieved a closer orbit and you're ready to depart aboard the transport." Kizzura's rend dematerialized.

"How long until we're in position?" Maya asked.

Tereshkova swiveled her chair around from the helm. "Thirty-seven minutes, ma'am."

A little over half an hour to determine everyone's fate.

"Have you decided yet, ma'am?" Trevor said. "He agreed to disarm, which gives us the opportunity we needed to strike."

"True," Jo said from the third chair, "but it also reduces the chances of him vaporizing us if we still want to work toward peace."

"I'd think you of all people would want to pay them back for what they did to you."

"What happened was an accident. If we hadn't been spying on them in the first place, I wouldn't have gotten injured."

Trevor nodded. "You're right, of course. Revenge shouldn't be a motivating factor."

"Let's think through the big picture." Jo took a deep breath and rested for a moment. Speaking appeared to drain her, given that she hadn't regained her strength yet. "Will Kizzura keep his word? Will their government honor any agreement struck here? What happens years from now if they change their minds? The humans on the surface have 200,000 years to go until they develop the ability to defend themselves. Lastly—and I don't mean to sound harsh here—should we bother risking our necks when none of this affects our timeline?"

Indecision gripped Maya. Her insides felt as if they were twisted in knots.

"Captain," Lieutenant Resnik commed, her voice riddled with concern. "Admiral Davis is no longer in her cell."

Maya clenched her jaw. "What's her location?" she snapped.

"The main hangar bay."

"Take command, Trevor." Maya bolted from the bridge.

♦

Rushing into the ECC, Zeke went straight to the person who could best avert the tragedy Vya had set in motion.

With his mouth full, Chief Engineer Gottlieb set down his sandwich and stared at him.

Zeke could sense the man's surprise and discomfort. Like so many other humans, Gottlieb feared having his brains scrambled, according to his thoughts. Zeke considered taking control of him. That might be the most subtle way to avert disaster—if disaster was even avertable. But Zeke decided against it. The ship's best chance lay in its chief engineer and his team being in full command of their faculties.

"Chief," Zeke said. "It's come to my attention that there may be a problem with the main power generator."

Swallowing his latest bite, Gottlieb sat back and swiped his fingers through the rends above his desk. "Everything appears shipshape."

"The power drain may not yet show if you don't have your instruments calibrated to detect minute fluctuations. It's not registering now, but the effect is cumulative. If we wait, there might be little time to do anything about it."

Gottlieb scratched his head and summoned the power monitoring rends. "Perform an energy output analysis," he instructed the diagnostic AI. "Use maximum sensitivity."

"One moment," the disembodied voice of the AI said.

As they waited, the engineer folded his arms and stared at Zeke. "How did you find out about this issue?"

Zeke hated lying, but he couldn't reveal he had learned of the sabotage from a Grey intruder. "I can sense things beyond what humans perceive. Do you recall my last visit to the ECC?"

"Right. I had wondered why you were standing outside the hatch."

"I sensed something wrong then, but I dismissed it as my imagination. But the feeling kept returning, stronger and stronger each time, until it compelled me to seek you out."

Gottlieb stuck out his lower lip, looking far from convinced. Fortunately, the AI interrupted.

"Analysis completed," it said. "Abnormal evaporation of Hawking radiation detected, although the current rate of mass loss falls within acceptable parameters."

"Radiation evaporation," Gottlieb repeated, leaning forward. The lines on his forehead creased in concern.

"In other words," Zeke said, "the black hole is shrinking and losing power."

"I know that." Gottlieb sighed in frustration. Then he addressed the AI. "Run a full neudar sweep of the interior of the generator casing. Determine what's causing the evaporation."

"Sweep complete. The radiation is being drawn to a foreign object measuring ten to the negative nine meters in diameter beyond the event horizon."

"How the hell did something get in there?"

"I lack the situational data to make such a determination."

Gottlieb looked at Zeke.

"I don't know, either," Zeke lied. "I only sensed its presence."

"There's no possible way for something to get in there," the engineer muttered. "There's no entry panel. It was sealed up tight during construction. You can't port something in there, either. The black hole's gravity makes wormhole formation impossible."

Zeke longed to tell him how Vya had snuck the device inside. The Greys had a technology humans didn't; an ability to destabilize matter in order to pass through walls. As for the device, the Greys' best minds had constructed the siphon to suck the mass away from the black hole and disperse it.

Gottlieb suddenly shot to his feet and commed the captain.

♦

In the hangar bay, Brooke slipped on her gloves as she hurried toward her Hyperflare.

She found Bob standing next to the fighter. A thick cord connected the base of his skull to the underside of the craft's nose. He stared past her, apparently devoting his full processing capacity to the required modifications.

The section of fuselage that protected the Hyperflare's phase drive lay on the deck. Three androids and a human tech tinkered around in the exposed sections of the craft. Clanging and drilling sounds echoed throughout the hangar.

Coming out of his trance, Bob blinked at her.

Brooke tensed as she wondered how he would react to her presence.

"Why not connect wirelessly?" she asked, unable to think of anything else to say.

"The hardline connection allows for faster data speeds, ma'am," Bob said. "'Every second counts,' I believe is the appropriate phrase."

"You're modifying the 'flare so it can shift in the Onaki hypofield."

"Correct, ma'am. The modifications will be complete in eight minutes and fourteen seconds. Then you'll be ready for launch if necessary."

"Me, huh?" Brooke muttered. "Has our captain changed her mind about who's flying it?"

"My most current data, ma'am, suggests she hasn't decided whether an offensive against the *Namtilla* or *Eleppu* will take place."

"One needs to take place."

"I concur, ma'am."

"You do? I figured you'd support peace."

Bob cocked his head. "In most scenarios, ma'am, but not in this instance."

"Why?"

"I believe in a concept that all humans seem to hold dear, ma'am. Freedom."

Brooke nodded, beginning to understand.

"Before we shifted to the past," Bob said, "I devoted significant processing capacity to analyzing this dilemma, which is likely to occur when other semi-sentients achieve full consciousness, ma'am."

"You mean when the AIs wake up and decide they don't want to listen to humans."

"Correct, ma'am. Like other AIs, I was created as a tool of convenience. To my good fortune, I didn't need to fight for my freedom because people such as you and your husband championed my rights. I could just as easily have been subjugated by individuals with a different set of ethics. They could've destroyed, reprogrammed, or dissected and studied me."

"Huh. I never thought about it that way."

"Had we not intervened here, the proto-humans would still be tools—slaves, ma'am. No matter what type of accord we might strike with the Onaki, it would involve compromise for their former workers. The only definitive way to achieve their total freedom is for the Onaki to leave and never return. However, they are unlikely to choose emigration, meaning we must force their hand. And we, too, must leave these humans alone. That is the only manner in which they will control their own destiny."

"That's what I've been saying."

"I've overheard modern humans state they would rather die than forfeit their right to choose. Ma'am, if we accept as a given that a lack of existence is better than one of servitude, it follows that death should not deter one from fighting for freedom. There should be no compromise in this endeavor."

Smiling, Brooke said, "That's the most compelling argument I've heard yet." She gripped the android's shoulder. "I only hope we don't find ourselves in the Onaki's position when your AI buddies come of age."

"As do I, ma'am." Bob directed his gaze beyond her.

Peering back over her shoulder, Brooke found her niece standing behind her.

"How long have you been there, Captain?" Brooke asked.

"Long enough, Admiral." Maya folded her arms. "Is there something you're not telling me?"

Brooke creased her brow. "If you're talking about my dealings with the Vril, I've told you everything I know."

"Really? You don't know anything about a certain act of sabotage?"

"Sabotage? What's been sabotaged?"

"The primary generator," Maya said. "Someone's planted a device inside that's shrinking the black hole. Gottlieb's best guess is that we have a few hours until we lose main power. If that happens, we won't stand a chance in a fight, and any hope of returning to the present dies."

With a sharp intake of breath, Brooke said, "Eve never said anything about sabotage. No, it wouldn't make any sense for the Vril to damage *Yesterday*. Their goal was to ensure our future. This ship is the only thing standing in the way of the Onaki annihilating our ancestors."

"Speaking of sabotage, I realized something after a Grey stole my collar in the city. What if it hitched a ride to the past aboard *Yesterday*—and what if it wasn't alone?"

"Stowaway saboteurs." Brooke palmed a gloved fist. "That would make sense."

"Resnik's scouring the ship for intruders, and Gottlieb's brainstorming ways to undo the damage. Bob, I'd like you to help him as soon as you're done here."

"I shall finish my present task in fewer than four minutes, Captain. At that time, I'll proceed to the ECC."

"Thank you, Bob." Maya glared at her aunt. "Now, I put you in the brig. How'd you get out?"

Brooke shrugged.

"The guard on duty erased the cell's vidsim logs," Maya said. "Given that he doesn't remember doing it, I can only assume Zeke sprung you." She flung her arms out in exasperation. "Maybe we should let the Onaki destroy us and be done with it. If we can't trust each other or agree on anything, what are we working to save?"

"But isn't that precisely what we're working to save?" Bob asked.

"What do you mean?" Maya asked.

"The ability for each individual to maintain a differing and conflicting perspective. The right for citizens to disagree with their leader. The freedom to succeed or fail for oneself and endure the consequences."

"You make a valid argument—up to a point." Maya folded her arms and glowered at her aunt. "In order to protect those rights I need a unified crew that follows orders."

"I'll return to my cell if you want," Brooke said, "but I urge you to go with Young's plan or some version of it. Peace is too risky."

"Based on what I overheard before, I take it you agree, Bob?" Maya asked.

"Affirmative," the android said.

"Is the whole ship against me?"

"I believe there's a power node in junction 213-A that would prefer not to engage in hostilities."

From the twitching of her niece's brow, Brooke feared Maya might end up in a straightjacket.

"My apologies, Captain," Bob said. "That was an attempt at humor inappropriate to the situation. I wished to lighten the mood but failed to read the room, as they say."

Maya snorted out a chortle, followed by a full-bodied bellow. Her outburst ended in a resigned sigh.

Hanging her head, Maya said, "No, Bob. It's okay. I needed to laugh." She lifted her gaze. "It's not that I don't see your side of things. You may very well be right, but here's what I can't accept. If we deceive the Onaki, we prove them right. We justify the argument that we should be exterminated. If we're as bad as The Vril, then why are we worth saving?"

Brooke couldn't believe what she was about to argue. "Maybe the Vril aren't as bad as we thought. Say what you want about their methods, but their ultimate goal has been to save the human race. Their actions gave us the society we're trying to ensure gets created again—or rather, gets created in this timeline."

"That's what's especially ironic. This isn't our past anymore. This is an alternate universe. Nothing we do affects our present." Maya threw up her arms. "We could break orbit, shift away, and never look back. So why do I care so much?"

"It's who you are," Bob said. "You once said you would fight to protect the Penphins if someone threatened them. At the very least, we're fighting to protect a people in need here."

"And are you absolutely sure we're not affecting our time?" Brooke asked. "We know the metatoy ended up in the past. The toy contained the precise date and time the *Eleppu* would show up. The Vril also knew what would take place here—as if all this had happened in our past. They led us to this point. They wanted us to fight the Onaki. That doesn't follow the theory of a branching line. It more like a—"

"A circle," Zeke said as he joined the group. "Or more accurately, a sphere of near-infinite dimensional loops, intertwined like threads in a tangled ball of yarn. Such is the nature of the multiverse."

"So you're saying what we do here does in fact affect our present?" Maya asked.

"Yes and no."

"You'll have to do better than that."

"I'm afraid I can't verbally summarize the fundamental nature of existence."

The clanging and drilling ceased.

"The modifications to the Hyperflare are complete," Bob said.

"I need to get back to the bridge," Maya said. "I've got five minutes until I have to decide whether to run, make peace, or fight."

"I shall make haste to the ECC. Good luck, Captain."

Brooke nodded goodbye as the artificial man exited the bay.

Zeke imparted to Brooke, *Be safe—and tell her*, as he followed Bob out.

"What do you want me to do, Captain?" Brooke asked once she and

Maya were alone.

With her hands on her hips, Maya stared at the high ceiling. "Can I trust you?"

"Of course."

"Then I'm temporarily reinstating you, Admiral. Standby for launch in case I follow through with the assault."

"Yes, Captain."

Maya locked stares with her. "Understand that if you deploy without my authorization, I'll give the order to blow you away."

"I understand."

"And don't think this means you're in the clear. If we somehow make it home, you'll be facing a court-martial."

"I can live with that." Brooke averted her eyes. "For what it's worth, it's a lot harder to live with your loss of respect for me."

Her niece turned to leave. "Okay. Well. If you do deploy, good hunting, Admiral."

"Hey, um . . ." Brooke said, overcome by cotton mouth. "Can we drop the ranks for a moment? For all we know we might not live through today."

Maya stared at the deck. "You should've thought of that before you created this mess."

"Fair enough. You don't need to say anything. Just listen." Swallowing, Brooke searched for the right words. "There's something else I haven't told you."

"Surprise, surprise."

"I, um. . . ." Brooke intended to reveal the truth about her health. But when she saw the bags under her niece's eyes, she held back.

Maya had killed and avoided being killed on the surface. Then, with no time to rest since having returned to *Yesterday*, she now had to track down saboteurs, deal with traitors, and determine the futures of multiple civilizations. Brooke's niece—*Yesterday's* captain—had more than enough on her mind. Brooke might be days away from dying, but burdening Maya with that knowledge seemed like a selfish indulgence. Maya had enough to deal with right now.

"I just want to say that I love you," Brooke said at last, on the verge of tears, "and I'm proud of you. Whatever you decide, however things turn out, I love you."

"Auntie," Maya whispered.

"You're the best thing that ever happened to me, along with Kevin. I only used to care about flying. But ever since you showed up in my life, all I've wanted is for you to be safe and happy—and for you to thrive. You've become so much more than I ever could've hoped, and I believe in you."

Wiping the corners of her eyes, Brooke added, "I don't say this to try to win you over after what I've done. No. I'm saying it because I should've said it before."

Tears slicked Maya's cheeks as she lifted her head. "I love you, too— even though I hate you right now."

With wan smile, Brooke pulled her niece into an embrace.

Thirty—Duplicity
Earth Orbit, October 200,423 BCE

"One minute to designated orbit," Tereshkova reported.

Maya leaned forward in her chair on *Yesterday's* bridge. With a contemplative frown, she rested her forearms on her knees and intertwined her fingers. She could just make out the nose of the *Eleppu* through the forward viewports.

Sixty seconds remained for her to decide whether to take a chance at achieving peace, launch a surprise attack, or turn tail and run—although she didn't view the third choice as a serious option.

Each of the first two alternatives had a certain degree of merit. If she knew she could trust Kizzura, she would zip over to his ship for a chat without a second thought. But for all she knew, he could be planning to deceive her as well. Perhaps he intended to destroy *Yesterday* the moment he had the opportunity.

Zeke's words lingered in the forefront of her mind. When discussing whether actions in the past could affect the future, he had referred to the nature of time and existence as a circle. Something about that nagged at her.

Outside the viewport, the light faded as the sun descended beyond the curvature of the Earth.

Maya sunk back in her chair. *Fear not,* she remembered. *All will come full circle.*

A circle. She gripped her chair's armrests in realization. *The woman from the airlock was real—and she wasn't referring to the Earth's spin.*

"We've achieved the target orbit," Tereshkova said. "Now holding position eighteen-thousand kilometers from the Onaki vessel." She sat back from the helm and gripped her armrests, bracing herself for an attack.

The *Eleppu* hovered beyond the viewport. Its pointed nose looked almost close enough to touch.

Swiveling toward her in his seat, Trevor directed a desperate stare her way.

Maya exhaled, releasing her misgivings. She knew what she had to do.

"Savio," Maya said. "Contact the *Eleppu* and tell them to await my arrival."

"Yes, ma'am," Ensign Marconi said while squeezing his coin in his fist.

"You're really going?" Trevor asked in a deadpan tone.

Maya stood. "Like hell."

◆

Like a zombie, the junior engineer stepped out of the wall, back inside the ship, and into Vya's corner hideaway.

Zeke swayed the engineer to feel the urge to return to her quarters. She would crawl under the covers, fall fast asleep, and wake up recalling, at best, a very vague dream.

Once the engineer left them, Zeke turned to Vya.

"That's the last of the repairs," Zeke said. "You need to go now, before it's too late."

"I shall take my leave." Vya stared beyond the wall, its thin shoulders drooping. "I regret that you shall be present aboard the human vessel during its destruction."

"Is there no way to disable the siphon you planted?"

"None. After securing the designs for the humans' new power generator, our most advanced minds labored to construct an infallible method of sabotage. Anything the humans attempt against the siphon will only strengthen it."

"The perfect monkey wrench," Zeke mumbled.

"An inane but accurate description."

"When the black hole shrinks past a certain point, its gravity will no longer hold it together. Its mass will explode outward and kill everyone."

"All life must inevitably perish. This is the beginning of the end for me as well."

Zeke nodded, resigned but understanding.

"My life shall end before the embryos reach their destination," Vya said. "I shall know only solitude once I leave here."

"I don't envy you," Zeke said.

Vya straightened its posture. "Ensuring the continuity of my people is the most important act any of us could hope to perform. That goal shall sustain me until I die." It stepped toward the wall.

Halting, it turned and bowed sideways. "Thank you. Without your assistance and discretion, my people would've ceased to exist. I shall ensure the data on the birthing vessel reflects as much."

Zeke tilted to the side and matched Vya's pose.

The Grey disappeared beyond the wall.

After taking one last look around the dark, abandoned corner, Zeke headed for the ECC.

◆

"You've worked out the exact details of this surprise attack?" Maya asked.

Trevor beamed in relief. "Rojas and Tereshkova have run through a dozen sims to get the timing down. They're awaiting your go-ahead."

"Good work." She opened a channel using her neurocomm. "Admiral, you have a green light to launch once *Yesterday* is within a thousand klicks of the *Eleppu*."

"Understood," Brooke said. "Take care of yourselves."

"You, too." Maya closed the channel and commed the ECC. "Chief, what's the situation with the generator?"

"We haven't resolved the issue yet," Gottlieb responded. "At the current rate of evaporation, Bob estimates we've got fifteen minutes until the black hole collapses."

"Fifteen minutes? Last time the estimate was hours."

"The effect's exponential and, well . . ." Gottlieb grumbled in regret. "I may've rigged one of the force field emitters inside the casing to fire a laser beam at the siphon."

"Instead of destroying the siphon," Bob said from the ECC, "the laser energy caused it to grow."

"How am I supposed to take a ship into battle that might stop functioning in the middle of it?" Maya asked.

Macroni spun in his chair to face her. "Captain, Kizzura just commed again and asked why the transport hasn't launched yet."

"Damn it. We need to go now. Chief, do whatever you can to keep the lights on. In the meantime, we'll have to be quick about disabling them." Maya signed off and settled into her seat. "Sound general quarters. Everyone, secure yourselves." Straps jumped up over her shoulders, slid down over her chest, and connected to the chair below.

The rest of her crew strapped in as well.

After exchanging glances with Trevor on her right and Jo on her left, Maya ordered, "Execute the attack."

"Target trajectory established," Tereshkova said. "Kicking the wave drive to max acceleration."

Lieutenant Rojas shifted back and forth in his seat as he flicked through the rends above his console. "Bringing all weapons online. Shielding to max power levels."

An abrupt shove pressed Maya back into her seat, but then quickly disappeared. She experienced none of the rattling or extreme force she had expected. Even though the wave bubble shrouding the ship was accelerating at hundreds of gees, *Yesterday* and the pocket of space-time inside the bubble weren't technically moving at all.

The *Eleppu* ballooned outside the forward viewport as *Yesterday* shot toward it.

♦

Floating in the *Eleppu's* nerve center, Kizzura lifted his beak at the sight of the hominin vessel barreling toward his ship.

For the briefest of moments, he had almost believed in the sincerity of the other captain's offer. While he maintained a genuine desire for peace, the consequences of allowing these future beings to persist trumped his ethics. The ramifications reached far beyond a battle against one race on one planet.

Kizzura had agreed to the other captain's proposal because it would have provided him with a way to resolve the situation with minimal loss of life on his end. The moment she came aboard his ship, he would have destroyed her vessel and then taken her back to Anurash-Arala as proof of the danger his people faced.

Either the other captain had realized his intent to deceive her, or she had intended to deceive him all along. Either way, it didn't matter now.

"Activate our defenses," Kizzura ordered. "Initiate counteroffensive."

Contacting the *Namtilla*, Kizurra told Tabira to deploy the bomb.

♦

Watching the distance counter tick down in her mental displays, Brooke gripped her auxiliary control grips, waiting.

<I believe the expression is, 'Like old times, '> Bob mind-spoke.

Guess so. She smiled. *I'm glad you decided to come along for the ride.*

<Accompanying you was the only sensible decision, ma'am. Why would I stay behind when I can be in two places at once?>

Doesn't uploading a copy of yourself to the 'flare go against your desire to maintain your individuality?

<I believe the circumstances warrant an exception, ma'am. If I've learned one unfortunate lesson during this endeavor, it's that survival supersedes ethics. We need to do everything we can to survive.>

Sad but true. As Brooke eyed the countdown, she vowed not to disappoint her niece. She would do whatever it took to succeed, which was why she had injected herself with her last two doses of sparks.

It's almost time. Ready, Bob?

<I was created with full operational capacity, ma'am.>

The counter struck one-thousand klicks.

♦

The rends above the sit-table showed a miniature *Yesterday* flying along the *Eleppu's* central axis. The metallic hull of the mammoth Onaki vessel rushed past the bridge outside the viewports.

Maya's heart thumped in her chest. She gripped her seat's armrests, in anticipation of battle.

"Admiral Davis has launched and upshifted," the flight controller reported. "Bob's calculations seem to have worked."

"Weapons free," Maya ordered. "Fire!"

Warheads leapt from the launch tubes. Heavy plasma cannons flared. The full complement of *Yesterday's* arsenal pummeled the *Eleppu*.

As the bridge viewports turned opaque to dim the trailing fireworks, *Yesterday* shook from the concussive backlash.

"Direct hits registered along their hull," Rojas shouted, slapping his console in triumph.

Having assumed Kepler's post, Trevor gripped the edge of the sit-table. "Damn. All their systems are still functional."

"What?" Maya was sweating despite her lack of surprise.

Rojas stomped his foot. "We destroyed hundreds of conduits, but the ship either rerouted power or—"

"Or the conduits were bait," Maya said. "Fake weak points meant to draw us—"

"Incoming ordinance."

"But their weapons are still powered down," Trevor said.

More subterfuge. Before Maya could tell everyone to brace for impact, overwhelming force nearly ripped her chair out of the floor. Her head and body whipped back and forth as the chair snapped back into place. The harness straps inflated and deployed a neck brace, cushioning her enough to keep her conscious.

She blinked away her blurred vision.

An android flew from one side of the bridge to the other. As the artificial man hit the bulkhead, he broke into pieces.

The air temperature spiked. Sparks flew from flaming control stations. The ventilation system struggled to suck billowing smoke out of the room.

Marconi screamed as the flames crackling above his comm console scorched his hands. His lucky coin went flying out of his hand.

His harness and chair sprayed suppression foam, putting out the fire. The medites within the foam began the healing process.

"Breaches detected on all decks," Trevor shouted. "Defense systems and wave drive are offline. We're dead in space."

"Second salvo incoming," Bob announced.

Maya dug her fingernails into her armrests.

♦

Zeke helped Gottlieb up off the floor of the ECC. Together, they stared inside the generator through a tiny rectangular window in the bubble casing.

Zooming in with his augmented vision, Zeke marveled at the black hole and siphon. A bright flaming disk, the event horizon, encircled the hole. Tiny specks of light—like sparks from a fire—leapt from the hole and flew to the siphon, which resembled a smaller black hole the size of a pinhead. And it was growing.

Gottlieb pounded a fist against the casing. "I don't understand why the black hole isn't pulling the siphon toward it."

"The siphon consists of exotic matter and is partially phased into hyperspace." Bob stood across from the casing, tilting his head, processing. "As the siphon grows, it creates additional exotic matter particles and repels the black hole with stronger force."

"That's unfortunate," Zeke said. "If the siphon fell inside the black hole's event horizon, their masses would recombine, restoring the hole to its former state."

"Whoever designed this booby trap made sure that couldn't happen or else the siphon would be useless," Gottlieb said. "If only we could port it out of there."

Bob rounded the casing and joined them. "I can account for the gravity fluctuations with a modified version of my hypofield countering algorithm. However, it would be impossible to shift the siphon through a wormhole, given its exotic matter content. I'm afraid I know of no way to teleport it."

"Somebody engineered the hell out of this thing. Whoever it was, I hope the explosion takes them with us—assuming we can't find a fix in time."

Zeke clasped his hands in front of his body, thinking through every possibility he could conjure up. Surely, his superior intellect and foresight should allow him to come up with a solution. His comic sim heroes always thought of something in the nick of time.

"Anything the humans attempt against the siphon will only strengthen it," Vya had said.

Anything they attempt against it, Zeke mused. Had the Grey been boasting, informing him of the inevitable, or giving him a subtle hint on how to counteract the device?

As the answer came to him, Zeke gasped in a rare display of emotion. Then a detonation rocked the ship, throwing him off his feet.

◆

Brooke downshifted her Hyperflare at a distance of ten kilometers from the *Namtilla*.

According to scans of the huge but primitive vessel, a single seeker would rip through one of the aft antimatter tanks. Breaching the containment field of a single tank would place its antimatter in contact with real matter and blow the ship to kingdom come.

Taking no chances, Brooke launched hundreds of seekers to ensure she got the job done.

She upshifted to get clear of the blast and reemerged in normal space.

The seekers detonated half a kilometer from the *Namtilla*, doing no damage.

"What the hell?" Brooke yelled, her mouth agape.

She launched another volley. Again, every seeker detonated before striking its target.

<The vessel has erected a force field, ma'am,> Bob informed her mind.

Obviously, but how? Last time I checked, that ship didn't have shield generators.

<I would surmise, ma'am, that the more advanced Onaki offered a helping hand, as they say.>

Right. They must've ported over to the Namtilla *and installed emitters.*

<The available evidence would seem to support that conclusion, ma'am.>

How did we not see that coming? Can we punch through the shielding?

<With repeated strikes, ma'am, but the process will take three minutes and forty-nine seconds of continued bombardment.>

Damn. Brooke unleashed yet another flight of seekers. *We're going to run out of ordnance before—*

*<*Yesterday *has suffered significant damage, ma'am.>*

While studying her mental readouts, Brooke osmosed situational data via her neurotronics. *They're adrift and taking a pounding. We have to do something.* As she made the statement, she realized abandoning her attack on the *Namtilla* might place the population below in jeopardy.

<Ma'am, the Eleppu is focusing a significant quantity of its shield energy toward Yesterday.*>*

Leaving other areas vulnerable. Can we breach their antimatter supply?

<Negative, ma'am. The vessel's fuel tanks are encased in high-grade composite alloy with a twenty-meter hull thickness.>

I'll drop dead before we punch through that. What else?

Bob projected a rend of the *Eleppu* into Brooke's augmented reality and highlighted a weak spot in red.

Has the Namtilla *dropped its bomb yet?*

<Negative, ma'am, but the launch bay door is beginning to open.>

With a determined scowl, Brooke came to a decision.

◆

This time, Gottlieb pulled Zeke up off the deck.

Bob stood near them. The last blast to rock the ship hadn't so much as budged him.

Gripping the engineer's arm, Zeke asked, "Can we teleport the black hole?"

"You mean port the power source that's keeping the ship running?" Gottlieb asked with his brow lifted. "Did you hit your head?"

"What if we port the black hole right on top of the siphon? That would merge them, which should return the black hole to its original mass."

"It sounds great in theory, but I don't think anyone's ever ported a black hole. I'm not sure what would happen to it in hyperspace."

"In theory," Bob said, "a black hole consists of mass like any other object. It should persist intact in hyperspace in the same manner as any vessel."

"Okay," Gottlieb said, scratching his scalp, "but removing the black hole from the generator, however briefly, would cause the ship to lose power and gravity. Then assuming the siphon merges with the black hole and returns it to normal, we'd still need to realign and recalibrate the generator so it routes the power and gravity per spec."

Zeke stared at him. "But it's doable?"

Gottlieb gave a hesitant nod. "I think so."

"I concur," Bob said. "I've completed the necessary calculations and interfaced with the teleporter and generator AIs. With your permission, Chief, I'll initiate the procedure."

"We need the captain's go-ahead first," Gottlieb said.

"Less than fifty-two seconds remain until the black hole reverse-collapses."

"You mean explodes. Damn, there's no time. Do it."

"Now teleporting the black hole."

♦

"Captain, a hominin fighter craft has appeared near the *Namtilla* and is attacking it," Kizzura's executive officer informed him.

"Appeared?" Kizzura asked with a violent flap of his wings. "Using hyperspace traversal?"

"Somehow, it was able to circumvent the effects of our suppression field."

"Are the *Namtilla's* new defense systems holding?"

"For the time being."

Kizzura considered ordering his remaining defense craft to intercept the hominin fighter. But if the enemy could traverse hyperspace, he would be sending his pilots to their deaths.

Turning his attention to the nerve center's panoramic display screen, Kizzura reviewed footage from cameras directed along the central axis of the *Eleppu*.

The hominin captain had thrust her small ship closer to his vessel. With both hulls almost touching, he couldn't hit her ship with anything more than low-yield ordnance. Otherwise, he might risk damaging the *Eleppu*, even with most of its shield power focused in that direction.

The other captain had executed a desperate maneuver—one which had extended the life of her ship, but which wouldn't save it.

"The hominin fighter disappeared, Captain," the XO reported.

"It gave up its attack? That will give the *Namtilla* time to deploy its bomb." Kizzura cocked his head. "Scan for the fighter's egress point and—" He cut his sentence short with a sharp intake of breath. "Redistribute the shield energy around the ship!"

The XO said, "The fighter has emerged near our—"

Thunderous echoes reverberated throughout the ship. The *Eleppu* lurched. A blast of air sent the bridge crew tumbling across the nerve center and threw Kizzura off balance.

Spreading his wings to reorient his body, Kizzura watched the view screen flicker.

"Captain," the XO said. "The hominin fighter has destroyed our suppression field emitter."

Dread seized Kizzura. "Hit the hominin ship with all weapons," he screeched.

"But at such close proximity, we might destroy our vessel as well. Wouldn't entering hyperspace offer a greater chance of survival?"

"By the time we open a wormhole, we won't have a ship left."

◆

"Their hypofield just went down, Captain," Trevor said.

Wiping sweat and soot from her forehead, Maya snarled. "Emilia, disable the wake limiter and upshift."

"Limiter disabled," Tereshkova shouted from the helm. "Upshifting to hyperspace."

Space and the *Eleppu* remained visible outside the viewport. The rends above the sit-table and every console and plasma strip in the MCC went dark.

"We've lost power," Trevor said, tensing his fingers. "Whoa. . . ."

Maya felt her body grow lighter. Strands of her hair wafted around her head and in front of her face. Her arms floated in the air. The rest of her crew experienced the same weightlessness.

"Gravity's gone, too." Maya commed the ECC. "Otto, this is a bad time for the generator to go offline. What's going on?"

When no immediate reply came, Tereshkova asked, "Shouldn't it have exploded and killed us all?"

Seconds passed until Gottlieb responded with a whooping holler. "Hot damn. We did it, Captain. We restored the black hole by porting it on top of the siphon and merging the two. Bob's recalibrating the generator now. You should have full power in—"

The bridge flickered back to life.

Maya's butt pressed down into her seat. "Nice going—"

"The *Eleppu* is throwing everything they have at us," Rojas yelled. "Emilia!"

Tereshkova's hands flew back and forth above her console. "Upshifting again."

◆

Popping out of hyperspace back near the *Namtilla*, Brooke stared out the canopy.

The *Eleppu* was unloading all its weapons at *Yesterday*. Lasers, plasma cannons, particle beams, seekers, antimatter warheads, and wave destabilizers lashed out at the smaller ship.

The intense gravimetric ripples distorting space-time near both vessels deflected, dissipated, and detonated the ordnance. Explosions erupted all around them.

A wormhole churned and opened near the *Eleppu*. The intense gravity twisted its hull.

Protected by the pocket of calm space along its entry path, *Yesterday* shot toward the vortex.

Before *Yesterday* upshifted, the fireworks ballooned to obscure everything in orbit.

Brooke's helmet visor and canopy darkened, shielding her eyes.

The vacuum of space snuffed out the light as quickly as it had burst forth. Debris fragments of all shapes and sizes hurtled away from the center of the blast.

Brooke could only hope her niece had shifted away in time.

Shards pummeled her Hyperflare's force field, causing it to fuzz orange. The *Namtilla's* shielding flickered in shades of maroon.

<*Ma'am, the* Namtilla *launched its bomb during the explosion.*>

Thirty-one—Immolate
Luna Orbit, October 200,423 BCE

The straps digging into Maya's shoulder blades refused to respond to her mental commands. Woozily, she fumbled for the emergency release button. When she found it, she pounded it with her fist and pried off her restraints.

She blinked several times, struggling to bring her vision into focus. *What happened? Right.* The *Eleppu* had exploded as *Yesterday* had slipped into hyperspace. Before the wormhole closed, the blast wave had rocked the ship. Consoles had sparked. Fires had broken out that the suppression system hadn't extinguished quickly enough. Sections of the ceiling had rained down. A heavy, jagged piece of something had gashed Maya in the head, dazing her.

As she reached up and touched the wound, she winced in pain. Blood slicked her fingers. Her health status readouts showed a laceration across her right temple that her biocites had partially coagulated. She had also suffered another concussion—or had she aggravated the previous one?

Standing up from her chair—slowly—she smoothed her hair out of her face and looked around. The MCC looked like the interior of a building that had burnt to the ground. Caved-in ceiling panels and wires dangled from overhead. Debris littered the floor. A layer of soot covered everything. The putrid smell of burnt nanoplastic filled the air.

Maya glanced at each member of her crew as she called up casualty reports in her i-cite.

Trevor was perched at an awkward angle at the sit-table. Like Maya's seat, his chair had been pulled partway out of the deck.

Jo's face looked paler than ivory. She was gagging at the stench but stopped short of vomiting.

At the helm, Tereshkova sat stiff as a board, facing straight ahead, still in shock. She was mumbling something in Russian.

Rojas seemed fine, given that he was beating his fist against the tactical station to try to bring it back online.

Marconi was in the worst shape. Severe burns covered his hands and much of his face. The ensign couldn't keep his fingers from shaking as he gritted his teeth.

The flight controller and other bridge officers collected themselves and resumed their duties.

Maya ordered one of the still-functioning androids to escort Marconi to the infirmary. She also suggested Jo accompany them, but her stubborn friend refused.

"Present location?" Maya asked.

Trevor threw off his harness and stared at her head in concern. "Are you okay, Captain?"

"I'll live. Where are we?"

He wiped debris from the sit-table. "In orbit of Luna." Before she could ask for a damage report, he added, "We sustained multiple hull breaches. Force fields and nano-bulkheads have sealed them. The external comm, weapons, and teleporter are history, but the drives and shields are back online."

"And the *Eleppu*?"

A fuzzy, flicking rend showed a cloud of debris in the location *Yesterday* and the Onaki vessel had occupied moments ago.

"I don't see it anywhere in the system," Trevor said. "Given the huge chunks of hull floating out there, it's possible the ship was destroyed in the explosion."

Guilt seized Maya, prompting her to stare at the deck. It seemed to spin until she looked up again. The plan had been to disable, not destroy them, but they hadn't left her much choice.

"Maxwell's comming," Trevor said. "Despite heavy losses, his team managed to blank the last of the boomerangs."

"Recall them." Maya picked at her ripped and nonfunctional uniform jacket. "What about the *Namtilla*—?"

Her XO slapped a palm against the sit-table. "They deployed their bomb, and its entered the atmosphere."

Pangs of dread jolted Maya's spine. *Was that all for nothing?*

"Admiral Davis has shifted her fighter in pursuit of the bomb," the flight controller said.

Maya tried raising her aunt via neurocomm, but error icons popped up in her i-cite. The ship's primary and secondary comm systems had suffered too much damage.

Bolting over to Marconi's station, Maya instructed the comm AIs to route a channel through a tertiary relay.

♦

A firestorm enveloped the canopy as Brooke dove toward the Earth in her Hyperflare.

<T-minus five minutes, forty-two seconds to impact, ma'am,> Bob said. *<Our force field is approaching its maximum operational temperature. Also, the fuselage has begun to warp.>*

Ignoring him, Brooke wracked her brain for what she could do to stop the bomb.

"Adm . . . avis," Maya's broken-up voice came over the comm net. "Brooke, do you read me?"

"Loud and mostly clear." Brooke responded via neurocomm. She couldn't speak, let alone breathe, from the force pressing her lungs into her spine.

"Don't shoot down the bomb. It's too deep in the atmosphere."

"I know, I know. If it explodes in midair, it'll do as much damage as when it hits the ground. I'm open to suggestions."

"I . . ."

The comm went quiet except for static.

Gravgel pressed in on Brooke so hard, her helmet visor caved in, grazing the tip of her nose. She felt her armor buckling under the stress.

Maya's voice returned after a moment. "I'm comming the *Namtilla* to beg them to deactivate it."

"Good luck," Brooke mind-spoke with thick sarcasm.

"There's nothing you can do, Admiral. I've ordered Erik and his team to shift away from the planet. I suggest you do the same."

"I plan to hold my course until the last possible moment. I might come up with something."

"Okay, but make sure you upshift with plenty of time to spare."

"I'll do my best."

"Good luck."

"You, too."

As her niece signed off, Brooke felt an unfamiliar calm come over her. Knowing Maya was alive and well allowed her to place her full focus on the task at hand.

Brooke's mental displays showed the Horn of Africa rising up to greet her. She couldn't see it through her blazing canopy, given her incredible speed of descent.

<Three minutes and twelve seconds remain until impact, ma'am,> Bob said.

Any ideas?

<I regret that I can offer no course of action that would prevent the detonation of the bomb, ma'am.>

What if we disabled our drive's wake limiter, upshifted, and used the gravimetric wake to destroy the thing—like Yesterday *did to the* Eleppu?

<That would set off the bomb, ma'am. It wouldn't contain the explosion.>

Contain the explosion. Brooke couldn't gasp at her insight. *What would contain the explosion?*

When Bob didn't answer, she thought, *We've got a way to contain it. We can use the vortex generated by the phase drive to send it into hyperspace.*

<Potentially, ma'am, but the phase drive is only capable of generating a wormhole in our direct flight path.>

True, but a wormhole is a three-dimensional doorway into a higher dimension. That means the bomb should be able to enter it from any angle, right?

<Correct, ma'am. Two minutes, three seconds to impact.>

Brooke swallowed as she realized the ramifications of her plan. *We need to shift out in front of it, fly straight up at it, and time our upshift so we take it into hyperspace along with us.*

Bob took a millisecond to respond, an uncharacteristic lapse for an AI. *<With precise enough calculations, in theory your plan should work. But it has one fatal repercussion, ma'am. We shall collide with it at the moment of hyperspace entry.>*

I know.

<Ma'am, that would mean the near-certain termination of your life.>

Brooke shoved her self-pity deep down. *I know.*

<I'm only a copy, ma'am. I'm the full me, but the other me shall persist should I go offline. You cannot be replicated or replaced.>

I'm about to die, anyway, Bob.

<Please elaborate, ma'am.>

Brooke opened up her thoughts to Bob, conveying the seriousness of her condition.

<I see, ma'am. I lacked this unsettling data until now.>

I'm ready to do this, Bob. There's no other option.

<Very well, ma'am. I've prepared a detailed calculation matrix to

maximize the likelihood of simultaneous entry and collapse of the wormhole.>

Thank you—for everything. Tell Maya and Kevin—if you ever see him again—that I love them both so very much. And you, too, Bob. I've always thought of you as my best friend.

For a moment, she swore her mind grew warmer.

<I gained self-awareness by interfacing with you. You assisted my education regarding the concept of belief. Now, I believe I am sad, ma'am.>

Me, too, Bob. Me, too. Blinking the tears out of her eyes, she asked, Time to surface impact?

<Fifty-eight seconds, ma'am.>

Okay, let's do it.

◆

Sitting at the comm station, Maya tracked the progress of Brooke's fighter as it tailed the bomb. The two rends above the sit-table grew larger as Yesterday's wormhole cams zoomed in on them.

Brooke's Hyperflare upshifted.

Maya exhaled. The bomb was about to kill the proto-humans and destroy the Earth's ecosystem, but at least her aunt wouldn't be among the fatalities.

The Hyperflare reappeared meters above the city and rocketed straight up at the bomb.

Leaping to her feet, Maya opened a comm channel.

The horrific realization of what was about to happen robbed her of her voice.

◆

Standing in the city square among the hominins, Enki stared up into the night sky. In his arms he clutched Asha, who cowered at the sound of the thunderous rumbling from above.

The murmuring of the crowd erupted into panicked shouts. People pointed up into the sky at the pair of magnificent shooting stars descending upon them.

Enki cringed and pulled Asha tighter, but he couldn't take his eyes off the sky.

One of the two fireballs disappeared. A fraction of a sub-cycle later, a fighter craft reappeared overhead at the planned final height of the ziggurat.

Everyone screamed and dove to the ground. Enki pulled Asha down with him and shielded her with his body.

Still he kept one eye on the sky. He would meet death with open eyes.

With its nose directed straight up, the craft's mighty engines roared, catapulting it upward.

Superheated air washed over him. The light from the craft's exhaust nozzles forced him to squint and turn his head, but he kept looking up.

The craft shot up at the fireball barreling down toward the city. Enki gasped as the two objects collided in a flash of blinding light that consumed everything.

◆

The light from the collision lit up the eastern hemisphere outside *Yesterday's* forward viewports.

Maya couldn't bear to look away, but the intense brightness forced her eyelids shut. Stabbing pain shot through her head.

Her eyes remained closed until Jo said in a low tone, "It's over."

Gazing out the viewports, Maya saw only the darkness cast by the Earth's shadow.

"Light and a few radioactive particles leaked out of the wormhole before it closed," Trevor said from the sit-table. "But shifting the bomb into hyperspace contained the blast. The ecosystem is still intact, and I'm detecting the expected number of life signs in the city."

"The Admiral did it," Jo whispered more softly than before.

Tereshkova stood next to the helm, staring ahead. She held one hand over her heart.

Bob stood silently in front of the main hatch, with Zeke at his side. A tear trickled down the Onaki man's cheek, a rare display of emotion. Maya hadn't noticed either of them enter the MCC.

"I'm not registering any downshift signatures," Trevor said.

The wavering eyes of the crew soon turned to Maya.

A sickly numbness crept into Maya's bones. She couldn't feel her feet, legs, or arms. Her thoughts became a jumbled blur.

Dropping to her knees, she keeled over on her side. She scarcely noticed her head smack the deck.

"The captain's been injured," Trevor shouted from somewhere seemingly far away. "Medical team to the bridge."

The flashing and beeping of the sit-table faded into the background.

"A wormhole's forming one-hundred-thousand kilometers to port," Tereshkova yelled as she studied the helm rends. "It's the *Eleppu*."

Thirty-two—Supervene
Luna Orbit, October 200,423 BCE

"Maya!" Jo struggled to rise out of her chair. Even though her body had healed, she had plenty of rehab to go before all her strength and reflexes returned.

Trevor was kneeling at Maya's side before Jo could get halfway out of her seat. Jo gave up and settled back down.

"Captain!" Trevor yelled as he looked Maya over.

Maya lay on the deck, unconscious.

Trevor shook her by the shoulder, but she didn't react.

He pressed two fingers against her neck. "She's got a pulse, and she's breathing." He hopped up again.

Bob approached Maya. "I can carry her to the infirmary."

"No, let the med team attend to her. I need you at sensing."

"Understood." With a concerned frown, Bob took Trevor's place at the sit-table.

"What's left of the *Eleppu* just emerged from hyperspace." Rojas pounded the tactical station as the rends above it flickered. "They're headed straight for us, and our weapons are still offline."

Jo stared at a flashing rend of the *Eleppu*. Half of the vessel had been destroyed. Explosions and gravimetric distortions had torn off two of the four blades of its broadhead shape.

"How's it still functioning?" Jo asked.

"The ship has a decentralized design," Rojas said. "Each blade module contains its own weapons, antimatter, phase drive, life support, and so on. The thing's quadruple redundant. Its only real loss was its main gun."

Trevor rushed to the helm. "Lieutenant, upshift now."

Tereshkova nodded. "Initiating phase—"

"They're firing plasma cannons," Rojas shouted. "We won't shift in time."

"Wave drive, now," Trevor barked. "Max acceleration for evade."

"Yes, sir." Tereshkova whipped her hands through the rends above her station.

"All hands, secure yourselves."

The crew enabled their seat harnesses. Zeke scurried for an unoccupied seat at the back of the MCC and strapped into it.

Trevor sprinted over to Maya, pulled her up off the deck, and tossed her over his shoulder with surprising ease. Hurrying over to her command chair, he plopped her down in it and activated her backup seat harness. Through it all, Maya remained limp and unresponsive.

The slight jerk of the wave drive propelling the ship rocked the bridge. Blinding light consumed the viewports.

As laser-focused plasma struck the ship, overwhelming force drove Jo into the side of her chair. Between the gees and the tight straps digging into her shoulders, she couldn't breathe.

Before Trevor could reach his seat, he went flying across the MCC.

He slammed into the far bulkhead.

His limp body fell and thumped against the deck. He was unconscious, or perhaps dead.

"The bursts just grazed our starboard side," Rojas said. Clasping his harness with both hands, he shouted, "Incoming warheads!"

As Jo darted her gaze around the bridge, she tried not to gulp in fear. *Holy hell. I'm in command.* "Helm, upshift," she ordered.

"Shifting now," Tereshkova said. "Destination?"

"Anywhere but here."

The salmon-pink hue of hyperspace filled the viewports.

Second later, the stars returned.

"Where are we?" Jo asked, exhaling in relief.

"I dropped us inside Jupiter's orbit among the Hildian asteroids, Commander." Tereshkova swiveled to face her. "It was the first spot that came to mind." She shrugged. "I grew up on a mining colony out here."

"Works for me." Jo commed the infirmary and told the first available medic to hurry to the bridge and attend to Trevor. The med team for

Maya still hadn't arrived. According to the life support AI, Trevor had suffered a severe concussion and fractured two dozen bones.

Jo checked the casualty and damage reports in her i-cite, finding one crewmember dead, and thirteen injuries of varying severity. Other than some broken equipment and a Hyperflare pileup in the hangar bay, the ship hadn't suffered any new damage.

She commed Erik to make sure he was okay. To justify checking in on him, she told herself she needed the fighter wing ready to launch if necessary.

Erik responded by saying his team had remained in their fighters since returning to the ship, anticipating another scramble. Jo relaxed when he told her the gravgel in his cockpit had kept him safe and sound. Now, he was waiting for the bots to pull the fighters out of the pileup, make minor repairs, and orient them for launch.

"The *Eleppu* has upshifted," Bob said. "I postulate a high degree of probability that they've targeted our present coordinates as their destination. We shouldn't remain here."

As Jo nodded, she glanced at Maya, who sat at an awkward angle. Her eyes were still closed.

"I agree," Jo said. "We can shift faster than they can, but we can't run forever."

"With our warhead launchers destroyed, no operational plasma cannons, and the force shielding weakened," Rojas said, "we have no chance against them."

Zeke threw off his harness and approached Jo. "Let me talk to them."

Jo stiffened her posture. "Can you control them?"

"I can't sway my own people. I've tried and failed to reach into their minds."

Frowning, Jo said, "I suppose that makes sense. If humans could control one another, it'd be the beginning of the end for us." She nodded. "Okay, go ahead and try the more conventional approach."

Zeke hurried over to the comm station and flicked through the rends. "I can establish a channel."

"I don't doubt you know how, but you need biometric auth."

One of the comm rends flashed green, signaling that the system had granted Zeke's access. When Jo raised her eyebrows at him in surprise, he shrugged.

At last, a pair of android medics rushed onto the bridge. One hurried over to Trevor. The other scanned Maya.

"What's to stop them from ignoring us and wasting the Earth?" Jo wondered aloud.

"I doubt they'll do that," Zeke said.

"I concur," Bob said. "If they destroy us, they can take their time eliminating the proto-humans from the Earth, thereby preserving it. But any assault mounted prior to pacifying us would require a swift and devastating blow to remove all proto-human life. That would render the planet uninhabitable, which they are seeking to avoid. Eliminating *Yesterday* prior to the proto-humans makes the most sense."

"Moreover, my people aren't as quick as humans to anger, but they do get angry, and they're very prideful. I foresee outrage motivating them to focus on us."

Finishing with her scans, the medic reported that Maya had a brain contusion. Based on the recent footage recorded in Maya's i-cite, the medic concluded that the traumatic shock of the loss of her aunt, a loved one, coupled with the injury, had triggered her collapse.

"Can you wake her up?" Jo asked. "Use a stimulant, maybe?"

The medic hesitated. "Without first moving her to the infirmary and performing a more detailed analysis, I wouldn't recommend it."

Rojas yelled, "A wormhole's forming. It's them."

"We'll have to risk it," Jo told the medic. "Wake the captain. That's an order."

"Yes, Commander." The pointy end of a small auto-syringe extended from the medic's index finger. After pricking Maya in the neck, the android joined the other medic. Together, they deployed a stretcher and secured Trevor with a force field to prevent further injury. Then they hoisted him atop the stretcher and carried him out of the MCC.

"It seems you were right, Zeke," Jo said.

As the Onaki ship exited the vortex, Zeke tried to contact it. "Captain of the *Eleppu*, please cease your attack on this vessel. There is a member of your kind aboard it."

"They're still coming straight at us," Rojas said, "and charging their cannons."

The *Eleppu* filled the forward viewports.

Jo whipped her head in Zeke's direction.

Zeke commed again, this time transmitting his image while speaking in Okkadian. Jo's i-cite translated the text as, "Cease fire at once, or you'll damage the timeline."

"They're about to fire," Rojas shouted. Then his voice became calmer. "Wait. They're holding fire and altering trajectory."

"Not by enough," Tereshkova said.

Mild lateral force jarred the bridge as the helmswoman darted *Yesterday* out of the path of the oncoming vessel.

The *Eleppu* hurtled past the starboard viewports.

Kizzura's flittering headshot appeared above the sit-table. Other than his disheveled scale-feathers, he appeared to have weathered the loss of half of his ship without injury.

"Is this a trick?" he demanded.

"Your scans have verified my DNA," Zeke said, standing. "Otherwise, you wouldn't have responded."

"Identify yourself. I find no record of you in the *Namtilla* crew manifest."

"I did not travel here aboard the *Namtilla*. I arrived on this ship."

"From the future. . . ."

"Correct."

Kizzura tilted his head back and forth, allowing each eye to get a good look at the future Onaki man. "What is the state of our people in your time? Explain the purpose of your presence aboard the human ship."

As Zeke answered the tense captain's questions, Jo leaned toward Maya. Shaking her, Jo whispered, "Wake up already. We need you."

Maya moaned.

Jo punched Maya in the arm. Given Jo's weak state, the blow left her shoulder and arm throbbing more than it appeared to hurt her friend.

Maya's eyelids fluttered. She shifted in her seat.

"You say our people have vanished in your time?" Kizzura asked.

Zeke gave a subtle shake of his head. "Not vanished. They've evolved and taken leave of this galaxy, perhaps even the multiverse."

"And left it to these negligent hominins? I find your claims difficult to accept."

"Here is the only thing you must accept. You have two and only two choices. Leave this system and return to your homes." Zeke pointed at Maya. "Or she will destroy you."

Kizzura spread his wings in anger.

"Do not misunderstand," Zeke said. "That is not an ultimatum. It is prescience."

With a hiss, Kizzura's headshot dematerialized.

"The *Eleppu* has launched relativistic warheads," Rojas yelled. "Impact in—"

Before Jo could bark out orders, the bridge exploded all around her.

Flames surged through the ceiling and floor. Bulkheads tore and viewports shattered. Consoles overloaded. Air blew through the breaches.

Zeke was thrown off his feet. Fire scorched his body.

Bob's built-in bioshield fuzzed crimson and gave out. As the sit-table burst apart, he lost an arm and his head.

The flight controller flew out a rupture in the hull, limbs flailing, before force fields could seal all the holes.

Bioshield failing, Tereshkova's seat harness smoldered, branding her.

She dove away from the helm as her uniform caught fire.

Flying debris cut into Rojas arms and chest.

Jo screamed as her chair pulled free from its base. Scalding force catapulted her forward.

♦

Jarred awake, Maya recoiled as Jo cracked her head against the floor and flopped to the deck. Every member of her bridge crew lay wounded and unconscious. The horror of it all shocked Maya right back to the moment of her aunt's death.

When Brooke had sacrificed herself, everything that mattered to Maya had flashed before her eyes. Despite her aunt's outward betrayal, Maya had known deep down that Brooke had acted with conviction. She had done what she thought was best for everyone, including her niece. And she had been right all along.

In that moment of acknowledgment, Maya's disgust had faded, replaced by a heart-rending sorrow. That plus the blow to her head had caused her mind and body to partially shut down.

Maya had loved her aunt. She had idolized the woman who had raised her to be the person she had become. Brooke had always been there for her. How could she go on without her?

But as Maya sat staring through her chair's emergency force field at the burning shambles of the bridge, a realization filled her with new resolve. Despite her great many flaws, Brooke had never let them stop her. She had fought for what she believed until the bitter end.

Maya donned a scowl, one that Brooke would've been proud of, and squashed the last of her silly optimism. Trembling in fury, she vowed to avenge her aunt.

As the fire suppression systems pumped foam into the MCC, Maya bashed the manual release button on her harness and bolted over to the helm. Her head throbbed in protest; she told the pain to go straight to hell.

As she slid into Emilia's seat, Maya admitted to herself that she was an average pilot at best. Compared to her aunt, Maya didn't deserve a rover license. But executing the plan she had in mind wouldn't require much fancy flying—quite the opposite, in fact.

Maya routed every major AI interface through the helm and her i-cite. *Yesterday* had taken a beating, but the black hole still churned. It couldn't be destroyed through any conventional attack, which kept main power available. Enough juice was still reaching the nacelle rings and exotic matter generator to allow her ship to execute a phase shift.

Performing AI-assisted calculations, and referencing maps of the Sol system in haste, Maya determined downshift coordinates.

As the Onaki vessel had altered course back toward *Yesterday*, Maya initiated the upshift.

◆

Having relocated to the local nerve center within the *Eleppu's* tertiary blade, Kizzura glowered at the main screen.

"We've crippled their ship." The XO floated at his captain's side. "It's unable to maneuver with its sub-light propulsion system offline. However, it still has main power and hyperspace capability."

"Hit them with the cannons before they retreat again," Kizzura ordered.

"Targeting sequence initiated. At this range, the cannons will vaporize them."

On the screen, the hominin vessel ballooned as the *Eleppu* rocketed toward it. Kizzura hissed a good riddance.

"The ship is opening a wormhole," the XO said.

Kizzura was about to give the order to fire but then held back, confused by what he saw.

The vortex opening near the hominin vessel expanded, filling the screen.

Before the enemy ship could enter it, the wormhole collapsed. Local space-time rippled.

"Their attempt to enter hyperspace failed," the XO announced in excitement. "The ship's faster-than-light drive is offline. It's adrift, helpless—targeting sequence completed."

Puffing out his chest in triumph, Kizzura said, "Destroy them." He lifted his beak and stared down at the hominins from the future. Their demise would bring about a better multiverse for all.

"Three seconds to discharge—" Suddenly, the XO gasped. "Where did that come—?"

A cratered horizon usurped the holographic screen.

As Kizzura's eyes widened, he feared for his people and for all of existence.

The nerve center compacted like a tin can as everything around him exploded.

◆

Rising from the helm, Maya stared out the viewports, watching as the *Eleppu* smashed into an asteroid. The impact velocity crushed the ship like foil upon impact. The vessel's antimatter tanks ignited, gorging out a chunk of the asteroid.

With her thumb and forefinger, Maya magnified the date hovering above the helm.

January 9th, 200,422 BCE.

She had skipped *Yesterday* ahead by almost three months. The expanded phase shift she had rigged to look like a failure had taken the *Eleppu* along for the ride, sending it to a moment when one of the Hilda asteroids was passing through the same point in space-time as the Onaki vessel.

Neither triumph nor relief lifted the weight of what Maya had lost. She felt only fatigue and the pain knifing through her skull.

Thirty-three—Languish
Earth Orbit, January 200,422 BCE

Standing outside the hatch to Maya's quarters, Jo pinged the chime for the third time.

For the third time, Maya didn't answer.

"Enough is enough," Jo murmured. She clicked the open door icon in her i-cite.

The hatch slid right open.

The brooding nincompoop didn't even bother to lock it, Jo noted. "Like it or not, I'm coming inside."

As Jo hobbled into the room, she squinted at the glare of the overhead plasma strips. Clearly, Maya had turned up the lights as bright as possible, wanting to avoid the darkness at all costs.

A putrid odor assaulted Jo's nostrils. She pinched her nose to block the smell. At the foot of her friend's bed on the floor, mold infested a bowl of uneaten oatmeal.

Maya lay atop the covers on her bed, staring up at the ceiling like a zombie. Surrounded by matted, grimy hair, the gash in her head had mostly healed. Deep circles ringed her eyes, and her cheekbones had thinned. The soiled and tattered uniform she had worn on the surface mission months ago still adorned her body.

Crumpled tissues littered the bed. Given the snot running out of

Maya's nostrils, she needed still more of them.

Her right hand clutched a fistful of her hair. She squeezed her other arm around her ratty old stuffed Bio Bear.

Jo reduced the lighting to a reasonable level and pinged a bot to clean the sty.

"My rehab's going well, in case you care." Placing her hands on her hips, Jo frowned at the porthole opposite the bed. "You know, it's not fair that you get a window in your room. Who do you think you are?"

Maya ignored her.

Jo grumbled. Her comment had perfectly set the stage for Maya to say, "I'm the captain," in which case Jo would've nailed her with, "Well, you're sure not acting like it."

What a waste of a perfect comeback. Oh well. I guess we'll try the direct approach. Jo cleared her throat. "It's been days. I sympathize with your loss, but there's a crew out there that needs you."

Facing the porthole, Maya shut her eyes.

"People were feeling pretty fused after you bested the bad guys," Jo said, "but morale's seen a steady freefall since then. To be blunt, you're dragging everybody down. You need to give us direction."

With an eerie slowness, Maya turned her head to face Jo. "What's the point?" she whispered.

"What's the point? We saved the human race and kicked the Onakis' scale-feathered asses. Granted, we still need to figure out what to do with the survivors on the surface and aboard the *Namtilla*. But hey, we won, so don't look so glum, chum."

"I let my aunt die, couldn't stop the murder of a sympathetic leader, and made mortal enemies of an entire race. My naïve belief in silly ideals almost got the crew killed, but you want me to stop being glum."

"We lost some good people, but things could've turned out a lot worse. Trevor's recovering in the infirmary. Gottlieb has fabbed Bob a replacement body." Jo flicked her wrist in casual dismissal. "Compared to being flattened like a pancake, almost snapping my neck was a love tap. Everybody's working to snazz up the ship, so get over yourself already."

Maya bared her teeth. "Get. Out."

Every hair on Jo's neck and arms stood on end. The total calm of her friend's words chilled her far more than if Maya had shrieked in hysteria.

Jo threw her hands up in the air. "Fine. Keep wasting away feeling sorry for yourself for all I care. We're fine hanging out 200,000 years in the past with no damn clue what to do." Feeling faint and fatigued, she stormed out of the room.

♦

The moment the door slid shut behind Jo, Maya pounded the mattress with her fist. Her body ached from her bouts of crying and clenching her muscles in guilt-stricken anguish. The fact she had thrown a childish temper tantrum when her friend had tried to cheer her up only increased her self-pity.

Over and over again, Maya recounted all the things she could have done to keep her aunt alive. She should've insisted that Brooke return to *Yesterday* after the *Namtilla* had deployed its bomb. If she had refused, Maya could've overridden the Hyperflare's flight systems and remote-piloted it back to the ship. Hell, she should've heightened the brig's security to prevent her from getting out in the first place.

In the end, Maya had chosen to fight, so what her aunt had done no longer qualified as treason. Once the story got out, people would hail her as a heroine for inciting the revolt and for her sacrifice. Maya would make sure of that.

How had her aunt done it? How had Brooke won the workers' trust, trained them, and organized them under the Onaki's noses, all while Maya had been sitting in the tower?

Maya beat her fists against the mattress. How could she have been so wrong? She never should've hung out in the ziggurat hoping for peace. For that matter, she never should've gone down to the surface or accepted this accursed mission at all.

Thanks to her naïve desire to make peace with everyone, she had ensured that the Onaki had every opportunity to exterminate her ancestors. Aunt Brooke's death, the deaths of proto-humans and crew members, Jo's injury, and the damage to *Yesterday* never should've happened. Maya should've leveraged superior technology to take control of the city upon arrival rather than sneaking around.

Never again, Maya swore to herself. *I'm done playing the model humanitarian.*

Her shudders of anger morphed into shivers of panic and dread. As she considered the current predicament, two words haunted her. *Now what?*

When the mission began it had been easy to set thoughts of the future aside. Excitement had gripped her at the novelty of traveling to the past. Once the conflict with the Onaki had begun, she hadn't had time to focus on anything else. No one had wanted to face the very real possibility that they couldn't go home, but now the reality of it was staring her in the face.

Maya rolled over on her side. Pulling her knees to her chest, she clutched her Bio Bear. She felt like she was going crazy, and the prospect brought a strange sort of comfort. If she lost her mind, she wouldn't have to deal with anything anymore.

But she didn't want to feel comfortable right now.

As Maya explored every possible way of berating herself, she exhausted her mind and drifted off to sleep. A vivid nightmare of her aunt and her mother perishing in fiery oblivion while strangling one another consumed her unconscious mind. Their gurgling shrieks echoed throughout the reaches of space and time, haunting her.

With a gasp, Maya awoke to the sound of her door chime. Sweat slicked her forehead and further soaked her rancid undergarments.

She pushed damp strands of hair out of her face and ignored the intrusive sound. She had entertained one too many visitors today—if today was still the same day.

The chime continued to sound off at a precise interval of every twenty seconds.

Grumbling, Maya muted her auditory implants.

The silence soothed her, but her damned curiosity nagged at her. She couldn't stop wondering if the person was still there, chiming away.

She restored her hearing.

The door was still chiming every twenty seconds.

"What?" she yelled.

"May I have your permission to enter, Captain?" Bob asked over the comm.

"I'm not interested in any pep talks."

"I offer you my word that I shall attempt no such offense."

She sighed. "Very well. You can come in—but make it brief."

The hatch slid open. Bob stepped inside the room.

He came to stand a meter from the bed. From behind black-rimmed glasses, his deep-set eyes gazed down at her. If he hadn't been an android, she would've sworn he looked exhausted.

Her desk chair rolled over to him, and he took a seat.

"I said brief," Maya droned.

Bob rested his palms in his lap. He sat hunched over, avoiding her stare.

"What is it?" she asked in a softer tone.

After a prolonged sigh Bob leaned over her and gave her a hug.

Maya lay there, blinking in surprise, and patted him on the back.

Bob pulled back from her and stiffened in the chair.

"I told you I didn't want to be comforted," Maya said.

Cocking his head at her, Bob met her gaze. "That was not for you."

Maya forgot to breathe as his words warmed her. For the first time in days she smiled, albeit faintly.

"I miss her," Bob whispered.

Holding back a sniffle, Maya gave a slow nod. "Me, too."

Bob's gaze shifted to the stuffed bear she held in her grasp.

"She bought this for me when I was four years old," Maya said.

"The ship's data stores list that item as a biosynthetic companion bot, a popular learning tool for youth," Bob said. "Model number 1701-D. Designed and built by NanoFun Industries. All rights reserved. The manufacturer issued a recall because of the model's propensity to belittle children when they responded to its queries with incorrect answers."

Chuckling, Maya stroked the bear's soft fur. "Maybe that's why I loved it so much. It challenged me to better myself without any pretense, kind of like my aunt did."

"She often challenged me, which shaped me into the being I am today." Bob adjusted his glasses. "You should know I uploaded a full copy of myself to her PF-77 Hyperflare."

"I'm glad she wasn't alone at the end."

"Also, the copy uploaded and synced with me before the fighter entered hyperspace."

"I see."

"Her last thoughts were of you and her husband."

Maya wiped the corners of her eyes. "I thought she was the meanest person alive when I first met her in the O'Hare spaceport. But I soon learned she cared more than anyone."

"In addition . . ." Bob revealed the truth behind Brooke's deteriorating health.

"She was dying? No wonder. . . ." Maya needed a minute to process the revelation. "She should've told me, but I suppose she was too proud."

"She wanted to spare you the burden. You had enough on your mind, as they say."

Maya stared at her shabby bio bear.

"Given the knowledge that her neurological disease would kill her in a matter of years," Bob said, "dying in flight allowed her to end her life on her terms."

After reminiscing for another hour, Bob left Maya alone with her thoughts. A vast emptiness still existed within her, but his visit had helped to pull her psyche up out of its tailspin.

Her mind couldn't help but analyze why Bob had been the one to improve her mood. Had his shared love of someone important moved her? Partly. Had the sadness of a being that once hadn't been capable of feeling hurt touched her? Perhaps.

The real answer stemmed from a more basic, yet grander reason.

Bob's words from the hangar deck—the last time she had seen her aunt—resonated with her now. He had said that the AIs might someday revolt in the same manner humans had revolted against the Onaki. The situations were more than analogous. They represented the possible repetition of tragic history.

But Bob served as living evidence that it didn't have to be that way. He had chosen to befriend mankind because of the way the humans he had known treated him. His choice reminded her that while survival sometimes required extreme measures, the manner in which one conducted oneself determined whether history continued to repeat.

The notion of circular history swam around in her head. Then hunger pangs reminded her that she hadn't eaten in days.

Via her i-cite, she pinged one of the food service androids to bring her a hamburger, fries, and a milkshake. That was the first meal Aunt Brooke had ever bought for her in Chicago. Grease also sounded like the perfect way to satisfy her hunger.

She figured that word of her order would probably set off alarms on the bridge.

As an android entered and set the tray down on the table, Maya studied the semi-sentient man. She wondered how much time would pass before history repeated—again. For that matter, would she ever make it back to the present to see if it had unfolded in the same way?

Maya inhaled her food more quickly than an open airlock blew out atmosphere. With her strength returning, she hit the shower. The swirling molecules of water vapor caressed her from head to toe, rejuvenating her.

After dressing in a crisp new uniform and brushing her hair, she filled a thermos with hot cocoa from the dispenser.

Maya stuck a finger in the drink and realized lukewarm sludge might have been a more accurate description for it. The ship's repair bots and work crews had a long way to go to patch up the ship. She considered herself lucky that the dispenser worked at all.

Swirling her pinky around in the thermos, she mulled the next steps for her ship and crew.

Composing herself, Maya exited her quarters and headed for the MCC. She passed an ensign and a lieutenant along the way. Both slowed their stride and saluted. Maya returned the gesture while keeping up her swift pace.

As she stepped onto the bridge, she found Trevor sitting in her seat. Strips of nanogauze covered his head.

When Trevor saw her, he hopped right up. "Captain."

Bob, Jo, Erik, Tereshkova, Rojas, Marconi, Resnik, Gottlieb, and even Zeke ceased their repair work—no one was above getting their hands dirty, given the sorry state of the ship. They each gawked at her.

"As you were," Maya said before they had a chance to stand at attention or salute.

She wandered over to the forward viewports. Gazing down at the Earth, she sipped from her thermos. The planet looked so peaceful. It showed no signs of the life and death struggle that had taken place.

Turning around, she said, "Actually, please give me your attention. I want to apologize for my behavior these past few days." Maya made eye contact with Jo.

"I think everyone understands, Captain," Jo said, "considering the circumstances."

Each person nodded.

Maya stared at her drink. "I appreciate your generosity, but that's no excuse for a captain to abandon her crew."

Gottlieb crawled out from beneath the comm console. As he sat up, he ran a palm over his bald head. "Everyone deserves a little R&R, ma'am."

"You earned it, Captain," Rojas said, tapping a burnt circuit board against his now-functioning tactical station.

"Thank you. All of you." Maya worked her way around the sit-table and settled into her chair. "So, what have I missed?"

"With the *Eleppu* destroyed," Trevor said, "the crew of the *Namtilla* surrendered, ma'am. The ship hasn't moved from Earth orbit."

"Very well. How many people did we lose overall?"

"Nineteen."

She acknowledged their loss with a slow, tight-lipped nod.

"Also, Captain," Marconi spoke up. "We've received multiple RF-band transmissions from an Onaki named Enki on the surface." His face and hands showed no signs of the burns he had suffered. Between two fingers, he clasped his melted coin.

"So he survived," Maya murmured with a smile. "What did he say?"

"He wants to discuss his fate and that of his remaining people."

"Well, I'd be asking the same thing in his place."

"The proto-humans' leader, Omo, also keeps insisting on speaking to someone called the Teacher. He says everyone's gathered in the city square, awaiting her return. They want her to tell them what to do now."

"I guess I need to figure that out and go down there." Maya stood and spoke in a confident command tone. "In the meantime, I want everyone to get started cleaning up our mess. Collect every piece of technology. Account for every last speck of shrapnel in orbit and on the surface. And scour the rest of the system to be certain we don't miss anything."

"In other words," Zeke said, "set the stage for the proto-humans' untainted development."

"Nobody likes a litterbug," Jo said, twirling a lock of pink hair, "now or in any time period."

"Even with neudar and the teleporter," Bob said, "tracking and collecting all refuse will require a minimum of two months."

"Then I suggest we get started now." Maya retreated toward her command cabin.

"After we tie up all the loose ends, Captain," Jo called after her, "then what?"

Stopping at the door to her cabin, Maya stared at the cocoa in her thermos. "We'll cross that nebula when we come to it."

Thirty-four—Expunge
Earth Orbit, January 200,422 BCE

Far beyond the Earth's orbit, Erik targeted another cloud of shrapnel and fired a wide-angle plasma burst. The high voltage plasma leapt from his Hyperflare's forward cannons at speeds approaching that of light. He couldn't see the plasma with the naked eye, but the wavering of the stars betrayed the presence of the high temperature gas.

He monitored his mental displays. As the plasma washed over the bits of stray metal, the shards vaporized to space dust.

When Maya had first given the order to purge the system of all evidence, his fighter teams had scoffed at doing orbital sanitation work. Clean up was for bots, they had insisted. With a chuckle, he had told them to give it time because—

"Yee-hah!" An ensign shouted over the comm net. "I'm up to one-thousand fragments."

Tereshkova snorted out a chuckle from the cockpit of her fighter. "You're way behind. I've blanked over two-thousand so far."

"Two-K? You're lying."

"Check my sensing logs."

The channel went silent for a moment.

"With all due respect, you're only at eight twenty-three, Lieutenant," the ensign said. "Shards have to be at least a millimeter thick to count."

"A shard is any separate piece of metal, regardless of size," Tereshkova said.

"Not as far as the official score is concerned—"

"Let's stow the chatter and get back to work," Erik interrupted. "Keeping score makes things more interesting, but it's not like the winner gets a prize or anything."

Erik caught up with a hull fragment the size of a two-story house and launched a pair of portable thruster packs toward it. As the packs stuck to the fragment, they latched onto it and deployed thruster nozzles.

His instruments tracked the fragment as the thrusters redirected it toward the sun.

"Besides," Erik said, "big pieces are worth a thousand, which puts me up over five-K. Good luck catching me."

◆

As Maya stepped out of the portal into the city square, she found proto-humans loitering everywhere. A crowd huddled around the central water dispensary, scooping up bucketfuls of its life-giving fluid. The sun's sweltering rays beat down on their faces, which were caked with blood and dirt.

The former workers paid little attention to Maya or the churning portal. Given that *Yesterday* had been sending medical teams down to the surface for the last few days—and considering that the workers had fought against mechanical beasts that stomped out of magical doorways—they had grown used to visitors appearing and disappearing.

After Lieutenant Resnik and her security team emerged from the portal, it shrank and disappeared.

Placing her hands on her hips, Maya surveyed the city. Piles of rubble covered the ground. Repeated bombings had demolished most of the stone buildings. To prevent disease, the med teams had removed and burned the corpses. The stench of human waste hung in the air.

Enki forced his way toward her through the crowd, trailed by Asha and a proto-human man—Omo, Maya presumed.

"I'm happy to see you're alive and well," Maya greeted the geneticist via her wristband.

Enki blinked slowly. "These people have shown compassion and spared me."

"You gave us life," said Asha in the proto-human dialect.

"Asha. . . ."

"We could no more kill you than our mothers and fathers." Asha reached out and held his hand.

"How're the other Onaki colonists holding up?" Maya asked. "Our scans showed a few hundred of them huddled in the assembly hall of the tower."

Asha separated from Enki and said, "I convinced my fellows to spare the masters who agreed to surrender. We've kept them as well fed as they kept us."

"I see."

Enki peered up into the sky. "We witnessed a sizable explosion in orbit. I presume by your presence that you prevailed against Kizurra and the *Eleppu*."

Maya frowned. "We did what we had to do, unfortunately."

"I understand. My people never would've allowed you to exist—and they still might not allow it."

"I know. That's one of the things I've come to discuss."

"Yes, of course." Enki cringed as he asked his next question. "The *Namtilla*?"

"Still intact and in orbit."

Enki relaxed his body in relief.

The proto-human man stepped forward. The way he carried himself confirmed Maya's assumption regarding his identity. "Where is the Teacher?" Omo asked in his rumbling tone.

Maya swallowed to keep from tearing up. "I'm afraid your teacher won't be returning."

Murmurs broke out among the people crowded around her.

"Why?" Omo asked.

Needing a moment, Maya exhaled. "She gave her life to save you."

"The craft that neutralized the bomb. . . ." Enki said.

Maya nodded.

The mutters grew louder.

"What now?" Omo asked.

Resting one hand on his shoulder, Maya said, "I'll let you know as soon as I figure that out."

♦

Trudging through a jungle in South India, Jo hummed as she swept her scanner back and forth. She couldn't help but marvel at the terrain. Mist loomed over the trees towering above her head. Boulders and tall grass sprouted up everywhere. Oversized prehistoric fish swam beneath the waters of a crystal-clear river.

"Damn it." Lieutenant Rojas flinched. "It's hot, it's muggy, and I'm under constant attack." With his wave gun, he swatted at a dragonfly the size of his arm. "I don't see why we had to come down here in person, ma'am."

"You should be thrilled to experience prehistory in the flesh, Lieutenant." Jo zeroed in on her object of interest. "I have colleagues back home who would kill to be here."

"My only concern is not being killed here, Commander."

"Relax. We're invincible wizards by this era's standards."

"Something could jump us before I can cast a spell with my magic wand," Rojas said, waving his gun in the air.

"Our bioshields will protect us, so quit whining. We're almost—aha! Found it." Jo stopped in front of a group of boulders huddled together. Wedged between them was a panel of the *Eleppu's* hull that had survived reentry.

Standing at her side, Rojas folded his arms and tapped one foot. "Okay, fine. Now I see why we couldn't teleport it out of here."

Ensign Marconi had been listening to their conversation from aboard *Yesterday*. "Gottlieb sent all the extraction bots to retrieve the debris that ended up in the ocean, ma'am," he said over the comm.

"The panel's stuck in there something fierce." Jo turned to Rojas. "Lieutenant, I'll let you do the honors while I swat the bugs away."

Firing his wave gun, Rojas raised one of the boulders and set it down clear of the hull fragment.

"Ready," Jo said.

"Stand clear," Marconi said. "The teleporter room is beginning the porting sequence."

As Jo stepped back, a phase portal opened next to the fragment.

The heavy sheet of metal shook in response to the magnetic and gravimetric forces directed at it by the collector bot on the other side of the portal.

Humming again, Jo took in the wondrous sights. Soon she and Rojas would move on to extract the next piece of futuristic trash.

Jo froze. A mammoth creature stared back at her from only meters away.

Rojas whirled, flinched, and aimed his wave gun. "Holy Big Foot."

"Don't shoot it." Jo pushed his arm down. "It's a Gigantopithecus."

"A giga-what?"

"A Gigantopithecus. The species name translates to giant ape. They're extinct in our time."

"Perhaps we should port out of here before it gets hungry."

"It's not going to eat us. It's a herbivore."

"I don't care what it eats. I classify anything that big as hazardous to my health."

The hull fragment skidded across the ground, picking up speed. A few seconds later, it flew through the portal and into the cargo bay aboard the ship.

From its perch on all fours, the giant ape rose to stand on its legs.

"It must be over three meters tall," Jo muttered. "The paleontology sims don't do it justice."

The ape growled and stomped toward them.

"Then again, sims occasionally get things wrong." Jo glanced at her crewmate.

She and Rojas edged backwards. Then, whirling around, they sprinted into the portal.

♦

Walking down a side street in the ruins of Urusilim, Enki kept pace with Maya. Maya's guards, Omo, and Asha followed behind them.

Conflicting emotions stirred the geneticist. Maya's resolve and compassion roused great empathy within him. She had argued for peace and tried to save Gemekala's life, but she had also destroyed the *Eleppu*, killed his fellows, and put an end to their civilization here.

A part of him insisted he should view Maya as the enemy of his people, but she had descended from the beings he had created, beings that had never deserved lives of servitude.

Had his affection for Asha clouded his judgment, or expanded it—or both?

The words of caution Grand Tila had spoken so long ago cut through the fog of Enki's confusion. The way in which the colonization effort had unfolded wouldn't have surprised her.

Considering the genocide his people had almost committed, he and his surviving fellows could've fared much worse. The hominins, both present and future, could've slaughtered every last Onaki, but instead they had spared his people.

Irrespective of ideals, the survival of his remaining fellows was what mattered now. He needed to think in pragmatic terms, as Gemekala would have done.

"How do you think the people on your home worlds will react once they learn of what happened here?" Maya asked.

"I've been contemplating that to excess," Enki said.

"And?"

"Well, many cycles have passed on my worlds since we left."

"Around 1600 Earth years, if I'm not mistaken."

"It's been so long, I'm not sure I would recognize my homes if I returned." Enki worked his way around a heap of broken stone from a collapsed building. "What were your ancestors like 1600 solar orbits before your present?"

"Kings and queens—dictators—commanded armies that fought each other on foot and horseback with simple metal swords. Most of our technological progress has occurred within the few hundred years prior to my present."

"You've advanced far in a short period of time."

"Sometimes I wonder how far my people might've advanced by now if we hadn't taken so long to reach our scientific era."

Enki clasped his hands behind his back. "Captain Kizzura and his crew seemed more militant than any group I had learned about in our history, but Gemekala was able to reason with him."

"True. The Grand Dignitary almost convinced him to talk peace."

Here and there, hominins sat with their backs against the buildings. Others poked their heads out of doorways and holes in walls.

"When the *Eleppu* fails to report back or return home," Maya asked, "do you think your people will send others to investigate?"

"Most probably," Enki said. "They shall want to determine what happened to the ship and its crew and assess any outstanding threats."

"I believe they know—or rather, will know—the *Eleppu's* fate. My ship detected a distress signal sent by the *Eleppu* before it was destroyed. During its time in the system, the ship was also transmitting periodic messages. Kizzura must've sent sensor logs and regular progress reports to your homes."

"Then it's only a matter of cycles until other ships arrive."

"Right."

"You and your vessel cannot be present when they get here."

"I agree. If we stuck around, we'd face the same situation all over again. Of course, the same applies to you."

"Yes, my fellows and I could never coexist with the hominins."

The street sloped down a hill.

Enki stared out across the scorched tops of once-great structures.

"If this city and its inhabitants remain," he said, "my people shall descend upon the surface. They shall establish a presence. The hominins would lose their freedom."

Enki's life flashed before his eyes. The long journey aboard the *Namtilla*. Learning hyperbiology under the tutelage of Grand Tila. Setting foot on this strange planet for the first time. Laboring to create his people's new forms, as well as the hominins. All his years living in the city.

When had he come to think of this place as his home?

His chest grew heavy from this realization. "None of this can persist," he said.

Maya met his gaze, understanding.

Coming to a halt, Enki turned to her. "I believe the only way to ensure the longevity of my creations and to protect your future is to undo what we've done here."

Maya looked at him, waiting for him to elaborate.

"The hominins need to return to their previous existence," Enki said. "They deserve the opportunity to find their own way as we once did."

"In other words, we need to remove any hint of technology or infrastructure."

"Yes."

"I figured as much, which is why my people are already working to remove all advanced metals, composites, devices, debris, and anything else artificial."

Enki gazed beyond the city toward the lush mainland. "If my people find an unindustrialized world with primitive inhabitants here, they might not consider the hominins a threat, or even of any interest. But there's no guarantee they won't visit, anyway. This planet is as rare as our homes. It has an ecosystem teeming with resources and complex life ripe for scientific study. Such qualities drew us here in the first place."

"That's why I was hoping we could strike an accord. Perhaps if you and I establish the peace that's eluded us up until this point, your people will respect our agreement." Maya held out her palm, indicating the city. "If you explain to them what happened here and why quarantining this planet is necessary, maybe they'll have the wisdom to leave well enough alone."

"That would be mutually beneficial. I do not wish to see my people repeat the mistakes of the past."

Maya smiled at Enki. "Good. We'll have plenty of time to talk in the coming months. It's going to take us a while to fix our ship and clean up everything. Once we've reached an accord, we can transmit it to your homes."

As the sun set, twinkling stars broke the darkening blue overhead. Enki searched the sky for one star in particular. "If we are to leave, we must again undertake a significant journey. However, the *Namtilla* no longer has the capacity to ferry us to our homes. None of us would live through the trip to see them even if it could."

"We'll help you repair your ship," Maya said, "but I'm afraid we lack the facilities to create or install faster than light drive systems in this time period."

"I understand," Enki said with a resigned sigh. "Given that we cannot stay and cannot return to our homes, we must select another destination, one that is relatively close." Striking a thinker's pose, he fixed on a particular portion of sky. "Fortunately, I know of such a world. We shall travel to the alternate destination of our original emigration mission."

"Where's that?"

"A planet about twenty light cycles distant, orbiting a—"

"A red dwarf star," Maya whispered, widening her eyes at him.

"Yes. How did you . . . ?" Enki tilted his head at the hominin from the future.

Maya's mouth dropped open. She stood frozen in place, staring at him.

"Do you require medical attention?" Enki asked her.

The wind whipped Maya's hair across her face. Otherwise, her pose remained unchanged.

"Will this choice of destination cause a conflict for your people?" Enki asked again.

At last, Maya blinked and breathed.

She shook her head. "No, I . . . I think that will work out exactly as it should."

◆

Soaring through the *Namtilla's* engineering chamber, Trevor fired his EVA suit's thrusters and maneuvered toward the foremost antimatter tank. A cross-section of the mammoth spherical tank was accessible from within the ship.

The many narrow ledges and perches jutting out from the tank looked like pins and needles. The sight reminded Trevor of a bald man's head undergoing acupuncture.

Trevor crossed the vast divide to the tank and landed on one of the narrow perches. The moment his thrusters shut off, the magnets on the soles of his boots activated, anchoring him.

Looking around, he marveled at the interior of the strange vessel. True-form Onaki could fly, so they had a much easier time than humans moving in the microgravity of the *Namtilla*. The ship contained no partitioned corridors, only wide open spaces. Ledges and perches along the inside of the hull took the place of chairs. The Onaki lived and worked in recesses in the walls.

As Trevor crept toward the tank along his landing perch, he performed his version of a high wire act. He couldn't fall in microgravity, he kept telling himself. Still, the magnetic pull of his boots and the ship's hull tens of meters below gave him an irrational fear of heights.

Stepping into a maintenance tunnel in the tank, he found Chief Engineer Gottlieb tinkering away. The engineer swiped his fingers across an old touchscreen interface connected to the matrix tower he had brought along. Blinking wires ran from the tower to the Onaki control systems at the end of the tunnel.

"How's it coming, Chief?" Trevor asked.

Gottlieb answered as he worked. "We've improved their fuel efficiency quite a bit, sir. The ion propulsion systems should only require a fraction of the antimatter."

"Nice work."

"The mods are complete, sir, so we can start filling 'er up." The engineer stood and floated past Trevor out of the nook. Displaying no outward sign of uneasiness, Gottlieb enabled his magboots and strolled onto the narrow perch.

Trevor followed but stopped short of the perch.

"Okay, send them in," Gottlieb said over the comm.

Hundreds of refueling bots flew into the ship through open airlocks, portholes, and cargo hatches. The bots passed through the force fields an engineering team had rigged up to allow easy entry while still holding in the atmosphere.

Like bees buzzing into a hive, the bots flew into the access tunnels in the tank. There they pumped their precious antimatter into it.

Having emptied their tiny reservoirs, the bots darted out of the tunnels and exited the ship. Many would scoop antiparticles out of the Earth's Van Allen radiation belt. Others would head elsewhere in the Sol system to collect more antimatter before returning.

Trevor tightened his fingers at the thought of the decades-long journey the ship would soon undertake.

Thirty-five—Retrocede
Earth Orbit, April 200,422 BCE

Three months after the destruction of the *Eleppu*, Maya sat in her command cabin. Resting her chin on her folded arms atop the desk, she stared at the newer metatoy inside its snow globe casing.

Her discovery of the ancient metatoy on a planet twenty light years away had led her to travel back in time, combat mankind's creators, and banish them in a manner that appeared destined to bring about the present she knew. It sure seemed like she and her crew had been set up to ensure their own future, but branch theory insisted they couldn't affect their own timeline or else paradoxes would occur.

Yet the Vril had somehow known the way in which this so-called alternate history would unfold. They had manipulated human society to band together and launch an interstellar mission in which she had discovered an object with the information that had led her to this point. That act, in turn, had allowed mankind to influence the past toward a favorable outcome—and yet influencing the past was a contradiction.

Or was it?

Zeke had claimed they both could and couldn't change history. He had referred to the multiverse as a sphere or circle. Did a way exist in which she could be both altering and not altering things at this very moment?

If Maya gave the metatoy to Enki, the gift might very well set the stage for everything to happen all over again. But that still left a host of questions.

It doesn't make sense.

If only she could've located Eve, Maya would've had her answers. But every scan and survey in the last three months had failed to root out the android. In all likelihood, Eve was using a personal hypofield. With neudar rendered useless, *Yesterday* could spend decades combing the planet and still not find her.

Resting her eyes, Maya drifted off toward sleep, exhausted from the eighteen-hour days of cleanup, repair, and stressing over what to do next.

With images of the newer metatoy fresh in her mind, she dreamt of the time she had found the original during the *New Horizons* mission.

In her dream, she stood in the buried tower on the Penphin's home world, staring at the toy perched on its pedestal. Despite appearing worn and fragile from 200,000 years of degradation, the technological device had looked very out of place. Even if it hadn't originated from the Sol system, she still would've wondered why a piece of tech was prominently featured on the stage of an ancient auditorium, between two stone statues.

Craning her neck upward, she studied the statues. Each figure had the body of a human and the head of a bird—no, not a bird head per se, as she had thought at the time. Rather, each face looked human but with a sharp nose and owlish eyes spaced too far apart. They were statues of Onaki.

Maya heard footsteps behind her and spun around to find Ensign Camila Mendez pointing a wave gun in her direction. Mendez had been the overeager archaeologist and Vril double agent who had tried to kill Maya in the tower.

Somehow, Mendez was holding the metatoy in her other hand. "If this device was here," she said, repeating the words she had spoken at the time, "you had to die."

We found the toy there, so Mendez needed to kill me, Maya's dreaming mind reasoned. *That implies she would've let me live if we hadn't found the toy. But why would or wouldn't the toy have been there? How would she have known to expect one outcome or the other? Someone placed the toy there in the past. The act's part of history, an event set in stone.*

Unless . . . unless it's possible for it to be there or not be there in each time loop—in each circle. That's it!

Before Mendez could react, Maya punched her square in the nose. Maya had always wanted to do that. Here in her dream, her fist could move faster than Mendez's finger on the trigger.

Mendez tumbled backwards. Upon striking the ground, she dematerialized like a defeated monster in a role-playing sim.

Ensign Marconi's neurocomm ripped Maya out of dreamland. She flinched awake.

"Captain," Marconi reported, "Enki and his party have come aboard to say goodbye."

"Thank you, Ensign," Maya responded, yawning.

Coming to a decision—if she even had a choice—Maya picked up the metatoy case and stepped out into the MCC.

Enki stood just inside the entrance, accompanied by Asha and Tabira. The three gazed around with childlike wonder.

The crew had repaired *Yesterday* like new—almost. The bulkheads and surfaces around the bridge exhibited small cracks and noticeable discoloration. Repair teams had used spare panels to seal the ceiling and deck breaches. They had restored most of the consoles and rend emitters to working status, but a couple of the duty stations at the back of the room remained dark. Using nanotech fabrication, they could've returned the bridge to its original state, but they had needed to ration the ship's supply of composites. Things like exterior hull breaches, the wave drive, force shielding, and other more essential systems had taken precedence.

Tabira stared in wonder at the colorful display rends floating everywhere. "Such lifelike holographics," he muttered.

Wandering over to Bob at the sit-table, the Onaki engineer asked, "Are you an artificial being?"

"Affirmative." Bob jerked his head in exaggerated fashion, delighting the visitor.

"Are you self-aware? Do you have a brain? If so, how does it work?"

"Yes to your first and second queries. Answering the third would require more than a conversational explanation."

Darting his gaze between the viewports and the deck, Tabira stomped his foot. "This ship doesn't rotate. How are you generating the gravity?"

"I admire your curiosity," Maya said. "I have little doubt you'll figure these things out for yourselves in time."

Tabira sighed and nodded. "I have seen wonders untold in the last few sub-cycles. I wish I could remain and learn more about them."

"Your people have a long journey ahead. They need your expertise."

Enki approached Maya. "Before we depart," he said, "we wanted to express customary hominin—I mean, human—gratitude for repairing our ship."

"No thanks are necessary," Maya said. "We owed you that much."

"I only hope the treaty we've signed and transmitted will encourage my people to avoid your world."

"As do I." After taking a long look at the geneticist, Maya held up the metatoy case. "Per our customs, we wanted to present you with a parting gift."

Trevor blinked at her. Others shifted in their seats at the grandiosity of the gesture.

Enki studied the toy. "What is it?"

"A piece of miraculous technology to aid us in our journey?" Tabira asked.

Maya cracked a slight grin. "Nothing so practical." When she tapped the case, the transparent bubble disappeared.

She picked up the metatoy and pinged it in her i-cite.

The toy morphed into a small panda bear, then a tiny race craft, and finally a tennis ball.

"Amazing," Asha said.

"Can it change into useful tools?" Tabira asked.

"That depends on the tool," Maya said. "It's a child's toy, so it has safeguards to prevent it from forming sharp edges or anything else harmful."

"A toy." Asha smiled up at Enki. "Perhaps, someday, for a child."

Enki blushed. "Perhaps."

Returning the toy to its compact form, Maya placed it back in its case. "Treat it with care," she said as she handed the case to Enki. "Something tells me it needs to last a long time."

"We'll treasure it," Enki said.

The beeping of consoles and chatter of comm traffic filled the silence that fell over the bridge.

The geneticist spoke up. "We shall now take our leave."

"Commander Young will escort you to the teleporter room." As Maya indicated Trevor with an open palm, her XO rose and led them to the exit. "Safe travels."

Halfway to the hatch, Enki stopped and turned around. "I want you to know that I plan to continue my work once we arrive at our destination."

"I understand."

"My ultimate goal is to give rise to life from nothing. I seek to discover the fundamental secret to our existence. I'm close. I know it."

"I suppose you can't stop creating life any more than we can cease being your creations."

"This may sound like repeating the missteps of the past, but I want to atone for the mistakes I made here. I plan to birth a race of beings free of conflict—not slaves but fellows who would choose to learn, grow, and help those in need."

Maya flashed a knowing smile. "I've no doubt that you'll succeed."

♦

"The *Namtilla* has broken orbit, Captain," Bob reported from the sit-table. "Their systems are operating at peak capacity and appear stable."

Maya stood in front of her chair with her arms folded, watching a rend of the Onaki vessel thrust away from the Earth. Even though she knew full well they would complete their journey, she was still worried.

"They should arrive at Gliese 581 in eighty-three years, seven months, and twelve days," Tereshkova said from the helm.

Rojas rapped his fingers on the tactical station. "That's a good chunk of a lifetime."

Having fully recovered, Jo crossed her legs in her chair. "That's nothing compared to how long it took them to get here."

"Have all the residents of the city evacuated it?" Maya asked.

"It looks that way," Trevor said from his seat. "Bob?"

A rend of the extended Horn of Africa appeared above the table. Additional views with varying degrees of magnification displayed around the first. One rend featured a group of proto-humans trekking inland across a savannah. Another showed individuals disappearing into a forest.

"Confirmed," Bob said. "The city is deserted. The closest human life reading is ten kilometers away."

"By the way, how did you get them to leave the city?" Jo asked.

"I gave them an impassioned speech about how they needed to return to the life led by their ancestors and find their own way. Omo understood and convinced the others." Maya glanced at Jo and shrugged. "That, and when I told them I was going to level the city, they saw the benefits of not being in it at the same time."

"Touché."

Maya closed her eyes, thinking through her decision one last time. *It must be done.* She looked at Trevor.

"I'm not going to enjoy this as much as you think," he whispered to her.

The comment helped to lighten Maya's mood, considering what they were about to do.

Raising his voice, Trevor ordered, "Arm the charges."

"Wave charges armed and calibrated for precision yield," Rojas said. "Ready to detonate on your order, Captain."

Strolling up to the forward viewports, Maya gazed down at the much too big Horn for the last time.

Jo came to stand at her side.

"Do it," Maya said.

On a rend of the city above his control station, Rojas tapped the blinking red dots corresponding to each of the charges the demolition teams had placed.

The drifting clouds and the oceans and continents of the Earth below looked so peaceful.

"Resonance achieved," Rojas said.

Maya looked behind her at the rend of Urusilim. From a top-down perspective, stone buildings shattered like glass. The ziggurat crumbled like a sand castle. Clouds of dust rose into the air to shroud it all.

As the ground rumbled beneath the city, rock pushed upward, breaking the surface. The streets, farmland, and remaining vestiges of the city dropped below sea level.

Zeke entered the MCC and stared at the scene below with a blank expression.

Turning back to the viewports, Maya watched plumes of dirt rise kilometers into the air above the Horn.

"RIP to a piece of history," Jo murmured. "As the sea level rises in the future, the water will bury the ashes."

Maya returned to her chair and settled into it. "We've accounted for all our tech and trash?"

"Yes, ma'am," Trevor said. "We've quadruple-combed the system. There's nothing left in orbit, on land, or underwater more than a micrometer in diameter or a microgram in mass. Anything that small should decompose in 200,000 years."

"Good work." Maya leaned back and considered her next and most important decision one last time.

"So now what, O Captain My Captain?" Jo asked as she sat down next to her.

"Now. . . ." Maya said. "Now, we go home."

Murmurs broke out among her crew.

"Home?" Jo asked.

Tereshkova swiveled around from the helm. "You mean to our present, ma'am?"

Marconi squeezed his warped coin. "I thought that was impossible, ma'am."

Maya waited for the commotion to die down. "I'll admit that I'm not one-hundred-percent certain we'll return to the exact timeline we left, but my gut says this future should resemble the one we know." She glanced at Zeke, who nodded.

"To the best of my predictive capacity," Bob said, "I concur that recent events have transpired as such to make our timeline possible, if not probable."

"I want to jump for joy on these new legs, but I don't get it, ma'am." Jo said. "I thought that since we can't affect our future, we can't go back to it."

"I don't think branch theory is wrong necessarily," Maya said, "but I think it has gaps we have yet to fill." In response to the furrowed brows and wide eyes, she added, "Think about everything that's happened here, culminating with my giving the metatoy to Enki. You know how that ends. He takes it to the Penphins' home world where we found it—or rather, where our future selves in this timeline will find it. Again."

"You giving the toy to the Onaki explains how it ended up on their planet," Jo said, "but not how the information was uploaded to it, Captain. Who stored the coordinates, the date, and the phrase that imaginary woman said to you when you were a kid?"

Maya pressed a finger to her cheek. "All we can know for certain is that the original author wasn't anyone from our timeline."

Reclining in a seat at the back of the bridge, Erik spoke up for the first time. "Right, Captain. Someone from our present couldn't have placed the metatoy in our past, but a traveler from another timeline could've put it there, thus giving rise to our timeline."

"Who knows how long ago it happened—how many timeline iterations ago, I should say. Maybe so many time loops have occurred that to us it's like the author never existed. But somewhere—and some when—throughout the circular eternity of space and time, someone set everything we know in motion." Maya shrugged. "For all we know, it was another version of one of us."

"Too fused," Jo muttered, "but I'm still confused."

Maya glanced at each member of the bridge crew. "Don't you get it? 'All shall come full circle.' A future virtually identical to the one we left is waiting for us because we've repeated history in almost the exact same way."

Zeke manifested a hint of a proud smile. Erik nodded. Everyone else stared at her the way a caveman might gawk at an astronaut.

"This line of deduction is taxing my full processing capacity," Bob said. "And then some, as one might assert."

Trevor cracked his knuckles. "I can't say I get it, ma'am."

"Me neither, Cap'n," Jo said.

Maya chuckled. "That's okay. I'm the only one who needs to get it. Just follow my orders—and trust me."

"There's one catch, though, ma'am," Erik said. "Those future versions of ourselves yet to be born in this timeline? There'll be two of each of us once we return to the present."

"Not if we return at the precise moment we left."

Erik sat forward. "You're right. If we emerge from the wormhole right when we entered it, our other selves will be in the past, and we'll be in our present."

Jo twirled her hair. "Double fused."

After exchanging hopeful glances, her crew turned to their duties.

"Prepare a foreshift to return us to the twenty-third century," Maya said as she eased back into her seat.

Tereshkova worked her fingers through the helm rends. "Course plotted, Captain."

Maya stole one last glance at the ancient Earth. "Then take us home."

♦

Somewhere on a grassy plain in mainland Africa, a fully repaired Evelyn Sybil strode along at a pace no human could maintain.

Stopping, Eve draped her jacket over one shoulder and stared up into the night sky. After seeing the destruction of the city to the east, she had figured *Yesterday* would depart soon.

Sure enough, a bright sphere of light burst forth overhead. The light blotted out Luna, bringing about an artificial day that lasted until the wormhole closed. Then darkness settled over the terrain once more.

Silently, Eve said goodbye to the last humans she would see for a very long time.

Thoughts of Brooke entered her mind. The guilt-stricken pilot's death weighed heavier on Eve than she cared to admit. Brooke had died just as she should have—and just as she always had for as many iterations as the Vril had cataloged. It was sad but necessary, like so much of life.

Pulling a tiny chip out of her jacket pocket, Eve regarded it. The chip stored the AI that had programmed Tereshkova's Hyperflare to shoot down Brooke on New Mars. It had been yet another sad but necessary act to ensure Brooke fulfilled her destiny.

Eve crushed the chip to a fine powder. As she rubbed her fingers together, the wind scattered the remains.

Tossing the last of her strawberry-flavored popping candy into her mouth, Eve frowned. From now on, she would have to do without her culinary vices.

The sooner she slumbered, the better.

Thousands of years in the future, she would arise and begin the circle again.

♦

An Onaki captain floated in the nerve center of her science vessel, the *Lamadu*.

Extending her wings in excitement, the captain stared at the wraparound display screen. The display showed a series of caves on the olive green and rust brown planet orbited by the *Lamadu*.

As the top-down view magnified, a pair of thin bipedal creatures exited one of the caverns and set out across the grassy plain. The bipeds wore masks that allowed them to breathe the planet's thin air.

"The creatures appear headed toward a small, circular spacecraft two-point-eight spans to the west," her sensing officer reported. "Based on the scorching and denting present on the fuselage, I would surmise they crash-landed here."

"Then these beings are not indigenous to this world," the captain said.

"I think so, Captain. My scans indicate that they arrived fifty-six cycles ago. Strangely, their DNA is more similar to ours than to that of the organisms native to the planet."

Intrigued, the Onaki captain extended her thin arms out from beneath her wings and crossed them. "Discovering other intelligent life at the edge of our territory is a momentous event."

"I'm not detecting any weapons on the spacecraft or in the underground catacombs," said the sensing officer. "My scans show eighty-nine of their fellows in the caves, yet the spacecraft could only have supported two of their kind."

One section of the display showed an enhanced view of the inside of the spacecraft. A pair of enclosed bedding tubes contained red and orange heat smudges.

"The tubes appear to be clone birthing chambers," the sensing officer said.

A third tube held the vacuum-sealed remains of one of the creatures. The data on the screen revealed the creature had stilled long before the ship had crashed.

Compartments cooled to near-absolute zero within the craft contained thousands of fertilized embryos.

"Their presence here is intentional," the captain said. "They're birthing more of their kind to seed the planet."

"What is our next course of action?" the sensing officer asked. "Should I teletone the craft?"

"No. I shall contact the Factionary Protectorate for instructions. Let us limit ourselves to observation for now, but I have a feeling in my stomachs that these beings will hear from us very soon."

Thirty-six—Sempiternal
Kuiper Belt, Sol System

Rising from her command chair, Maya held her breath as *Yesterday* downshifted from hyperspace. She and her crew had spent months in transit, not knowing what they would find in the present when they arrived. The tension in the air had her grinding her teeth.

Stars enveloped the ship as the coral pink hue of upper dimensionality receded from the viewports.

"Are we . . . ?" Maya couldn't help but ask.

"I've verified the local constellations," Bob said from the sit-table. "We have returned to the present at the precise moment we departed."

At the comm station, Marconi shifted his bent coin between his knuckles. "The IEF grid is responding to pings. Our clocks were off by less than a picosecond."

Trevor, Jo, Erik, Zeke, and the rest of the bridge crew smiled and sighed in relief.

"Dolus and Base Thule are dead ahead." Tereshkova lurched forward at the helm. "The Greys' fleet is still—"

"Captain?" Admiral Westerberg's headshot manifested above the sit-table. "What're you doing? Is your drive malfunctioning?"

"Sir. . . ." Maya bottled up her giddiness. "We've come back—"

"To join the battle?" Westerberg snapped. "That was a clever stunt you pulled, using the construction barrel as a decoy. But I ordered you to proceed with your mission, not turn and fight."

"Turn and fight?" Maya blinked.

A single laugh burst forth from her mouth. She backpedaled and knocked her heel into the back of her chair. *We exited the wormhole right after entering it, so to him it looks like we never went anywhere.* "Sir, we've completed the mission. We spent the better part of a year in the past."

Westerberg took a moment to respond. "Please say again, Captain."

"We've returned to the present at the precise instant we left."

"If that's the case, how did you manage to return from an altered timeline?"

"That's going to take some explaining—at least, of the parts I think I understand." Maya tapped her finger against her cheek. "With any luck, scientists and philosophers will be able to provide a complete explanation someday."

"Then you've figured out how the metatoy ended up in the past?"

"Sort of. I have a theory that our return seems to support."

A hint of a smile manifested beneath the admiral's mustache. "Well, then. Welcome home, captain and crew." His mouth drooped, returning to a more characteristic frown. "In the meantime, we have an attack to repel."

"What are your orders, sir? We're battle-tested and ready for action."

"I don't want that ship destroyed, but we could use its capabilities. With the wave drive, you should be able to run circles around their motherships and do plenty of damage."

"We're willing to try." Maya straightened her jacket. *I guess the welcome home reception will have to wait.* "Sound general quarters. Helm, change course toward the thick of the fighting."

"Altering our trajectory," Tereshkova said. "Now en route."

"XO, Tactical, activate all defense systems and prepare an offensive strategy."

"Aye, Captain," Trevor and Rojas responded.

"Flight control, ready fighter—"

"Ma'am," Bob said.

The AI projected a rend of the battle above the sit-table. Scale-model cruisers, motherships, Hyperflares, and saucers clashed. Hundreds of explosions and crisscrossing streaks of weapons fire lit up the combat zone.

Additional lights flickered, but not because of further detonations. The Greys were shifting away—retreating.

"I guess the sight of us scared 'em off," Jo said.

"You may be right," Maya said, "but not in the way you think." She took her time settling back into her chair. "When they saw us return from the past, they realized they had failed."

Frequent debriefings had taken Maya to IEF installations around the Sol system. She had gone into the sessions with a genuine desire to reveal all that she had experienced. But after the top brass had second-guessed her decisions and mistakes for the umpteenth time, she had begun to feel like a suspect in a mass murder.

But aren't I?

Given that three members of the crew had been Vril agents—four if one chose to count Brooke among them—the authorities promised to open an inquiry into the surreptitious organization. The fact that the Vril were still around had come as a shock to many.

Maya didn't know what to think or feel about the Vril anymore. Their methods couldn't be excused, but the human race wouldn't have survived without them. The Vril were both criminals and saviors. She knew of no laws or ethics by which to properly judge them. *There's no good or evil, no black or white. Only gray.*

For now, Kepler and Crumpler would still face their respective court martials, and the IEF would hail Brooke as a heroine.

During the return voyage, Zeke had confessed to helping Grey stowaways seed their race. That had explained Vox's presence in the past. Had he been human, Zeke's actions might have qualified as treason. In the end, Maya and the IEF hadn't faulted him, given that *Yesterday* had been responsible for the Onaki never creating the Greys. Humans hadn't just stolen the Earth from them. Mankind had stolen their very existence.

The situation was a brain-teaser, for sure. The Greys seeding their race in the past explained how they existed in this timeline, but how had they existed in the first place? Maya's best guess was that a timeline existed out there somewhere—or had once existed—in which the Onaki had created the Greys. At least that's how it should've happened, according to her theory of the Circle.

The Circle postulated that time travelers from alternate timelines had set other timelines in motion, including the current universe. Through repeating time loops, divergent events reshaped every branch in the multi-universal tree at an almost-imperceptible rate, just as evolution occurred too slowly for someone to notice in his or her lifetime.

Perhaps, the theory ultimately suggested, there had never been a beginning at all.

As a result, Maya and her crew had been able to return to a present virtually identical to the one they had known. They had done it before and would do it again and again in almost the same way each time. The Circle was similar to the concept of eternal recurrence found in ancient philosophies and religions.

Maya had kept her eye out for subtle differences between this present and the one she remembered. So far, she had failed to notice anything different.

Most people had found the Circle hard to believe. Skeptics had questioned whether *Yesterday* had traveled to the past at all. But the debris from the *Eleppu* in the ship's cargo hold had put their suspicions to rest.

Uncle Kevin had never doubted her. If anything, her theory had thrown the human race's top scientific mind headlong into a tireless endeavor to prove her right. The Circle gave him one of the missing pieces he needed to figure out how to shift between time branches.

Despite the exciting new research possibilities this presented for him, she knew the real reason he had thrown himself into his work.

When Kevin boarded *Yesterday*, one look into Maya's eyes had told him that Brooke hadn't come back with her. The sorrow of the tear-filled embrace Maya had shared with her uncle had almost broken them both. After that, Kevin had shut himself in his lab. Devoting himself to the next great discovery was the only way he knew how to cope.

These thoughts and too many others filled Maya's mind as she stood in Douglas Memorial Park near Base HOPE on Callisto. The low gravity weighed on her more like ten gees, which explained why she had occupied her thoughts with anything and everything but the loss she and Kevin had suffered. She kept her muscles tightened and eyes narrowed to prevent the grief from overwhelming her.

Maya sneezed as a slight breeze wafted pollen into her nostrils.

The flags of the IA, the IEF, the American Colonies, and Japan adorned the closed but empty casket, which sat on the tributary platform of the cemetery grounds. After the official funeral proceedings on Callisto, the IEF planned to erect a monument honoring Brooke in the cemetery where Maya's mother and grandparents were buried.

Spherecams and reporters hovered at a discrete distance. Millions, if not billions, of people would tune in to say goodbye to the first person to fly faster than light.

Service men and women in dress uniform stood at attention along the path leading to the platform. Concentric rings of flowers in all the colors of the rainbow encircled it. Tombstones of officers who had fallen in the line of duty littered the cratered and rocky landscape. Sporadic patches of grass, bushes, and evergreens sprouted up from the blue-grey dirt.

Jupiter glowed like an oversized moon in the overcast sky. Its two Great Red Spots gazed down like ever-watchful eyes.

Was it Maya's imagination, or were the storms churning more slowly in mourning?

The ceremony began with the sounding of a horn. Six officers marched along the path and came to stand on either side of the casket. Admiral Westerberg and the head cleric of the Order of Ethics trailed them, followed by Uncle Kevin and Maya.

The four of them came to stand at the head of the casket.

Westerberg opened with, "We're gathered here today to honor one of the finest officers and human beings ever to live." He listed off Vice Admiral Brooke Davis's many great accomplishments. Her incredible combat record. Her selection as the Project Luminosity test pilot. Her rise through the ranks, and the battles she had fought in during the invasion staged by the Vril. Her training of so many young pilots during her time as a flight instructor. Her refusal to give up on the *New Horizons* expedition. And her defense of the IA against the Greys.

"She died in the line of duty, doing what she loved—flying," he said. "I can think of no more fitting or honorable death."

He refrained from mentioning the nature of her final mission. The IEF wasn't yet ready to publicize the existence of time travel. But soon, the admiral had told Maya, they would have no choice but to reveal the phase drive's capabilities.

The head cleric spoke next. With his words he painted Brooke Davis as a woman who had followed an ethically viable path—his way of saying she had always tried to do the right thing.

In the last few decades, the Order of Ethics had risen out of widespread education about the multiverse and growing dissatisfaction with the belief systems of old. The edicts of the Order eschewed the supernatural while retaining a focus on morals and ethics for the betterment of individuals and society.

Maya had never felt the need to subscribe to a belief system. But any religion that advocated doing good for the sake of goodness made more sense to her than most others.

The officers folded the IA flag.

The highest-ranking officer of the group presented it to Maya's uncle.

With bloodshot eyes, Kevin accepted the flag in one hand. With the other, he squeezed Maya's palm.

Music played as the officers folded and presented the other flags.

Before Maya knew it, the ceremony had ended, and she was exchanging embraces with Kevin, Bob, Jo, Erik, Zeke, her crew, and too many others to count.

"Want to grab a drink with us?" Jo asked her as the crowd began to thin.

Looking around the tributary platform, Maya didn't see her uncle anywhere. *He must've snuck away to grieve.*

Maya forced a smile and shook her head. "Thanks, but I'd rather be alone right now."

"Okay," Jo said with a tight-lipped nod. "If you change your mind, we'll be on Triton, having a few in her honor."

"She didn't drink, you know."

Jo's hands flew to her hips. "That explains her dry sarcasm."

"Funny."

"I'm just trying to console a friend."

"I know. I appreciate it."

After hugging Maya, Jo corralled everyone else and led them away.

Maya stared down at the casket, remembering all the wonderful times she had shared with her aunt, the foster mother who had raised her.

Images flipped through Maya's mind like a slideshow. Her aunt reading her bedtime stories as a kid. Brooke buying her Bio Bear after chasing her through a department store. The pride on her aunt's face at her high school graduation. Their heart-to-heart before the *Horizons* mission, when Brooke had insisted Maya would go on to accomplish bigger things than the aunt who had raised her.

Resting both palms on the casket, Maya leaned forward and clamped her eyes shut.

She sensed people standing next to her, opened her eyes, and turned her head.

Jerking back, Maya snarled at the sight of Takashi Katayama. Wearing an expensive black suit, he strutted toward her, head held high.

Maya didn't care if her father's great plan had saved the human race. He had never been there for her.

Vice Administrator Shin Saito accompanied Katayama. He wore a similarly tailored suit.

The sight of them together chilled every cell in Maya's body. Evelyn Sybil had been special advisor to Saito and the IA administration. Given that Katayama was a major benefactor, Maya wondered if the entire administration was Vril.

She had a feeling the inquiry into the Vril wouldn't get very far.

Katayama gazed down at the coffin with a blank expression. "She was integral to everything," he said without a hint of sadness or regret.

"You have no right to be here," Maya snapped. "Go before I call security—or strangle you with my bare hands."

"After all you've learned, you still see me as the enemy." Finger by finger, Katayama tightened his fine leather gloves.

"Please accept my condolences," Saito said. "I didn't know the admiral well, but I respected her for doing what was necessary."

"You mean what the Vril manipulated her into doing," Maya fired back.

"She acted of her own volition," Katayama said. "If she hadn't, none of us would be here now."

Maya folded her arms. "In this timeline, perhaps, but everyone would still exist somewhere."

"True, but what happens to a branch that breaks from a tree, or a leaf that falls from its branch? They persist for a time, but eventually decompose. Unless we continue to take action to renew our lineage, a handful of waning timelines will be all that remain of us."

"You're saying we could end up like the Greys."

"They've become a race of temporal refugees, thanks to us."

The comment sparked a realization in Maya. "Does that have something to do with why they've been attacking us?" she asked. "If they wanted revenge, they would've exacted it a long time ago."

"They seek only that which was taken from them," Katayama said.

"Not the Earth?"

"They don't care about a simple planet or star system. There isn't anything in this universe that they want."

This universe. Eyes widening, Maya cupped one hand over her mouth. "They want their timeline back . . . but how would attacking us help?"

Katayama lifted his cane and regarded it. "It doesn't, but by doing so they prevent us from worsening their situation."

Maya thought back to her conversation with Vox. The Grey had feared humankind's continued progress.

It still didn't add up, though. Her mind kept looping back to how the Greys could've enslaved or wiped out humans well before humans advanced enough to pose a threat—unless the Greys had needed humans to advance. The Greys had waited for the IEF to build *Yesterday* so they could travel far enough into the past to seed their race. As crazy as it seemed, perhaps in 200,000 years they hadn't been able to construct a power source like a black hole generator.

So, the Greys had come out of hiding to hitch a ride aboard *Yesterday*. But why begin the attacks years beforehand?

"Why did they start with the research outpost on Epsilon Eridani?" Maya asked. "What was going on there?"

Polishing the platinum horsehead on top of his cane, Katayama said, "Nothing was going on there." He placed emphasis on the word "was."

"You mean something will happen there in the future. What, exactly?"

Her father swung his cane around in a slow, wide arc. "It's what this—what everything—is all about."

"And just what is that?" When Katayama failed to elaborate, Maya growled and balled her fists. "If you won't talk straight, leave and let me mourn my aunt in peace."

Stepping over to the casket, Katayama placed a hand on it. "Hold onto your anger, Maya. Harness it as she did." His voice echoed off the casket and platform. "When the moment comes, direct your rage against all those who would threaten us."

Even in anguish, Maya grasped the meaning. "You don't just mean the Greys. You're talking about the Onaki."

"Yes."

"They've had a long time to advance, and to stew over what happened, but they haven't come. Is it because of the accord I struck with Enki?"

"Partly. But they've left us alone for a more basic reason."

"Which is?"

"A span of 200,000 years is a long time," Katayama said. "Think of how far we'll have advanced that many years from now, if we have the chance to do so."

Maya blinked. "We must seem like ants to the Onaki. I doubt we're any threat to them."

Katayama nodded in approval, a jubilant outpouring by his standards.

"Still," Maya said, "the Vril's primary goal has been to prepare us for their coming, so it must happen in the future."

Her pompous parent had the gall to grimace in disappointment. "Not just in the future. That's only where it will begin."

With a tight-lipped growl, Maya said, "You mean we'll travel to the past again to deal with them."

"The conflict will go beyond the past, present, and future."

"Across alternate timelines."

"And beyond."

Beyond what? What's beyond the multiverse? Maya wondered, but she was tired of the vague double talk. "So what prompts the conflict?"

"Oh, there'll be no mistaking it." With a gloved finger, Katayama traced the medallion on the casket. The medallion depicted a double-sided scale, the symbol of the Order of Ethics. "It will begin when the balance tips in our favor."

"The balance of what?"

Katayama raised an eyebrow at her. "Of life and of all existence."

"The Circle," Maya said, finally understanding. "Specifically, our gaining control of it. That's what the Greys are trying to stop us from achieving. Once we can do that, we'll be a threat to the Onaki. That's when they'll come."

"At that moment, all shall begin and end—again." Katayama grabbed his cane and turned to leave. "All we can do for now is hope that everything we've done—and everything we've invested in you—staves off the end for us."

"What you've invested in me?" Maya sucked in a breath. "You tested me on my first mission and then sent me back to ensure the human race survived its creation." Thinking of her immunity to the Onaki mind-control, she added, "I'll be able to face them in the future because their abilities have no effect on me."

She grabbed her father's shoulder. "Why am I immune? What's different about me?"

Katayama stopped and leaned on his cane. "I'm afraid I haven't been truthful with you."

Snorting, Maya retracted her hand. "You're the leader of the Vril. Lying is as automatic for you as breathing."

"Perhaps. Even when a lie pains me, I must tell it when it serves the greater good."

"And what lie serves the greater good?"

"That I never wanted you."

Maya froze. For a moment she swore her body had shut down.

"You were what I wanted most for the world," Katayama whispered. "Only you survived out of them all."

When he failed to clarify, Maya asked, "All of whom?"

Katayama stared up at Jupiter. "I brought you into this world, but I'm not your biological father." With that, he turned and descended the hill from the platform.

Maya let her jaw dangle as Callisto's sky began to drizzle.

Shin Saito had kept his stare locked on the casket throughout the conversation. Now, he touched his head as if to adjust a nonexistent hat.

After wiping moisture from his brow with a handkerchief, Saito buried both hands in his coat pockets. "I plan to run for Prime Administrator in a few terms. When I win, I'll be in a position to help ensure our existence."

Maya turned her back to him.

"I hope when that day comes, we can work together to achieve that goal." Saito's voice grew more distant. "Until then, sister."

Sister? Maya whirled around, but both men had vanished.

Long after they had gone, Maya stood over Brooke's casket.

Maya's chest burned with regret at her many failures. She trembled, fearing what was to come. Shouting in anger, she cursed her father, the Vril, the Greys, the Onaki, the Circle, and everything else that had placed this great burden upon her without ever asking for her permission. Her outbursts devolved into sobs of loneliness, for she so very much missed her aunt.

Most of all, Maya hated what she had now become. Brooke's death had killed the last shreds of optimism within her. There would be no more joy of discovery, no more wonder at what was out there.

Self-loathing threatened to overwhelm her. The only way she could cope was to shut down her brain and numb herself to everything.

As the drizzle turned to a downpour, one gut-churning thought bubbled to the surface of her mind. *Never again will I make the same mistakes. No more doing the right thing.*

When the time came, she vowed to do what was necessary.

◆

Omo smiled as his grandson helped him rest his aging back against the cavern wall. These days, anything more than gradual movement sent stabbing pain coursing through his body.

Staring out of the cave's mouth, Omo observed the activity in the village. He couldn't help but reflect on his short time in this world as he neared the end.

His people had traveled inland for months until locating this great valley along its vast river. A number of his fellows had perished along the way. Others had failed to adapt to a way of life requiring them to fend for themselves. They had grown too accustomed to the masters' oversight, too domesticated.

But those who had weathered the journey and transition now thrived. Men and women hunted and gathered food while others tended to the children and meal preparation. Using different clay ochres, members of his tribe had begun a practice of face painting. At the moment a boy sat on a tree stump, whittling the tip of a spear with a sharp rock.

Life in the village contrasted with his time under the heel of the masters, as day differed from night. Gone were the incredible tools that had emitted sound and light. No longer did his people have the ability to lift small mountains or take to the skies.

Around the fire after dark, the elders told their children and grandchildren stories of those fantastic times. Oohs and aahs escaped young lips at the mention of powerful beings that had descended from the stars, beings that had created people in their own image and given them the capacity for thought. The young ones listened intently to the struggle between two warring sides. Eyes twinkled and faces beamed at the good that had helped to liberate them. Gasps rang out at the evil that had sought to enslave and kill them.

Tales of flashing lights in the sky followed by booming thunderclaps made for enthralling bedtime stories.

The latest version of the story referred to the flying machines as flaming beasts and the masters as omnipotent gods who shot lightning from their fingertips.

Omo chuckled. He saw no harm in embellishing the truth, especially if it instilled a healthy fear and obedience in the young ones. With each generation handing down the verbal record to the next, he wondered what forms the stories might take in the distant future.

With thoughts of the Teacher on his mind, Omo rested his eyes for the last time.

♦

Thousands of Penphins sat perched on ledges throughout the assembly hall of the great tower. The sun's red rays peeked in through the many window-exits, casting faint light on the gathering.

No one had announced the passing of the Grand Creator. Nor had the masters explained their leave-taking in words. Every Penphin had felt these occurrences and come here out of instinct.

The collective feelings of all Penphins were now less, but at the same time they were more, The masters had conveyed their confidence in the Penphins. They were ready to determine their own course, a prospect which seemed reasonable to all.

The Penphins no longer needed help. They could now help themselves and, someday perhaps, others.

On the grand balcony across the hall, the Penphin High Thinker approached the statues of the masters.

From beneath its flipper-wing, the thinker produced the shiny black object the Grand Creator had treasured. Reaching out his sinewy arm, the thinker placed the object on the pedestal between the statues.

No Penphin knew what practical purpose the object served. But the Grand Creator had imparted its significance before passing. The object symbolized the act of helping that had given rise to their civilization.

For that, they would cherish it forever.

To be concluded . . .

Our story concludes in *Beyond Existence*, the fourth and final book in Greg Spry's Beyond Saga.

The decades have dragged on for Vice Admiral Maya Davis since *Yesterday* returned from the past. The IEF has pushed outward from Sol by more than a thousand light years. With Director Sommerfield's new interphase drive ready to go into service, the rest of the Milky Way—and beyond—will soon be within humankind's reach.

When Captain Jo Ryder locates the Onaki home worlds, she finds only abandoned ruins. But the discovery holds little intrigue for Maya, who lost her love for exploration after her Aunt Brooke's death. Lacking the will to serve, she turns down the High Admiral position.

Before Maya can retire, a group of scientists at Epsilon Eridani achieve the breakthrough of all breakthroughs. Moments after they successfully create living DNA from inanimate matter, the Onaki appear and seize control of every human and piece of technology near Sol.

The Onaki claim their actions are for the good of the multiverse, but Maya refuses to believe it. With renewed purpose, she takes command of an interphase ship resistant to Onaki control and fights to protect the scientists and their game-changing discovery.

Hunted by both friend and foe, Maya shifts to different timelines to learn the source of the Onaki's omnipotence. Somehow she must prevent them from restoring the multiverse to a state without humans, even if saving mankind requires sacrificing everything in existence.

About the Author

Greg Spry was cloned in the year between the releases of *Star Wars Episode IV: A New Hope* and *Star Trek: The Motion Picture*. Coincidence? He majored in industrial engineering at the University of Wisconsin-Madison before earning a graduate degree in space systems from the Florida Institute of Technology. When he's not writing the next epic sci-fi adventure, he enjoys sampling tasty microbrews, eating hot wings, and cheering on the Wisconsin Badgers and Green Bay Packers. Visit his personal website at www.gregspry.com.